A LATE
DIVORCE

Books by A. B. Yehoshua

A LATE DIVORCE
BETWEEN RIGHT AND RIGHT
THE LOVER
EARLY IN THE SUMMER OF 1970
THREE DAYS AND A CHILD

A LATE DIVORCE

A. B. YEHOSHUA

TRANSLATED FROM THE HEBREW BY
HILLEL HALKIN

DOUBLEDAY & COMPANY, INC.
GARDEN CITY, NEW YORK
1984

8407

Excerpt from "The Second Coming" from *Collected Poems* by William Butler Yeats.
Copyright 1924 by Macmillan Publishing Co., Inc., renewed 1952 by Bertha Georgie
Yeats.

Library of Congress Cataloging in Publication Data
Yehoshua, Abraham B.
    A late divorce.
    Translation of: Gerushim me' uharim.
    I. Title.
PJ5054.Y42G413   1984   892.4'36

ISBN: 0-385-15574-3
Library of Congress Catalog Card Number 82–45830

SUNDAY

Benjy knew it when Da Muddy died. He
cried. He smell hit. He smell hit.
　　　　　　　　　　Willam Faulkner

Grandpa really has come I thought it's raining outside it wasn't a
dream I remembered how they woke me and showed me to him
because they promised me they would as soon as he came from the
airplane even if I was sleeping that's why I agreed to go to bed. At
first I heard them argue in the dark because dad didn't want them
turning on the light but mom said I promised and dad said so what
he'll have plenty of time to see him. But mom insisted just for a
second come see him father he's done nothing but wait and ask about
you for the last three days. Which wasn't even so. And the light went
on but I couldn't open my eyes because it hurt and I heard a hoarse
new voice it was grandpa's I don't believe that's really Gaddi why I
still think of him as a baby you're raising a giant here. A giant he
called me not fat but dad laughed time hasn't stood still he's not your
tribe's he's ours big fat and solid the blanket's hiding him now you'll
see him better later the kids in his class call him Boxer he's really a
sweetheart the pain shot through my heart again. How could he?
Why?

　　Shh Kedmi shh whispered mom the child's up already she patted
my head and tried sitting me up but she was too late she always is
grandpa already had heard. Who told dad? He knows everything. If

only mom had told grandpa now about my glands but she just propped me up in bed with her hand to keep me from falling get up Gaddi it's grandpa he's here open your eyes I opened them and saw Uncle Tsvi in a hat but all wrinkled and taller full of hair he was crying ma passed me to him he tried lifting me he staggered and almost dropped me he kissed me he got me wet with his tears. He doesn't remember me. Do you remember me Gaddi? We told you he would come in the end laughed mom her eyes were wet too. You wanted us to wake you. So I put my lips on his rough dry cheeks for a kiss. That's enough said dad he took me from grandpa and swung me back into bed they were already by the baby to look at her too they didn't wake her though because once she's up she never goes back to sleep. Enough said dad you'll see so much of them you'll be sick of them yet. He turned off the light I was almost asleep again when he came back and pulled off the blanket as long as you're up why don't you try to pee we don't want any more little messes. I don't have to I whispered. Try anyway there's always something he helped me up and into my slippers he led me to the bathroom and pulled down my pajamas I saw the whole house lit bags and suitcases and grandpa's back he was drinking tea with his hat on. But there wasn't any pee my head kept dropping to the little pool of clear water dad whistled standing guard by the door. Well? I made already I whispered and flushed right away. I didn't hear you he said but I made I pulled up my pants and went back to bed what does he want he trails me like a policeman he covered me and said give me a kiss so I gave him one and he kissed me back hard and left then I felt if I waited some more I might have peed after all it was all because of that whistling and I fell asleep.

And now it was warm and wet down there with that sweet like smell of the mess and the rain I could hear it dripping all the time even though it was nearly Passover it was the day of our class seder. There wasn't a sound in the house not even the radio till dad stood in the doorway it's seven o'clock aren't you getting up he came to pull off the blanket but I held on to it tight. I'm getting up I said he didn't smell a thing the minute he left I part-closed the door I pulled off my wet bottoms real quick and stuffed them into my schoolbag and covered them with books I took an old wool blanket and spread it on the stain to absorb it the baby opened her eyes. Then I went to the bathroom to wash up. Grandpa's bags were all gone only his hat was still on the kitchen table there was a smell of coffee dad sat behind his paper.

"Where's mom?"

"She's sleeping. They were up all night. C'mon, get a move on. It's raining, I'll drive you to school. Do you want an egg?"

"Yes." And I sat down at the table that was full of food while he went to fry me an egg. "Will grandpa live with us now?"

"Of course not."

"Will he go live with grandma?"

Dad laughed. "Where is that?"

"Where she is."

But I was never in that place she doesn't really live in just nearby.

"No. He's only come for a few days to take care of some business. He'll stay with Tsvi too, and with Asa in Jerusalem. Then he'll go back to America."

"For good?"

"For the time being."

He gave me the egg and some cocoa and Rice Krispies and two slices of bread. He always gives me a lot and expects me to finish it all.

"Why did grandpa cry?"

"When?"

"Last night."

"Did he? I didn't notice. I guess he felt like it. Let's go, enough questions. Hurry up, I don't have time . . ."

I began to eat listening to the quiet in the house watching the raindrops run down the windowpane. I said:

"It was just one boy who called me Boxer once. It wasn't every-one."

He put down his paper and looked at me and laughed.

"All right, all right. It was just something I said. I didn't mean anything by it. Even if they do call you Boxer why should you care? Tell them to go to hell. I'm on the chubby side myself, and you can see there's nothing wrong with it, especially if you're tall."

He stood up to show me his stomach letting it hang out on purpose beating it with his fist.

"Don't worry, you'll be big and strong just like me."

But I didn't want to be just like him not that I said so. It was already past seven-thirty. I finished eating and went back to my room to pack my schoolbag and to see if the stain was gone but it wasn't so I sort of made the bed while the baby looked on it's a good thing she can't talk I stuck the pacifier in her mouth and walked out past the shut door where grandpa was sleeping I looked around to see if he had left something for me but there wasn't anything that looked like it. I went to mom and dad's room and touched mom she opened her eyes right away she smiled but dad was right behind me leave her alone Gaddi hands off let her sleep what is it that you want?

"I need matzos, lettuce and wine. We're having a class seder this morning."

"Why didn't you say so yesterday?"

"I told mom."

"Maybe you can get along without it. Borrow some from another boy."

"I'm getting up," said mom.

"You don't have to. I'll take care of it. Come on, just get a move on."

He went to the kitchen and wrapped two matzos in a newspaper he looked in the closet and found a bottle of old wine he tasted it and made a face he looked at me and said what difference does it make you won't drink it anyway it's just symbolic and he poured some into an old jar that used to have olives in it. Forget about the lettuce he said you can borrow a leaf from someone. So I started back toward mom don't be stubborn he said it's getting late but I said I need lettuce so he searched in the vegetable bin and found some old leaves and gave them to me was he sore. Since when did you get so religious? I put it all in my schoolbag my watch already said ten to eight.

"What else do you need?"

"A snack for school."

"What about the matzo?"

"It's for the seder at the end."

"Okay, I won't let you starve." He cut two thick slices of bread in a hurry and put chocolate spread on them he jangled his keys then mom was there she told me to put on my boots I went to get them she combed my hair I'm counting to three and going dad shouted the baby cried I strapped on my schoolbag and started downstairs half-

way down I remembered I ran back up mom opened the door the
baby was already in her arms.

"What's wrong?"

"Nothing."

I ran to the bathroom and opened my schoolbag and took out the
wet pajamas and stuffed them deep into the laundry bin on the way
out I passed grandpa's door I opened it quietly and saw him sleeping
by a suitcase full of clothes but nothing in it seemed to be for me.

I felt mom's hand. "You'll see him later when you come home
from school." I ran down the stairs. Dad's car was running the
wipers were on white smoke came out from the back.

"What the hell's the matter with you? What did you forget this
time?"

"Nothing."

"It's enough to drive a person up the wall."

The cars whizzed down the hill without stopping for dad they
honked their brakes squealed in the end though he swore and swung
into the traffic and let me off by my school.

It was raining harder the children were running someone ran by
me and said look at Boxer in boots he was gone before I could grab
him I was sure it was the boy from 3A who had called me that
before. There wasn't any lineup we went straight to our rooms the
bell rang our teacher Galya talked about the rain which might be the
last of the year she wrote last rain on the blackboard we opened our
Bibles before she even began hands were up to answer questions that
no one had asked we have kids like that in our class. We read about
Jacob who thought Joseph was eaten alive because all his brothers
lied I was thinking of grandpa was he up yet when Galya told me to
read next read what I said the chapter's finished then start the next
one she said and I did. And the famine was sore in the land and it
came to pass when they had eaten up the provender which they had
brought out of Egypt. Galya stopped me to ask what provender was
I said it was some kind of food I didn't know which then Sigal raised
her hand and said it was wheat because that's what they ate in those
days and Galya said wheat and other things too so we talked about
making flour from wheat and about baking bread and I opened my
schoolbag to see if the bread was still there. At last the bell rang and
I took out my sandwich because I was hungry but Galya made me
put it back because we don't eat in first recess.

During recess we stayed in the halls because it was muddy outside the janitor wouldn't let us out the children were wild I went looking for the boy who called me Boxer just let him try again in the end I spotted him running around a small skinny kid I went up to him he just smiled with his big dark eyes I wanted to hear him say it again so I'd know for sure I could sock him but he didn't say anything then the bell rang and he went back to his class it was really 3A.

The next class was drawing. Right off I drew a sun and a fence and a house like where grandma lives a man by the fence held a boy's hand but the boy came out very big almost bigger than the man so I gave him a beard and made a man of him too and gave the first man braids and made him a woman and drew a new boy a baby on the ground with big flowers all around. I showed it to the teacher that's nice she said but why is the sun so low it's almost touching the people so I went back to my desk and drew a black cloud over it with rain coming out and wrote last rain on it and gave the man and the woman an umbrella but not the baby he couldn't hold one he'd have to get wet but by then I was bored so I wrote Gaddi underneath and took out my sandwich and ate it because the drawing teacher doesn't care if we eat in her class and then I stripped to my gym shorts. The rain had stopped so I went out to the yard we shot marbles in the mud the boy from 3A who never seems to play with boys his own age just with smaller ones was there too he didn't say a word to me it was like he never had or would he just took out two marbles and shot them sharp and fast. It was a weird game because the marbles kept sticking in the mud they got bigger and bigger like big slow brown balls we all laughed at the fatsos rolling in the puddles there was mud all over us too we really had a good time. But when the bell rang and we started picking up the marbles and putting them back in our pockets Ido from my class thought that one of mine was his and wanted to know where it was and this little kid says just like that Boxer took it while sticking close to a teacher passing by I made believe I didn't hear but something ached inside I went to look for a stick because once the others learn to call me Boxer there won't be any stopping it.

Then we had gym it's the class I hate most because the teacher always picks on me for not touching my toes or raising my arms high enough when my turn came to jump over the horse I went around it at the last second and ran my hand over it when they raised it higher

I didn't even try I just dragged along at the end of the line and let the other kids pass me. The gym teacher called me over try Gaddi he said I'll help you I said I can't. If you'd lose some weight you could jump he said so I said it's not the food it's my glands there's something wrong with them. What glands he said who put that into your head? So I explained to him about the glands that make me fat the doctor said so he even gave me a note at the beginning of the year that I wasn't supposed to jump. The gym teacher gave me such a hopeless look that it's a wonder I didn't cry I usually do when he starts up but today he was too tired to yell maybe because it was almost spring vacation. All he said was they'll get you in the army then he blew his whistle and said now choose teams for dodge ball. I was chosen last and counted out first so I went looking for a stick again I found a short iron rod that I hid behind a fence I hoped it would rain some more so that gym might end early.

At last the bell rang and we went inside to set our desks for the seder we spread them with sheets and took out the matzos and the wine and the lettuce from our schoolbags and put them on the sheets. The music teacher came with her accordion to play Passover songs and we sang and when she went to the next class for them to sing too we said The Four Questions and the blessing for the wine and some other stuff and picked up the matzos and put them down and wrapped them in the lettuce and picked them up again and ate them. I even drank the wine dad gave me at first I made a face but something made me drink it and I finished it all and suddenly felt a bit drunk. Honestly. I even ate Ido's matzo and lettuce because he didn't want them.

Then we cleared our desks it was vacation by now because tomorrow we only get report cards. I was so drunk I nearly fell down the stairs I went to my hiding place and took the iron rod and walked slowly home by way of my old kindergarten I stood by the window and looked at the room with all the toys I knew so well and at the teacher who used to be mine sitting on a little chair and telling all the little kids a story it was dumb and for babies but I listened anyway because I remembered it except for the end the parents stood around me with raincoats for their children they kept pushing me 'cause they wanted to hear too so I walked up the street a bit and sat down on the fence to see what would happen just then the boy from 3A came out of the alleyway from school he said goodbye to some

older kid who went into his house and started walking toward me.
When he saw me on the fence he stopped to think for a second then
he crossed to the other side of the street and smiled to himself as
soon as he got close still watching me I jumped down and pulled the
rod from my coat all at once he was running shouting you fat Boxer
I chased him but he was too fast he kept gaining on me all of a
sudden he tripped by the time he got up I had grabbed his schoolbag
I tore the strap with one pull I knew then I was right he was weaker
than me I knocked him back down and threw myself on him because
my weight was my strong point he tried biting me but couldn't I
swung the rod because I meant to kill him maybe now. But a
grownup standing by ran up and grabbed me that's enough he said
you should be ashamed of yourself hitting little children I started to
cry let me go he's older than me he had already squirmed free he was
crying too he was really freaked out there was blood on his face he
barked like a dog you fucking Boxer you he picked up a stone from
the ground that's enough you two the grownup said he took the rod
away and tossed it into an empty lot he gave the kid a push go home
he said he kept his grip on me let me go I said it was raining so the
last rain wasn't the last after all maybe this was. The boy from 3A
walked up the street he was crying he was scared of his own blood he
kept cursing me I sat down on the fence to dry my face and wait till
he was gone the children came out of the kindergarten all the way
home I walked close to a neighbor of ours who had come to get her
child.

Mom opened the door. Shh shh she said grandpa's still sleeping
what took you so long? I need you she said. I had forgotten all about
grandpa she didn't even see the mud and the tears. She was nervous
not like herself the baby lay in the playpen in the middle of the living
room and cried Di Di when she saw me that's her name for me so I
went to give her a pacifier but mom said don't touch her you're filthy
go wash and come quick to eat I need you today so I went to wash
up and saw my red eyes in the mirror and thought of the kid squirming under me how he cried I dried my hands and went to eat.

Have you been crying mom asked. What made you think that I
said. Did anything happen? No nothing. I had made up my mind not
to tell her because she tells everything to dad.

"Don't eat so fast."

The house was quiet only the baby talking to a toy.

"Has grandpa been asleep all the time?"

"Yes. He's very tired from the trip and from the difference in time. What happened in school today?"

"Nothing."

"Don't eat so fast. Did you have your seder?"

"Yes."

"What did you do in it?"

"Nothing."

"What do you mean, nothing? Didn't you sing? Didn't you say any prayers?"

"Yes."

"Then why do you say nothing? Where are you going?"

"Just to feed the worms."

"Leave them alone now. First finish eating."

"It'll just take a minute."

I went to look at my silkworms a new one had spun a cocoon in the night so I put it aside and gave the others fresh mulberry leaves. Since I started second grade mom can't handle me anymore she lets me do what I want she isn't strict with me like dad. I went back to the table it was really storming outside the telephone rang it must be dad he always checks up at this time of day to see if I'm home. The baby started crying go take care of her said mom I went to her there there I said but still she cried I blew out my cheeks and made a mouth-fart to get her to laugh she stopped crying at once and looked at me her blue eyes full of tears she even smiled a bit then changed her mind and cried some more so I made a mouth-fart again.

Mom was arguing on the telephone lately they argue all the time she hung up she came and picked up the baby she took her to the bathroom to change her I followed her there. The baby had a little yellow crumb of BM.

"Is that all you've got for us?" asked mom disappointed but the baby didn't answer her. She just kicked her feet fast in the air.

"The baby will be fat too."

"She isn't fat. All babies are like that. And stop calling her the baby, she has a name . . ."

"Dad calls her the baby too."

"You're not your father and not everything your father does is right. Stop calling her the baby. She has such a sweet name."

I didn't say anything.

"Why do you keep putting your hand on your chest?"

"My heart kind of hurts."

"Your heart? Show me where."

I opened my shirt and showed her.

"That's not where your heart is."

"Then where is it?"

She showed me. I moved my hand there.

"Right. That's where it hurts."

"You're being silly."

"No, I mean it."

"Since when?"

"It kind of always has."

"It's nothing. You had gym today."

"It's not gym, that's for sure."

"Do you want me to take you to the doctor?"

"Okay."

"What are you doing this afternoon?"

"Nothing."

"I have to go somewhere."

"Where?"

"It's not important. To do some shopping. You'll look after Rakefet."

"But I have to go somewhere too."

"Where? What are you talking about?"

"To pick mulberry leaves."

"You can pick them later. It's raining now anyway. Rakefet will go to sleep soon, I kept her up purposely this morning so that she should have a long nap. She won't bother you."

"What if she cries?"

"She won't. And if she does let her have a pacifier, you can always quiet her down. Make one of those funny faces that she likes. Be a good boy, Gaddi, I know you can be."

I walked out of the bathroom.

She diapered the baby as fast as she could she put her in her crib she dressed quickly and put a bowl of clean pacifiers on the living-room table and some crackers and a bottle of water and some old keys that Rakefet likes to chew on even three diapers though she told me not to lift her if I had to I should wake up grandpa.

"Does he know how to take care of babies?"

"Of course. He's going to have one soon himself."

"Where?"

"Never mind." She was already sorry she had told me.

"But where?"

"In America."

"How come?"

"He's going to have one."

"But why?"

"He's going to. What difference does it make?"

She hugged me.

"All right, Gaddi, I'm going. He'll wake up soon but don't bother him. Rakefet is sure to sleep. If she cries give her a pacifier and she'll fall asleep again. Just don't touch her with dirty hands."

She seemed awfully nervous.

"Will you bring me something?"

"What?"

"An airplane."

"All right."

"An airplane, not a helicopter, because I've already got one. You know the difference?"

"Of course."

"Why did he cry last night?"

"Grandpa? Because it's been years since he's seen us. Since he's seen you."

"But why did he cry?"

"From excitement. From joy. You can cry from joy too."

She was sad she always is but now she was sadder. She turned off the heater you'll be warm enough without it she kissed me and left she said she'd be back in two or three hours. I went to the kitchen and opened the fridge to see what was in it I looked in the pantry not that I was hungry but just in case I found some nuts and chocolates that dad had bought to eat by the TV after supper and put them on the table. It was quiet in the house I turned on the TV there was nothing but lines I turned it off. I took my cars from the drawer and arranged them all in a row. Suddenly I stopped and went to look at grandpa I stood by the door and heard nothing so I opened it a crack and saw the darkness and the open suitcase just like in the morning and grandpa crumpled in bed as though his head wasn't part of his body. On the table was the welcome sign with the flowers that I'd made him. I closed the door I went to my room the baby was sleeping just then she turned and sighed all funny like an old woman who's had a tough life I took the box of silkworms and left. I took a worm and put it on the fire engine and gave it a piece of mulberry leaf for the ride and drove it around to see how it would feel. Suddenly the phone rang it was Uncle Asi from Jerusalem he wanted grandpa he couldn't believe it when I said he was sleeping what he fell asleep again? He never woke up I said mom's not home. Do you want me to wake him he thought for a minute no he said he'd call again tonight. I wrote Asi on the pad by the phone I picked up the worm it had dropped off the fire engine and put it back in the box I took out another and put it in the helicopter and gave it a piece of leaf too and flew it to the kitchen.

There I drank some juice and ate some of dad's nuts it was rainy and gray out a real winter day what kind of seder would it be. The worm wanted out of the helicopter I gave it a little bit of nut it didn't eat so I pushed it back in and flew it to mom and dad's room where I pulled down the blinds and took out a blanket and lay on the bed with the helicopter beside me. I pulled out the little ladder and that fat white worm that I call Sigal actually slid down it onto the white blanket and poked around there among the lumps it must have thought it had landed on the moon. The phone rang again I picked it up dad's put a telephone in nearly every room. It was him he was really surprised to hear that grandpa was still sleeping he's spaced out he said I said maybe he's sick. Suddenly he asked where are you now what telephone are you talking from he can always sense where I am and what I'm doing even when he's far away. So I said I'm talking from the phone in your room what are you doing there he asked I said nothing don't turn the house upside down he said maybe you'll lie down and rest. Maybe I said. And I tried dozing off because the house was so quiet the dark rainy outside made me want to sleep or maybe it was the queer wine I had drunk. All at once though the baby started crying at first she only whimpered dad's calling and being upset must have waked her so I waited for her to stop because sometimes she does if it's just a bad dream like that someone's stolen her bottle or something like that. And she did but soon she started again even louder she cried and cried in the quiet house it was up to me to do something so I got off mom and dad's bed and went to our room and stuck the pacifier in her mouth.

She didn't want it though she wanted to cry she spat it out so I put it back in she shook her head and tried throwing it away so I grabbed her head gently and stuck it in her mouth and held it there until she got used to it like mom does she froze for a minute and looked at me wondering what to do next she really did begin to suck too she sucked more and more as though she had no choice but then she got tired and threw it down as soon as I took my hand away she started to cry again she wouldn't take it anymore she fought it all red with anger. There there I said stop that crying but she just cried even harder. So I left the room and shut the door behind me and let her cry I looked at my watch to make sure that she didn't do it too long dad once explained to mom that when you think the baby's been crying forever it's only five minutes if you can bear to let her cry for five minutes more she'll stop by herself. I turned on the radio and went to the kitchen I shut the door to keep from hearing but just then the telephone rang it was Uncle Tsvi from Tel Aviv he's not so serious like Asi he chats with me and asks me things he asked me now too how I felt and what happened in school and what were my plans for the vacation and I answered everything because I know he really cares it's a fact that he remembers even long after meanwhile I kept hearing the baby's screams who's screaming there he finally asked it's little Rakefet I said. Is your mom with her? No mom isn't home I'm all alone with grandpa. He thought it over all right he said let me talk to the old man he's sleeping I said all right then he said don't wake him go take care of Rakefet it breaks my heart even in Tel Aviv to hear her crying in Haifa you're a terrific kid he said he'd call back at night.

I went to the baby she was red screaming in her cage her blanket thrown off waving her hands in the air you'd think she was being murdered I tried talking to her but she wouldn't even look at me I brought her a bottle of water she punched it so hard that it fell on the floor so I stood on a chair and turned her on her tummy she quieted down for a second then she began to groan and tried crawling forward as if she were going somewhere. I thought at least that will tire her out but she started choking on the sheet so I turned her back on her back she was really sobbing now I was so mad at mom for leaving me with her without permission even to lift her so I went and slowly opened the door of the room where grandpa was sleeping maybe he'd hear and come help.

He didn't move though he didn't hear a thing he lay like a pile of rags by the wall covered by a white blanket with only his skinny feet sticking out. Grandpa I whispered to this man I didn't know I almost cried but he was in an awfully deep sleep.

The baby kept crying she didn't mean to stop at all. I brought her a cracker she didn't want it I crumbled it and sifted it into her open mouth she didn't even know it was there she didn't look at me she just screamed and bawled at the ceiling with her arms in the air. I tried pulling down the bars of her crib but I couldn't I never did get the hang of it. So I ate the cracker I took off my shoes I stood on the chair and climbed over the bars into the crib that once was mine. What is it Rakefet? There there that's enough but she was screaming too hard to hear me so I picked her up carefully so as not to crush her head in the place mom warns dad about because there's an opening there where her brains are going to grow. She cried a little less and then she stopped. I sat in the crib feeling the rubber sheet under me with the baby on my knees I raised her head a bit and gave her the pacifier she sucked it and gave me a worried look like I was the problem not her the tears stopped all at once mom once explained to me that crying is talking for babies that's their language just then she shut her eyes and turned red again at first I didn't realize then I smelled what she was doing. She kept straining harder and harder her forehead all creased like an old lady's. So I slid my knees out from under her and eased her back into the crib she was happy now she put her fist in her mouth to eat I climbed back over the bars and left the room. It was quiet for maybe five minutes she even sang and talked out loud until I heard a little sob she was calling me again so I closed the door maybe she'd wear herself out and go to sleep mom said that she'd been up all morning. I went to mom and dad's room to look for the silkworm I found it crawling in the dark beneath the bed I picked it up and put it in the helicopter to fly it back to earth. The telephone rang it was Grandma Rachel our other grandma never calls because she's sick.

Gaddi darling she said do you know who this is. Yes I said. So she said this is grandma on the phone so I said yes. So she said it's been ages since I've seen you Gaddi why don't you come to visit me don't you know it's hard for grandma to come to you because of those stairs. So I said yes. So she said why don't you ask your father and mother to bring you to me you have vacation now don't you want to

spend some time with me so I said yes. So she said your grandpa
came last night from America aren't you glad that your grandpa is
here so I said yes. What did he bring you will you tell grandma so I
said yes. It must be a new toy or something to wear will you show me
so I said yes. Now darling tell me how Rakefet is. She's fine I said.
You love her don't you do you help your mother with her so I said
yes. I really hope you love her now please put your mother on the
phone. So I said mom wasn't home. So she asked for grandpa to say
hello to him so I said that he was asleep. Sleeping *now?* Yes I said it's
nighttime for him now. What do you mean nighttime? So I told her
about the earth and the sun and the differences in time. I don't think
she believed me all she said was you're just like your father you have
an answer for everything. The silkworm had escaped from the helicopter again and was crossing the room fast so I whispered just a
minute grandma it was already under the closet I couldn't find it so I
shut the door tight because the baby was crying in that awful way
again and I went back to the telephone. Where were you grandma
asked I didn't want to tell her about the worm because she wouldn't
understand it would disgust her so I said I thought Rakefet was
crying but she isn't. I always lie to her the lies come all by themselves
it's like she wants to be lied to.

"Rakefet's there? Your mother didn't take her with her?"

"No, she's asleep."

"And you're all alone with her. They left you all alone with her."

"What's wrong with that? Grandpa's here too."

"But he's sleeping."

"He'll get up if I ask him to."

"Gaddi, darling, be careful. Where is she?"

"In her crib."

"Whatever you do don't lift her. You might drop her."

"I won't."

"And when your father and mother come home tell them that I
just called to say hello and that they shouldn't leave you alone with
the baby."

"I will."

"And be sure you don't lift her. You might drop her and paralyze
her for life. You wouldn't want a paralyzed sister, would you?"

"No."

"So be careful, darling. Isn't that her crying now?"

I covered the receiver with my hand to keep her from hearing the awful screams.

"No."

I waited for her to say something else but she didn't so slowly I hung up.

The baby really was crying again not just crying but one long loud wail. I didn't know what to do I went back to her with a pacifier and the bottle and the ring of keys but she just pushed them away so I left the room and turned on the TV to drown her out I watched an English lesson but Rakefet was louder than it she even started calling my name Di Di Di her troubles were making her smarter. I couldn't take it anymore. I went back to her she was purple tears ran down her face she stank from what she had done. I really felt sorry for her. And so then I made up my mind. I went to the clothes closet and found an old raincoat of mine and put it on I put on a woolen hat and dad's leather gloves and tied a kerchief of mom's over my mouth. Then I went to the kitchen and took the sugar tongs and pushed the chair against the crib again but this time I kept on my shoes I climbed over the bars and got back in with her. I opened her diaper without getting too near I turned her on her side with the tongs together with the full wet diaper I pulled it away from her without looking all at once she was half naked and kicking her legs in the air. I threw the tongs into a corner of the room I gave her the water bottle she grabbed it and drank almost all of it right away she was feeling fine now she started to sing. So I said you feel better now don't you Di Di got rid of all that doody for you she listened and made a surprised sort of sound as though to get me to laugh she turned her head to look at the diaper lying beside her. I took the blanket and covered her to keep her warm and ran out of the room ahead of the smell. It was already five o'clock and still raining. I looked at myself in the mirror I was awfully funny-looking with those gloves and the hat and the coat though they hadn't scared Rakefet maybe they'd go well with a rifle I thought so I took my gun and lay down behind the armchair in an ambush. Now and then I fired a shot it's a game that once I liked better. The house was quiet. The baby didn't make a sound. Suddenly I thought she might be naked and catch cold. So I tiptoed in and saw that the blanket had really fallen off she had moved to another part of the bed and dragged the diaper with her everything smelled pieces of BM were everywhere she was trying to grab one she was talking to it I was afraid that next she'd want to eat it.

So I ran to grandpa's room to wake him I touched him and said grandpa get up quick something's happened to the baby. It was weird to be talking to him like I knew him when I'd never talked to him before. He turned toward me he opened his eyes you could see right away he didn't know where he was he stared at me wondering who I was he put his hand on his forehead he must have thought he was dreaming. I'm Gaddi I said to give him a hint he smiled and held out his hand he pulled me to his warm bed what time is it he asked it's five p.m. I said but what day is it he asked is it still Sunday. He looked at his watch it said ten o'clock that's right he said it's five I've been sleeping all this time.

"The baby's dirty. We have to clean her because mom's not home and there's a mess. You've got to help me. Mom said to wake you because I'm not allowed to lift her by myself."

He got up right away in his red pajamas and went to have a look at her it made him smile. Look how she undressed herself he said she must be freezing never mind we'll run her a bath right away and clean her up. She doesn't need a bath I said you won't be able to even dad can't you just have to clean her with this lotion I showed him the white bottle. Don't worry he said there's no problem just show me where her bathtub is and give me a towel you'll help me a bit and then you can go. Go where I said. Aren't you on your way out he asked. My way out where I said. He said I thought you were dressed to go out so I took off the hat and the gloves and the coat they were just for some game I was playing I said and he patted me on the head.

It really was strange how a minute ago he was fast asleep and now he was running around the house in pajamas tall and queer with a big head of white hair and bright eyes not stooped or slow hardly old-looking at all. And the baby too who'd been quiet after maybe eating some of her own crap looked curiously at her new grandpa she was finished crying she just babbled on and on. Grandpa wrapped her in a sheet and lifted her out of the crib she kept watching me to see if it was all right.

"It's all right," I said. "This is your new grandpa from America."

Grandpa laughed I'd better drink some coffee first to wake me up he said otherwise I'll make a mess of it can you find where things are in the kitchen? He had this fast way of talking that reminded me of Tsvi's I took out a cup and the sugar I brought him milk and instant coffee I even put the kettle on the stove and told him to light it he did with one hand I took some cake from the bread box he smiled I see you know your way around here I didn't answer though I knew what he was getting at he cut a piece of cake for us both and gave me mine as though the guest was me and not him. The water boiled he poured it with one hand he held the baby with the other he sat down to drink. The rain was quiet outside it ran down the window what's all this rain he said. It's the last one I said so he said it doesn't look like the last one to me it's plain rain and there's going to be plenty more he seemed sore at it so I asked have you had the last rain in America yet there's no last rain there he said that's an Israeli invention so now he was sore at all of Israel. The baby lay on his knees watching him put cake in his mouth and drink his coffee. Every now and then her eyes closed from sleepiness but she kept moving her mouth as though she were eating along with him. All at once she sat up with a whimper so he put some cake on his fork and stuck it in her mouth at first the fork scared her but then she started to suck on the cake because she has no teeth so he gave her some more and she ate that too she didn't know what to make of it. I don't know if mom would have allowed it but he was in charge now he was from the minute he got up.

She kept eating and he fed her with a smile she really reeks he said we have to wash her. He pushed the plate away. Who baked this cake your mother? Your grandmother baked wonderful cakes.

"My grandma in the hospital?"

"Yes."

I didn't say anything. He looked at me.

"No one's ever taken you to see her?"

"No. They don't want me to catch it from her."

"Catch it?!" he almost shouted. "Catch what?"

"What she's got."

"That's ridiculous. Who told you that?"

"My dad."

"What does your father know about such things!"

I didn't say anything. He looked at me.

"I'll tell your mother to take you to see your grandmother. She loved you so much when you were a baby."

I didn't say anything.

All of a sudden Rakefet fell asleep with her open mouth smeared with chocolate. She's already asleep I said maybe you don't have to bathe her.

"Doesn't she like baths?"

"Sometimes. She likes it when mom sings to her."

It was awfully weird to be talking like that with a new grandpa I didn't even know. The baby was really asleep all that chocolate cake must have pooped her out. Grandpa was thinking. I guess he was afraid to give her a bath too but when he smelled her he made up his mind we have to he said you'll help me. All right I said but I hope you realize that she'll start screaming again.

"We'll survive. When you were little your father and mother once left you with us in Tel Aviv and you screamed all night long. Your grandmother didn't sleep a wink."

"Did she take care of me?"

"You bet."

"Was she sick then too?"

"Of course not."

"Why did mom and dad bring me to you?"

"They just wanted a little rest from you."

He bent over again to smell the baby sleeping in her BM like the smell was supposed to tell him what to do all of a sudden I thought suppose I really caught what grandma has she must have had it then too. And just then something hurt near my heart it was even right in my heart. Why did mom and dad have to leave me with them? Grandpa stood up and put Rakefet in her crib I showed him where everything was and how to fill the bath he opened the closet and began taking out clothes and diapers and a towel it was weird how he poked around in there as though he needn't even ask all the time he kept pulling out clothes and opening and smelling them and checking how the buttons and the zippers worked. So I gave him the soap and of course he smelled that too I helped him fill the tub he brought an electric heater to the bathroom and turned it on. We put the thermometer in the water but I didn't know where the mercury should be he went to get his glasses when he put them on and looked at it he didn't know either. So he told me to keep my hand in the bath and tell him how it felt I kept telling him hot until he checked it himself you call this hot he said it's ice cold at last he told me to bring him a spoon so he could taste it. When he was finally ready he went to get the baby she was fast asleep wrapped in a sheet the telephone rang I wanted to get it don't leave me now he said I need you too much. And he told me to close the bathroom door.

He took the sheet off the baby who was really filthy he swabbed her with moist absorbent cotton I held the garbage pail up so he could throw the dirty pieces in it. The baby slept her head drooping down the telephone kept ringing on and on. He took off her shirt and fumbled with her undershirt he couldn't undo the knot it was making him nervous who tied this damn thing run bring some scissors he said the baby was still asleep. I ran to get them but couldn't find them the telephone kept ringing as though it were chasing me it must be mom or dad and awfully mad that no one was answering so I picked up the receiver and left it off the hook at least let them think it was busy. I went back to grandpa he'd taken his pajama tops off to keep them dry his chest was covered with white hair I can't find the scissors I said so he said run get me a knife quick Gaddi. I raced to the kitchen and brought him a sharp knife he put his glasses back on and tried cutting the knot he flipped over the baby who was still asleep but he couldn't see very well turn on the light he yelled quick Gaddi before there's an accident I turned it on he slashed open the whole undershirt and peeled it off just then Rakefet woke up and started to cry. He picked her up he bent down to the water and licked it to make sure it wasn't too hot he put her in but she was screaming she was fighting him something fierce. Here she had gotten used to being asleep and all of a sudden she was in the bathtub she really wriggled and squirmed maybe he was holding her too hard for fear of losing his grip for sheer panic sing to her Gaddi he said so I sang what mom sings blue are the waters of the sea sea sea while he hummed the melody he told me to hold her legs and pour soap into the water I tried grabbing them they kicked like crazy and got away Rakefet was battling the two of us like a lion she was shrieking suddenly there was blood in the water grandpa I said there's blood in the water he turned pale quick take the towel he said and I'll hand her to you I'm not allowed to lift her I said I'll put the towel on the chest and you lay her on it that's what we did he wrapped her up quick looking at his bloody hand it was his blood not Rakefet's he'd cut himself with the knife without knowing it. Rakefet stopped crying and rubbed her eyes grandpa sucked his cut finger and said thank

God he shut his eyes he dried her carefully and started to dress her you have to put powder on first I said that's what mom always does. If I have to I have to he said I'll do what you tell me where would I be without you. I gave him the box of powder and he poured it on her tush and on her weewee and rubbed it over them and over her fat thighs. Do you think she'll always be fat I asked she's not fat he laughed all babies are like that. Yours too I wanted to ask but I didn't the baby looked grandpa in the eyes while he tried dressing her cocking her head to one side as though wondering why an old man like him was bathing her in the middle of the day. But grandpa was in a good mood from time to time he sang some song he stopped to suck more blood from his cut laughing at her talking baby talk even bending down to kiss her tummy.

"She looks like grandma."

I didn't ask it I said it. I was sure he knew. He stopped kissing her and straightened up.

"What???"

"Once when Tsvi was here he told mom that she looks just like grandma. I mean like their mother . . ."

I said it quickly so he'd realize that that's what Tsvi said that meant it was so.

He smiled a funny smile and gave the baby a scared look.

"Tsvi said that?"

"Yes."

"And what did your mother say?"

"Mom didn't say anything but dad said it was nonsense."

He stood there sucking his cut like a boy smiling a dumb smile as though I'd said something bad. I handed him the undershirt he finally took it his hands shaking a bit he put it on her inside out then took it off and tried it differently he put her shirt over it just how old is she he asked about six months I said. He took a sweater and put it on her too he rummaged in the medicine cabinet until he found a big bandage I thought it was for himself but he wrapped it round her tummy even though she wasn't hurt there. I'd never seen mom do anything like it but he did it so quickly you'd think that he did it all the time.

What's the bandage for I asked. Mom doesn't do that. It's to strengthen her stomach he said.

"To keep her from getting fat?"

"No, that has nothing to do with it. Why do you think she's so fat? She isn't and neither are you."

"It's because of my glands," I whispered but he didn't hear.

The baby liked having the bandage on her tummy she was babbling for joy at the top of her voice. Grandpa was feeling good too.

"Do you do that to your baby in America too?"

He dropped what he was holding.

"Is there anything you don't know? They've told you everything!"

"Not everything."

"Who told you that? Your father? Your dad? He can't keep his mouth shut."

He was mad at me for saying he had a baby maybe he was ashamed of it.

"No." I whispered. "It was mom who told me." I wanted to drop the subject. He finished diapering Rakefet and even put a little jacket on her and wrapped her in a blanket and put her in her crib which still was a mess so he told me to sit with her in my arms while he cleaned it out and arranged it. She began to cry again the afternoon had spoiled her completely what a brat she'd become she thought she could just cry and cry so I made my funny face with the crazy hands and grandpa turned around to watch me.

"I used to be able to calm her like this when she was little," I explained.

He laughed. "If it was me it would just make me more nervous."

Suddenly she fell asleep all at once she just closed her eyes in the middle of one of my faces grandpa put her in her crib and covered her thank God I said and we tiptoed out and shut the door behind us. He went to his room and sat on the bed there to rest while I walked around the house I went back to the bathroom the kitchen wherever we had been until I came to the line of cars in the living room I took the worms from them and put them back in their box I noticed one was missing it was the one that escaped I looked for it everywhere in all the toys but I couldn't find it instead I found a little old boat I had forgotten all about so I took it to the baby's bathtub which still was full of water to see if it would float and it did. Grandpa was still in his room it was so quiet there that I went to see what he was up to he was lying down in bed again still thinking and sucking on his finger.

"Is anything the matter, Gaddi?"

"No."

"The baby's asleep?"

"Yes."

"Be careful you don't wake her."

"I won't."

"I'll get up soon. I just need to rest a bit. I seem to have blown some sort of fuse inside."

"That's okay."

I could feel he was angry with me for having mentioned his baby. So I went to the kitchen and finished off the cake I switched on the TV with the volume turned low to watch some program then I went back to look at grandpa he'd fallen asleep again he was curled up in bed it was getting dark I went back to the bathroom to see if the boat was still afloat it had sunk I wanted to fish it out but there was blood grandpa's blood in the water. So I left the bathroom and went to have a drink in the kitchen and walked quietly around the house until I saw that the telephone was still off the hook that's why it was so quiet it rang the minute I replaced it as though that ring were waiting all along. It was dad. What happened? He began to shout. Have you gone crazy? Who's been on the phone for so long? Grandpa? I've been trying to get you for the last hour.

No one's been on the phone I said so he said what are you talking about then you didn't hang up right go get mom quick.

"Mom's not back yet."

"She isn't? Where's your grandpa?"

"He's sleeping."

"He's still asleep?"

I didn't want to tell him about the bath and all that because it would just make him mad. Let him hear it all from mom.

"Tell me, has he gone off his rocker completely?"

I didn't answer.

"What are you doing now?"

"Nothing."

"Then why did you take the phone off the hook?"

"I just took it off for a minute. The baby was crying and I didn't want it to wake her."

"Why on earth should it wake her? Don't ever let me catch you doing that again. You're driving me batty, do you hear?"

"Yes."

"You better watch it, have you got that?"

He hung up. As soon as I did too it rang again as though another ring were patiently waiting its turn it was mom she sounded like she was underground so far away shouting in a faint voice saying that she couldn't hear me that she was on her way home then she hung up also.

It was really dark in the house but I didn't turn on the lights sometimes it's nice to walk around in the dark I went to look at the baby she was in a deep sleep so peaceful a bomb wouldn't wake her now. I passed grandpa's door he was lying in bed on his back his hands behind his head still thinking smoking a cigarette.

"Gaddi?" he called to me. "Who was that who called?"

"First dad, then mom."

"What did your mother want?"

"To say that she's on her way home."

"Where has she gone to?"

"She didn't say."

I stood in the doorway maybe he had more questions.

"Come here a minute."

I stepped into the room I went to his bed I thought maybe now he wants to give me my present. He grabbed hold of my hand and looked at me like he was seeing me for the first time.

"Why are you so sad all the time?"

"I'm not sad."

"Are you always somber like this?"

I knew what he meant but I didn't know what to say. Mom once called me that too but couldn't explain it exactly.

"Is something bothering or worrying you?"

I didn't know what to say maybe about the boy who called me Boxer who I hit he might try getting even with me tomorrow though right after report cards was vacation I didn't want to tell him he might think there were lots of kids like that it's not my being fat that makes me somber because it isn't my fault there's a reason for it maybe someday they'll fix my glands. So I said:

"It's because of mom, she left me with the baby. She said Rakefet would sleep after lunch but she didn't. It isn't fair because I'm not allowed to lift her and I can't quiet her if she's lying down. No one can."

He listened he didn't look old he was still wearing his pajamas all at once he sat up and bent over his suitcase he looked there for something at last I thought he's giving me what he brought because it can't be that he didn't dad said for sure he did but all he took out was a pack of cigarettes he tore off the wrapper and pulled out a cigarette and lit it he lay down again in bed with his hands behind his head and the cigarette in his mouth. He was looking at me but thinking of something else.

And then he started asking me about mom and dad what they did and how they lived and what they were like and whether they fought with each other. I told him that sometimes they did that it was always dad who started but mom was to blame because she forgot to do things he told her I told him everything I told him too much he made me tell him things I didn't know that I knew everything interested him he sat up in bed and listened bent over toward me he didn't always understand what I said so I had to explain and repeat things he kept holding my hand and asking me to talk more slowly more clearly I guess it must have been important to him. Like that mom was getting fat and that made dad sore even though he was fat himself but mom didn't care. And he asked me all these exact little questions as though he wanted to live over with me all the time he'd been away. I even told him things that happened more than a year ago like the car accident and the night that mom cried and things that maybe I shouldn't have like the time mom lost her purse with over two thousand pounds in it and dad didn't talk to her for a week until he did again when the baby was born. Grandpa was wound up he listened to every detail he kept asking me questions it was really dark outside in the house too except for the glow of his cigarette he flicked the ashes into his palm as though it were an ashtray doesn't it hurt you I asked no he said old people don't feel heat anymore because they're cold inside. But you're not an old man I said because you have a baby. So he laughed and said I'll be an old man with a baby but bring me an ashtray anyway I brought him one and he stubbed out the cigarette in it he turned on the light and got up and looked in his suitcase again I thought maybe now but he only took out some underpants and took off his pajamas first the tops and then the bottoms he stood naked in front of me before I could look away I saw what I didn't want to his long skinny body with the scary white hair and a wrinkled cock below I hardly saw it though I couldn't understand how he wasn't ashamed to let me see as though I was a baby I left the room feeling sick. I turned on all the lights I filled the house with light I even turned on the TV what had I been expecting I thought what was in it for me I wouldn't even have cared if he'd brought me something cheap I watched the TV to forget that white hair down below after a while he came to the living room washed and dressed and shaved with a checked shirt and green pants he even smelled of perfume he sat in the armchair watching Mickey Mouse with me in silence. I got down on my knees to collect my cars aren't you watching TV he asked no I said it's for babies. That made him laugh so it's true what they say he said that there's a new generation that isn't addicted to television anymore you're a member of that generation. I'm glad to see that. Suddenly I knew that he hadn't brought me anything that he just yakety-yakked all the time. That he thought my generation didn't need presents. He sat watching TV like a little boy there were sounds of people getting hit and of things being broken I wanted to get up now and watch too but I couldn't after saying it was baby stuff. Finally it ended some Arabic program came on so I asked if he knew Arabic and turned off the set. Then I sat watching him maybe he wanted to ask me something else.

Just then the door opened and mom walked in with her arms full of packages she was wet from the rain. She smiled at us both. I see you're up father. I went to her I could see from the shape of the bags that she hadn't bought me my airplane just flat things like clothes grandpa went to kiss her she took off her coat and wanted to kiss me too.

"How's Rakefet?"

"She didn't sleep. You were wrong again. We had terrible problems with her, grandpa too, and it's all your fault. Where did you disappear to? We had to give her a bath and grandpa cut himself."

"It's nothing." Grandpa laughed. Mom was all confused.

"You gave her a bath?" She laughed. I left them I went to the kitchen I took a knife I put on my coat I opened the front door.

"Where are you going?"

"I have to pick mulberry leaves," I said. "Do you want all my worms to die?"

"Now? In the dark? In the rain?" She tried stopping me but I slipped past her down the stairs to the street. It wasn't raining I crossed to the other side I walked toward the bus stop I reached the mulberry tree and tried shinnying up it but it was too slippery a man with a hat on was standing at the bus stop he saw me and helped me grab a branch it was an old man who limped a little I took out my knife and quickly cut the fresh wet leaves.

I gathered a bunch of them and stuck them inside my coat.

"Do you raise silkworms?"

"That's right."

He approached me now in the light I could see he was a dirty miserable old man. I started home he turned around and came with me kind of limping.

"Do you have cocoons yet?"

"Yes, five."

"Soon you'll have butterflies."

"I guess so."

I couldn't figure out what he wanted.

"Do you know how a cocoon turns into a butterfly?"

"Yes."

"How?"

But I didn't. So he began explaining to me what happens inside the sealed white cocoon. He wouldn't leave me alone he limped along beside me he even offered me candy. Just then the lights of dad's car shone on us he had driven up quickly. He flung open the door and stepped out with his briefcase.

"Gaddi, what are you doing here?"

The old man stepped to the side.

"Yes? Can I help you?" dad asked.

The man started to mumble something.

"What does he want from you?"

"Nothing."

"Where do you live?" dad asked him harshly.

The old man didn't answer he turned to go.

"Beat it! This isn't the place for you . . . get a move on, mister! . . . What did he want from you? How could you have let him accost you like that? Be more careful, Gaddi, don't you realize whom you're dealing with? What's come over you lately?"

"He helped me pick mulberry leaves. He held the branch for me."

"All right, come on home. Is grandpa up?"

"Yes."

"It's about time."

I followed him up the stairs how could I have told grandpa all about them now he must be telling mom. I saw her face in the doorway looking at me seriously I went to my room.

It was dark the baby was sleeping you couldn't even tell she was there I put the new leaves in the box and took out the old ones suddenly I remembered the worm that was lost I went to look for it dad was talking to grandpa by the door of grandpa's room he gave him some papers the radio was on in the kitchen mom was setting the table in the dining nook. I went to look for the worm in the kitchen.

"What's the matter, Gaddi?" Her voice was gentle. "Grandpa says you were a wonderful helper."

I didn't answer I was looking for that worm maybe it had spun a cocoon. Finally I said:

"You promised the baby would sleep. She cried all the time and even made in her crib."

"I thought she would sleep. She was up all morning. How was I to know?"

"But you promised."

"What do you mean, I promised? Don't be idiotic. How can I promise what she'll do?"

"Then don't. But you did."

She looked tired. Why did I say bad things about her to grandpa? I went to the toy basket I turned it over the worm wasn't there. I took all my cars and went back to the kitchen and started to throw them in the garbage pail.

"What's going on there?"

"I'm throwing out some old toys I don't need."

"Must you do it now?"

"Yes."

Dad came to butt in to check up to take over.

"What are you throwing out there? Are you out of your mind?"

"I don't need them anymore."

He stood watching the garbage pail fill up.

"Now go empty it downstairs."

I went down with the plastic bag. Cars sped along the wet street but the rain had stopped the sky was clear. I opened the garbage bin a cat jumped out I dumped the plastic bag in a can the cat stood meowing as soon as I moved away it jumped back into the can I covered it with the lid. Suddenly I didn't want to go home. What made me tell grandpa everything he didn't bring me anything he didn't give me a thing. The old man saw me he came out from the doorway of another house he'd been poking around in the garbage there. I ran up the stairs I felt sorry now about some of those toys.

Dad was eating already grandpa was sitting beside him at the table with an empty plate. I sat down to eat but they made me wash my hands when I returned dad was making some joke about the government grandpa smiled then he talked about America. I didn't listen I ate as fast as I could. Then I was sent to wash up. When I came back in my pajamas they were sitting in the living room. Dad was saying something nasty to grandpa they were talking about grandma grandpa was hunched in the armchair looking at the floor I wanted to hear but mom put her hand on me.

"Go to bed."

"I want to watch TV."

"Absolutely not tonight."

I went to bed. Rakefet was sleeping like a log she'd sleep on and on like grandpa now like she'd come from America too. Mom took off the bedspread she took a pillow from the closet she pulled back the blanket I crawled quickly into bed before she could see the faint stains from the morning. She covered me all at once she put her lips on my forehead.

"Are you warm? I have a feeling that you're coming down with something."

But I wasn't.

"There are report cards tomorrow," I reminded her.

She didn't hear me though she was sad. Had grandpa told her what I told him?

"Grandpa thinks the world of you. He says that you know so much, that you understand so much . . ."

I didn't say anything. She turned off the light and went out. I lay there in the dark. Then I got up and went barefoot to pee. In the hallway I saw them dad was showing grandpa some more papers and grandpa was reading them. Mom stood off to one side. They were talking about grandma I understood it right away. She wasn't in a hospital she was in a prison I knew it I knew it all along. Grandpa had come to get her out. Suddenly dad felt me standing in the dark.

"Scram! Back to bed," he said.

I ran to my room. I felt sorry for grandpa. I looked at the worms they had nibbled the fresh leaves. One of them was loose in the house it would turn into a cocoon and then into a butterfly if dad didn't squash it on purpose.

I covered myself with the blanket. The baby sighed. All at once her breath came in jerks. She must want to wake up and cry again. If I'm quick enough I'll fall asleep before it starts.

MONDAY

Things fall apart; the centre cannot hold;
Mere anarchy is loosed upon the world . . .
                                    W. B. Yeats

What do I care? We have to talk in whispers in the morning to keep
the radio down to hold the baby all the time so she won't cry when I
called at noon yesterday and she said he was still sleeping I warned
her she better wake him or he'd never sleep at night it's not jet lag
anymore it's depression but she said let him sleep what do you care. I
don't but I do that all last night he was up around the house again
and wouldn't let us sleep. There's no night or day around here anymore by the time his inner clock is reset he'll be on his way back to
America and meanwhile our clock is off too not mine but Ya'el's
because I won't give in to this lunacy no one keeps me from sleeping
once in the army I even dozed off under fire. Someone has to stay
sane in all this chaos I have an office to run and a murder trial
waiting for me I can't afford to be a shadow of myself like her for the
past three days getting maybe five hours' sleep how can I even think
of sex with her. But it's almost over. Tomorrow we'll ship the old
man to Jerusalem let Mr. Young Ph.D. and his little nun of a wife
look after their dad for a while and I'll look after my biological
accounts don't think I've forgotten the pleasures outstanding how
much pleasure is left in this goddamn life anyway. As long as we're
alive and kicking we've got a lay coming to us now and then what we

don't do now we'll never make up for later. The real loser will be Gaddi. All week long he's heard nothing but grandpa grandpa he must have thought a good angel was coming down from heaven I told her why put ideas in his head what good's all this grandpa stuff to him what good's your whole family to us there hasn't been a day in the last seven years when we could even leave the boy with them and take a vacation for ourselves. Some families come with grand-mothers free of charge to raise the children while the parents run around the world but what's your mother ever done for us except get herself locked up thirty kilometers from here so that we can burn ten liters of gas to go visit her twice a month. Still not even to have brought the boy some kind of present is really too much. He forgot. He wanted to forget. His own self he never forgets. Let alone that during twelve hours in an airplane where every minute someone's trying to sell you whiskey or cigarettes for a song he might have thought of me too it's me after all who's getting him his freedom who's treating him to a new life what would it have cost him to bring me a nice little bottle of French cognac he lives in dollarland anyway life's so much easier for him. But leave me out of it forget about me I don't count I don't need his damn liquor how many grandchildren do you have grandpa? Just one besides the baby. The baby you can forget she'll never know you were here but the boy's gone gaga over you all week long he kept looking at the globe to see how you would come he made you a big welcome grandpa sign with flowers as tall as trees I mean he was ecstatic so how the hell could you forget to bring him even a small toy something symbolic it's not that he needs things you can go to his room and see for yourself but you live in toy universe couldn't you have brought him something we'd all get a kick out of a remote-control car or some tank that shoots little shells? Two grandchildren here in Haifa are all you have there won't be any more so soon trust Kedmi's intuition on that you'd need the Holy Ghost to make one in Jerusalem and some new facts of life in Tel Aviv. So at eleven o'clock last night after the boy's hung silently around you all day you actually remember that you should have brought him something and begin to apologize that the trip wasn't planned and that you had no time to shop and could I please buy him something for you that's my latest job to buy the presents you've forgotten and in the end you won't even pay me back for them I could see it the minute you got up to look for your wallet as soon as

just to be polite I whispered don't bother you collapsed right back
into your chair looking for wallets must fatigue you.

All right then so we'll buy him something to remember you by
when you're gone maybe he will. The poor kid has only one grandfather I've got a stake in your image and believe me presents are important to kids. They remember the times they've had by the
presents they've gotten I know what goes on in his mind we're like
the same person I handle him like I handle myself. The boy knows
where it's at he's got a good head for sums. You should have heard
what his arithmetic teacher told me he even found some mistake that
she'd made. He's from my side of the family not yours he's like me
that's why I'm so crazy about him. If only he weren't growing up too
serious for this ridiculous world.

"So who's this boy who calls you Boxer?"

"He's from 3A."

"What's his name? Who are his parents?"

"I don't know."

"But what's he like?"

"Kind of skinny. Small."

"So what are you afraid of him for? Sock it to him where it hurts."

"I already did."

"When??"

"Yesterday. I knocked him down. He even bled."

"Easy there, Gaddi, easy. We don't want to leave any marks.
Don't forget that you're in a special class already."

But you've got to hand it to him. He can take care of himself even
if I do now notice a black-and-blue mark on his forehead. The way
those quiet brown eyes take me in that mouth quickly shoveling it
away it's the same nervous hunger that shot me up to a meter eighty-
one even if I have ten kids someday and I won't the fat little sweetheart will always have a special place in my heart.

"C'mon, Gaddi, that's enough. I've got to go. I have a crazy day
ahead of me."

A crazy day with crazy people. But what do I care I said I'd do it
and I will as long as they let me do it my way. Just let the family
keep out of it and I'll hand the old folks their divorce all signed
sealed and delivered. A really neat job. Just all of you keep out of it.
If there's an ounce of sanity among you you'll leave it to me to find a
painless way out of this forty-year-old neurotic mess. You're lucky to

have found a lawyer to marry into this family of yours so have a little faith in him after all you're not paying me a cent for this relax I wouldn't think of taking it anyway.

"C'mon, Gaddi, you've had enough. You'll be late for school. Leave room for your ten o'clock snack."

The kid's gotten used to eating too much when no one's looking. Ya'el comes into the kitchen half asleep gray these last few days have been the death of her I get up to give her a big hug and a kiss not that I feel like it just to show her I'm still boss.

"You're sure you don't want me to come with you?"

"Absolutely not. You'll only complicate things. As soon as she sees you she'll think of some new way to be crazy. With me she talks plain prose, with you she starts spouting poetry. Let me do it my way, for God's sake. Why don't you spend some time with your father? You haven't seen him for three years. What did you take off from work for? And there's still the family seder to think of, why should you run around with me all day? I'm going. If the secretary calls, tell her to sit tight and that I'm on my way. . . . Yes, I'll see the doctor first. It's not just a medical issue, it's a legal one too. What's this? What's in this bag? . . . Vitamin powder for the dog? I swear to God . . . All right, all right, I'll give it to her. A work of genius could be written about that dog if only you could find the genius to write it. Don't you have some new novel for her to read? . . . All right, all right. I'll call during the day. We'll be in touch. Don't worry, and whatever you do don't forget to tell the secretary to wait. Gaddi, I'm off!"

Yesterday it rained and gusted today the sun's beating down how can you expect stability in a country with such weather? The cars keep streaming down the hill no one stops to let you in you might think from the rush that people actually work around here they just want to punch in quick so they can go moonlight somewhere else. Honk you stinking Subaru screech till your brakes burn it's my road too I pay enough taxes for it.

To think that once I went to this school too I'd kill myself if I had to go back how scared I was of those shitassed teachers but he looks like he actually enjoys it the jaunty way he bounces out of the car. Where are those traffic monitors they promised? Don't tell me young kids have started striking too. I'll just wait to watch him cross the street. I don't like to think of his walking home by himself with all these crazy cars zooming around. Honk honk your head off you fucking Volvo you just wait till my son crosses the street you bitch if you're itching to kill some child this morning go find another one than mine.

That's it. I can't see him anymore among the children. When they're babies you don't feel a thing for them but the older they get the wilder you become about them. That's all life is in the end just a few people no matter how grand no matter how complicated no matter how wretched so spare them a smile if you can.

"Morning."

My secretary is huddled by the electric heater small dark and bitter if she goes on like this only the heater will want to marry her.

"Are you cold, Levana? And here I was thinking I'd actually seen a little bit of sunlight outside—or was I mistaken?"

She glances up at me darkly with that look that's already driven more than one client away.

"For the forty thousand pounds that I pay you per month plus all the fringe benefits don't I at least deserve one smile in the morning? Or do I have to pay extra for that?"

By the time she gets it and gives me a twisted smile I feel sorry for having made fun of her. And it's only on her good days that she gets one out of every ten jokes that I tell her. When I opened a private practice two years ago after getting fed up with financing a new Cadillac for Mr. Advocate Gordon each year I was advised by those in the know to take an old maid with two years of high school it will cost you less they said and you can be sure she'll sit faithfully in the office and not run to the doctor every day with a sick baby what they forgot to mention was that you can also be sure of perpetual gloom stuck to a chair a foot away from you and of a big hike in the electric bill.

"Was there any mail?"

"No."

That aggrieved tone of voice. They can't forgive us for having rescued them from the caves of the Atlas Mountains and introduced them to civilization.

"Did anyone call from the district court to let us know if they've set a date for our murder trial?"

"No."

"Did Mr. Goren call to tell us when he sent that check of his that he never sent?"

"No."

"Did anyone call this morning, was anyone in the office?"

"No."

I pay her forty thousand pounds a month to hear her say no all day long. Two hundred pounds for each no.

"All right, then. Call Goren right away and tell him that I still haven't gotten his check and that if he doesn't get it to me this morning I'm not going to the rabbinical court tomorrow and he can stay married a few years more."

A fancy divorce settlement that I finished two months ago. In the end it upsets people to realize that they've gone to a lawyer when they could have gotten the same deal on their own if only they'd kept their cool. Maybe they could have but it takes a certain amount of intelligence to know when you've run into a blank wall most people prefer to bang their heads against it and then hire a lawyer to explain to them that it can't be moved. Why is she looking at me like that in a minute she'll be asking me what Goren's number is.

"I don't know Mr. Goren's telephone number."

"And why indeed should you? I've only given it to you thirty times. It's a pity you can't move away from that heater, because if you could you might free your legs enough to get to the telephone book. When is your birthday?"

"Why?"

"I want to know. Is it a secret? Do I have to find it out from the police?"

"June tenth."

"Then maybe you could move it up a bit so that I can buy you the present I've been meaning to—an electric blanket to wrap yourself in so as not to be addicted to that heater . . ."

Those dark Moroccan eyes regard me does she get it or am I jerking off another joke in vain she's already cried more than once over my jokes in a second she'll cry again I'll have to add the cost of all that Kleenex to the electric bill.

"I was only kidding. Don't take me so seriously. I see you're feeling low this morning. Did something happen at home?"

"No."

Her father must have beat her. Those primitives run amuck before each Jewish holiday or maybe one of them's in jail I already once had to bail out a brother of hers after he socked somebody in the market that's how I made the acquaintance of a family of greengrocers for my fee they sent me a check drawn on eggplant we ate them for a whole month now when I see one I cross to the other side of the street. It was clever of them to plant a daughter in a lawyer's office though if you intend to run regularly afoul of the law you need dependable legal coverage.

She gets up and goes to the stack of telephone books she turns their pages as though they were the Talmud. Let's see how long it takes her.

"I won't be in the office this morning. I told you yesterday that I'd be out today, didn't I?"

"Yes."

Yes? Did she really say yes? All is not lost there's still hope.

"Did you finish typing that agreement that I gave you the day before yesterday?"

"Yes. It's on your desk."

Yes again. If she keeps it up she'll find a husband after all the agreement is in fact on my desk I can't deny she makes clean copies she works slowly but surely.

"Did you guess who the parties in it are?"

"No."

"That's just as well."

She looks at me with huge surprised eyes like a witness japped by the prosecution she won't have any peace of mind until she japs me back.

"If you'd look for Goren in the Haifa phone book instead of in the Tel Aviv one you might find him there before noon."

She's so alarmed she drops the phone book but I look at my feet to avoid embarrassing her the phone book's not made out of glass after all the phone company's taken her into account.

I quickly read the divorce agreement I drew up. A good one a really good one. In a few years I can publish a treatise on divorce and get a university chair. Everybody's uncle writes a book in this country and everybody's cousin praises it in the newspapers so why not let the world see for itself the grade-A work that I do. I just hope the old lady signs today with no problems. When I was alone with him in the living room last night I said be a sport don't quibble over each cent don't forget you live in dollars now the Messiah himself when he comes couldn't up the value of the Israeli pound against them do you know how many men over sixty would love to get a divorce like this and trade in the old jalopy? He sat shocked in the shadow of the unlit lamp looking at me angrily a savage glitter in his glasses he jumped up shaking flushed with rage I was sure he was going to hit me. Maybe it's true that I come on as a bastard I've got a big mouth my poor dead father used to say there's no clutch between your brain and your tongue though it was he who taught me that style it's just that he had to aim most of his jokes at himself since who'd have laughed at them if he hadn't? How he used to lose his temper with me yet secretly pleased with me too two hours before he died with twenty tubes stuck up him I still got a laugh out of him but he had a sense of humor how many people like that do you find nowadays? I have to be more careful. Once I made a gag in court I waited for the merry tinkle of laughter it was so quiet you could hear a pin drop one of the judges was so stunned he nearly fell off the dais. I thought I'd be debarred for it in the end I got off with a reprimand. What can you do? That's the world we live in. The trouble is that sometimes I regret having said things myself it's not that I really think of her like that I've learned to respect and even to like her although those first years she wasn't totally human I mean the way it's defined in the encyclopedias.

But what could I tell him that I'm sorry then he'd think I'd really meant it so I just waited for him to insult me back because at least if I hurt people's feelings I'm willing to have mine hurt too let him say what he wants that I'm fat that I'm clumsy that I'm a very mediocre lawyer I'll even write his lines for him something really mean he'll see I'm the first to applaud him but he didn't say a thing he just spun around dumbstruck in the room how I hate all these people with thin skins.

"Maybe you'd like a glass of some good, special cognac?"

But he refused with an angry wave of his hand as though chasing away a fly and left the room. Let him suit himself. Afterwards when I undressed in the bedroom Ya'el kept asking me what did you say to him. What did you say? Did you say something to him? I only said he should be a little more generous. That's all? Yes that's all. For sensitive souls like him that's apparently too much come to sleep do you know how many nights it's been since you've fulfilled your connubial duty I could get a rabbinical permit for adultery but she just looked at me mournfully and walked out in the middle of the sentence. The family's falling apart. The last bastion.

Should I go or wait for the mail?

Levana comes to tell me that Goren insists that he sent me the check four days ago. The thought that a check for a hundred thousand in my name is making the rounds of this town in the hands of those morons in the post office is enough to give me the willies. I asked him the day before yesterday didn't you at least send it registered. It turned out it hadn't even occurred to him. When he married his wife ten years ago it didn't occur to him that he might want to dump her one day either. Should I go or wait for the mail?

It's so quiet. What's going on here? No one needs me today? No one killed anyone last night? No one stole no one burgled no one cheated no one put his hand in the till? No one wants to sell an apartment or to rent anything? Anyone reading the newspapers might think that half of Israel does nothing but earn a living for us let him come and see the quiet in the lawyers' offices there are too many of us wolves all waiting for the same prey. Well if nobody needs me I'll go visit my murderer and from there to the loony bin. A charming itinerary isn't it?

"All right, Levana, I'm on my way. If the check comes, deposit it right away in the bank before it can bounce. And when you've warmed up, take a wet rag and clean off our sign below. All that soot on it doesn't make us look good. The whole world thinks that all lawyers are shysters; we'll never convince it otherwise, but at least it needn't think that we're dirty ones."

Suddenly the phone rings I can tell from the sound that it's someone in the family still I let Levana answer if she doesn't keep busy she'll degenerate completely it's part of what I'm paying her for I've had to teach myself not to grab at the phone people think more of you if they have to ask a secretary for you.

It's Tsvi from Tel Aviv. All in a tizzy. A few minutes ago he spoke with Ya'el and heard that I was going there alone and he thinks (why shouldn't he have thoughts too?) that it's out of the question someone from the family must come with me if not Ya'el then himself he'll come right away he'll cancel everything (what could he possibly have to cancel?) and join me because we have to break it gently it's not just a formality there's the doctor to talk to as well she may get emotional when she hears that he's in Israel it will be very painful for her . . .

I let him talk the call from Tel Aviv is on him so what's the rush. He can talk all he wants. I'm listening. It's his right. In the family they say that he's the problematic middle child that he's very close to his mother not that I've ever seen proof of it it's all purely theoretical long-distance sympathy. Since she was put away five years ago he and his brother have kept the fifth commandment strictly by phone. If Moses had thought of such a possibility he could have gotten by with nine. I the stranger who thank God doesn't have a drop of her blood in my body have visited her more often than her two sons put together and now they want to mess things up for me.

"Do you hear me, Kedmi? Wait there and I'll come with you."

"Don't bother. Either I go see her by myself or else you can count me out. You can find yourselves another lawyer, it will cost you fifty thousand smackers plus tax just for the right to talk to him. You have no idea how lucky you are that I'm both in the business and a member of this family. If I didn't exist you'd have to invent me. You're wrong if you think that I'm nothing but a big oaf with a loose tongue. You have no monopoly on either pain or gentleness." I glance at my secretary sitting silently with her head down playing with her pencil lapping up every goddamn word. "I have an old mother too and I know what it's like. I'll know how to handle her. I've already talked to her several times, I've done the groundwork and prepared her. She's a lot stronger and saner than you think. We have a good, unsentimental, working relationship, even the dog's taken a liking to me lately. . . . Where are you talking from, home? Then there's time to explain to you exactly what my plan is. . . ."

In the end he manages to hang up on me. It's almost ten o'clock am I going or not. Maybe the check will still come I'll feel better if I deposit it myself. I dial Ya'el.

"Yes, Tsvi called me. . . . No, he's not coming with me. . . . Yes, I'm being stubborn. If someone has to be stubborn, it damn well better be me. Is your father still sleeping? . . . He had to come all the way to Israel to learn the fine art of slumber. . . . What did I say to him? I already told you, I didn't say a thing. Tell me what he said that I said, go on, I want to hear. . . . If you don't know stop hassling me, I'm hassled enough as it is. . . . Because I'll go see her by myself. I'll get her to sign, you'll see it will all work out. . . . All

right. . . . All right. . . . All right. . . . All right. . . . I'll only
say what's absolutely necessary. Ten percent of my average output."

I know she's smiling now into the phone that wise tender smile
that I married her for not like Levana's who isn't missing a word her
curly African head down grinning to herself for sheer joy. Hats off to
her I never would have thought that she knew what average output
meant. I can see that if I want to keep up her morale I have to crack
some joke at my own expense every hour on the hour.

"Just a minute, Ya'el." I cover the receiver with my hand. "If you
don't mind, Levana, as long as I'm still in the office . . . that wet
rag we talked about . . . the sign down below . . ."

She rises grudgingly she takes a rag and goes out while I get back
to Ya'el I say a few sweet words and remind her to reserve a place for
her father on the limousine to Jerusalem tomorrow.

I'd really better go or should I wait some more but what for. It
doesn't look like there'll be any mail today. I sit down and open a
locked drawer I take out the murder file and leaf through it. By now
I know every detail by heart but still it obsesses me. This is my
chance this is my hope this is my ticket to get ahead. The rest is
garbage. Three months ago when Steiner died his office divvied up
his cases. I got a young murderer a television repairman it looks like
he really did it though he insists that he didn't since then he's all I
think about. I've slept with him dreamed of him spent dozens of
hours with him. His family has no money but they've called in a rich
uncle from Belgium to help and help is what he'll need. He made
sure to leave his fingerprints all over the apartment everywhere except on the television that he never got around to fixing. But did he
murder the old man or did he just find the corpse there I'm going
nuts trying to figure it out I'll drive the judges nuts too. I phone the
prison and ask them to get him ready for me I'll stop off on my way
to have a chat with him.

So now I really have to move. Only where's Levana? I step into
the dark corridor into its underworld mold. A few unsavory characters are sitting on the bench by the door to Mizrachi's office for the
past year the media have been arguing whether there's organized
crime in this country if they could see who's being licensed to practice law these days they would realize that the organization is the
government.

So where has she gone to? I should never have sent her out. All I

want now is to move to get going to do something. I return to the
office glance at the telephone gather up my papers wipe a little dust
with my finger from the volumes of the proceedings of the supreme
court smear it on an old map of Israel on the wall rummage through
Levana's pocketbook hanging from her chair photographs of movie
stars clipped from the newspapers crumpled tissues a vial of cheap
perfume what a wasteland in keeping with the grayness of this office
with its high mildewed British ceiling that smells of failure once I
said to Ya'el give me some bright new idea here some fresh direction
of paint but I dropped it when I saw what it would cost. I call my
mother to let off some steam.

"It's you at last. I thought you'd forgotten me." (Since Ya'el's
father arrived she hasn't had a moment of peace.) "What's happening." (It's not a question, it's a statement of fact.) "I called yesterday
afternoon, did they tell you? What kind of business is that, leaving
Gaddi alone with the baby, he's only six." (Seven.) "He sounded so
sad." (He always does to her.) "And the old man was sleeping."
(That's what she calls him, even though he's a year younger than she
is.) "What's the matter with him? Is he sick or is there something up
his sleeve? He didn't even bring Gaddi a present. What sort of ego-
tism is that? Did he bring anything for you?"

"No. It's not important."

"I knew he wouldn't, and here you are trying to get him his divorce. Is that poor crazy thing really ready to agree?" (She's always
made her out to be sicker than she is.) "To think of him throwing her
to the dogs like that." (I hold the telephone away from my ear and
stare out the window.) "Why must you involve yourself in it?" (Here
I can't deny she has a point.) "He isn't paying you after all, is he? Is
he?"

"No. Why should he?"

"I knew it. So why get involved. If afterwards there's trouble,
you'll be held responsible. Don't you have enough work in the office
without looking for more? In the end there's bound to be bad feelings
and who will he hate for it? You. They'll take it out on you because
you're not one of theirs, so why are you wasting your time always
running to see her? Don't you have an important trial coming up?
You know, the one your career depends on, that trial you're preparing for, that if you get that rapist acquitted . . ."

"Murderer."

"That makes it even bigger. It will make you famous, you'll be able to open a big office. So instead of getting ready for all the questions you'll be asked you go running gratis to insane asylums. What will come of it all? Yesterday I thought I'd go say hello to him, but all this sleeping of his scared me off. And what's with Ya'el? Smiling her quiet smile, I'll bet. Didn't you once tell me that you fell in love with her because of it? Didn't you, Yisra'el?"

"I did."

"Well, you're free to decide what you want. Your poor father once said something deadly about that smile, something you're not going to want to hear. Do you want to hear it?"

"Not now, mother."

"So I'll see him the night of the seder then. It's rather strange to insist on a divorce at his age, don't you think? What does he need it for? He's separated from her anyway. But I suppose he wants to get married over there in America. People have no idea what sex does to old people. Your own father when he was in the hospital . . . do you want to hear about it?"

"Not now, mother. I'm in a hurry. Some other time."

Levana enters noiselessly she puts the rag by the sink she washes her hands.

"Will you drop by today? I've made those meat patties that you like."

"I don't think so. I have a crazy day today."

"I have a delicious pie too."

"I'm afraid I can't. What sort of pie?"

"Apple."

"Well, I'll see. Goodbye."

She's still washing her hands.

"Are you done?" I ask gently. "You seem to have misunderstood. I meant you should just clean the sign, not the whole street . . ."

She flushes her eyes going wild.

"You have to comment on everything!"

"What??"

But she doesn't answer.

"What??"

But she doesn't answer her head is bowed her hands twist a piece of paper she's actually trembling.

And I'm already outside. Feeling hassled. They've hassled the hell out of me Ya'el my mother and now this little darkie too. Just imagine if every darkie around here should start opening his mouth and saying dark things. It's not enough that ninety percent of them are in court all the time. They want to give us lessons in etiquette too. My mood is shot now. Suddenly I'm all jelly inside. My father went and left me with this nosy venomous woman and I have to carry her on my back. An only child. Everybody's favorite target. They were too busy sleeping at night to have time to make me a brother. I'll show that little darkie yet. When the right moment comes I'll turn off that heater and fire her. My mood's shot to hell. And outside it's cloudy again and everyone's beeping their horns the traffic's moving at a crawl the whole world's in a rush maybe I'll find some peace there in the prison.

Thank God that Haifa is at least a pretty town they haven't managed to ruin it yet. Screened by pine trees that help filter out the general filth. I drive along the ridge of the Carmel into the forest ocean down below on either side bathing my eyes in the green air eddying over the lush wadis.

Everyone knows me here at the prison I'm not even asked for my papers. These past few months I've spent whole days here if ever I'm imprisoned myself I can ask the judge for time off retroactively from my sentence.

What bedlam. Every other door is unlocked the jailers just jingle their keys for form's sake and then wonder why prisoners escape. Escape isn't the word they just have to open the door and walk out.

An old Druse jailer brings me to a dark cubbyhole it's a good thing there are still Druse and Cherkesses to keep order in this country my young murderer sits waiting by a bare wooden table short slender and sullen but very muscular when he was still in handcuffs the first time I met him I noticed how easily he stretched them. I shake his hand. God is my witness that I've tried to like him but he's an unfriendly fantasizing type to top it all off they found some marijuana in his house.

"What's doing?" He looks at me with his mousy eyes.

"Is everything all right?"

He nods.

I toss my attaché case on the table I sit across from him I leaf through the file that I practically know by heart. The forty thousand pounds that I've gotten so far from his family have barely covered the ink and paper that I've wasted on him.

"Have you heard anything from that uncle of yours . . . that diamond dealer in Belgium?"

"He's supposed to arrive any day."

"He's been supposed to arrive for three months now. Apparently he's decided to come from Belgium on foot."

He gives me a hard sullen stare. I should know by now that I have to be careful with my jokes here.

I begin to ask a few questions going over once more details of his testimony about the great day in his life that I've lived every minute of and know better by now than any day in my own. That's my secret strategy for his defense I'll break time down under the legal microscope into its tiniest particles I'll wage war over each second. The prosecution has no idea what's in store for it. I've catalogued the minutes one by one and I'll prove that he couldn't have done it. This trial will yet be a textbook case to be studied with astonishment and awe. It was Kedmi who first taught us to think in milliseconds . . .

I interrogate him and he answers briefly and to the point. He's a lone wolf all that damn day he hardly talked to anyone but stupid he's not. I already know all his answers I simply have to polish them here and there to put him through his paces once again. I want this trial in the worst possible way. Just the look of him is suspicious at least let him be clear and precise. But what's the truth? I'm still groping in the dark for it. It's enough to make me despair. The truth is hiding inside his skull like some wriggly slimy gray worm let's hope the prosecution can't get at it either.

The old jailer comes into the room with a note.

"Advocate Yisra'el Degmi? Your secretary wants you to call your wife."

My murderer looks at me sharply.

"Thank you but the name is Kedmi."

"You better finish with him soon, he has to go eat lunch."

Everybody wants to give orders.

"I heard you. Now if you don't mind, I'd like to be alone with him."

I continue the questioning. He begins to lose patience he's worried about missing his meal the smell of food drifts up the corridor the clink of dishes but I press on relentlessly if suddenly he gets hungry and is short with the prosecution he'll be eating his meals in prison for the rest of his life.

Finally I'm done. I'm getting hungry too. We stand facing each other. Did he or didn't he? God knows. But I have to be tough with him to spring him from here.

"Do you need anything? Is there anything that you'd like?"

He thinks it over and asks me to arrange to get him out for the night of the seder he wants to be with his parents they'll be lonely without him.

He's too much. Behind that hard-nosed exterior he's so innocent I could plotz. He's barely been in jail for three months and already he wants a vacation.

"Forget it. But maybe you could invite your parents to have the seder here with you in prison. It will be an unforgettable experience for them to hear some rapist sing the Four Questions."

I begin to hum the tune to myself.

His fists ball in anger. Did he or didn't he? Meanwhile it's my duty to defend him as well and as cunningly as I can.

"You don't believe me," he whispers hopelessly his eyes growing red.

An actor in the bargain.

"Of course I do. Leave it to me, you'll see that everything will be all right. Now go eat."

I hurry out past rows of prisoners in gray uniforms murderers thieves terrorists each holding a plate and a spoon. I should eat here myself sometime and see what the food is like. There's no one in the office I head straight for the telephone. My mother is right I shouldn't have gotten involved. Ya'el. Her father is up. He doesn't want me to go by myself. It's immoral to send me in his name while he begs off. He has to talk to her or at least to be there with me.

"Fine. I'm not going. I'm chucking the whole business. Do what you please. Now it's morality. Do you know what morality is? Do you? It's a pebble in somebody's shoe. I've had it! I'm tearing up the papers I drew up and going back to the office. There's enough work for me there. I'm jumpy and I'm hungry. In a minute I'll eat the dog's vitamins and start to bark."

I could always get the better of her by quietly beginning to rave. They're used to giving in to hysteria. When Asa was a little boy he'd lie flailing his arms and legs on the floor and the whole family would kneel in homage.

All right all right. She'll talk to her father. Maybe she'll go herself tomorrow. I'm right. It's best for me to go first. I should just be careful.

At the gate I'm stopped and sent back to have my exit card stamped. Getting in is easier than getting out. I have to waste fifteen minutes looking for the clerk with the stamp. Meanwhile the head warden gets hold of me a sly old bugger who has this ironic thing with lawyers. "What's the matter with you people? You're not helping us to solve the overcrowding here. Where are your golden tongues? Come, let me show you some drawings made by one of our high-security prisoners. They're absolutely marvelous."

It isn't easy to shake him off.

Then down from the mountain from the forest to the sea I'll zip through the bay area past the refinery driving thou art my comfort my desire my only love. I hug the curves of the-wounded-the-quarried-mountain road silently racing the cable cars that pass over my head with gravel for the big cement plant down below the panorama spreading out in the valley beneath me there's the Galilee there's Acre there are the white cliffs of the Lebanese border it's like flying a plane coming in for a landing in the clear spring air the car wheels gently touching down on the tarmac of the highway to Acre I could get a free lunch if I stopped at my mother's but there's another woman that I'd rather see.

I've never cheated on Ya'el nor do I intend to but here and there I keep a few women on standby. In restaurants in cafés in the offices of courts and colleagues I see them now and then I exchange a few words with them I touch them lightly I drop a few soft promises. If only in thought I wish to be a candidate for love. A restaurant with glass walls by the highway near a gas station. Across the road a ceramics plant and beyond it the sea. Here I used to wait for Ya'el those first years she went to visit her mother when she preferred I didn't come with her. Right away I noticed the round waitress with her slow challenging walk. Where is she now? I order lunch from the proprietor and go to call the office.

"Did your wife get in touch with you?"

"Yes, I've spoken to her. Is there anything new? Are you still warming yourself by the heater? Did the check come? . . . What, I don't believe it! For how much, a hundred thousand? . . . Fine, put it in the bank. . . . I have to endorse it first? Right you are. All right, then put it in the drawer and lock it. I'll come by later to pick it up. . . . What, when will I be back? Why do you ask?"

All at once she asks shyly if she can leave work early today. It's almost Passover and she has to help out at home. I gallantly agree. Think of the electricity bill that I'll save. I tell her again where to put the check and how to lock the drawer. Now I see the narrow ankles stepping slowly the pretty eyes open wide to see me she remembers me she better not drop my meal.

At last I'm putting something into my mouth until now it's all been outgoing. I'm the only customer in the place I keep sending her back for salt for pepper for beer for a clean fork enjoying her slow challenging walk the dumb blond animal. She blushes each time she returns. Do I arouse desire in her with my big mug and pot? The thought amuses me. Every day you suffer on account of those you lust for you never think of those who suffer on account of you. In the end she sits down near me with her legs innocently crossed we're all alone except for the music on the radio. I cut my meat and devour her white hands I dip my bread in her eyes and suck them she sits there passively pliantly she brings me coffee a newspaper she unties her apron and bends to clear the table showing me her breasts that I have no time for not now.

Kissinger dining before the next delicate phase of his Middle East shuttle invisible reporters all around him. The quiet restaurant the highway the cars zooming past behind the glass. The sea and the spring and this cup of fragrant coffee. A short nap. A hundred thousand waiting for me in the drawer my little murderer who'll be firm on the witness stand about the elementary particles of time my brilliant strategy brought to the world care of his uncle in Belgium. My mood's on the upswing again. I ask for a cigar and more coffee. And why not? I deserve them. My eyes grow moist. Finally I rise to go I pat her shoulder. There's warmth in my largesse. It was very good. The proprietor is called to add the bill. I leave a generous tip and register her silent gratitude.

Ten after three. A light gentle breeze. I always call by now to see if Gaddi's safely home but I don't want any more truck with the moralists not when this salty breeze from the sea is busy caressing me. I walk slowly to my car. A strawberry vendor has a stand nearby I buy the old woman a bag of them let her have a little pleasure that's all of it she'll get from me today. I check the air in the tires moving softly thinking of the children at home swelling with love even for this ludicrous land. I get into my car.

A leisurely drive along the coast to the hospital. I turn into a side road straight toward the sea toward little cottages surrounded by broad lawns. The thin line between a bungalow colony and an insane asylum is no more than this guard at the gate he must be a rehabilitated nut himself they've given him a visored cap a tin badge and a pistol every third person in this country is either a policeman a security guard or a secret agent. I step on the gas honking the horn keeping my head down maybe he'll think I'm a doctor and open the gate so I won't have to walk half a kilometer but he won't give up his one chance to wield authority. Open up you moron I whisper but he doesn't he jumps from his chair to point out the parking lot before I know it he'll put a bullet in me.

I haven't been in many loony bins Ya'el but if ever I go crazy myself this is the place for me. Perfect silence. The sweet sound of the surf lovely white cottages gorgeous lawns. They build prisons in forests way up in the Carmel and lock up crazies by an enchanted beach they've given them the nicest places in this country and left the rest of us the crumbs.

A nurse in white walks quickly down a path she vanishes through a doorway a man is standing in a distant field suddenly around a bend I find myself facing a crazy giant even taller than I am a colossus with a straw broom on one shoulder staring at me in bewilderment I smile magnanimously at him and pass him quickly leaving him standing there turning to gape at me his mouth hanging open a thread of spittle running down it as though a million-dollar sports car had just gone by him. A small group of patients is sitting on wicker chairs by her cottage I keep smiling as though in a trance a pale old man in a white smock jumps up from his chair he knows me a few months ago I chatted with him about Begin and Sadat.

"Mr. Kedmi, Mr. Kedmi, she's in the garden by the woods. She's waiting for you."

We shake hands warmly.

But first I go look for the doctor as I promised. The large bare room is full of bright light a few women are sitting there each by herself the TV in the middle looks demented too. I already have a guide he grabs my arm and steers me toward a small side room. A smell of medicine.

"Thanks, I can manage by myself now."

The sharp light is everywhere a blue patch of sea fills the windows. A young doctor is lying on a bed his arm flung over his eyes quietly sleeping among the crazies but the patient steps right up to him and wakes him. "Here's Mr. Kedmi, here's Mr. Kedmi, he's come to see his mother."

"My mother-in-law," I whisper damn his eyes. "Mrs. Kaminka. I wanted first of all to know how she was."

The young doctor lowers his arm from his eyes and smiles up at me.

"Is her husband here? Is he with you?"

"No, he'll come the day after tomorrow. He's already in Israel, though. I see you know all about it."

"We know everything," says the patient right away. "She told the nurses . . . they're getting divorced . . ." His eyes sparkle.

"That's fine, Yehezkel, that's fine. Now leave us alone for a while."

But nothing can make him budge. He already wants to know what's in the bags I'm holding.

"What do you have there, candy?"

"Later, Yehezkel, later . . ."

But he must know what's in the bags. "What is it? What is it?"

"It's for the dog."

Only then does he back off violently blinking his eyes chewing on his tongue his voice changes he rocks back and forth as though shaken by something inside. "That dog. That dog."

"That's enough, Yehezkel, that's enough." Without sitting up the doctor tries to calm him. "Why don't you write a letter to the Prime Minister? You haven't written him in ages. Come, sit down at the table, I'll give you some hospital stationery."

"Is it all right if I talk with her . . . is she . . . ?"

"In good shape? Definitely. She had a cold last week but now she's better. She's been waiting for you, your wife phoned two hours ago. She's behind the cottage. . . . Yehezkel, come here . . ."

The doctor gets up and grabs the old man in a bear hug.

I leave the room I walk down the path to the little woods I see the loony giant with his straw broom standing just where I left him still searching for me. And then I see her among the tall trees watering something with a hose a broad straw hat on her head as soon as I start toward her I hear a muffled growl that seems to come from the earth she turns her head in my direction the glitter in her eyes like droplets of water in the air. I walk uncertainly toward her not knowing if the dog is tied the last time I was here he attacked me I ask you gentlemen what other lawyer would agree to work in such conditions.

I never did understand exactly what was wrong with her not that I ever really tried to. I'm not sure that even Ya'el knows there are things that this family has hidden. And I know from the courtroom what rigmaroles psychiatrists are capable of it hasn't made me think any more highly of them. The last few years I've gladly forgone the pleasure of visiting her I've usually waited somewhere with Gaddi while Ya'el went in to see her. Still she must be better if they've started treating her now with water therapy instead of electric shock. Apparently she's taken to working in the garden hosing down the big trees that the Turks forgot to chop down in World War I to stoke their troop trains drenching everything in sight with Noah's floods if the hose were any longer she'd be watering the sea.

I pick my way through the bushes the divorce file in one hand and two paper bags that are already coming apart in the other. If the dog jumps me I'll throw him the strawberries. They needed special permission from the department of health to hospitalize him here the first time I set eyes on him when Ya'el introduced me to her family he was in the prime of life I said right away this dog needs either psychoanalysis or a bullet in the brain and the first he can get only in America they thought I was making another one of my jokes. All joking aside I can now make out the big mangy beast through the bushes part shepherd part bulldog and part monster getting slowly to his feet rattling his chain which I hope is attached at the other end to something solider than grass.

"Hi, there!" I call bizarrely jolly coming to a halt waving the file of documents moving slowly forward again to within a few feet of the dog who isn't looking at me but knows that I'm there. After the wedding I tried calling her mother for a while but soon got over that aberration I even used to kiss her now and then. I was one confused person after that wedding.

She tosses the hose into an irrigation hole she bends down among the weeds to turn off the water and comes forward to greet me in the loose cotton shift that Ya'el bought her last year her strong legs in farm boots her uncombed blond hair that's turned white with an odd luster falling gaily around her wrinkled freckled sunburned face. The day they all started saying that the baby looks like her was the day they spoiled the baby for me.

I press her hand.

"How are you?"

She smiles gently she ducks her head pertly she doesn't answer.

"Ya'el sent this powder for the dog. It's some kind of vitamins, I'm not sure which. I guess you mix it with his food. And these are some strawberries that I bought for you . . . I saw them on the way . . . luscious berries . . ."

She thanks me with a nod her eyes smiling she carefully takes the bags from me the smile is still there. If I had time I'd write a book about the connection between smiling and madness. We stand there for an awkward moment then lead each other to a bench beneath the trees we sit down she smiles uncertainly shaking her head with a slightly automatic motion.

"So he arrived the day before yesterday," I begin in my most grandly auspicious even epic manner.

She listens still saying nothing.

"He looks well. Of course, he's gotten older . . . but who hasn't . . ."

Her eyes light up.

"Is he still complaining about that cramp in his neck?"

At last she's said something. Although it remains to be seen what frequency she's transmitting on.

"In his neck? I didn't notice."

What can she be talking about?

"A cramp?"

But she doesn't answer she's staring off into the distance.

"He still hasn't gotten over the jet lag. He's up all night and sleeps all day."

She regards me searchingly.

"He doesn't bother you . . . the children . . ."

"Of course not. Why should he? Gaddi is so happy to see him."

The name Gaddi soothes her she shuts her eyes.

The dog charges quickly out of the bushes wagging his tail dragging the chain behind him sniffing the ground around me sniffing me loudly licking the bags on the bench whining a bit circling then lying down against my legs beneath the bench.

"And Ya'el must be terribly tired."

"No . . . a little bit . . . it's all right, though . . ."

"Let her rest. Don't pressure her."

"In what way?"

But she doesn't answer. What does she really feel toward me? At first when she was well a slight disdain now in recent years a soft loony affection. Asa and even Tsvi have grown remote from her only Ya'el still looks after her and I look after Ya'el.

Silence. The crystal-clear spring air. A trickle of water still running out of the hose.

"It's so lovely here. The breeze, the sea . . . everything, in fact. Did it rain here yesterday?"

Her head is cocked to one side her hands in the lap of her clean cotton shift strands of gold in the tresses of her hair she sits very straight.

"Whenever I think of you I tell myself how lucky we were to find such a quiet place. If ever I needed . . . this is the place . . . that is, I'd want to be put here . . . I mean . . ."

My big mouth again. That last sentence was uncalled for I have to shift into reverse now. But she's listening to me carefully her fingers picking at the fabric of her dress nervously winding a loose thread. Far off in the middle of the path stands the giant with the broom rooted to one spot his blank face turned toward us.

At least here no one interrupts me when I talk.

I hand her the document.

"This is the agreement." Suddenly I feel emotion. "I drew it up. It's your divorce settlement."

She regards me thoughtfully but doesn't reach out to take it. I lay it carefully on her knees. The dog begins to whine he comes out from under the bench he rubs his red matted coat against me saliva dripping from his snout he lays his head in her lap sniffing the papers.

She looks at me. "He wants to read it."

I smile caustically. Is she joking or being mad or both? She has a right to her mad jokes if I were her I'd make them too how tempting to be absolved of all legal responsibility for one's words.

She opens the bag of strawberries she takes out a ripe berry she smells it and gives it to the dog who gulps it down.

"You've written so much here . . . must I read all of it?"

"I'm afraid you must before you sign. That's how we generally do it."

"We?"

"I mean we lawyers."

She holds the document close to her eyes trying to make something of it but grows tired at once and hands it back to me.

"Maybe you'll read it to me. I can't see a thing. My glasses broke
. . . I told Ya'el . . . I couldn't read that book she gave me either
. . ."

I take the document from her carefully wipe off the traces of the
dog's saliva and begin to read slowly. The dog gobbles ripe strawberries from her hand nuzzling the torn bag. Kissinger sits in a palatial
garden by the Nile explaining the disengagement agreement while
the photographers scramble with their telescopic lenses through the
distant bushes. Here and there I pause to analyze the hidden meaning of some passage to point out a pitfall I've avoided or a loophole
I've managed to close. But what does she understand? She doesn't
say a word just tightly grips the collar on the dog's neck. At last I'm
done.

"And the baby?" she asks. "She doesn't wake you up at night
anymore?"

"The baby?? Hardly ever."

"I keep forgetting her name."

"Rakefet."

"That's right, Rakefet. Write it down for me here, please."

I write it down on a small piece of paper and give it to her.

Silence. The suspense is killing me.

"Why didn't Ya'el come with you? Why did they send you by
yourself?"

"She'll be here tomorrow. So will he. We thought that . . . that it
would be best . . . professionally speaking . . . if I'd explain
things quietly to you first . . ."

"Why didn't Ya'el come? Something's happened to her . . ."

"Nothing has happened. She'll come tomorrow or the day after.
I'll bring her."

All at once the dog growls he's already eaten the paper bag now
he's eating the air that was inside it. Once again total silence. It's
time for her to sign now I know these silences well.

"All you need to do now is sign here in the corner. At the bottom. Unless you have any comments to make."

But suddenly she gets up the papers fall to the ground she's having an anxiety attack.

"Why didn't Ya'el come with you? Something's happened to her . . ."

Well well well good morning. The devils have woken up.

I quickly gather up the papers.

"I swear to you nothing's happened. She just didn't sleep well last night. She was tired. Now if you would sign here . . . we don't have much time . . . the rabbi's expected by the end of the week. He came back from America especially . . . you agreed by mail . . . you promised . . ."

I'm getting into hot water. The dog senses my agitation he pricks up his ears and growls loudly. The golem standing on the path shuffles toward us his straw broom aimed at the sky. How can I leave without her signature? My mother was right why did I get involved in their affairs. No one ever taught me in law school how to give legal advice to the insane someone should write a book about it the obvious candidate is me.

"I say it's best to sign now. That's all there is to it. Because it's a good agreement that guarantees all your needs. Even if you should remarry someday, he'll still have to support you."

And I take hold of her shoulder.

But she backs away in a fright still gripping the dog's collar he's barking now he lunges at me clumsily. The filthy old mutt. I let go of her at once.

"Maybe you'd like to think about it some more . . ."

She nods like a little girl.

"I'll leave it here with you and tomorrow or the day after Ya'el will pick it up. Perhaps the two of them will come together."

"Ya'el will come?"

"Of course."

She beams radiantly. I'm careful not to touch her again I don't want the dog to get the wrong idea. Suddenly something straw-like tickles the back of my neck the golem has arrived he's standing silently behind me. I smile forbearingly and grab the broom that's prodding my head. The dog's whining again he won't attack him though he'll attack me he's lost all his family instincts.

"Well, then, I'll be off. Is there anything you'd like to ask or request before I go?"

She smiles affectionately at me.

This is where true liberalism began. I could write an interesting book about it. Thirty years ago they still tied up the crazies today they tie up anyone sane who gets in their way. I make a fast getaway. Not that it hasn't been an experience. It certainly has been. But from a legal point of view I haven't accomplished very much. I hurry to the gate it's already half past four. Time's flown like crazy today. It's not ideas I'm lacking it's time. If I had the time I could have written three books already but what would Gaddi and Rakefet eat? Books. It's a good thing that check for a hundred thousand is waiting for me otherwise it would have been a wasted day one without a single legal orgasm.

It's already twilight when I get back to the office. The corridors are dark. More shady customers are still waiting on the bench outside Mizrachi's office. What brings them to him I ask myself it's not his brains he doesn't have any it must be his cut-rate prices. I open my office and turn on the light. She's gone. I open the drawer right away I can feel there's no check in it. What's going on here? Good Lord! Where is it? Where did the bitch put it? I go through all the files and papers. This is all I needed. The end will be a heart attack. I'll kill her I'll really kill her let's see what court will dare to convict me I expressly said put it in the drawer so she put it somewhere else and someone came and stole it. God in heaven have pity! I jump for the telephone to dial the police but I know them they'll just send me some illiterate Ali Baba. If only I could cry I'd sell tickets to the thousands who'd like to see me I've ransacked the office she must have stolen it herself. Why not? For the past month she's been warming herself by the heater and plotting it.

"Gaddi, quick, get me mom, on the double, not a word out of you. . . . Ya'el, I'll tell you all about it afterwards, now I just have one question, do you know anything, did my secretary call about some check? . . . No? All right then, goodbye. I'll explain it all later. If I don't come home tonight, look for me in intensive care. It's nothing to worry about, just a hundred thousand pounds down the drain. . . . What? . . . Later!"

I hang up madness coming over me. I yank all the drawers from their grooves I search the inside of the desk I tear the map off the wall and look for the check behind it. I go through the office like a storm I have to get my hands on her but how? Her family of cavemen doesn't have a telephone finally I find her address written in a little notebook thank God I was smart enough to jot it down when I hired her only what kind of address is it some housing project with two numbers and no street I call the police to get directions I switch off the light leaving the office in a shambles behind me.

It's already evening I drive down to the lower city through Wadi Salib through Wadi Nisnas through Rushmiyya where the hell am I. Don't they even have Hebrew names for all these wadis all this desolate earth these narrow crooked streets stuck to the mountainside all at once the road comes to an end. I begin climbing up and down stairs I've never been here before a government project grafted onto deserted Arab houses twining grapevines water in the gutters sand weeds bursting through broken sidewalks farmland turned into a slum a dark store here and there lit by a kerosene lamp groceries where they spike the cottage cheese with hashish it looks like I'm in for another adventure. What a wasteland. Such quiet passive people how slowly they walk it's only on television that they start to shout they're all carrying packages now matzos for Passover when I grab them to ask the address they look at me calmly what family is it that you want. Pinto? But which Pinto? A good question that I feel I'm going to cry the Pintos who sell eggplant in the market the night's still young if I have to I'll visit every Pinto within miles.

And I do climbing up massive stone stairs to wildly constructed houses entering kitchens bedrooms living rooms until I get to some doorway where I'm shown a hundred-year-old Pinto in pajamas or a three-year-old Pintoette in her underpants all the Pintos I could wish for just not the one who has my hundred thousand a small gang of boys and one adult have become my escort they must get a kick out of seeing a big paleface like me running frantically around their neighborhood.

At last I'm brought to a small cobbled courtyard surrounded by blue walls full of furniture and empty vegetable crates I climb the steps to a little apartment whose front door is open at first I don't recognize her barefoot and in a pair of shorts wearing a light sailor shirt how small she looks holding a small rubber hose cleaning the back stairs she stares at me astounded I must look as pale as I feel I'm ready to faint my big heart is beating so hard that it hurts.

"I have it," she shouts. "Don't be upset, Mr. Kedmi . . . everything's all right . . . I couldn't open the drawer . . . the only key
was with you . . . I didn't want to leave the check in the office . . .
I was afraid that something might happen to it . . ."

I don't say a word I just shut my eyes and finish fainting she dries
her hands and runs to an inner room full of colorful pictures of her
ancestors dressed like sheikhs she brings me an envelope I grab it
from her I tear it open I pull out the check I look at it quickly and
stick it in my shirt pocket throwing the torn envelope on the wet
floor.

"I hope you weren't frightened."

I manage an ironic smile by now the whole family has me surrounded half a dozen short swarthy gangsters invite me to sit down
but I still can't get a word out I'm dazed from fatigue and excitement
I raise one hand in a crazy salute and whisper thank you. I'm in a
hurry all I need now's to have to sit down and eat eggplant I turn to
go opening a small door they rush to my side but already I'm in a
tiny bathroom facing an old witch sitting naked in yellow water lit by
the lurid glare of a heater Lord have mercy she whispers in terror
already gentle hands are pulling me out she takes my arm lightly and
steers me to the exit leading me down the stairs she's worked a year
for me now and I never knew she had such straight lithe legs they
make me feel for her how was I to know when she's always bundled
up behind the desk we're standing in the dark street now.

"I can see you were really frightened." She does her best not to
laugh. "You really were."

I stand shaken in the desolate darkness.

"What a pity it didn't occur to you that I know how to read. You
might have left me a note."

"You're right. I didn't think of it."

I pat her head careful not to choke her.

IQ. That's what it all boils down to. Their IQ evaporated in the
Islamic sun. And that's something you can't give them along with
their social security. Again I'm running through the alleyways looking for my car I've already got a title for my fifth book *The Secret
Life of the Underprivileged* in the end I'll write a book with nothing
but the titles of the books I never wrote I'm lost in the sands of this
ruined wadi at last I find my car I turn on the light I take out the

check to make sure that it still has all the zeros I start the motor and depart from this vale of tears.

Gaddi opens the door for me now I remember what I've forgotten it's his present. The lights are all on in the house the baby's in her high chair in the living room surrounded by toys facing the TV watching Begin on the Arabic news the dining table is full of dirty dishes scattered papers a tube of paint grandpa is sitting drinking coffee Gaddi runs to bring me a big picture Ya'el comes out of the kitchen in an apron.

"What happened? We were so worried. I didn't understand a thing. What hundred thousand pounds went down the drain?"

"It didn't. It came back up again."

"Did you see my mother?"

"Of course."

"Did something go wrong?"

"No. Everything's fine."

I head for the bathroom with her on my heels and Gaddi on hers.

"We didn't know when you'd come, so we ate without you."

"That's okay. I just hope you left something for me."

"Of course we did. Did something go wrong, Kedmi?"

"If you'd allow me to take a leak there might be some prospect of your serving me supper."

I shut the door in Gaddi's face to keep him from gate-crashing with his picture. I pee I wash my hands and face at the sink I go around the house turning off unneeded lights finally I sit down at the table. Grandpa moves his chair closer to me his face pale and serious.

"So tell us . . ."

"In a minute. Just let me first put something in my stomach to draw the blood down there so that it doesn't explode in my brain. If Kedmi gets a stroke, the Kaminkas will pay dearly."

I settle into my chair take the check from my pocket place it on the table read it like the morning paper it's certainly better news. He gets up stricken and walks about the room Ya'el sends Gaddi to the bathroom the baby quiets down so does Begin there's just background music now. Ya'el looks pitifully gray and tired.

"Didn't you eat all day long? Your mother called a few times to say she was waiting for you for lunch. Where did you disappear to? Did something happen? . . . Why don't you say something? . . . She was terribly worried."

"Then call her and tell her that I'm here with my mouth full of food. You can spare me the pleasure and her the worry . . ."

All at once he stops pacing the room and bursts out:

"What happened? Did you see her?"

"Of course I did. Could I have some more egg, please?"

"How is she?"

"She's fine. She was watering the trees."

"But what did she say? How did she receive you?"

"Very hospitably. By the way, you have regards from the dog. He thanks you for the powder, Ya'el."

I take a last look at the check I fold it and replace it in my pocket.

"Did she sign?"

"Almost. She wants to think about it some more."

"To think?"

"Such things happen."

Why am I doing this to them? Is it just my lousy character?

At last Ya'el exclaims almost in tears:

"Can't you talk like a human being? You insisted on going by yourself and now it's like pulling teeth to get a word out of you."

"All right, all right. I only wanted to eat in peace. I'm sorry, I didn't realize that you were so impatient." (Kissinger presents his report to the Israeli government.) "I arrived there at three-thirty. I spoke with a young doctor whom I had to wake up. He said she was in good shape. A few of her friends in the hospital knew what I had come for too. I found her tanned and spry-looking, watering the trees. I don't know if that's some new sort of therapy but in any case it definitely works. There's no comparing the way she is now with her condition several years ago. Do you remember that time I was with you, Ya'el?"

Her father leans toward me his legs spread menacingly Ya'el looks at me with loathing.

"I told her you had arrived and that you looked well. She asked if you still had a cramp in your neck and I said that I hadn't noticed any cramp there. Then she asked if you were bothering the children. I said on the contrary, the children are happy that you're here. I did tell her that you were finding it difficult to adjust to Israeli time. I gave her the agreement and recommended it. She asked if she had to read it. I said yes because that's our professional duty, not to let people sign any contract or document that they haven't read. They won't understand it anyway, but it's better for them to feel that they've read it without understanding it than that they haven't understood it without reading it, ha ha . . ." (No one laughs.) "She tried to read it but she couldn't because her glasses are broken. Or maybe the dog ate them. You really should take care of it, Ya'el. So I read it to her. She listened quietly while I explained all the fine points to her, how her rights are all guaranteed. I really did talk carefully and gently but she hardly seemed to respond. She just asked once about you, Ya'el . . ."

"Why I hadn't come . . ."

"Precisely. But I explained why and she understood. I told her you'd come tomorrow or the day after and meanwhile we agreed that she'd think it over and sign and give the agreement to you. Of course we're pressed for time. I tried telling her that as gently as I could. . . . Could I have another cup of tea? I'm totally bushed. I've been running all evening after this check . . ."

"She won't agree," blurts the old man hopelessly. He leaves the room. Deep down I know that he's right.

"Why won't she?" I object. "That's not my impression. Can I have some more tea or do I have to request it in writing?"

Ya'el brings me tea her hands shaking she takes the baby from her chair and puts her into her crib Gaddi shows me his picture some tall women standing in the rain.

"It's a terrific picture." I kiss him and send him off to bed.

Ya'el's father has disappeared. She looks at me hostilely.

"What's gotten into you?"

"I don't know. I've been a wreck all day."

"That's obvious."

"It was all just too much for me."

And really I'm dead on my feet it can't be just that damn check something scared me today the world itself. Those broken alleyways . . . that nude old woman in the yellow water . . . that feeling of straw in my hair . . .

I get up to look at the mail I turn on the TV I'm exhausted my eyes close I can't make out the words Ya'el is cleaning the table the baby's already asleep. I turn off the light and get into pajamas I put the check in my pajama pocket and look for a newspaper I can hardly move I get into bed and pull the big blanket over me.

It's ten o'clock. The telephone rings it's my mother yes says Ya'el to her as though I were a three-year-old yes he's eaten and now he's in bed. Her father returns from a walk with a pack of cigarettes he whispers something to her. My eyes shut the newspaper slips to the floor. The old man comes into the bedroom to ask if I bought the present for Gaddi.

"I'm sorry. I forgot."

He takes thirty dollars from his pocket and puts the bills on the night table by the bed.

"You don't have to," I whisper.

But he lays an ashtray on them. He stands there morosely. Ya'el is washing dishes in the kitchen.

"What should I buy him?"

He doesn't answer.

"If it's all right with you, I'll find some little electric train. He's never even ridden in a train . . ." He stands silently by my bed tall a handsome man a mane of graying hair bohemian-style on his neck. Fitted into his American suit his fingers stained with nicotine what does he want from me of course to ask about her but he's afraid to talk.

"You're going to Jerusalem tomorrow. To Asa's."

He gives me a hard look deep in thought he wants to talk but something won't let him he puffs greedily on his cigarette.

Suddenly he sits down on the bed. Something draws him to me. The fact that I was with her but what more can I tell him. Silence I'm fading out I curl up in the blanket and close my eyes from time to time to see what effect it has. But he goes on sitting there smoking his head in his hand. He's a worried man. He needs the divorce he has a woman waiting for him there and if I let my intuition run free I'd guess that he's made a little uncle for Gaddi. It's quiet except for the dishes my body's turning to lead.

"If you don't mind turning off the light, we could sit in the dark for the same price . . ." I smile weakly hoping it's my last joke of the day.

He draws back. "What?"

He's gotten the hint though he straightens up looking down on me from above he turns off the light and leaves the room I bury myself underneath the blanket.

Once upon a time I used to feel desire at this hour but lately someone's seen to it that I don't. The baby's begun to cry but I'm not getting up for her I've already put in a full day the title of my next best seller will be *How to Subtly Get Your Marriage Partner to Take Care of the Crying Baby.* I snuggle deeper into bed. They must be going over my agreement in the loony bin now assuming that the dog hasn't eaten it why half asleep do I think of her again in the sharp light by the sea you've caught some of her madness Kedmi dear Kedmi poor Yisra'el Kedmi you aging hyperactive child who needs to sleep . . .

TUESDAY

Imagination protects sight
And taking art for act
Protects all life.
Wisdom's pearls protect the tongue
A ring
The finger. . . .
And so I think of wherewith to protect
Myself against the self's own self-reversal.

Yona Vallach

Is this where he lives? On purpose in so drab a neighborhood or are
such the meager rewards of a literary career? And does he really
write his books facing that ugly peeling wall? He has three different
mailboxes two broken and the third a giant new one its upraised slit
hungry for mail. A man bounds quickly down the stairs he slows and
stops in wonder pirouetting by the mailboxes fondling the air around
me he steals a look at me and steps outside turning to look once more
before he's gone. *The pain of your beauty* wrote one of the boys in my
high-school class who used to write to me and which of them didn't
try. Anonymous notes slipped into my schoolbag devious love poems
intricately concocted from biblical verses and the sayings of our
blessed rabbis with here and there a drop of plain hard filth when one
of them beneath his knitted skullcap couldn't stand it anymore. The
Tartar cheeks the blue twinkle that smote their hearts. Because how

could one not be in love with you tell me? I will tell you. You cannot
be in love with me because you do not know the first thing about me
but why shouldn't you fall in love anyway and meanwhile can I look
at your math homework I didn't understand one single question.

Five minutes to ten. Wait. It's gauche to come early even coming
on time is bad form he'll think how important I must be to her if
she's timed it so exactly I'm sure I'm not the first or last to pester
him like this he's too big a man for a novice like me but Asi had to
prove what wonderful contacts he has. Perhaps he can help you
make some contacts. A code word. From contact to contact we'll all
stay in contact until we're a contact ourselves. My (even if I am
being punished) love. My love verily my husband. What shall we do?
If you fear my pain how shall I not fear it too?

So I'll walk down the street a bit I'll give him ten minutes more. A
cloudy morning a chill breeze Jerusalem of cold. *Frail cloud.* So
many young mothers out strolling with their babies all gone down in
quick pain sweet perhaps too the whole world. It's not the penetra-
tion that I know but the pain not the pain but the blood. Two years
and running out of patience. Put me to sleep and then you can . . .

And then my mother:

I don't want to interfere but sometimes a mother must and I can't
sleep at night because of it. You've been married for over two years
you want your freedom I realize that but perhaps one has to think
further ahead.

And my father:

It's not so much the sin although that too but Asi believes in
nothing and he's managed to convert you you've given up the religious faith that we raised you in too easily still it isn't that although . . .

And mother:

Don't start with all that now it's the medical side of it just the
medical side of it that concerns me. You were once very sick I hope
you haven't forgotten and I read in the newspaper don't laugh that
sometimes women put it off because they think that they have all the
time in the world but then when they want to they find out that they
can't the sooner the better it doesn't happen by itself that's only in
novels and even there . . .

Father:

Why must you always make everything sound so complicated! Yes we want a grandchild. What's wrong with that? Is it forbidden to want one? We deserve that much happiness God gave us an only child and He knows how hard we tried to have another but your mother couldn't . . .

Mother:

Don't start with all that now for God's sake let me talk this over calmly it's not for our sake it's for yours. We're in a position to help we're not like his family which simply isn't. We've actually thought of moving closer to you but it makes more sense for you to move closer to us we've even found you an apartment not far from here.

Father:

It's not just evenings we'll be able to help it's days too business is so bad thank God that I can manage to lose money in the store by myself and spare mother for you her time will be yours.

Mother:

In terms of Asa's getting ahead we're thinking of his career if that's the reason.

Father:

You won't have to worry with mother around look how she raised you to be such a beauty when you were born we wondered where a monkey like you came from but little by little . . .

Mother:

That's enough you'll annoy her and ruin everything. You think that it's me but you can see that it's him he doesn't stop talking I don't get a moment's peace. Yesterday I spoke to Sarah's mother that girl from your class who was married a few months before you they're already expecting a second grandchild. Don't be angry I wasn't making comparisons I know that's all that she's good for but you have to realize that time's not standing still it never does . . .

A soft enclasping pleading cunning duet if only they knew how we're still stuck at the starting line. They do but don't know what they know.

But he does have a view on the other side of these houses a deep broad cleft toward the mountains and sky for inspiration is that west east or north I'm so bad at directions Asi can take one step in any room and know just which way he's facing. *Down dropping heavens.* And in the plural too. Sometimes unexpectedly in a Talmudic text such a precise sense of landscape the boys would chop logic with the Talmud teacher while I dropped down heavens. *A frail snake by a drowsing old man.* Perhaps. We'll have to see. In the end only words and the pain of words. And yet no blood of words.

It's really cold and me in this light spring dress and open shoes. Is this icy wind supposed to be spring? Why it's almost time for the seder. A few pale weak glizzly days and summer will be on us all at once. *This land of all at once.* A line for a poem. I must write it down. Some poet quoted in the paper as saying that he always carries a little notebook with him. Useful. What can he possibly say to me? Dina Kaminka you are a great talent. Yours is a name to remember. The great hope of a declining literature. Where have you been hiding until now? Baloney. Wanton women with shopping bags stare at me as they pass. Some women's glances are more piercing than men's as though I'd robbed them of something. But those who know me know the threat's sheer bluff.

A small child backs against a wall of the stairway. His. You can tell right away the same curls the same look all he's missing is the pipe. I put my hand on his shoulder your father is isn't he? But he's not impressed he's used to being spotted to having a famous father he kicks a ball and trips down the stairs after it.

Two facing doors on each (how odd) his name. I ring the bell of the one on the right a young faded woman in jeans holding a baby rock music inside before I can say a word she points to the other door softly retreating it opens while I'm still looking for the bell and out steps an older woman with another baby (his third child?) and a shopping basket.

(Does he really have two wives? But why not? The apartments are low-income. In the middle of the night he runs naked from one to the other.)

"I have an appointment with Mr. . . ."

Mister?

"Come in."

She studies my fancy dress with an ironic smile and points to an inner door. It was an error in judgment to come traipsing into this hotbed of bohemia in high heels. I enter a small hallway the front door slams rudely cynically behind me the dim light is congested amid the low bookcases there's a smell of mold and wet laundry a lyrical overture to a literary tribunal my head is a pennant in the flaking mirror among the winter coats the sharp slanty blue the open doggy mouth the curly until-two-weeks-ago-soft-honey-braided head my makeup's come off in the wind. What have I gotten myself into? I pass the kitchen piles of dirty dishes on the stained marble counter of the sink. Maybe he's looking for a third wife to do them.

What can he possibly say to me?

My wife has been secretly *(secretly?)* writing stories and poems for a while now I mean just for her own satisfaction maybe you'd be willing to read them and tell her what they're worth. A professional opinion and a kind word from you. (Perhaps you can even talk her out of the obsession.) She admires you greatly.

Why did you say I admired him who allowed you. Then you don't? I admire no one. Not even me? You I love. What do you care if I said you admired him it will make him read your material *(material?)* I mean what you've written more sympathetically. I don't need sympathy I need truth. Truth is different when told with sympathy. But what kind of a writer is he? What sort of stuff does he write? Read it yourself. I don't have time for literature I'll read what books time has been kind to when I retire but what does he write about what subjects describe one book. Don't be absurd you can't describe books like his. That's what must make him so important.

Important. Another code word.

I knock on the door and open it softly. A small room with a big blond baby girl on dirty linen gnawing on a doll behind crib bars. I push open the next door. An old snake in a shabby black turtleneck shorter than I imagined sturdier than I imagined older than I imagined leaning over some page proofs with a tall young man. A huge dilapidated light-colored armchair ravaged like an old woman a clutter of pipes a large desk a poorly lit wood-paneled room with books on the windowsill beyond them the peaks of mountains a lambskin rug a record soundlessly spinning a deep un-Israeli room full of dark wooden figurines and sharp male tension.

"Excuse me . . . your wife said I should come in . . . I don't know if you remembered . . . my husband . . . at ten o'clock . . . my name is Dina Kaminka . . ."

Coffee dregs in tall glasses ashtrays full of burnt tobacco an airless room the smell of literature in action. His eyes beam at me brightly the young man glowers. I'll let them take in (what else do I have to show?) my beauty.

"My wife? Well, never mind. Is it ten o'clock already? You're right, we do have an appointment. Come in, sit down . . . I'll be

with you right away . . ." I make a beeline for the tumbledown
chair and flop right into it sinking all the way to the floor. Reliably
precise-looking in his worn corduroy pants he clears papers and the
coffee glasses off his desk and tells the young man with the proofs to
step out it won't take long he whispers sympathetically regarding my
flaming face with its strained smile trapped in this armchair still
sinking lower I cross my legs and bare the cause of so much pain.
Not mine.

He remains standing there contemplating me genially objectively
seeking to cope with what the morning has unexpectedly turned up.

"Would you like something to drink?"

"No, thank you."

He closes the door behind the tall young man who has left without
a word or glance he puts on his glasses and begins going through
drawers and moving piles of paper until at last he finds a yellowish
sheaf and starts to read silently. He turns the pages beaming he sits
down and takes off his glasses.

"You know, your poems made a great impression on me."

Can it be? The miracle. And so painlessly.

"Honestly?" I sink soundlessly ecstatically deeper into the chair.

"Where have you been until now? Your poem *Pleasantly My Body*
is absolutely marvelous."

"Which poem?"

"Pleasantly My Body . . ." He leans ceremoniously toward me to
read with me from the yellowish manuscript that's covered with a
strange curvy disturbed scrawl. He's mixed me up he's thinking of
someone else.

Pleasantly My Body?

"Amid all the junk that comes my way at last I find a new sound,
the prospect of a new linguistic key."

In a crumbling yet courageous voice:

"One minute, I think you're mistaken . . . those pages aren't
mine . . . Dina Kaminka . . . you're mixing me up . . . my husband gave you a notebook with a floral design . . ."

He's stunned. Turns red. He drops the manuscript smiles (what's
so funny?) grabs hold of his head and slaps it lightly gets up sits
down gets up bends over mumbling just a minute excuse me that's
right how could I have confused you. He kneels to pull out a bottom
drawer talking to himself just a minute everything's all jumbled up

here they've turned this room into an editorial office yes Dina Kaminka of course your husband Asa's in the history department of course I remember . . .

"You didn't get around to reading it . . . it doesn't matter . . ." With a sudden feeling of relief I seek to extract myself from the jelly-like armchair and vanish.

"No, just one moment. I did read it. I'm sure I did . . ." He rummages feverishly through some papers. "There was a story there, wasn't there? About a young woman . . . just one minute . . . it takes place in a shop on a winter day . . . one minute . . ."

One minute for what? Some other woman has already found a new linguistic key amid all the junk that's being written. She can look forward to the joyous prospect of hearing it from you perhaps she's already coming up the stairs. But behold he has my notebook in his hands triumphantly he shows it to me. My first mistake was to copy everything out into a high-school notebook. I should have written on yellow disturbed paper *yea to take and bring forth the tokens of the damsel's virginity unto the elders of the city in the gate and they shall spread the cloth* . . .

Silence.

He clutches the notebook predatorily racing through it quickly filming digesting with supreme concentration he's not embarrassed to read it now in front of me. At last he shuts it puts it down stands up and smiles at me kindly.

"Which will it be, Turkish or instant? Or perhaps you'd like something cold?"

"No, thank you. I really don't want anything."

"Turkish or instant?" he persists, still smiling his patronizing smile. "I wanted to make some for myself anyway."

"No, thank you, really . . ."

He steps up to me and takes the liberty of laying a warm hand on my shoulder.

"You're angry at me. But I really did read it . . . it was just one of those things. If you don't have coffee with me, I'll feel hurt. Turkish or instant?"

"Turkish."

He energetically loads the glasses and the remains of some crackers on a tray lays my notebook on top of them and leaves the room.

I rise from the bottomless depths of the armchair and loiter by the

row of books drawn to the yellow manuscript left on the desk with
its strong curvy scrawl.

> *Death can fall from the dark*
> *Like a poem—*
> *But a poem was all that it was.*

Laughter from the kitchen. I return to the books unable to read
even their titles my eyes on the watery light swirling over the mountains.

The door opens and he carries in a tray with coffee cups cookies
and my notebook. The stage is set he glances hesitantly toward me at
the other end of the room I'm still rooted to my place by the window
have a seat he smiles and I float to another chair (enough of that
mortifying armchair) and sit down by the steaming cup while he
offers me sugar. He lays my notebook on his knees picks up his cup
and drinks from it vigorously.

"My first question is just out of curiosity. Are you religious? Do
you come from a religious background?"

"I went to religious schools."

"High school too?"

"Yes. Why do you ask?"

He's tickled pink with himself.

"It's something one senses in your language, your imagery, your
values, your way of dealing with things, of approving or disapprov-
ing. It's something one can smell. It's a new phenomenon, this writing of literature by religious Jews. There's already a whole school of
you."

He's classed me with a whole school, and a religious one yet. He's
got the world all figured out.

"But I'm not so observant anymore . . ."

"That doesn't matter. These things run too deep to be easily cast
off. It's a whole outlook."

"Is that good or bad?" I inquire submissively trying to grasp the
steaming-hot cup.

"On the whole, it's a welcome new source. Not that I myself can
subscribe . . . on the contrary . . . but it's a new climate for literature, a new possibility. How old are you? Please, drink your coffee,
why aren't you drinking?"

He was asked for a literary opinion and he's already made himself my guardian he thinks he can ask what he wants he does have a technique though for dealing with young scribblers.

"I'm twenty-two."

"Are you a student?"

"I finished a year ago."

"In what field?"

"Social work."

"Not literature?"

"No."

"That's good. But how did you manage to finish so quickly?"

"I was exempted from the army." I look straight at him waiting for the scornful smile of the injured solid citizen. He says nothing suddenly blushing at a loss.

"But drink something. It will get cold. Have a cookie."

"Thank you." I lift the cup noticing with revulsion the lip prints on the rim I quickly slurp a drop of bitter Turkish coffee and put it down again.

"Do you have any children?"

"What? No, not yet."

"Do you have a job?"

"Yes. In the municipal department of social work."

Why all these questions? Is he playing for time or gathering material for a diagnosis?

"How long have you been writing?"

"For quite some time. I began in the eighth grade. I was sick for a few months . . . some kind of rheumatic fever . . . that's why I didn't serve in the army. It wasn't on religious grounds." (Take that, you varmint!) "I was bedridden for a long while, and it was then that I started to write. To this day when I want to concentrate on writing I get into bed and write on the pillows."

I'm talking too much.

"Into bed?" He laughs amazedly warmly excitedly leaning toward me.

"To tell you the truth" (just lay it on me gently please) "your story is weak, still juvenile. It gets too involved for no good reason in the middle and lets itself off too easily in the end. Basically, the poems are better. This one here . . . *For You Raised Me Like a Thistle* . . . it really sings, it even deserves to be published. At any rate, it's no worse than a lot of poetry that does get published these days. So if you've come to ask me which to devote yourself to, prose or poetry" (I didn't) "I should obviously say to you: poetry. And yet still . . . I can't help thinking . . . that you shouldn't stop writing fiction either. There are definitely some good passages in this story, not all that many, but a few. The descriptive ones in particular. What's the one that I'm thinking of . . . ah yes, in a grocery store, isn't it? An old-fashioned sort of grocery. Something in your description of it struck me." (I shut my eyes.) "The shelves, the dim bread compartment. There was a wonderful, humorous bit about a hunk of white goat cheese—you captured the absurd shape of it perfectly, you used a precise image there, I can't remember it, but I recall having marked it." He rapidly leafs through the notebook. "Well, never mind . . ."

"A pale brain."

"That's it. With that married old grocer couple. Good, concrete prose, even funny . . . it's too bad, though, that your heroine moves in such a vague, undefined vacuum . . . that you saddle her with all those emotional clichés . . ."

Earnestly:

"I hope you're not upset with me for telling you what I think. It's only my opinion, of course, and it would be less than honest of me to conceal it behind empty compliments . . ."

"That's quite all right."

He reaches out to hand me the open notebook.

"It's as though you were afraid to touch on the real problem . . . if there is one, that is, and of course I know nothing about you . . . but I did feel that there was one, especially in that comic sketch in the dark grocery. I felt some sort of bitterness there. You have to get more deeply into it, to open it up. Even in your poems . . ."

"In my poems too?" I sound crushed.

"Yes. In your poems too." Suddenly he's annoyed. "Wherever an emotion is called for you retreat into scenery, into some neutral description of nature. *All alone all alone O vain seeker bent over that small body frail clouds of morning in the window.* When someone is bending over the body of a dead child . . ."

"A dead child?"

"Dead or sick, it doesn't matter. That small body demands a response, not frail clouds of morning in the window. That's an evasion, an aesthetic indulgence. You can't write without the willingness to expose yourself, and even then nothing is ever certain. But without it you're wasting time and paper. And in general, you overwork the word 'frail.' I counted it five times on the first page alone."

Hail frail snake.

He reads aloud. He reads well. A seasoned professional. He's gotten the feel of it right off even if he did probably read it for the first time in the kitchen between the kettle and the coffee cups.

Silence.

"Is it important to you?"

"What?"

"Writing."

"Yes, I think so."

"Then give it all you have, please. Otherwise . . ." His voice dies softly away his glance caresses my legs. A baby bursts out crying in the hallway there's a scraping of chairs. Suddenly I have a bad taste in my mouth. All in all a negative opinion.

"You say that my story isn't developed, but in your own fiction . . ."

He bristles. "What about my fiction?"

"Never mind . . ." I don't pursue it. I get up to go the baby is still screaming. His head is bowed with a wise understanding smile. I reach out again for the notebook.

"I think someone is calling you."

But he's distracted still deep in his chair he won't let go of the notebook he leafs through it again quickly loath to part with it.

"First things, objects, physical realities, only afterwards ideas and symbols derived from them. That's literature. The full immediacy of the moment as it happens to you or others, the ability to empathize rather than abstract, to be down-to-earth . . . to keep closing the gap between life and the written word . . ."

I smile my hand still out to take my story. The baby is having a tantrum I hear the young man's steps utensils are falling. He rises slowly still holding on to the notebook. Now that we stand facing each other I can see that he's actually shorter than I am not that that keeps him from stalling still more.

"Give my regards to Asa. When he first approached me at the university I didn't realize who he was. I remember him as a small boy. His father, old man Kaminka, was my teacher in high school."

"Really? I didn't know that."

"He was a sharp fellow. An odd person, though. And one who got on your nerves. Still, he did make me think. What's with him? Is he still alive?"

"Of course. He's been in America the last few years."

"Kaminka? What is he doing there?"

"Teaching at some half-Jewish college. I've actually never met him. He was already there when we were married."

"And he didn't come back for your wedding?"

"No."

"That sounds just like him. An odd fellow. Complicated. He made life tough for us. You never met him?"

"No. But he's here now on a visit. In fact he's due in Jerusalem today."

"Is his wife still alive? I believe she was ill or something."

"Yes. There was something."

"A strange man. Talented but wasted. There were times when he drove us up the wall."

(And you? *Odd, strange*—three times on the same page.)

"Give him my best. He'll remember me if he wants to. Our relationship was never very good. And if you'd ever like me to read other things of yours, I'll be glad to. You don't have to ask me through Asa."

I catch a whiff of his tobacco-smelling breath. He ushers me outside his hand on my shoulder he gives me my notebook back.

"That poem you said deserved to be published . . . whom shall I send it to? Do you think that you might . . . that is, perhaps you . . . might give it to someone . . ."

He steps back his hand slips from my shoulder. But I give him a soft look mustering all my beauty.

"You already want to be published?"

"Just if I deserve to be . . . if you think . . ." The page is torn from the notebook and given to him. He takes it reluctantly then hands it back and asks me to write my address on it. We are in the hallway by the kitchen door the tall young man is standing with the baby in his arms. Her face is wet with tears she emits a muffled gasp reaching out for him but he ignores her and continues seeing me out my page of poetry crumpling in his hands.

A big sharp-eyed woman opens the door with a key she enters quickly and snatches the baby at once. Through an open door at the rear of the house two youngsters are blowing up a ball. I tiptoe back out to the madding crowd unable to restrain myself any longer.

"Excuse me for asking, but how many children do you have?"

He turns around quickly.

"Two. Why?"

"Nothing. I just wondered."

A slight bespectacled mouse of a girl ascends the stairs. Perhaps it's she who has found the new linguistic key. My provisional mark: an honorable failure with hope for the future. My best effort so far is that hunk of white cheese the dimness of the bread shelf that's where I'm most at home. Yet I did feel the warmth of the truth when I wrote it. To look hard not to fear self-exposure to dig deeper into the problem if it's there. Farewell frail clouds. He's right. Though what will I do without "frail" that magic word that helps in hard transitions? *An old snake on a rock an old errant snake?* I must find a substitute.

Meanwhile the hunk of cheese has come to life out of the pages of my story. Here's my father slicing it with a long knife his large handsome face so weary tall blond a skullcap pushed back on his head. Objects give me of yourselves come you breads you biscuits you smoked fishes you jars of jam you yoghurt containers come smells I need your inspiration. Joking with the fat voracious short-tempered lady customers struggling with stained little chits of bills I slip silently by him to the storeroom in the back where amid beer crates oil bottles and bags of powdered detergent mother bends in the gloom with her glasses on writing new prices on items.

"Raising prices again?"

"Ah, Dinaleh, it's good you came. Asa called. He's been trying to get hold of you."

Father is already hugging me from behind he's left the customers.

"Be careful, you'll get her pretty dress dirty!"

"I'll buy her a new one. So what did he say?"

"Who?"

"That author, what's his name . . ."

"Let her catch her breath first!"

"How do you know about it?"

"Asa told us."

My room never had a lock or a key no bolt even in the bathroom they just barged in without knocking without asking in my bed in my drawers no secrets no privacy an all-loving all-knowing omnipresent world invading every pore choking me with embraces yet I'm to blame I ask for it I collaborate going out of my way to come see them each day if I didn't they'd turn up in disgrace at suppertime wanting to know if their daughter is still alive or has she gone up in smoke.

"So what did he say? Did he like . . . ?"

"Yes . . . more or less . . . he had some comments but . . . yes . . . on the whole . . ."

"Leave her alone. Mrs. Goldberg is waiting for her bill. Don't make her nervous."

He kisses me and goes back into the store.

"Do you want me to help you, mama?"

"No, darling, absolutely not. Sit down and rest a bit. I'll make you something to eat in a minute. Just get in touch with Asa. He's already called three times today. His father is coming this afternoon."

"I know."

"Call him now, he's only in his office until noon. We promised you'd call him right away."

"All right."

I sit on a beer crate feeling weak as though I'd just had a tooth pulled.

"Would you like me to dial for you?"

"In a minute, mama."

"Are you feeling all right? Come, I'll make you a cup of tea."

"Not right now. One minute, mama."

"His father is coming today at three o'clock, so we thought we'd invite the three of you for supper, that way you wouldn't have to cook. And we have to see him once anyway . . . he is our in-law, after all . . . no one understands how we've never met him. Of course, I imagine he'd like to meet us too . . ."

"Not tonight, though, mama. He'll want to be alone with Asi. They haven't seen each other for years."

"But it's already been settled with Asi."

"Will you stop badgering me! No . . . please don't feel hurt, it's just that . . . one minute . . . I need to think . . ."

One minute one minute . . .

Father comes back he can't keep himself away.

"So you're eating with us tonight! You won't have to cook."

He returns to the store.

They cling to me without sticking they flutter apprehensively around me.

"No, mama, not tonight. Another time."

"It's for your sake. Do you have anything to make dinner with at home?"

"Yes. I'll manage. Don't worry."

"It's not for us, we don't need it. We just wanted to help. And of course, he'll want to meet us socially . . ."

"Of course he will. I'll bring him. But not tonight. Maybe tomorrow."

"Maybe for the seder."

"I don't think he can. He'll want to be with Ya'el and the grandchildren. We may have to be with them too."

She turns pale.

"You're not planning to leave us all alone for the seder?"

"We've been with you every year. It would be just this one time, and even that isn't definite."

On one only child's back two whole parents whither thou goest and the pain the hot twinge inside and old age and only the light in the eyes that you feel that you see how bossy they are yet they're the ones who spoiled me without end to protect me from all pain why should he tear the light that glows and him surrounded by women wanting me exposed no wonder that I'm here among these bottles of cooking oil times have changed the sexual revolution group orgies hard porn a married virgin in Jerusalem with white cheese on the scales and a barrel of pickled mackerel never alone never never alone tracked by radar from afar they know all see all when I write they'll stand by my side to hold the pen to be of help they mean so well and the onus is mine I'm to blame he's started to punish me now he'll go mad in the end what good is all my beauty everything will go up in smoke if I don't let him in and I won't my friend my love my true heart try my mouth if you want but not there.

"Dinaleh, you're not feeling well. Maybe you'd like to go upstairs and lie down."

Couldn't you please be sick so that we could take care of you put you to bed undress you cover you up. Be a good sick girl. I feel as though I've turned to stone.

"Then call Asa."

"In a minute . . . that must be him ringing now . . ."

"Dina? When did you get there?"

"Just this minute, Asi. Just now. A minute ago."

"It took so long?"

"It didn't take so long."

"How did it go with him?"

"Later."

"In one word."

"All right."

"In what sense?"

"Later."

"My father's coming today."

"I've been told."

"Something seems to have gone wrong there. Kedmi stepped in and insisted on going to get her signature by himself and messed things up. I warned them not to let him go alone but with Ya'el he does what he wants. That's not for now, though. . . . He's coming at three on the one o'clock car from Haifa but I don't finish teaching until three-thirty, so you'll have to meet him at the taxi station and take him home with you."

"All right."

"You know that the house is in total chaos. There's nothing to eat. Your parents invited us for dinner tonight. Maybe we should accept so that you won't have to cook."

"Don't worry, I'll make something and you'll help. He'll want to spend a quiet evening with you."

"As you like. I was just thinking of you."

"It's okay. You didn't leave me any money in my purse again, though."

"I can't be responsible for your purse. I don't have any money either. You can borrow some from your parents."

"I'm not borrowing any money from them. You know they never take it back. Why did you take all the money from my purse?"

"I didn't take a cent from you. I'm broke too. But take five thousand pounds from your parents. That much they'll agree to take back."

"I won't. Stop giving me advice. I'll go to the bank and take money out myself. Who do I have to see there?"

"Anyone. It makes no difference."

"Where exactly is our branch?"

"On the corner of Arlosoroff Street, where it always has been."

"Fine. Now I remember."

"Take out two thousand pounds."

"I'll take out as much as I feel like."

"All right, all right. Just don't be late. Be there by three. Will you recognize him?"

"Yes. Don't worry."

"I'll come straight home from the university."

"Maybe you'd like to meet us in some café downtown."

"No. That's too complicated."

"But why?"

"What on earth do you want to meet in a café for? He'll be tired. I'll be home by four-thirty. Go straight there, all right?"

"All right. Say something."

"What am I supposed to say?"

"Am I still being punished?"

A long pause.

"It's not a punishment. It's despair."

He hangs up.

Father and mother have already gotten the message into a shopping net go some rolls cans of spreads and sliced yellow cheese teary in its plastic wrapper down from a shelf come spongy gray mushrooms the refrigerator is flung open they take they cut they wrap in a singsong Hungarian duet silently they consult each other just a few things to put on the table swish into the bag with them why should you go to the supermarket where everything is so expensive do you really enjoy being cheated anyway it's Tuesday everything closes early the banks too already the cash register has sprung open with a rustle of bills here's some money you can return it when you want it's yours in any case so you'll inherit that much less why should you care if we give you an advance money is worthless nowadays anyhow how much do you have here why it's nothing if it's heavy papa will help carry it to the bus stop why don't you take it what's the matter? Take your father and mother too squirming in the net missing you before you're even gone counting the hours until they see you again tomorrow don't hurt our feelings how can you refuse we've already sliced it we've already packed it everything will spoil.

But for once I do refuse. Stubbornly adamantly. No money either.

I have my own. I'm not taking a thing. Out of the question. I don't want advances you won't take them back anyway. All I want if you don't mind is that hunk of white cheese.

"What do you want that for? It's dry as a stone. It's not fresh."

"I'll grate it and make a soufflé."

"You'll never get a soufflé out of that. Dinaleh, don't be a child."

"I saw some recipe in a cookbook. Are you saving it for someone? How much does it cost?"

Father is in a rage you're doing it to insult me he wraps it up angrily and flings it at me. The store is full of irritable customers the shopping net with the food lies on the counter father is red in the face mother is beside herself I've never said no to them like this before I kiss her and reach out my hand to him I slip away down the alley behind the Edison Theater walking by a high blank wall on whose other side is the movie screen recessed in its far end is a run-down kiosk with a leaky soda fountain and a few cartons of yellow chewing gum and dry wafers next to some thin writing pads and notebooks. Fat lame and inert the kiosk owner sits on his stool his back to the wall the sounds of the movie behind him a roar of cars of explosions all that American bang-bang he sits absorbed in the noise. I reach for a writing pad and choose an orange one with faded lines a product of the Jerusalem Paper Company.

"Are these the only writing pads you have?"

He doesn't answer. He doesn't see me. In a trance he listens to the sounds from behind the heavy concrete wall.

"All right, then. I'll take this one."

He takes the pad from me to check its price. I hand him some change he counts it suspiciously I grab the pad back all at once my fingers are itching to write here on the border of downtown to one side of me the stone houses of Ge'ula a spiritual watershed down one slope of which flows a thickening stream of black coats before them a last display window with photos of leather-booted women a neighborhood of uglies who no longer turn to stare at me. I riffle through the small blank pages.

"Do you have a pen or a pencil?"

He produces a dusty pen I pay him he hands me back some moist change. I can feel an attack coming on. On one side I write *Poetry* I turn it over and write *Prose* on the other I lay the pad on the wet marble counter and write quickly.

Rockdrowsing snake. Rustling bleeding. Venomous skull soft bald head.

The kiosk owner looks up at me.

"Not here, lady. This isn't a desk."

But I pay no attention I flip it over quickly to the prose side. *Father in knots large gloomy wall beyond the hum of projector muffled booms. Zombie-like kiosk owner selling soda in shade of banyan tree. She buys a small pad from him.*

"Hey, lady, not here!"

A bus pulls up across the street the driver looks at me the doors hiss open and shut I signal him he brakes sharply I grab the pad and my bag and the cheese and dart to the opposite sidewalk the door opens again I'm safely inside. Thank you. He grins. He deserves to have me sit near him so I do smiling back sweetly as I pay him the fare but before he can get a word in I've whipped out my pad and plunged into it. *The speedy recognition of beauty.* And on the poetry side I write *I saw her as she danced her body deep in soft melody.*

It's something else today.

The keys are already turning in the glass door of the bank but I manage to worm my way in. No one knows me though we have a joint account because Asi takes care of all our bank business but a nervous young teller takes me under his wing and manages to give me five thousand pounds even though I don't have a checkbook he fills out the forms for me and carefully has me sign he runs to bring me my money in new bills and a new checkbook too I can feel him falling for me head over heels he's the clean skinny intellectual type crushed by an ambitious mother he scents the tender virgin in me like a moth attracted to the light.

His thin wings beat against the counter of the emptying bank while the rest of the staff files away its papers and regards us with a smile. All of a sudden I must know exactly how much we have in our account. It turns out that we have several accounts he writes each down on a piece of paper and goes to check the computerized listings explaining everything precisely. Here you have twenty thousand pounds and here you have some German marks and here you even have a few stocks. I never knew or else I wasn't listening when Asi told me. The amazing thing is that I've co-signed every one of them. Some little female clerk is impatiently jingling the keys but my moth with glasses has decided that now is the perfect time to sell me some new savings plan for the thrifty woman. I let him tell me about it acting docile even a little dumb nodding dependently but forced in the end to confess that my financial authority does not extend beyond five thousand pounds. I promise to send him my husband for a pep talk and slip the money into my purse letting my glance linger over him. He opens the glass door wide careful not to touch me.

I buy a cake and some flowers and board another bus. It's already one o'clock I'd better hurry. I sit in the back I take out my pad and write *noon light in an empty bank* and on the flip side *silver moth.*

At home I take off my dress and change into pants I make the beds wash the dishes dust and air out the house. The refrigerator is practically empty. The white cheese has been left behind on the bus or in the bank. How stupid of me to say no to my parents they were so hurt perhaps I should call them. I run down to the corner grocery but it's already closed. How could I have forgotten that it's Tuesday? But the weather's clearing up a bright blue sky is being unfurled the day that started glumly with such a cold wind is filling with warm clear light now.

I return to the apartment throw out old newspapers put Asi's papers into drawers arrange the books change my pants put on makeup the time flies by. At two-thirty I'm downstairs again a bus roars by me without stopping. I step to the curb and stick out my hand to thumb a ride. A car screeches to a stop. I hate to hitch just because it's so easy. The driver in dark glasses looks like a pimp. Downtown? At your service. I press against the door gently laying my hand with the wedding ring on the dashboard. A deterrent or an invitation? These days one never knows. He tries striking up a conversation I answer politely but more and more drily the closer we get to downtown. We stop for a light. May I? I open the door and slip out.

It's five minutes to three. Suddenly I feel a burst of emotion. Asi's father. Kaminka himself. This man whom I've known only from stories from arguments from short letters bearing the usual political dirges with the requests for books and journals at the end. Asi's father a processed element within Asi tumbling in our sheets with us thrashing about in the throes of our marriage. In a few more minutes I'll see him alive and in person at the bottom of Ben-Yehuda Street a subject for inquiry and interrogation. The number of the one o'clock cab from Haifa is five-thirty-two sit down right here miss I'll find your party the minute it arrives what did you say his name was? I sit among parcels in the open office facing the busy street the sun at the top of it flooding the rooftops like a sea. People press around me the festive commotion of the approaching holiday I take out my darling pad the attack won't let up today it's been one continual rush of excitement. In prose *throes of marriage*. In poetry I cross out *silver moth*.

A taxi pulls up across the street. That's it miss. The door opens I recognize him at once because it's Tsvi. Amazing. Even uncanny. The most obvious thing about him they never mentioned to me that he's the spitting image of Tsvi. Tall erect even powerfully built he stands by the car in rumpled clothes looking about glancing up at the sky his gray hair uncombed a little mustache what does he need it for. Something menacing about him. He looks tired confused but I'm frozen where I am. I watch him try catching the attention of the fat driver who's taking parcels off the baggage rack shouting and joking with the office personnel across the street. Kaminka looks at me but doesn't see me. At last the trunk is opened he takes out a coat hat and a small leather valise gathering them up while saying something to the driver he turns to look at the sun hanging at the top of the street. I must go to him but the pen won't leave my hand I turn the page and write *sun in the creases of a hat*. He starts toward the office across Ben-Yehuda Street but abruptly veers and begins walking down it instead. Passing cars screen him from me I stuff the pad into my bag and jump to my feet the flow of cars keeps me from crossing the street he's gone but at once I see him again about to turn into some side street by a traffic light he stops to ask something and light a cigarette I jaywalk quickly over to him and reach out to him in the middle of the street.

I put my arm around him and embrace him. Dina. He leans over me radiantly the lights keep changing next to us. At last. Asi is teaching at the university he'll go straight home from there. I drag him back to the sidewalk slow-moving cars barely missing our feet. He throws his cigarette into the street he's confused he can't get over me he leans heavily on my shoulder pedestrians jostle us stopping to watch us meet. I reach the sidewalk first I stand on tiptoe and kiss his face warmly generously. He's moved he drops his valise at his feet and hugs me with tears in his eyes. It's about time I laugh it's about time he repeats mesmerized his eyes shut as he steps up onto the sidewalk.

"Let me carry your bag for you."

"Don't even think of it!"

"Then at least your coat and hat."

"They're no trouble. I'll wear the hat."

He puts it on smiling surveying his surroundings. The crowd presses against us sweeping us along toward Zion Square. We drift aimlessly with it.

"Where to now?"

"To the bus stop and home."

"Maybe we should have something to drink first. Are you in a hurry?"

"Not at all. It's just that Asi will be home soon."

"It won't kill him to wait. Come, I want to talk with you. Isn't there some nice café around here? Let's get out of this mob scene. Were there always such crowds in this place?"

He tucks his arm in mine and youthfully but with surprising brute force spins me around into a dark little street as though he had his bearings exactly he stops by the glass door of a bank walks on turns back crosses to the opposite sidewalk looks up and down and returns to me. "It's become a bank," he murmurs. "Let's go to the Atara then. Is it still there?"

His speech is a quick clipped Hebrew with a slight musical Russian accent.

"When were you last in Jerusalem?"

"Long ago. I skipped over it on my last visit three years ago. That must make it five years or more. Over there, in America, I often wonder about this city. There's a photograph of it in all the offices of the Jewish community centers and it's always the same: the towers of the Old City, the Wailing Wall, the Israel Museum, all in the same pretty colors. No one ever photographs this shabby, gray, congested triangle of streets in which the real life of Jerusalem goes on and all those little bombs keep exploding."

We elbow our way into the Atara Café people turn to stare at us we're a curious-looking couple. We find a small table at the back and he takes off his hat. A waitress appears he orders coffee for us and gravely asks about the cakes he even decides to have a look at them he consults with the waitress smiling at me from afar. Finally he points a long finger at his choice and disappears into the men's room. I take out my pad a wave of warm words in my gut.

She gives off warmth she kisses the old man generously. She opens patiently to him listening suspending judgment refusing to categorize. A crushed felt hat a little mustache a warm yet violent exterior. A touch of the hand. His lust for cake. Describe a cake. Between two worlds. His different father.

He sits down next to me his hair combed and slightly damp beads of water still on his brows looking quizzically at the writing pad as it slipped back into my bag.

"Now then. At last I can take a good look at you. Relate the reality to the picture. So here you are. It's really you. Where did he find you?"

"Asi? In the university, where else."

"They tried to prepare me for you in their letters. Asi wrote: 'I think she's very pretty but that's not the main thing.' Just what the main thing was, though, he never said. And Ya'el in her cut-and-dried manner: 'We don't know much about her. She's retiring and doesn't talk much. Her family is very religious but it doesn't show on her. Extremely pretty.' End quote. After the wedding Tsvi wrote me too: 'The bride is beautiful.' As if they wanted to give me over there something tangible to take hold of, inasmuch as no one seemed able to explain, not even to himself, why Asa was in such a hurry to get married or who the young woman was. But if she was beautiful, perhaps I'd understand and accept. To tell you the truth, though, it wasn't much help to me. In fact, it only confused me more. Why, of all people, a religious beauty—those being the two things that everyone referred to? Either the combination was accidental or else it was supposed to tell me something. Was it mere caprice on his part? A misjudgment? Something temporary or a genuine decision? Because when I last saw him three years ago he had another girlfriend, a student from one of his classes. You must have heard of her. A girl with character, they had known each other since childhood. And then out of the blue I get an invitation to a wedding with a religious beauty! What was I to make of it? I'm not blaming anyone, but it was as though I wasn't wanted. That kind little note that you added at the end didn't amount to much either. You'll forgive me, but I'm sensitive to language. As if it didn't really matter whether I came or not. And there it was winter, in the middle of the academic year, and with no money set aside for the trip. Was I supposed to show up here just to stand arm in arm under the wedding canopy with the woman who tried to murder me while the rest of them stood by . . . was that it, eh?"

Coffee and cake are brought I'm in a daze I feel dizzy from this fantastical outburst. This sudden show of frankness. This violence. He keeps his eyes on me they're Asi's that split-level look but in light brown. The musical direct uninhibited speech that flows so powerfully. They wanted to murder him? My God, what can he be talking about? Did I hear right? Then he must be ill too. What kind of family have I landed in? Delicious tremor of fright. He bends over to sniff his cake sensually. He takes out two greenish pills and swallows them.

"To wake me up. I'm still limping along seven hours behind you and I can't seem to catch up. I've never suffered this way from jet lag before. I suppose I must be getting old, eh?"

He takes a bite of cake.

"I wanted to write a letter of apology to your parents, and of course to you too. I did manage to find out a bit about them through a friend of mine in Jerusalem. I understand that they own a grocery store. That they're decent, unassuming people. Hungarians?"

He stops to sip his coffee cuts himself another piece of cake and crams it in his mouth wrinkled desire suffusing his face.

"But in the end you didn't," I almost whisper.

He seizes my hand.

"I wasn't sure they'd understand . . . and to have to start explaining it all . . . with what they already knew about me . . . after all, such people put great stress on family life. I wrote a page and threw it away . . . but I told myself then that one day I still would explain myself. And now here I am alone with you . . . and you are very lovely . . . the way you stopped to kiss me with such feeling in the middle of the street, without giving it a second thought! You're not only beautiful, you have character. And I'm glad that we're alone and my first meeting with you is tête-à-tête, because Asa would have begun arguing right away. He's spent his whole life arguing with me from the minute he was born, he already started in the cradle. Well, he's got his students to argue with now, I suppose . . ."

The speed of it the honesty the crankiness the torrent of talk is too

much for me I'm shaking I'm blushing the sun is in my eyes there's a
hubbub of people around me. Soon Asi will be home. It's all burst on
me so suddenly. This vertigo. This deep emotion. He gulps down the
last of his cake he drains his coffee with his eyes closed he smiles and
looks around.

"But I don't understand . . . who tried to murder you?"

He stares at me. He takes out a cigarette lights it and snaps the
burnt match with strong fingers.

"You really don't know? No one ever told you? I see Asi has been
protecting our good name. How long have you been married? Nearly
two years, isn't it? Well, if you haven't left him until now, you won't
leave him because of this, ha ha ha . . ."

His sudden burst of depraved laughter astounds me.

"This?"

"Never mind. If they didn't tell you, it doesn't matter. It's all past
history now."

All at once though he changes his mind he leans toward me veiled
in smoke he sticks his face close to mine and murmurs feverishly:

"Who did? She did, of course. Why do you think that she's in
there and I'm out here? You mean they never even referred to it in
front of you? No, I suppose they didn't. . . . Well, someday, years
from now, when I'm dead and gone, Tsvi will tell you how he saw
me with his own eyes wallowing in my blood in the hallway outside
the kitchen . . ."

He loosens his tie opens two buttons in his shirt and displays a
pink stripe through the gray hair a ragged scar like a scribble now I
see it now I don't. The sunbeams play over his face. He takes my
hand again.

"Now where was I? Ah, why I didn't come to your wedding. The
question kept bothering me too. Here my son was getting married
and I sat in some faraway city in the middle of a black winter trying
to punish you when I was only punishing myself. What were they
thinking back there about the missing father of the groom? What did
the bride think? Someday, I told myself, I'll explain it all to her. A
few years from now I'll go back and explain. When all the fuss is
over I'll sit with her in some café in Jerusalem—that's exactly how I
imagined it—and we'll have an intimate talk. I didn't have this particular place in mind; I was thinking of that nice little café that's
been turned into a bank. I and the religious beauty—because you

really are beautiful, I can see now why they all made a point of it. Only who really are you? We'll have to try to understand you, to get to know you better . . ."

Customers are staring at us. Next to us sits a couple holding hands but the man can't take his eyes off me.

It's clear to me now. A character for a story. Better yet, for a whole novel. If only he'd stay with us in Israel I'd put him to good use I'd take him apart and spread whole chunks of him on paper I'd copy down entire sentences unchanged. The ineptness of that Asi. I've asked him a thousand times what's your father like and all he could offer me was a jaded stereotype. Why the man's a human gold mine! The looks of him the thick brows the little mustache the flow of his talk candid and crafty at once. Strong. I grip the hot cup of coffee hard. A warm trickle in the dark gut. Asi hasn't touched me for two weeks. The valise squeezed between my legs caressing my flesh. Customers walk back and forth brushing my hair. It's getting warmer. All at once a strong scent of spring. I open a button of my blouse suddenly aroused. The pain of words. I can't control myself I take the pad from my bag and quickly write *wrinkled desire. A human gold mine.* I close it and replace it. He smiles at me sagely.

"Found a phrase? When I was young I went around with a pad like that too."

He's already reaching out for it.

"We'd better go. It's getting late. Asi will be upset."

He asks for the bill. Five hundred pounds? He's stunned then he smiles. You must have it good here if such crazy prices don't faze you. He takes out his wallet and extracts a few American dollars but the waitress doesn't want to take them. I pay instead firmly refusing the dollars he offers me. The only one in this family who knows the value of a dollar is Kedmi he says the taxi driver didn't want any either Ya'el had to pay him for me and wouldn't take them herself. I must go to a bank and change money. Asi will change some for you let's not waste any time he'll kill me for keeping you so long. We walk to the bus stop and join the throng waiting by the iron pole I try hailing a cab that doesn't stop. He observes the hectic street amused. A bus comes the crowd surges toward the door. I take his hat to help him pushing him ahead of me he boards and disappears inside I get on too and pay for both of us. The whole bus is pushing and shoving. He's swept to the back he even manages to find a seat there he borrows a newspaper from the person next to him and opens it winking at me. Where have I landed? He's soft in the head himself he just pretends to be sane they want to force their madness down me drop by slimy drop. I don't mean you O man of gloom. It's not prudery it's self-protection but I'll write up your father to make up for it. My subject at last. Prose of course only prose will do there'll be a child too I promise it can be done scientifically with anesthesia what thou hast made pure I have made impure and what thou hast made impure I have made pure what thou hast forbidden I have permitted and what thou hast permitted I have forbidden what thou hast loved I have hated and what thou hast hated I have loved what thou hast condoned I have condemned and what thou has condemned I have condoned what thou hast rejected I have accepted and what thou hast accepted I have rejected yet none of it to make thee wroth. What did he do to make them want to kill him the brilliant light and the sea I saw the fear the disgust right away in Asi's eyes her fierce look the white cotton dress and the smell of old medicines the jar of jam that my mother gave Asi that I put at her feet on the grass he leaned toward her he said mother this is Dina we've come to invite you to the wedding that was the first time on a clear winter day she sat wrapped in a blanket in a chair by a tall tree she listened she asked questions she even smiled she seemed so normal until the sun went down then she tuned out what did he do to make her want to kill him so that's the skeleton they've been hiding in the closet wallowing in his blood by the kitchen how horrid but there is a story here there's got to be one and me so close to it if only I'm up to it one step at a time God give me strength I've married into a subject for at least a novella. The bus lurches forward the passengers topple on each other. A large man is thrown against me or maybe throws himself he's all red doesn't know what to do I'm draped by the warmth of his body I let it bear down on me the whole bus is shouting and laughing the human swarm.

At the university a mob of passengers tumbles out and another mob pours in. In line I spot Asi standing by himself in a plaid jacket and a thin intellectual tie careful not to touch or be touched looking angrily at the packed bus. I lean over toward the window banging my head against the bars. Asi! He hears me but can't see me he springs forward and presses ahead with the crowd. The despairing shriek of the door trying vainly to shut. What's happened to the buses today? Asi just makes it he's thin and wiry the last one in with his back against the door his briefcase clutched to his chest searching the passengers for me irritated worried at last he spies me and makes a terrible face. I smile and nod reassuringly I put his father's hat on my head the passengers near me grin broadly he gets it and looks for his father I point to the back of the bus. At Ramat Eshkol a large crowd gets off all at once. I shout to Asi's father that it's our stop Asi is already waiting by the rear door I step down first and go straight to his side waiting to see their reunion. His father staggers out holding his crushed coat Asi reaches for his bag the old man's confused but sees Asi right away they embrace on the bus steps behind them people are still struggling to get out the doors shriek encouragement.

"Were you waiting for us here?"

"No, I was on the same bus you were. I got on a few stops back."

"What's with these buses? You don't have a car, you don't even have a telephone—what kind of university professor are you?"

"I'm only a lecturer."

"It's lunacy to travel in these buses, with these crowds. You need a car."

"On my salary? Don't you have any idea what life's like here?"

"Then what has all your genius gotten us?"

The pushing continues the bus moves. All of a sudden we're alone on the sidewalk at the large intersection.

"Fame." Asi smiles his wonderfully wise ironic smile.

"Whose?"

"Yours too, father."

They embrace and kiss again his father rumples his hair. And I how can I not be happy too clinging to Asi hugging him putting my arm through his seizing the chance to hold his thin wriggly body he shrinks back a bit then relents. A marvelous moment the neighborhood in such a gentle light. Asi at his worldliest cleverest best. Father and son release one another each takes a step back the father slightly the taller of the two. They grin at each other without words yet perhaps a slight antagonism already brewing a certain distance. I feel a hot flash. Where is my pad my muse is signaling again. The poetess throbs with inspiration.

"What happened to your finger? Did you cut it?"

Is Asi just trying to break the ice or is this a serious checkup?

"Oh, that." He lifts up the finger with its gray bandage and laughs. "The day before yesterday I cut myself bathing Ya'el's baby."

"You bathed her? How come?"

"Ya'el went out shopping and I was still sleeping off the trip. Gaddi was taking care of Rakefet and couldn't handle her. She made in bed and cried, so he woke me and we bathed her together . . ."

"Did the two of you know each other?"

"Of course, what do you think? But I hadn't seen him for three years and he's grown. He looks a lot like Kedmi, tubby but bright. He has an eye for things and knows how to express himself. He's just a bit on the sad side, a bit . . . somber. Kedmi doesn't make life easy for anyone, although he does love the boy, that's evident. And you, Asa, how good it was of you to send your wife to fetch me! It was an excellent idea. We had a chance to get acquainted . . . we sat for a while in a café . . ."

"So that's where you were. I've been wondering what took you so long."

"What are all these new buildings? Is everything here one big development?"

We cross the street and pass the open supermarket.

"You two go on and I'll run in here."

"Maybe we should come with you." Asi is anxious not to lose control.

"No, you go ahead. Can't you see your father is tired? I'll manage by myself."

They walk ahead. No longer touching grown distant conversing Asi must be explaining the neighborhood to him his father halts from time to time to look around. Did she really want to kill him? Truly? God give me strength. *Yea the hand of the Lord was upon me and He brought me forth in the spirit of the Lord . . .*

The supermarket is crowded. It's a busy time of day people go berserk before each holiday at last I find a wagon and begin cruising the long shelves. Pardon me pardon me wagons bump together pass each other front back right and left. I stick my frail hands into piles of fruit and vegetables in line by the scales I remember my pad wearily uninspiredly automatically I write in it a few words. *On her head a man's hat. Happiness gone m(b?)ad. An orange peel. Son sniffs father.*

"You're next." A large woman peers tiredly over my shoulder.

I push my wagon down an aisle of wine bottles the sunbeams light the glowing liquid. I run my hand over them and take an expensively wrapped one down off a shelf *Old Judean Dessert Nectar* says the label in antique rabbinic script. Six hundred eighty pounds. Suitably impressed I put it in my wagon. Everyone around me is snatching items off the shelves you'd think the whole country was about to close down on Passover. I get into the spirit of it grabbing cheeses bread eggs canned foods a jar of olives frozen meats heading with the stream for the check-out counter. Here and there someone joins me on my way with his wagon trailing slowly after me among the aisles staring at me then drifting away.

"Dina!"

An old classmate by the name of Yehiel holding a sweet blue-eyed baby with a tiny skullcap on his head beside him a woman with a wagon full of food. He comes up to me all excited aglow already a bit gone to seed with a tummy a perspiring paterfamilias but the baby is soft and sweet. He tells me about himself with bumpkinish delight he's almost finished law school maybe they'll move to a new settlement on the West Bank he can work as its legal adviser. His wife a pale shrew a tight coif on her head examines me hostilely. "This is Dina," he says. "From my class . . . Once I told you about her . . ."

"You have a little boy already?" I can't get over it. Something suddenly draws me to the little tot. "Can I hold him for a minute?" I ask. Happily proudly he hands him to me while his wife's eyes widen with alarm. He too fell hard for me once. *The glory of Israel is slain upon high places how the mighty have fallen* a long long line of them the baby is light and warm all at once I'm overcome by desire I stroke his silken hair he clings to me watching me quietly reaching up for his skullcap with his small hand and giving it to me I smile at him I kiss him and hand him back replacing the skullcap I kiss him once more. He doesn't mind me at all I say softly to them. And all this while Yehiel chatters excitedly on about old classmates of ours whom I've forgotten he even writes his name and phone number on a piece of paper he informs me that once he met my husband. He teaches in the university, doesn't he?

A whole hour has passed by the time the supermarket's disgorged me. And with a lethal bill. Father and mother were right. At least I've been given an Arab boy to push the shopping wagon home for

me. A fresh warm wind is blowing outside a coppery twilight buses
pull up from downtown releasing their human beehives. The gay
shrieks of children. I walk in front the wagon rumbling after me.
Arab boys come back the other way with empty wagons they call out
to my boy and clap him on the back. He smiles uncomfortably he
steals a look at me is my beauty clear to them too? By a lamppost in
the busy street I make up my mind to stop a strong hand massages
my heart. Here it comes. I take out my already worn pad and leaf
through it to a fresh page.

*The plot begins in a supermarket. Age thirty-plus. An intellectual,
unsuccessful type. Once briefly married before. She steals the child
from a wagon by the door of the store. The time is dusk, people pass in
the street, coppery twilight. The boy is eight, nine months old. In the
end she'll have to return him!!!! She wears glasses, her hair is clipped
short. Deep down she doesn't know what she's doing. A description of
the warm bursting forth of spring. Nature means a great deal to her.
Only her mother is still alive. A heavy smoker.*

The Arab boy watches me good-humoredly his foot on the wheel
of the wagon. I stick the pad excitedly back in my bag. Why on earth
a heavy smoker?

At home I find Asi sitting with his father in the dark living room
tensely talking smoke drifting between them. His father wears a
checked shirt his tie is pulled loose. I've noticed that he dresses in
good taste he knows how to choose his clothes. I walk in the Arab
boy after me with the large cartons. Asi jumps up. Have you gone
out of your mind? Where have you been? The boy cringes and looks
at the floor. What got into you? What have you bought here? He
begins poking through everything. We already have cheese! He
throws the box of it aside. What's all this for? Who's going to eat it?
Where did you get the money from? I'm so mad I could kill him. The
boy brings in the rest of it stealthily watching us with wide eyes.
How dare he. Be quiet I hiss how dare you in front of your father.
Go back inside. Already I hear the hoarse musical voice from the
terrace.

"I'm a Tel Avivian, and with all due respect to Jerusalem, when
evening comes on here I feel a slight metaphysical angst. I always
tried to get back to the coast before it, to the scent of the orange
groves. In Jerusalem I feel afraid that some prophet will come to
haunt me in my sleep, ha ha . . . You do have a grand view here,

though. Just don't let anyone build on that empty lot in front of you. What are those lights over there on the hillside?"

I join him and stand by his side.

"Someone once told me, but I forget. It's some place in the West Bank."

The smell of his sweat. Asi is still rummaging through my purchases in the kitchen. He's taller and broader than Asi. He leans powerfully on the balcony his checked flannel shirt stirring slightly in the breeze.

As the grass that hath dried as the blossom that hath faded as the shadow that hath passed as the cloud that hath fled as the wind that hath blown as the dust that hath scattered as the dream that hath vanished forever.

I touch him lightly on the shoulder.

"You have regards from Ehud Levin."

"Which Levin? The author?"

"He said he was once a student of yours."

"That's right, he was. I've got them scattered all over."

"What was he like?"

"Oh, I don't know. Bright enough . . . rather sure of himself . . . always surrounded by girls . . ."

"He still is." I laugh.

Asi gloomily joins us.

"Where do you know him from?"

"Asi sent me to show him some things that I'd written."

"Do you write, then?" He eyes me with a warm smile.

"I try to."

"What did he say to you?"

"He made a few comments."

"But the gist of it." That's Asi no-nonsense impatient.

"He was somewhat encouraging."

Silence. I wish they'd drop the subject.

"He said that you gave him a lot as a teacher. That you meant a great deal to him."

He turns to look at me glowing in the dark.

"What, Levin? Really? I don't believe it. He actually said that?"

"I swear. He spoke of you with great respect."

He's bewildered he smiles and wants to say something but is so taken aback that the words stick in his throat.

He takes out a handkerchief and mops his brow.

"Suppose you get around to making supper," says Asi brutally.

"Are you hungry?"

"Of course."

"All right. In a minute."

I lean on the balcony grinding my stomach hard against the grillwork bending down toward the street below. Digging in.

"Come on, Dina, let's go. You certainly bought enough food."

His father watches from the side assessing us.

"Is there anything I can do to help? I've learned to cook in America . . . Connie actually depends on me to . . . ."

"No, nothing, father."

"Why isn't there? You could teach us some new recipe. Asi likes to fool around in the kitchen too, he's just too embarrassed to admit it."

I steer them both into the kitchen. I hand Asi a knife and some vegetables. His father rolls up his sleeves opens the refrigerator and sticks his head in to ferret out what's there. Finally he spiritedly suggests making some special egg dish. Do you have any rice? Not much. Where do you keep your spices Dina? And already he's in the pantry going through old containers sniffing at bags tasting things. He asks me to light the stove he takes a bowl and cracks egg after egg he begins to scramble them. Asi stands darkly in the corner watching resentfully but I'm utterly charmed. First you bathed Ya'el's baby now you're making us supper what will you do for Tsvi sew new buttons on his shirts?

He laughs rubbing his hands.

"Connie isn't much for housework, she's always held down a job. And I'm at home a lot these days, especially in the winter when you can't go out. I don't teach many hours at the college, so I have time to be in the kitchen."

He stirs forcefully trying to resuscitate the spices. I watch his long agile precise movements understanding all at once how he drove that bulky woman crazy feeling fear I leave the kitchen and begin to set the table halfway through I leave that too I have the need to write again I can't hold it in the words press on some tender bladder bobbing taut and smooth in my chest I go to the bedroom I kick off my shoes I shut the door I take off my pants I undo the hook on my bra I throw back the covers baring the white sheets I jump into bed and cover myself with a blanket my pad in my hand the pen gliding between my fingers my eyes are moist I warm up the paper with a torrent of remembered words . . .

Thou my strength thee the length of my days I shall praise thee implore all the more as I knock on thy door to thee sigh when I cry as each day goeth by and I pray yea I say O keep me from harm's way.

A baby carriage by the entrance to the supermarket. The baby's hair the color of honey. A description of his mother through her eyes. Worn-looking, talkative, her third child. The candy has been prepared in advance. She follows her through the aisles. Her first planned hiding place. A dark stairwell. Describe precisely the run-down entrance, the peeling plaster. A broom and a bucket in one corner. The objects with realistic verisimilitude to balance her great excitement when she picks up the baby with the candy stuck wonderingly in its mouth. At first all it shows is surprise. A passive collaborator.

Asi comes in and sees me bundled in the blanket. I hide the pad immediately.

"What are you doing there? Have you gone out of your mind?"

"I'm just resting for a minute. I'm bushed today."

"But you haven't done anything!"

"I've had a lot of excitement. That's work too. First the morning with you, then your father. I'll be up in a jiffy."

"What is he doing in there? Is he done cooking? I swear, he's too much! Go set the table. At least do that."

"In a minute. I already set part of it. He's an unusual person, your father. Did he cook for you when you were little too?"

Asi doesn't answer he looks at me grimly he goes to the closet.

"What are you looking for?"

"For a towel for him."

"Take the red one."

His father stands smiling in the doorway peering jovially in.

"Are you resting?"

"Yes. Just for a minute."

"I'm going to wash up. Don't touch the pot. Let it simmer."

Asi gives him the towel and he shuts himself up in the bathroom.

"You know, he's a good-looking man. It's no wonder that he found a young wife over there. He's better-looking than you are." Asi makes a face at me. "You aren't so good-looking, but you're sweet. Just don't be so gloomy. In the end you'll go crazy from all that tension and gloom. I can't stand how tense you are. Come, give me a kiss. Lie down for a minute. Let's take time out from the punishment."

"What punishment? What are you talking about?"

"You haven't touched me for two weeks. Come, give me one teeny kiss. Tonight we'll sleep together in honor of your father. You can do what you want with me. What needs to be done. You're right. It struck me today how crazy we've been. My fear of you, your fear of my fear . . . it's no way to have a child. Come, let me kiss you. I'll do anything."

It's as though he wants to step toward me but won't let himself hanging his head. I hear singing and water running in the bathroom.

"Are you lying to me now?"

"Why would I lie to you? You can see that it's you who's avoiding it. That it's you who can't."

"Me?" He twitches scornfully.

"Then do what you want. I won't move. I'll let you do anything. Come here a minute. At least let me give you a kiss."

But he's stubborn belligerent.

"Try me. I know I have to. Just be gentle and slow. Maybe we could work up to it slowly, night by night . . . Come, let me kiss you."

I get out of bed and hug him pressing against him twining my legs about his climbing up him kissing him. The water stops running. His father calls out something. Asi pushes me away. "Set the table this minute!" He leaves the room.

The stirred eggs and rice were delicious I couldn't stop praising his father. They've been discussing people I don't know at first I tried listening drowsily lethargically suddenly thinking hopelessly of my story how will I ever manage to explain the girl and her motives. Thinking should I make her a primitive or half crazy to make her more credible. The doorbell rings. Asi goes to answer it. Somebody wants you. Who is it? Somebody. He has a small package. I get up and walk down the hall the little bank teller who took care of me today is standing there with the bag of cheese that I forgot. Crimson frail in love an arrow lodged in his heart he hands me the cheese so choked up I can't understand what he says the stairway light goes off. I try touching him gently but he's scared of his own self he retreats down the stairs hardly waiting to hear me say thank you.

"Who was that?"

"A teller from our bank."

"That's right, I thought I recognized him. What did he want? What did he bring?"

"Nothing. I forgot a piece of cheese there today that my parents had given me."

"And that's why he came? There must be something the matter with him."

"I wouldn't know." I smile absentmindedly. "I suppose there must be. I'm not to blame for it, am I?"

He doesn't answer. He's used to such types all the lovesick souls who run after me but the unexpected appearance of this unobtrusive clerk has left him dumbstruck.

I lay the hunk of cheese down in the kitchen and unwrap it. Wrinkled crumbly soft and damp how hard and dry it was on the shelf in the grocery this teller has revived it with the warmth of his feverish hand. I rinse it in a dish of water. Sometimes I'm afraid of my own powers to go running at night with it to a far-off address just so as to see me again. Asi springs tensely into the kitchen and stares at the white hunk immersed in water.

"What are you going to do with that cheese?"

"Paint it, what else is it good for? It certainly can't be eaten."

"The worst part of it," he whispers with sudden venom, "is this new smart-alecky style of yours . . . the terrible tease you've become. The poor kid had to drag himself all the way out here to bring you this crumbling piece of cheese . . . and you actually smile . . . you enjoy it . . . it's too much, what kind of a person . . ."

"What?"

But he's stalked out again.

I serve coffee and cake. His father is smoking heavily looking detachedly at the books on the shelves only half listening. I'm already so used to having him with us.

"When do you think you can see my parents? They'd like so much to meet you."

"Of course." He turns to Asi. "Of course I should meet them. But when?"

"Maybe tomorrow evening," I suggest. "We can have dinner with them. Have you ever eaten Hungarian cuisine?"

"Tomorrow evening? No, tomorrow I'm going back to Haifa . . .

I mean to the hospital . . . and from there to Tel Aviv. I haven't been in Tel Aviv yet. I saw Tsvi only briefly at the airport . . . he's expecting me . . . I really don't know if I'll be in Jerusalem again on this trip."

"I'm going with you," says Asi.

"You're going tomorrow?" I'm thunderstruck. "Why?"

"I want to go with my father. Ya'el will come too. I haven't been there for ages."

"Is something the matter? Don't you teach a class tomorrow at the university?"

"We'll leave after it. It's over at ten."

"But what's the matter? Why should you want to go all together?"

"Because we do."

But his father abruptly bursts out:

"Kedmi insisted on going to her with the written agreement! Everything was already decided by mail . . . I even phoned several times from America to settle things with Ya'el . . . she had promised in so many words . . . we had talked with the doctor and invited the rabbi for next Sunday morning . . . and I wanted to see her before then . . . to say hello . . . but Kedmi insisted that she sign first, since she might change her mind if she saw me. Because we need her signature on the document, otherwise it isn't valid . . . which means the rabbi won't come . . . as it is, he's doing us a favor. So in the end Kedmi went by himself. Ya'el wanted to join him but he insisted on going alone. You know him, don't you? A rare specimen, always telling bad jokes and sure that he's the world's leading expert on everything. And I was so out of it my first day here that I agreed. Well, it looks like he made a mess of it, because she didn't sign. She told him she wanted to think about it . . ."

"To think about it?"

"Yes. All of a sudden she has to think. After everything was all settled and I had phoned all those times from America and made this trip. The rabbi even agreed to come especially with his assistants on the eve of the holiday . . . it wasn't easy to get him to do it . . . and next Tuesday I have to fly back. I don't know. Perhaps her feelings were hurt because I didn't come to see her but sent Kedmi straight off with the agreement. I suppose he made some careless remark—he's a simple man really and from a very uncultured family, even if he does have a glib tongue. So now I'm at my wits' end. I

thought that perhaps Asa and I should go see her tomorrow with
Ya'el . . . my fears may be groundless, but still it's better to see her
. . . it will be good for her . . ."

"But must you absolutely divorce her on this trip?" I ask with soft
surprise unable to comprehend all this rush.

Asi kicks me hard beneath the table. His father's face falls growing
tired and creased there's a silent plea in his eyes.

"Yes, of course. You see, Connie . . . it can't go on this way
. . ." At a loss he looks at Asi who says nothing.

"Then maybe you can see them for a few minutes tomorrow morning."

"See who?"

"My parents."

"Right, your parents. I don't know. Tomorrow morning? Will
there be time? I had wanted to get something done at the university
. . . but perhaps . . ."

"You won't have time," declares Asi drily sharply head down.

"And you won't be back in Jerusalem?"

"In Jerusalem? I doubt it. I haven't been in Tel Aviv yet. I have so
much to do there . . . this visit is so short and Tsvi is expecting me.
But you'll be at the seder at Ya'el's . . . we'll all meet again there
. . ."

"No. We have to be with my parents. They have no one else."

Asi wants to say something but doesn't.

"Perhaps the day after then, on the holiday itself . . ."

"We could try . . ."

Silence. I suddenly grasp that I may not see him anymore that he's
about to vanish again.

"Maybe I'll come too tomorrow."

He looks at Asi.

"No. You can't," says Asi determinedly. "Not tomorrow. There'll
be too many people. She won't be able to cope."

"But I want to see her too."

"No. It's impossible. Not tomorrow."

We trade blows via his father.

"What will I tell my parents then? They'll feel so disappointed."
I fight bravely on for them.

"My father will phone them tomorrow to say hello. He'll apologize and explain."

All at once such loneliness engulfs me. Asi is casting me vilely aside. He'll always do just what he wants to. His father smokes thoughtfully.

"I really did want to meet them but I don't see how it will work out. This trip's been so rushed . . . the time has sped by. I will call them, though. That's a good idea. And I'll tell them that on my next visit . . . because I'll come again next year with Connie . . . yes, I'll certainly call them. Someone told me that they're very religious. Where do you live? . . . In Ge'ula? Are they followers of some Hasidic rabbi? . . . You don't say! How interesting. One could never tell by looking at you, there's not a trace left. How could they have let you? Have you lost faith yourself? I mean . . ."

Asi regards me intensely.

"Asi dislikes God. It's that simple. Like someone who can't stand a certain food and won't allow it into the house." His father smiles and nods. "It's a matter of taste. But sometimes when I'm alone I buy it and cook it and eat it in secret, and wash out my mouth so he won't know. I've lost faith but sometimes I'm still afraid . . ."

Asi's eyes glitter with mirth. He's cruelly amused.

"Apart from that, we keep a kosher home: the dishes, the pots, the silver . . . so that my parents can eat here with us, although in fact they never do."

"Over there, this past year, I've begun attending synagogue now and then."

"I always figured it would come to that someday," Asi jabs drily still staring down.

His father flushes hard-pressed to explain.

"Simply as an onlooker. As a sociological observer of the vagaries of Jewish history. Besides, the temple has a wonderful choir. All Gentile, of course. You should hear how beautifully it sings. Absolutely professional."

> *O he knows that he has sinned, he knows that it's no use,*
> *In vain he strums the burst strings of his heart.*
> *He's silent as a shadow and equally elus-*
> *ive, & he shivers when the Sabbath prayers start.*

Suddenly there's an awkward feeling in the air. Asi projects hostility toward both of us. I clear the table and put the dishes in the sink I soap them and run the water. The two of them sit silently smoking by the table. So what? The distant mother the mortally wounded parents. All that counts is *she. Waiting for me. Where did I leave her? Coming out of the supermarket with the baby in her arms. Twilight. I have to dress her. A skirt or pants? Pants, soft velvety ones. People in the street brush lightly against her, quickly she slips into the stairwell with the broom, yes I see it clearly, there's a dusty old baby carriage there. She puts him in it and begins to wheel him. Her name should be simple, drab, nothing special or too modern. On the stairs she encounters a neighbor. Our banalities are the most incriminating things about us. She pulls down the blinds, she gathers pillows and builds a wall of them on her bed, she puts the child inside it. Make him younger. Four months old. His first fit of crying. Until now he's been quiet. She goes to look for milk. She doesn't have enough? She runs down to the grocery, it's open until late. Another grocery? More objects. Where does the plot go from here? All right, in the end she returns him, but why? A purely internal decision?*

Someone's at the door. Who is it now? Telephone for Dina. I wipe my hands and descend to the floor below the door is open the family is eating invisibly in the kitchen where I hear hoarse adolescent voices. The receiver is dangling from a hook. Father and mother each on a different phone. Do not forsake us O our darling. They had to install a second phone because each kept grabbing the first from the other. Their voices mingle in the identical accent one finishes the other's sentence one answers the questions asked me by the other.

"So how was supper?"

I astound them with its story. They disapprove. "You should have made it. If you had taken the groceries from us, you would have been spared the embarrassment. What are his plans now?"

"He's heading back north tomorrow. He has to visit her in the hospital. But he'll call you in the morning."

"He'll call? That's all he'll do, call? He can't come?"

"It seems not. He's leaving early in the morning. The whole visit's very rushed." (I should have invited them tonight really I'm not ashamed of them.)

There's a long silence on both phones.

"How is he?"

"Fine. Just fine. He's young-looking, likable, friendly. He resembles Tsvi more than Asi. He even goes to synagogue in America."

(Now what did I tell them that for? To please them? To make them like him? As their consolation prize?)

And indeed they're in seventh heaven. Religion wins the day.

"How do you like that! . . . You see? . . . Just a minute, what? . . ." (A brief pause while they consult.) "Maybe we'll come over for a few minutes now . . . we could even take a taxi . . . or is he too tired? . . ."

I say nothing. My heart goes out to them so lonely in their old neighborhood. But how can I possibly have them over now? Delicately they probe my silence. "Dina? Are you there? What do you think? We'll take a taxi . . ." (The ultimate for them in dissipation.)

I still don't answer. I can't tell them not to. In a minute they'll understand by themselves. "Dina?" Father raps on the phone. In the end they give up.

"Perhaps I'll bring him to you for a short while in the morning. We'll see. The main thing is that we'll be with you for the seder."

I hang up.

Asi and his father are already finishing the dishes in the kitchen putting everything away. No wonder she went mad. The old man's crafty glance alights on me as though asking for help. Asi is getting moodier by the minute their silence percolates between them.

"You really needn't have!" I do my best to sound thrilled. "Asi, why did you?"

He makes a despairing gesture with his hand. I go to the bedroom and look for my pad between the sheets. Where are you my dear sitting moodily in your room shuttered by your growing fear fatigued from listening to the ceaseless crying of the baby. Asi enters after me I snatch the pad and escape with it to the bathroom I undress there and take a long shower blissful in the vaporous spray I slowly advance upon the mirror from time to time kissing a breast nibbling a shoulder with dainty bites licking my fragrant skin. I put on my bathrobe and brush a few droplets of water from the pad where some words have blurred like frail spiders on tiny shelves. I dry them with my breath I return to the bedroom and climb into bed. Away with all inhibition! I begin to write. *Stress my character's fright after the initial steely excitement of the kidnapping itself, which took place with surprising ease and speed. Her modest room? A poster of a dog. The baby cries and cries. She's afraid someone will hear. She boils milk and waits for it to cool. Describe the moment and the quality of the light. Her violent inner conflict. The telephone rings, it must be her mother. She doesn't answer for fear the cries will be heard.*

I let the bed warm me rereading what I've written. So thin and lifeless. I turn to the poetry side. How different.

Soft venomous bald skull old snake napping on Jerusalem rock. Frail spring

Hot air.

I close my eyes. Asi calls from the next room. Just a minute I answer without opening them. The TV is on. Light glares on me something is snatched from my hands. My bathrobe slips freezingly off of me. Asi stands by the bed holding the pad thumbing it reading it. I must have fallen asleep what time is it?

"Put that down!" I jump naked out of bed shivering with cold but he goes on reading with cold eyes. Put it down! He shuts it and puts it on the table the pen slips from beneath my legs to the floor he bends down to pick it up and lays it by the pad.

"Stop snooping, I tell you!"

"I'm sorry," he whispers. "I didn't know what it was. You never had a pad like this."

"What time is it?"

"After eleven. How could you have fallen asleep like that?"

"Where's your father?"

"Watching the news. I'm looking for some sheets."

"I'll give them to you. Just close the door."

I put on a skirt and blouse. "What have you been doing?"

"Talking and watching TV. But what's with you today?"

"I don't know."

"Where are the pillowcases?"

"In a minute. I'll make his bed. Let me do it."

But Asi won't leave he wants to say something he's terribly upset he paces the room restlessly.

"Is something the matter? Did he tell you anything?"

He stares at me a thin smile on his lips he exclaims:

"It turns out that . . . you won't believe this . . . he's going to have a baby over there. That's why he's in such a hurry to get divorced. That woman of his . . . that Connie . . . is pregnant . . ."

"Pregnant? How old is she?"

"I don't know. What difference does it make? He's going to have a baby, just imagine . . ."

"Asa?" The musical voice drifts in from the living room. "How do you turn off this television?"

"I'll be right there."

Asi goes out followed by me carrying sheets and a blanket. In the smoke-filled living room are dirty teacups and a small bottle of brandy. It's as though I haven't been here for days. Asi's father stands tall and upright by the flickering white screen his fingers sliding over the buttons. Asi turns off the set and takes the cushions from the sofa.

"I'll take care of it, Asi. Go wash up. I'm so sorry I fell asleep like that."

"Never mind. You needn't have bothered to get up." Asi's father reaches out to take the sheets from me but I hug them tight not letting them go.

My conking out like that must have hurt his feelings he gives me a remote look. He smells sharply of sweat again. Didn't he just shower a few hours ago? And yet again this sour masculine odor. What is he secreting all the time it's as if his body wished to tell us something. A strong a very vital man he's going to have a baby well why not?

He helps me move the sofa he catches the end of the sheet and tucks it under the mattress. He looks at me fondly.

"You needn't have bothered to get up."

"I have this way of collapsing when I'm emotionally excited . . . because of your coming . . . I was all worked up . . . because of that meeting this morning too . . ."

"This morning?" he wanders his arm around me.

"With that author. Your old student."

"Ah, him." His grip on me weakens. "Were you afraid of him? What did he talk to you about?"

"It's hard to explain. About what I showed him, about literature in general . . ."

"He was a loudmouth back when I taught him, so sure of himself, so . . . doctrinaire. Every few months he'd come up with some new theory and make a religion out of it. What was it this time?"

"That one has to work from the concrete, from immediate physical objects, to find significance in them . . . if there is any . . ."

"From the concrete? What is he talking about? What does he

know about it? Don't set him up as an authority. He's a fellow who loves to have disciples, to have a court full of followers—I've heard all about him. Listen only to your own self! You know, I'd also like to read what you've written . . . that is, if you'd have the confidence in me to let me . . . I know a bit about these things too. Maybe you'll show me something now . . . or better yet, mail it to me. I can feel that I'll like it, especially now that we've gotten to know each other. . . . Don't pay attention to Asa. He's a cynic. There's so much to see in the world—me, I'm always curious for more. I've told him that the two of you should come stay with us for a while in America. I'll find him some work there, some postgraduate position. After all, I am his father. And you too, my dear child . . . as soon as the pressure lets up . . . as soon as I'm rid of this bane of my life . . ."

His eyes glow fiercely he flushes and grabs my hand pushing me against the wall whispering excitedly carried away with himself.

"I don't know what Asa has told you, and he doesn't know everything himself. Not that it's his fault. It was I who decided to wait patiently until he grew up and left home . . . but now that I see him with a home of his own, with a wife, with all the makings of a serious, creative, successful career . . . I can't tell you how happy I am that I came to Jerusalem today even for these few hours. At last I'm at peace and can think of myself. Do you know what all that I want is? Simply to have and to give a little happiness. Even a small apartment like this would be big enough for me if it were inhabited by sane people. You have no idea how hard it's been . . . and I honestly tried my very best until she stuck that knife into me."

His hand gropes again for his shirt buttons.

All at once I feel terror. Standing pressed against the wall with him looming over me his eyes full of tears a gusty night outside and Asi locked in the bathroom.

"I don't blame them. She's their mother. But did they really think that I would live out the rest of my life chained to her . . . to the long twilight of a mad glob of living matter, to put it concretely, as our dear author advises us to . . . and there is no significance here, it's simply a concrete, physical fact, the sum of its own physicality. I, to whom things of the spirit . . . and I'm not that old, you can see for yourself, I'm only sixty-four . . . people realize who I am, they make contact with me, love me . . . I still have the strength, the potential . . . Asi can tell you . . ."

Unnoticed Asi stands listening palely in the doorway in his pajamas. His father smiles at him the tears gone.

"We've been waiting for you to say good night."

He kisses me very gently on the forehead.

"Open the window a bit, Yehuda, to air out the room. It's full of smoke."

He hesitates. I'm surprised at myself for calling him by his first name.

"Afterwards you can close it again."

"All right."

"If we're up early tomorrow we'll leave here with Asi and the two of us can go say hello to my parents. They were so disappointed when they heard you were leaving already."

I want to say more but he's heard the entreaty in my voice.

"That's fine. That's perfectly all right. I'll get up early. You'll wake me."

I open the window and look out at the dark blocks of apartment houses. A strong half-wintry half-springlike wind is blowing outside. I collect the cups from the living room and glide out of it. What matters most more than anything is my heroine for whom the time has come she demands it to be given a name. Sarah plain Sarah it's an awful one but exotic-sounding like a character's on TV. And if the story is ever translated it won't be a problem. Where are you my dear? Wretchedly cooped up in her room with that baby whom she is slowly discovering is retarded slightly brain-damaged his mother was probably glad to get rid of him. Whan an incredible idea a whole new slant the ironic possibilities! It will help make it credible. I can stay with the absurdly tragic and not have to get so deeply personal.

Asi is already in bed with his head on the pillow looking at some book he has to lecture on tomorrow. My little orange pad is on the night table by the bed. He's touched it it's fouled I want to pick it up but I can't. I close the door soundlessly turning the key and switch off the light. Light from the living room creeps under the door. I strip off my clothes I lift the blanket from him and whisper:

"Call off the punishment. I'm ready now. I promised you . . ."

He smiles stroking my face and neck distractedly.

"Not now, we can't. He's in the next room. Tomorrow."

"You mean you can't."

"Of course I can. You know that perfectly well. Watch it . . . but why now when he's practically on top of us? You know you'll scream the way you always do. Think about it, do you really want him to hear you . . . is that what you want . . . ?"

"I won't scream this time. I promise."

"Yes, you will. It's not up to you. But never mind." He hugs me powerfully. "Tomorrow. If we've waited this long, we can wait another day."

"Then I want you to know that means you can't."

He's furious now. "Don't start that again. You know what the real truth is . . . all right then, come on! I'll prove it to you."

All of a sudden he throws himself on me savagely spread-eagling me mounting me right away I contract as hard as I can locking the little door he's a frail snake gliding groping slithering drily away.

"You crazy woman, now do you see?"

All at once my anger melts I have to force myself not to cry. I get out of bed and put on a nightgown.

"All right then, tomorrow. But call off the punishment."

"Do me a favor, stop talking idiotically."

"Tell me it's called off."

"There's nothing to call off."

"There is. You know how you've behaved toward me these last two weeks. You've picked on me, you haven't touched me . . ."

"All right, all right . . ."

I kiss his face I get into bed I turn my back to him and snuggle up like a fetus asking him to put his hand on my belly. The warmth of it in that deep pit of tiredness. The mind's last gasps. My heroine Sarah she's stuck in her room without moving. Where will she sleep? She won't talk she won't think. A flop of a character. The whole story's a washout. Where can it go from here? A dead end. And now I don't know what to do with her. Tomorrow I'll try to breathe some life into her I'll give her of my own flesh and blood. The light goes out in the living room. Fatigue courses through her like a river wave after wave of it rocking over soft bottomless depths a towering dull blue wall of water beneath her the quiet hum of the traffic in the wind. But someone keeps bothering her there's no quiet a murmured sob blankets are tugged back and forth he moves her about lifts a hand or a leg the light keeps going on and off. Asi are you up? What time

is it? It's already three o'clock what's the matter with you? I can't
sleep he sobs. Put your arms around me. That won't help I'm boiling
mad inside. What's wrong? Everything everything. Is it me? It's you
and it's him. He has to go have another child hasn't he done enough
harm already? Goddamn him . . . where does he get the strength
. . . the man has no sense of shame . . . he'll make a laughing-
stock of us all. I'm finally beginning to understand. Ya'el suspected
all along. But sleep is getting the better of her. What will she do? An
old a prolonged cough pierces the silence from the other room. She's
so sleepy she's sleeping but he keeps bothering her. Stop thinking
you think too much if you don't think you can't go mad she says it
without knowing if she really has said it or if she only has slept
it . . .

WEDNESDAY

Family, I hate you!
André Gide

". . . so that as consistently as these youngsters rejected the idea of the state, and of all public bodies and institutions, they also rejected, at least initially, the idea of organized terror. Their terror was individual, and so they wished it to remain. A private rather than a collective act. Authority could reside only in the individual acting by himself and flowed from his great sense of inner freedom that sought to bestow itself upon the nation as a whole. The decision to commit a terrorist act could not be made by any organized forum proceeding by majority vote or some other resolution-passing process. Thus, despite their enormous feeling of camaraderie for each other, their marvelous sense of shared humanity that made up in part for their lack of contact with a sympathetic public, the terrorists remained radically isolated. In the first place, you must remember that they were very young—much younger than you yourselves. Pisarev, the leading theoretician of Russian nihilism, once remarked that children and teen-agers made the greatest fanatics. Russia was at this time a youthful nation that had been essentially reconstituted barely one hundred years before, and its terrorists were youthful too. 'A proletariat of high-school graduates,' they were called. And yet it was they who held high the torch of freedom and took a stand against a brutal dictatorial regime in order to liberate a people that was far from eager to collaborate with them. Nearly every one of these youngsters paid the price of suicide, public execution, imprisonment or insanity. A handful of intellectuals struggled alone while an entire nation kept silent. On the twenty-seventh of January 1878, what is called the First Wave of Russian Terror began. A young woman named Vera Zasulich shot General Tarpov, the vicious head of the St. Petersburg police. She had received orders from no one and was acting completely on her own, impelled by her own moral conscience. Ideologically, however, she was well prepared for what she did. She had read many underground writings, among them an essay called *Murder* by the German Karl Heinsen that was published as early as 1849 and was well known in her circles. She was also familiar with Mikhail Bakunin's famous treatise *Revolution, Terrorism and Gangsterism,* which appeared in Geneva in 1856. These were the two selections that I asked you to read for today in Walter Laqueur's anthology . . ."

But as usual they haven't. The pens stop moving. Outside the wind howls in the sudden silence. Their eyes avoid mine breaking off contact. What do they care about treatises? I should be grateful that they're willing to listen to me at all. You tell us about it. Whatever you say. But unless I get a discussion going now I'll have to eat into my next lesson. There are still fifteen minutes to go. If only that old fusspot had come today: he doesn't bother with the reading list either but he always has something to say and knows the oddest details and old books. He's the only one here with some vague idea of what I'm getting at even if he is always protesting in the name of his absurd sense of values. I can always kill some time with him. Shadowbox with him in a corner. But he didn't come to class this morning and he wasn't here last week either. Sick? Dead? Dropped the course? Neither did those old women auditors show up today because of the holiday. I have a small audience and that always annoys me. I've gotten used to standing room only.

"Can somebody please tell me then what Heinsen's basic thesis is? Who'll sum it up for us?"

A scraping of chairs.

"Who read it?"

They avoid my glance leafing through their notebooks looking out the windows deep in thought.

"Perhaps I'd better ask who hasn't read it."

A limp hand goes up. Several others hesitantly follow it. They grin at each other.

"The book wasn't in the library because you have it," calls a voice from the corner.

Relieved laughter.

"But there are two other copies. I put them on the reserved shelf myself at the beginning of the year."

They frown bewilderedly.

"I really did look for it but it wasn't there."

In her dreams.

Yes, a student announces, they were once on reserve but they're gone. The librarian can't understand it herself.

"Gone where?"

"Who knows? They're gone."

The relief is general now. As long as the books aren't there.

"But why didn't you let me know? I asked you to read those selections a month ago. Why didn't you say something then? This is a discussion class, not a lecture . . ."

The door opens silently and Dina's curly head peeks in. "May we?" she whispers amiably and without waiting for an answer turns and says in a clear voice that echoes down the corridor, "It's here!" She glides to the last row and slips silently into a seat while father tiptoes in behind her head down as though entering a low tunnel careful not to meet my eyes his little valise clutched to his chest and picks his way through the jumble of empty chairs to the last one in the corner. Everyone turns to look at them. Several students recognize her and start whispering to each other while giving me doting looks. The blood goes to my head. Goddamn her. Why did she have to come in now? The room buzzes irritatingly.

"Karl Heinsen's essay *Der Mord, Murder,* is considered the most important ideological document of the early terrorist movement. Reprinted several times and widely quoted from, it first appeared in 1849 in a newspaper put out by a German political exile in Switzerland. In it Heinsen, who was exiled himself, seeks a moral justification for terror. He himself was not a socialist but a radical bourgeois, for which both Marx and Engels attacked him; it was his rejection of socialism rather than his espousal of terror that offended them. In later life Heinsen emigrated to America, where he edited several

German newspapers. He died in 1880 in Boston, a city that he considered the one refuge of culture in the United States."

A faint smile darts over father's tense face when I relate Heinsen's opinion of Boston but at once he starts and stares down.

Dina isn't listening. She's still beaming with dumb pleasure. She had no time to put on makeup this morning and her face looks all splotchy. She has an old childish blue dress on. She peeks at the notebook of the student sitting next to her who offers her his notes right away. They exchange whispers. Is she going to make a public nuisance of herself?

"Heinsen begins by reviewing several historical cases of primitive terrorism in which individuals sought to strike down tyrants on their own initiative. He describes the respect and admiration we feel for such figures as Harmodius and Aristogiton, who murdered the tyrant Hipparchus . . ."

I've learned their names by heart and don't even have to sneak a look at my notes. Father bends marvelingly forward. I'm taut as a spring driven by an intellectual anger.

"He demonstrates that, historically, terror in itself has never been repudiated as long as the wickedness of the tyrant or regime it is aimed at has been acknowledged. On the contrary, terrorists throughout history have earned our approbation. If the young German named Stacz who tried to kill Napoleon, asks Heinsen, had succeeded and not been caught at the last minute, would not he be a world-famous figure today?"

Again you can hear a pin drop. I pace back and forth looking down at the floor tiles.

"Heinsen develops his theory further by arguing that the difference between state and individual terror is to the moral advantage of the latter. The state employs weapons of destruction that indiscriminately kill people by the hundreds, whereas the terrorist strikes only at a specified target. The moral contrast between an artillery shell and a pistol shot is entirely in the pistol shot's favor."

They're bent over their notes. They'll write down whatever I tell them.

"Indeed, a well-aimed pistol shot . . ."

I stand facing them. I raise one arm and make a pistol with my thumb and forefinger. The silence deepens.

"In those days care was still taken to avoid injuring the innocent bystander. When the final touches were being put to the planned assassination of Admiral Dubasov, the terrorist Vinarovsky declared: 'If Dubasov's wife is there with him, I won't throw the bomb.' Karl Heinsen makes his own position clear. You'll read it for yourselves. Tomorrow the vacation begins and you'll have plenty of time. I'll return my copy of the book to the library."

"But put it on the reserved shelf before it disappears too . . ."

The familiar ripple of laughter. Only the technicalities concern them. Their pettily practical souls.

"All right. But I want you to read two more selections in the anthology. One by Sergei Nichaev and the other by Morozov."

I angrily write their names on the blackboard.

"Is that clear? Those two selections too, and I'm warning you that you'll be tested on them. I've had enough of this monkey business. If you don't read everything you'll never understand the intellectual background of young Vera Zasulich, the daughter of aristocrats, who served two years in jail even before she decided that she was honor-bound to make Tarpov pay for his bestiality. She loaded her pistol, stuck it in her coat pocket, and gained admission to Tarpov's suite on the pretext that she had an appointment with him . . ."

The bell. At last. Father looks pale. He props his head on one hand while holding the valise on his knees with the other.

"She waited quietly in the vestibule outside his office. She knew him well—in fact, she had visited his house many times with her parents as a small girl. I've mentioned that she was of aristocratic stock, and relations among the terrorists between children of nobility and children of commoners were deep and fraught with consequences. As soon as he stepped out of his office surrounded by his assistants she rose and shot him in the chest. She didn't kill him, though; he was only wounded. She made no attempt to escape. She threw her pistol on the floor and calmly let herself be arrested."

Dina stops whispering. All eyes are on me in the sweetly deepening silence. They want adventure stories not history.

"The government did not try Zasulich before a regular court but rather before a special jury of magistrates that was appointed to give her sentence moral standing. To everyone's amazement, however, this jury acquitted and freed her. And when afterwards the police sought to arrest her administratively in the street, a crowd of admirers rescued her from their hands. Eventually she illegally left Russia and became a leading figure among Russian revolutionary exiles abroad. Vera Zasulich's pistol shot and dramatic acquittal paved the way for many more assassinations. A wave of terror swept over Russia. That same year Krabchinsky, a strange but talented man about whom we shall yet have much to say, laid still another tier in the growing edifice of terror with the publication of a small pamphlet entitled *A Death for a Death.*"

Father's eyes shut. The valise almost slips off his knees. The door opens. The next class's students are trying to get in.

He shuts his folder with a flourish. He takes out the cigarette prepared in advance and lights it with the ritual gesture that marks the end of the lesson. A cloud of smoke envelops him as the dry tension slowly eases. The students rise to go. Two of them ask him for the book. He hands it to them in silence, answering their questions distantly, laconically, almost brutally. He throws his papers and other books one by one into his briefcase, bristling as new students fill the room. Already I'm making my way out through the crowd head down careful to touch no one passing without a glance by Dina who stands giggling by the door with two students. Neither do I look at father who leans uncertainly against the wall unable to find a place for his valise. Gingerly I lay my hand on him: "Come, we'll be late." And without looking back I hurry down the corridor and skip quickly down the stairs. He feels my anger as he hurries after me.

"I hope we didn't disturb you," he murmurs. "Dina insisted that we drop in to watch you teach. I myself didn't want to . . ."

"It's all right."

He smells faintly of eau de cologne. What's gotten into the man?

"You're so intense that you scared me. But I'm glad to have seen you lecture. Marvelous! You're a real orator. And with those dramatic hand gestures . . . I thought you were really going to shoot. Bravo! Go on being tough with them. Give them exams. That's the only way they'll respect you. What was the subject of today's lesson, terrorism? How interesting. Are you lecturing on that all year long?"

"No. The course is on late-nineteenth-century Russia."

"Of course. That's what your doctorate's about."

"No, it's about the 1820s. I sent it to you . . . but I don't suppose you ever looked at it . . ."

I weave in and out lightly fending off bodies like a submarine in a busy harbor.

"But I did. Of course I read it . . . that is, the parts that I could understand . . . it's just that . . ."

Now he's trying to stammer his way out of it. But then I didn't hear a single word from him. We stand facing a strong dry wind in the plaza outside. Dina rushes to catch up with us. She clings to me hugging and kissing me for all the students to see.

"It was such a lovely class!"

"But you kept disturbing me."

She giggles.

"He started up with me. It wasn't my fault. He's one of those eternal students. He was once even in a class of mine. But we talked in a whisper."

"Forget it." I take a step back from her. "Were your parents happy to see you?"

"At least now they're sure that you weren't immaculately conceived . . . even if you would have liked to be."

Father laughs.

"I'm glad Dina made me go. It was a must. They were so happy to see me. It was a short but successful visit, wasn't it, Dina? They're very likable people."

"That's good, father, but we have to move. We have a long trip ahead of us."

Again I feel the sting of the lost day. My precious time . . . and it almost Passover and the library soon to be closed . . .

"Yes, let's go," says Dina animatedly.

"You're coming too?"

"Of course."

"But how can you? Aren't you going to work today?"

"I'm taking the day off. I'm coming with you."

My wife the playgirl.

"Absolutely not. There's no reason for you to be there."

"Then I'll wait outside."

"But what on earth for? I don't get it. You haven't gone to work for several days. In the end you'll be fired, you do know that, don't you?"

"Don't worry about me."

The selfishness to keep taking off from work and coming home at the end of the month with hardly any paycheck. If it weren't for what we get from her parents . . .

"Then I'm coming." She turns beseechingly to father who says nothing.

"You are not!"

"I haven't seen your mother for so long."

"You'll have plenty of time to see her. She's not going anywhere. And neither are you today."

I squeeze her arm hard to show her I mean it. She has new little pimples on her face. Brackish blue eyes. Cheekbones that protrude as though about to puncture her thin skin. How did I ever get stuck with her? A stubborn Mongoloid child.

"Why don't you go to work."

She retracts her arm from me.

"I don't want to. And you can't make me."

Father turns away smiling faintly half listening to our enjoyable little spat.

"Of course I can't. Who can make you do anything? Come, father, we'll be late."

She stands there stunned flushed with rage. Students stare at us as they pass. Father lays a light hand on her.

"So we'll see you on the holiday? You'll come to say goodbye . . . we'll be in touch . . ."

She doesn't hear him though. Doesn't look at him. She stares at me floored by my refusal.

"Then give me some money, Asa."

"What for?"

"I need some."

"But just yesterday . . ."

"It's all gone."

"Do you two need money?"

"No, father, it's all right." I take out my wallet and give her five hundred pounds.

"That's all?"

"That's all I have. I need some for myself."

"If you two need money, say so."

"Fine. I'll go to the bank."

"There's none left there either."

"He'll give me some anyway."

"Who?"

"The teller who brought me the cheese last night."

All at once she bursts out laughing gaily. Warmly she throws herself on father's neck then shakes my hand stiffly and disappears among the students.

"Very simple people. I was in their grocery store. Straight out of a nineteenth-century Hebrew novel, with a barrel of pickled fish by the door. A genuinely literary grocery! A most depressing one too. And they're very religious, even if her father doesn't grow long sidelocks. *Very* religious, I tell you: I have a sixth sense for that sort of thing and I could feel it right away. In fact, in no time they were telling me that they belong to a small sect of Hungarian Hasidim with some very old rabbi whom they consult about everything and who tells them just what to do and think. Were you aware of that? You too, my dear Dr. Kaminka, are in his hands. You too are being manipulated by him by means of some hidden string, heh heh . . ."

(Why is he carrying on like this?)

"Is this our bus? The express to Haifa? You'd better make sure. . . . Let me pay for us. It's frightful that I still haven't gotten to the bank to change dollars. . . . All right, then, I'll pay you back in Haifa. The main thing is to be in the station there by one o'clock. Ya'el and Kedmi will be waiting for us. . . . It makes no difference to me, you can sit by the window. . . . What I've been asking myself since my fascinating visit with your in-laws this morning is whether you knew what you were getting into or whether you simply saw a pretty young thing at the university and didn't bother to ask what she came with. What a hodgepodge world it's become! Twenty years ago a young girl from such a family would never have left the streets of her neighborhood; she would have gone about so muffled up in long dresses that you wouldn't have bothered to look twice at her in the street. But today there are such astonishing leaps and transitions . . . the barriers have all come down. A total chaos. Just look what an anarchist like you has gotten involved with! But I suppose you manage to get along with them . . . leave it to you. From the time you were in nursery school you always had the knack of getting along. Asa knows how to minimize conflict, mother and I used to say to each other. . . . When is this bus going to leave? I'm glad I went to see them, they would have been hurt if I hadn't. I really don't understand why you were so against it. After all, we got back in perfectly good time. Your Dina can be a bit childish, and I'm happy you didn't let her join us for the drama that's in store for us today. You saw that I kept out of it. But this morning she was right. Why should you have been angry? After all, I did it for your sake too. I really don't follow you there. Are you ashamed of them? They may be simple folk, but they're certainly decent ones. And your own father is no model of perfection either, heh heh . . ."

(He's got this new way of laughing. Almost reedy. What's come over him?)

"Well, someday they'll be gone, and you'll be left with a wife who ten years from now will be a notorious beauty. I've noticed how people stare at her . . . right now she's still half-baked, but give her a few years' time. She'll open a lot of doors for you . . . your father has some knowledge of these things . . ."

(Did he really wink at me? How revolting!)

"Of course, we talked about you too. They're very fond of you. Maybe fond isn't the word, but they do respect you, perhaps even fear you a bit. And her they absolutely adore. If you treat her like a little girl, they still treat her like a baby, waiting on her hand and foot, thrilled with every step and bite of food that she takes. I'm glad you don't live any nearer to them—if you did they'd crawl into bed with you at night from sheer concern and devotion. . . . Perhaps if you gave them a grandchild they might bother you less. Take my advice, think it over. I know how you value your time, but it's still worth considering. She doesn't really have a steady job anyway . . . so why not let her raise a child and write her poems? They alluded to it a few times themselves, trying to get me on their side. I suppose you must hear it all the time from them. Perhaps their rabbi is after them, heh heh . . . and yet they're good, simple people. We must seem like freaks to them. I saw how they kept looking at me, and I couldn't help wondering whether they knew the whole story about mother or whether you had spared them the gory details. . . . Don't think they're not in awe of you, though. You can consider yourself lucky that they didn't come to hear you lecture about that young Miss Zasulevich whom you described so vividly, as though she were a friend of yours . . .

"Zasulich, right, excuse me. Zasulich? What really could she have been like? Most likely simply another one of your disturbed young persons—after all, you yourself said that that general was a friend of her parents. To go and shoot him just because of something she had read . . . oh no, you can't convince me that it was a matter of ideology. What I look for in such cases is always the personal angle, and I wish my historian friends would get off their high horses and look for it too. Connie has taught me to pay more attention to the psychological fine points, and believe me, it's as though a curtain had gone up on my world. But to do that you'd have to read in the original . . . in Russian . . ."

"I'm studying it now."

"Are you! I'm glad to hear that. I'm sorry I don't live close enough to help with it. . . . What was that?"

"What?"

"Those metal things sticking up back there."

"It's an air force memorial."

"A new one?"

"No. It was there in your time too."

"I've never noticed it before."

"How often were you ever in Jerusalem?"

"That's so. Those last years I was hardly there. I was imprisoned with her in the house. Every time I went out was a production. But you've forgotten all that, and now you blame me for trying to salvage what's still left of my life. . . . What's the matter?"

"Nothing. I'm just tired. I didn't sleep well last night."

"I know. I heard you tossing in bed. Why don't you close your eyes? I promise you I'll shut up . . ."

"You don't have to. I'll never sleep on this bus."

"You're driving yourself too hard . . . deliberately . . . I could see it in your class. You're so intense, like a bowstring . . . you'll burn out quickly, old man. And where did you get all that pathos from? Is it really from me? Certainly not the power of it, though . . . and you've chosen such gloomy subjects. Although you do have a talent for making things seem important. Even when you were a tot you'd come home from school and have the whole family breathless with some account of a cat or a fly that you'd seen on your way. . . . Where are we now? What happened to the Trappist monastery that used to be here? Or am I completely confused?"

"We're on a new bypass now."

"Ah, yes, the famous new road. I read about it. There was even some picture in the paper of the ceremony when the Prime Minister or the President cut the ribbon. Zionism isn't dead yet if we still hold such pageants for a few kilometers of paved road."

"You were on it yesterday too."

"I didn't notice. I've no head for landscape, old fellow. I hardly know where I am yet, though I've been here four days. All right, the first day I slept right through, I was simply dead on my feet. Day Two I waited for Kedmi, who insisted on going alone to the hospital and came back empty-handed. Yesterday I spent with you, and today I'm going back again. God only knows what she's cooked up for us. I don't trust anyone anymore. And I was so sure that it would only be a matter of a day or two, the signatures, the divorce ceremony, everything, and that I'd be free to spend some time with you afterwards, to see old friends, to look for books. Everything was supposed to be settled. All those letters back and forth, the long-distance phone calls . . . Kedmi drove me crazy with the tiniest details, he'd call me about them in the middle of the night—collect, of course. He enjoyed torturing me. . . . What's that over there?"

"I don't know. What? That forest?"

"No, over there."

"It's just some little army camp."

"Do you think you could close your window a bit? It's terribly windy outside. Don't tell me it's raining again!"

"I can't tell."

"Ya'el told me that there hasn't been a winter like this here for years. I know you're angry at me for dragging you up there today. You've always made people feel that your time is a valuable commodity. Never mind, though: you can lose a day of your life for your father's sake—and for your mother's too. Believe me, it's also for her. So you'll get your professorship one day later. . . . I simply couldn't bear the thought of having to face her all by myself. And Ya'el is immobilized whenever the two of us start to quarrel. If only Tsvi had been willing to come. But he wasn't. . . . Well, it doesn't matter. You haven't seen her for so long that you owe her a visit anyway. Kedmi claims that he's seen more of her these past few years than you and Tsvi put together. And even if he's exaggerating as usual, we can't let ourselves be talked about like that. People will say that we've thrown her to the dogs. After all, Tsvi was always close to her, and you should visit her too now and then even if it is far away. Where are we turning off to now?"

"To the airport. From there we take the Petah Tiqva road."

"Ah, I see. And this four-lane highway continues to Tel Aviv?"

"Yes."

"Tel Aviv is the place I miss most, and in four days this is the closest that I've gotten to it. The humidity . . . the sea smells . . . the broad sidewalks with the café tables already set out on them in early afternoon . . . Jews who visit this country always talk up Jerusalem and run down Tel Aviv—and I let them. Just try telling them that Zionism began with men who left Jerusalem for the coastal swamps. Who can appreciate that today? Jerusalem, Jerusalem, it's a regular cult. . . . I want you to do the talking for me there. Explain to her that it's all finished. Talk about freedom, human values. Your moral judgments always counted a great deal with her. Be gentle but firm in that imposing way that you have. . . . After all, you're on my side, we see eye to eye. Ya'el gets too emotional, that's why it's best for her not to talk. I won't say any more than I have to either. Because once I start, everything will flare up . . . I'll keep my mouth shut, you'll see . . ."

(Then why don't you start now?)

"Don't say anything about another woman or a baby. Don't talk about the past or even about me. Talk about principles. I'm glad Tsvi isn't with us . . . God only knows what he thinks. Kedmi can stay out of it too, there's no need for him. The four of us will sit and talk quietly . . . it's all up to you. What will you say, have you decided?"

"More or less."

"We'll hear her out first, and then we'll do some explaining. I want you to know, though, that I'm not at all dependent on her. She's the one who will have problems if she doesn't agree. I'll manage, there are all kinds of ways . . . if necessary, the child can be legally adopted by me. Don't let her feel that I need her . . . it will only bring out the cruelty in her. She still can't accept the fact that I'm no longer under her thumb. Talk about principles in that logical way you're so good at . . . unsentimentally, as though it were a lecture to your students. I'm counting on you. . . . Isn't there going to be a rest stop?"

"No."

"Once they used to stop at some diner on this trip."

"There's no point in it anymore. The whole ride barely takes two hours now."

"You look so pale."

"I'm just tired."

"Then why don't you try to sleep? You can rest your head here, I'll squeeze over."

"No, I can't sleep on buses."

"That's because you're afraid of losing control."

"Where did you get that idea from? You've suddenly become this big psychologist."

"I'm afraid to fall asleep when I travel too. But never mind. I've been meaning to ask you: do you have enough money?"

"For what?"

"In general. I've noticed that you worry about money a lot. If you're hard-pressed, let me know. I'll scrape up something over there and send it."

"Hard-pressed? Whatever made you think . . . ?"

"All right, all right, don't be upset. I really enjoyed my stay with you. I'm sorry it had to be so short. . . . What are you working on these days, tell me. I apologize for not responding when you sent me your doctorate. I was actually very proud of it. After all, that's something I dreamed of myself and never managed to achieve . . ."

"I didn't expect you to read it. I just wanted you to have a copy. I knew it wouldn't interest you."

"No, I should have responded. I should have made the effort to understand at least part of it. Not that I didn't thumb through it. I even read that poem of Pushkin's that you quote . . . it's a good one . . . but my mind was somewhere else."

(It always is. That's why he's never gotten anywhere.)

"Never mind."

"But I do mind. When I get back I'll read it and write you what I think."

"Don't bother. Really, father. It will bore you."

"I'll do it for my own sake. What are you working on now, those Russian terrorists?"

"No. That was just today's lesson."

"What then?"

"It wouldn't mean anything to you."

"Try me anyway."

"On the question of historical necessity. On the possibility of shortcutting historical processes. Something having to do with the nineteenth century. A kind of a model."

"But that's very interesting. Why wouldn't it mean anything to me?"

"Because it involves a controversy about theories that you know nothing about."

"You and your controversies. You waste too much energy arguing with everyone."

"I had a good teacher to learn from."

"Maybe I once did let myself be goaded against my better nature . . . but it happens less often now. I'm more on my guard. Connie . . . well, never mind. Shortcutting history? Can it be done?"

"It can."

"For example?"

"Not now, father. Not on this bus."

"Right you are. But this, Asa, you must send me to read. Do you promise?"

"All right."

"After all, how can I allow myself not to know what you're doing, even if I am so far away? I'm sure to understand parts of it . . ."

"Parts of it, certainly."

"I myself, you'll be surprised to hear, am in a very productive period. I'm constantly doing new things. I have my little linguistic projects . . . it's very peaceful there . . . and in the winter you can't go out anyhow. And recently—I'll let you in on a secret—I've been writing this . . . these memoirs . . . maybe one day they'll turn into a . . ."

"Novel? I always thought you'd write one someday."

"Why shouldn't I try? There's no need to be so scornful."

"Who's being scornful?"

"You are. You keep parading this intellectual scorn for me."

"I was never intellectually scornful of you."

"But I keep feeling it. Well, it doesn't matter. You're like a small boy, angry because I've left you . . ."

"Since when? You're totally mistaken."

"But I'll return. You may not believe me, but I'll return to live here someday."

"I never said you wouldn't."

"I keep feeling that you're judging me."

"I'm not."

"For all it mattered to you, I could have stayed locked up with her in that house until I died. Just as long as I didn't bother you."

"Did I ever tell you to stay there?"

"If I had stayed, could I ever have hoped for such a relationship with a woman . . . for such an intellectual renaissance? Tell me . . . when I see your angry looks . . . why, you would gladly have seen me taken away and locked up there with her! . . . What's this, already the new road to Haifa?"

"It's the old road. The inland route."

"But it's so wide. It looks new too."

"They've widened it."

"How soft and lovely everything seems . . . these orange groves on either side . . . it's a beautiful country, we should be kinder to it . . . But where was I? Enough, let's change the subject . . ."

(Now! I can feel it coming over me. Right smack in his puss.)

"Did you tell Dina that mother tried attacking you?"

"Murdering me, not just attacking. You know perfectly well . . . please . . ."

"You know that's not so."

"What are you talking about? How can you keep insisting? . . . Tsvi saw me lying there in my own blood . . ."

"All right, forget it. Don't let's start with that again. So she wanted to murder you. Why did you tell her yesterday . . . ?"

"I just mentioned it in passing. What was wrong with that? So she'd understand why I didn't come to your wedding. I owed her that much of an explanation."

"Did you also owe it to her to open your shirt and show her your scar?"

"I don't remember showing her . . . did you say that I opened my shirt? How can that be . . . is that really what she told you? Perhaps I just outlined it with my hand. She really said that? But you know what she's like. Terribly childish, she lives in fantasies . . . or call it the literary imagination . . . and even if I did show her, so what? I suppose she thought it was a big joke."

"No."

"Then what did I do wrong? For better or worse she's one of us now. Let her know. It's not something that can be kept hidden. Why must you keep feeling ashamed?"

"I'm not ashamed. I just want you to know that if I feel scorn, it's for that. It's not intellectual. I never looked down on you intellectually. On the contrary, I learned a great deal from you. You were a teacher too, and I've followed in your footsteps, although in a somewhat different field. But this sentimentality of yours . . . this uncontrollable need to talk . . . without the slightest sense of discrimination . . ."

"Where are we turning now?"

"I don't know. Why are you so worried about the bus?"

"I don't want to be late. Are you sure he's going straight to Haifa?"

"Of course."

"But that's how I am. That's my nature. Take me or leave me, as the Americans say. It's my nature to be frank."

"Don't be absurd. Frankness has nothing to do with it. Nobody asked you about it. Don't you see why I didn't want you to visit her parents? I was afraid you'd start telling them everything, that you'd stand there and open your shirt . . ."

"Did you really think I was capable . . . ?"

"Why not? Recently you've proven yourself capable of astounding things."

"That's Connie. It's she who gave me new hope. It's she who saw the potential still in me when I came there a beaten, desperate man . . . who restored my faith to me. I'd like so much for you to meet her. You'd understand me much better if you did. It would be wonderful if you and Dina could come spend some time with us . . . if you could see our little Jew-child when it's born . . . what a miracle! I still haven't told you everything . . . I have grand plans for you . . . it's just that . . . Look, there's the ocean at last! It will be a chance for you to get out into the world . . . I'll arrange something for you at the university . . . how is your English? You can lecture about your terrorists, or about Judaism and Jewish history— that's a hot item there now, and they pay well. We'll live together for a while. . . . Could you open the window a bit or is it too windy? I'm suddenly gagging . . . I feel nauseous . . . you've really done a job on me . . . squelched me completely . . . you don't know the meaning of compassion . . . why can't you understand what I've been going through?"

"That's enough, father. Never mind. Let's drop it for now. Close your eyes. Take a deep breath. I'll try to sleep too."

And the pale young man so rudely plucked from his work—that thinker of never-before-thought thoughts that were to astound the few intellects of his age that could grasp them—that man shut his eyes. He sat with his head thrown back in the speeding bus that drove one dull spring day through hot dusty winds toward the ridges of the Carmel and the bay that looped at their feet, passed on the left by soundless cars whose drivers, sprawled limply at their black wheels, had not the slightest inkling who it was they had passed sitting at the window by his father, that blurred, concupiscent figure of a man now wiping away tears whose traces too would be stalked one hundred years from now by an eager young biographer, who—if he meant to do the job properly—would have to travel all the way to Minneapolis and burrow there through old papers to determine what, if any, had been the paternal influence on that world-shaking, seminal mind. He curled up in his seat, savagely kneading his own silence, upgrading raw libido into intellectual power, contemplating space rushing by upon the face of the historical time that meandered within him. Flowing past borders, shooting white water, navigating the hydra-headed river, crossing the alluvial swamp in the midst of dead cosmic time, there he would find the bottom, the true bed in which it all flowed. The time had come to make order, to gather the defiant facts into one grand system, to bare the underlying laws, the sudden cascades, the disappointing channels that blindly petered out only to burst forth unexpectedly again, the missed, the impossible opportunities.

To understand the pulsing shuttle of the historical grid: with that he was to begin the first of his series of essays, which, appearing one by one at regular intervals, were eagerly snatched up by his few mental compeers . . . The theoretical approach to history and its laws is still alive. No doubt it has suffered a severe setback in the course of this century, in which certain malignant phenomena in the human organism have revived absurdly chaotic ideologies of a mythical, religious or fatalistic nature that exist side by side with the most banal sociological generalities. Yet the historical process itself has continued; it is inherent in human behavior and has its own laws that render it both predictable and quantifiable. It moves irreversibly forward, never revolv-

*ing in place, though increasingly complex and tortuous attempts to
shortcut it have frequently blurred its clear course. Is it possible to
construct a reliable and measurable method that will account for the
success or failure of such shortcuts, which are the essence of practical
politics, within the readily discernible outlines of the historical process
itself? Are even the most chimerical attempts to oppose or circumvent
this process governed by laws of their own? In this series of essays I
shall attempt to build and verify such a model based on a study of the
history of the nineteenth century taken as one homogeneous unit. Un-
deniably I have taken upon myself a highly ambitious task . . .*

We were exhausted when we got off the bus in Haifa. Father stum-
bled going down the stairs and had to shut his eyes and lean against
one of the big concrete columns of the terminal. I took his valise and
he walked slowly on, head down and arms dangling, through the
dark wide passageways that echoed with the screeches of the buses.
All at once Kedmi popped out of some exit.

"It's about time! What happened to you? I was about to try the
lost-and-found department. The two of you look as depressed as
though you'd just landed on the moon."

Father looked right through him. He glanced about, then left us
without a word and crossed the passageway to the men's room.
Kedmi winked jovially.

"This is his big day. Believe me, though, he never should have
come. All I needed was one more time alone with your mother to get
her to finish thinking. But who can stand up to you all? Come,
there's another Kaminka-and-a-half eagerly awaiting you."

He took me to a corner table in the cafeteria. Once again I was
struck by the sheer size of Gaddi, who sat there with a big shiny
bright toy locomotive. I smiled at him and mussed his hair. He didn't
smile back.

"We're old phone pals, aren't we, Gaddi?"

He nodded.

Ya'el sat hunched, soft and pensive, in a big gray windbreaker, her
smooth, unlined face looking broader than ever. I dropped into a
chair by her side. Should I kiss her? She made a face, then shut her
eyes, put her arms around my head, and kissed me. Her so feminine
skin.

"Who's looking after the baby?"

"Kedmi's mother," answered Kedmi with a twinkle.

"Dina couldn't come with you today?"

"No. And it wouldn't have been a good idea."

"I don't suppose it would have. How is she? I haven't seen her for so long."

"The same. She's still working on and off at the same place."

Kedmi chuckled abruptly at a joke he'd just told himself. Ya'el smiled nebulously. She started to say something but Kedmi beat her to it.

"You'd better hustle, Asa, if you want to eat something. The train is leaving soon. We've got our work cut out for us."

"The train? What train?"

"Surprisingly enough"—he laughed—"there is one. And you're going to Acre on it. Relax. I promised Gaddi. It will be an experience for you too. The station in Acre is near the rabbinate building. From there you'll take a cab to the hospital, and I'll pick you up at five. It's been all decided. I've got to run to see my murderer now. I still have to earn a little money here and there, your father hasn't put me on a retainer yet . . ."

Through the plate glass I saw father come out of the men's room. He halted confusedly, then headed in the wrong direction. Kedmi grinned and roused Gaddi. "Go get your grandpa before we lose him."

"What's with him?" asked Ya'el. "How was his visit with you?"

"Fine. He actually seemed in good spirits."

"Yes. He seems happy."

Gaddi ran up to father and poked him in the back. Father bent and hugged him warmly, then picked him up and kissed him with an emotion that surprised me. The boy looked excited too and kept pointing at the locomotive that he held. They returned to us with their arms around each other. Ya'el got up to hug father. His face was wet, his hair damp. There was a faint smell of vomit about him.

"I didn't feel good. I don't know what happened to me all of a sudden."

"It was your fear," blurted Kedmi without looking at him.

"Fear of what?"

"Never mind . . ."

A nauseating man with a nauseating sense of humor.

Father made a move to sit down but Kedmi began giving him orders too.

"Go eat something. It won't help any to be hungry."

"Sit, father," I said. "I'll bring you something. What would you like?"

"Just tea and cake or something. But wait a minute . . ."

He reached for his wallet and took out some dollar bills.

"I don't need them," I said.

Kedmi hovered jocularly around us. "You still haven't changed your dollars, eh, Yehuda? You're a rational man, you know a dollar changed tomorrow is worth two changed today . . ."

Father interrupted him short-temperedly. "Where is there a bank around here?"

"Not now . . . not now . . ." we all exclaimed together.

"But I have to. I must."

"Come here, I'll change them for you. How much do you want?"

Father gave Kedmi a hundred-dollar bill. Kedmi held it up to the light, grinning impishly. "There are counterfeits making the rounds." He picked up a newspaper to check the exchange rate and showed it to father.

"Fine, whatever you say," mumbled father with loathing.

I went to get lunch and returned with it. I said nothing, watching them remotely from some tenuous, still point inside me. Gaddi stared at the loaded tray that I'd brought. Father forced some pound notes on me. Kedmi grinned. Ya'el kept her eyes silently on father. Where is Dina now? People came and went. Dishes clattered. Jerusalem seemed a world away. The morning's lesson. Kedmi scurried about, conversing with people, scanning newspapers. At one point he furtively slipped me some document. "If you can catch her between the acts, see if you can't gently get her to sign this. It's a copy of the agreement that I gave her. If you don't stay cool, who will?"

I said nothing.

At two o'clock we were standing by the train. Kedmi put us aboard as though we were luggage, finding us our seats, buying us our tickets. He'd put father's valise in his car and given him a yellow cardboard file holder which said *Chief Rabbinate* on it. There was nothing he hadn't made his business in his revoltingly jovial way. How did the two of them live together? But Ya'el was her usual patient, passive self, thoroughly held in check, always ready to give in, to let him poke his nose everywhere, even go through her purse.

"Why do you all look so alarmed?" he called to us from the platform. "Don't worry. It's an honest-to-goodness train. It will be an experience. I'll come to get you at five, five-thirty. Gaddi, don't forget your locomotive on the train. And ask your uncle to show you around it."

He waved at us and departed, leaving us out of time in the still, empty train. A hell of an experience to have to go through for the boy's sake. What was I doing here? I wondered. I felt paralyzed, dog-tired. I watched Ya'el open a large plastic bag and take out a big blue woolen shawl and a flowery robe to give father to give mother as presents. He accepted them gratefully, and together they removed the Israeli labels. Slowly the train began to move. It crept along through the freight yards of the port, among cranes, past ugly factories, warehouses and grim garages, stopping for no reason and starting up again, nearing some blocks of public housing. Father was restless. He chain-smoked, asked about relatives, sighed, combed his hair. "I won't say a word there," he promised again. "I'll let you do the talking. Asa will go first." He opened the cardboard file holder that Kedmi had given him and studied its contents.

I took Gaddi for a tour of the train. We walked to the last car and, from a rattling passage by the rear window, watched the unweeded rails slowly receding. The boy stood silently by me, a softer edition of Kedmi but terribly earnest, the locomotive still in one hand and the other on his chest. He stood glued to the window. I took out the document that Kedmi had given me and leafed through it. Their divorce agreement. Brutal legal phraseology spelled here and there by sentimental clichés. The last page enumerated the joint property to be divided. With what perverse pleasure Kedmi had listed all the furniture, inventoried everything, estimated its value down to the last cent. I shook with anger. Where is Dina now? What am I going to do with her?

It took us a ridiculous hour to reach Acre. At the station we found a taxi and drove to the rabbinate building in the walled seaport, not far from the old citadel. "Here you'll leave it to me," announced father with a sudden show of firmness. "It won't take me long." And so we waited in the taxi, bus stops and felafel stands around us, old stones from the citadel piled on the curb. The driver got out to clean

the windshield. Gaddi drove his locomotive back and forth in the
front seat. Ya'el sat huddled next to me with a guilty look on her
face. Does she ever actually think? Think, Ya'el, think, we used to
beg her whenever she would suddenly go blank.

"You know . . . he's going to have a baby over there . . . with
that woman . . ."

"Yes. He told me."

"Have you told Tsvi?"

"He knows."

"What did he say?"

"He just laughed."

"He did? Why didn't he come with us today? I phoned him last
night but got no answer."

"I spoke to him."

"Why didn't he come with us?"

"I don't know. Maybe he doesn't want them to get divorced. He
likes having their apartment . . ." She didn't finish the thought. But
it was Kedmi's anyway, not hers.

"Is that what he said?"

"No. All he said was that he didn't like hospitals."

"I couldn't sleep last night. I kept tossing in bed. That baby slays
me. . . . Who would have thought it of him?"

She didn't understand, though. Her eyes grew large with wonder.

"What makes you say that?"

I shook with anger again. My lost time. I missed Jerusalem as
though it were years since I had last seen it. Father was taking his
time. The driver had gone to sit in a nearby café. I glanced at the
vaults of the citadel, at a strip of sea on the horizon. I opened the car
door.

"Come on, Gaddi. I'll show you something."

We strode along the seawall until we came to some steps that
zigzagged down to a recessed apse at one end of it. A dry, gray day,
with a hot desert wind from the east. The U-shaped bay was a blur,
the Carmel range a purple mass. I grasped Gaddi's fat hand to keep
him from slipping on the guttered stones, the locomotive still under
his arm, explaining to him what we saw and showing him the hills
across the water where he lived, although he preferred looking at a
column of flame rising from the oil refinery on the bay to flicker in
the foul wind.

1799. From a hillock nearby Napoleon gazed down on these walls, reached out his hand to them. Had he wished to take them or merely to comprehend, to palpate the pulsebeat of history with his sensitive touch? And then he retreated. This was not the place. Never mind. It was through this trivial defeat that he came to know himself, his true powers, the mission entrusted him. That he found the necessary point of connection. The last years of the eighteenth century were where I must begin.

I wanted to *he* myself again but could not. The boy was in the way. Scrutinizing me. My trampled time, my papers left by my books. In far, clear Jerusalem. Clear thought. Hard light. Dina in its streets, free with our money, free with strange men. And you, stranded high and dry here.

We descended the wall. Ya'el was still in the taxi, eyes shut, arms folded on her chest. The driver looked at us.

"Father isn't back yet? What's going on in there!"

I climbed the steps of the rabbinate building. A large, long hallway with narrow doors. From somewhere came a sound of muffled sobs. Father's? In a fit I opened one of the doors. A dark young woman sat at a bare desk in a room that made the sobs resound like a weird echo chamber. She rose to speak to me as though I were an office clerk, but I beat a hasty retreat, letting go of the door, which slammed behind me. At the end of the corridor, through another door, I saw father's head beneath a black skullcap. Two young, dark-bearded rabbis sat on either side of him, evidently explaining something to him while he nodded his agreement. I collapsed onto a bench in the hallway, my head in my hands. An endless day. Two black-suited men climbed the stairs with a folded stretcher, threw it on the floor at my feet, and continued up another flight. At last father emerged, seen out by the rabbis, to whom he hadn't stopped nodding. He bowed his head and shook their hands with submissive gratitude. "Everything will be all right, Professor Kaminka," they assured him. I rose quickly and started down the stairs with him hurrying after me while removing the skullcap and sticking it into his pocket.

"Really, they're being most considerate. They'll bring the rabbinical court to the hospital. They'll arrange it with the management, even though it's Passover eve."

The exit below was blocked by the yawning doors of a hearse.

With an angry movement I slammed them shut. It was already half past three. We were late. The taxi drove to the hospital and left us at the front gate. Suddenly I had second thoughts: shouldn't Gaddi wait for us outside? But father insisted.

"Why shouldn't he come? She'll be happy to see him. He's a big boy already and can understand."

Did he want him there to be a buffer? We started down the paved path among the lawns and cottages, the sea glinting beyond them, the strong dry wind at our backs. My last visit here was late last autumn. I had lectured to some history teachers at a local regional high school and stopped off to see her on my way back. It was dusk when I arrived. She was thrilled by my unexpected appearance. She was as lucid as could be, hardly talked about herself, wanted only to hear about me, even asked about the lecture I had given. I felt that she knew what was going on in my mind, in my life. I had already been told of her unforeseen improvement, which hadn't surprised me at all, because I had never really believed in her illness. When it began to get dark she suggested that I stay the night and even went to see if there was a room, but I was in a hurry to get back to Jerusalem. In the end she walked me in the darkness to the gate. Horatio ran wide circles around us, coming back to us each time to sniff our footprints, lick my shoes, tug at their laces with his teeth. And she walked by my side, heavy but erect, stopping now and then to look at me, wanting something from me that I never could give. We didn't argue or quarrel even once. She was unusually tender, thoughtful, uncomplaining, unaccusing. We were standing by the gate when she first told me that she had been getting mail from father. She took out a rustling packet of envelopes from her handbag and showed them to me without letting me hold them. What does he want? I asked anxiously. A divorce, she said. A weak light shone from the gatekeeper's hut. The dog passed under the barrier and stood in the middle of the road with his ears back and his tail wagging softly, drawn bow-like by the sounds of the night, the white fields of cotton, a distant bark. Now and then he glanced our way as though following our conversation from afar.

I began talking in favor of it, enthusiastically even. It's high time. It should have been done long ago, you've just enmeshed each other more and more. She heard me out in silence, her profile turned to me, until she interrupted coldly:

"But he didn't want to."

"When didn't he?"

"Years ago. Before you were born. I begged him. He didn't want to. There are things you don't know. He wouldn't let me go."

"But when?"

"There are things you don't know. You wouldn't believe how he clung to me."

"But you yourself say that now . . ."

"We shall see. Now be on your way." She was discounting me, dismissing me. "You'll never get to Jerusalem tonight like this."

And I left her, walking down the empty road in the dark. Horatio set out at a lope next to me, turned suddenly around to look for mother, and rejoined me once more. Finally he stood halfway between us in the middle of the road, emitting a long angry howl until he was gone in the night.

And now the four of us were going to see her, a family delegation to this hospital that was once a World War II British army base. Gaddi gripped father's hand, Ya'el went ahead, and I brought up the rear with my briefcase. Again the urge to *he* myself and again the need to forgo it. He. What is a he? And what was the collective consciousness of the four of us, did it add up to a single whole? Gaddi's terror combined with his curiosity to see the forbidden he had barely even heard talked of, Ya'el's sadness, father's apprehension, the pain in store for him, his hopes and his fears—and I, feeling only anger at their pointless mulishness and the desire to tell them both off, to expose them, to pillory them, to have done with it, mourning my wasted day. I quickened my pace. Suddenly the paths around us were full of people. Patients and visitors spilled out of the cottages, nurses bearing trays crossed the old lawns still frost-burned from the hard winter, all slightly doubled over in the wind. A shrunken little yellow sun peered through the haze. Will I someday remember this moment, will it have any meaning? Can it be maintained as something tangibly, necessarily alive or must it shrivel too with the dead husk of time?

And then all at once there was a howling shriek as though a tramcar were flying through the branches, something galumphed through the air, someone screamed, the people in front of us scrambled out of the way, someone fell, someone shouted with laughter—and out from the bushes he charged, throwing himself upon us, his torn chain dragging behind him, whining, howling, first jumping on Ya'el and then quitting her, next sinking down at my feet to bite my shoes, then running into Gaddi, bowling him over on the grass, licking him and romping on again, at last spying father and sprawling all over him, pawing his face, clasping him, slobbering on him with choked whimpers, spattering him with mud, rattling the chain still wound around him. Father lost his footing and fell to his knees, white-faced and startled, but only when he screamed did I realize that he didn't know it was Horatio. He had completely forgotten his own dog, who had now streaked so suddenly back into his life and begun to writhe in a demonic dance, circling tightly around him on the pavement where he sat with his arms shielding his face, sprawling on him again like a thing possessed, yipping in a throttled falsetto as though trying to force out a bark that was stuck in the throat.

I rushed over to them. "It's Horatio, father! It's just Horatio. Don't be afraid."

Ya'el ran to pick up Gaddi, who was too bewildered to cry, and the locomotive that had gone flying on the lawn.

"*This* is 'Ratio?" Father was stunned, disheveled, covered with mud. " 'Ratio? He's here?"

Father had always called him 'Ratio.

He rose and tried grabbing the uncontrollable dog by its head, as though struggling to make out his once-beloved pet in this mangy old beast.

"Down, Horatio!" I tried calming him. "Down . . ."

Just then we glanced up and saw mother watching us in silence a few steps away. Her hair was loose, her face was rouged, and she wore a long brown dress. In one hand she held the other half of the torn chain. The wild look of her shocked me, the glare in her eyes, the splotches of makeup on her tanned cheeks. It was twenty minutes to four. Had she had a relapse? Silently she watched father struggling with the dog.

"He's here? He's alive?" He laughed, still in a daze. "Didn't you write me that he'd died long ago?" he asked mother.

"Who did?"

"I had already mourned for him . . . I was sure he was long dead . . ." He gripped the hairy head that nuzzled in his lap.

"He was sure that you were dead too."

They kept their distance, she solidly planted where she stood, a

wrinkled old nurse in a blue uniform behind her. Her answer, though
clear, did not bode well, I thought.

Ya'el kissed her and led Gaddi to her. She bent and hugged him
feelingly.

"Gaddi . . . darling Gaddi . . . do you know who I am? Do
you remember? And where is your little sister"—she fumbled in her
pocket, took out a slip of paper and read from it—"Rakefet?"

Still whining, the dog broke away from father and ran wagging to
join the embraces. Gaddi clung to Ya'el, too frightened of Horatio to
move, his face stained red from mother's kisses.

"Don't let him frighten you . . . he's ours . . . when you were a
baby and your mother left you with us, the two of you even played
together . . ."

Gaddi looked unbelievingly at the huge animal, amazed at himself.

Then it was my turn to embrace her, bussing the air about her
rouged cheeks, my head tilted skyward, eyes shut.

"Asa . . . at last a visit from you . . . in honor of your father
. . ."

She hugged me powerfully.

"Where is your wife?"

"She couldn't come. But she'll be here on the holiday."

"On Passover?"

"Yes."

Now father finally stepped up to her, the dog tagging after him, his
arms spread wide with Russian pathos.

"Mother . . . at last . . ."

Did he know what he was doing? Had he planned it this way or
had the shock of events unnerved him? I cringed while he hugged
her, pressing her to him, gathering in the strong erect woman, planting kisses on her face. "You look so well . . . there's been a great
change . . ." he murmured as though come for a reconciliation
rather than a divorce. He even whispered something in her ear and
laughed with tears in his eyes. Could he really be that shallow or did
he have some ulterior motive? Mother froze in his arms, staring into
space with dilated eyes, a hint of amusement on her lips.

Horatio gave a loud bark. At last he had gotten it out. Then father
stepped back and mother introduced him to the wrinkled old nurse,
who stood there without ceasing to smile. "I want you to meet Mir-

iam . . . she's my good angel . . . Miriam, this is my husband
. . . the man from America . . ."

"Yes, I know. We've all been waiting for you." The lines in her
face reddened sharply as father turned to her and quickly embraced
her too with the same somnambulistic zeal.

And indeed, to our horror, they were waiting for us. Much of the
hospital already knew of our arrival. A crowd streamed toward
mother's cottage, men and women in bathrobes and pajamas
swarmed around her, a young doctor stepped up to greet us. As we
passed the row of beds inside someone even broke out into applause.
Father went first, nodding to everyone, shaking the hands that were
extended to him, that conducted him to mother's bed, which was
piled high with big white pillows. There he stood, declaring how
moved he was until I thought I would go mad myself. The patients
reached out to touch Gaddi and pat his head—one could see how he
attracted them, they had probably not seen a child in ages. Then the
doctor explained about the ward and its routine while father listened
devoutly and the nurses pushed back the curious patients—one of
whom, a little old fellow, kept elbowing forward again and interrupt-
ing the conversation with eager hand gestures. At last we all trooped
outside, the crowd of patients still behind us, and were led to a small
building that served as the hospital library. Some tables with chairs
stood inside, on the largest of which, in the middle of the cracked
concrete floor, was a white cloth set with an electric kettle and several white cups and saucers stamped *Property of the Bureau of Public
Health.* Beside them was a big, yellowish, lopsided cake, very high on
one side and totally caved in on the other, so that it formed a steep
inclined plane at the base of which glittered a knife. A few of the
patients tried following us in, but the nurses kept them clear of the
doors. And again that skinny, rotten-toothed old fellow made the
most fuss; he seemed very agitated and kept trying to catch father's
attention while pulling behind him a moronic-looking giant who carried a rake on one shoulder.

In the end they were all persuaded to leave. The door closed on us.
We took off our coats and Horatio ran happily wagging his tail
around the room. My eyes scanned the books that lined the walls but
it was impossible to read their titles because they were all covered
with the same brown wrapping paper. What a dump. We stood
around the cake, eyeing it nervously as though it concealed some

harsh message. "Mother baked it for you all by herself," said the old nurse, as though apprising us of a major psychiatric feat. A silent, younger nurse poured tea into the cups while Horatio thrashed restlessly about among our legs. I tried grabbing him by the collar and dragging him outside, but he growled aggressively and shook free, trying to bite me.

"Let go of him!" mother cried.

The old nurse handed her the knife. She made a movement to wield it, then suddenly shrank back, stealing a quick glance at father and releasing it.

"No, you cut it," she said.

Quickly the cake was sliced into thick heavy pieces and we sat down to eat. Horatio climbed on a chair too, climbed down again, still rattling his broken chain, and jumped once more on father, as if the years that had elapsed since their parting were now running amuck in him and giving him no peace. Father smiled, lifting a full, shaky cup to his mouth. Mother rose, went over to Horatio, gave him a quick hard slap with the chain, and pushed him beneath father's chair. She threw him a slice of cake there, which he sniffed at suspiciously and licked a little without eating.

No one spoke, not even to utter the simplest, most ordinary words. The cake had struck us dumb. I tensed like a bowstring each time I heard a noise outside the door. The giant's face appeared at the window, staring in at us. We drank the lukewarm tea and ate the half-raw cake, which was a mishmash of colors and tastes. The two nurses ate too, the younger one chewing away at her end of the table as though compelled by a strong inner code, yet not quite certain what she was ingesting. Like in some relentless ceremony that we were all called upon to perform. The cake turned to a sickening goo in my mouth. Mother fed Gaddi, who sat beside her, but did not eat herself.

"You don't have to feed him, mother," said Ya'el softly. But she didn't hear. She went on tearing off pieces of cake with her fingers and cramming them into Gaddi's mouth while the rays of the setting sun slanted sharply off her painted cheeks.

"What a wind there was today," sighed father all of a sudden. "All the way from Jerusalem."

He resumed chewing his cake. Mother regarded him thoughtfully

before turning back to look at Gaddi's mouth, which hung slightly
open.

Where are you, Asa? In a little cottage, a library for the insane, an
abstract thought deflected from its path, shanghaied from its desk,
on which an old lamp casts its light on papers and books, a sole
beacon shining in the dark. The irretrievably lost hours. If only they
would die already! If only the two of them would die. Why can't they
understand? Their nightly quarrels, like two old children, all their
cursing and shouting each time I came home from friends or the
Scouts. Ya'el was married already. Tsvi was in the army. I would slip
off to bed but they would follow me there, sit down on the blanket,
pull it off me, anything to have a referee.

"Aren't you eating your cake?"

"No, mother, I'm not hungry."

Ya'el rolled her eyes at me.

"You don't have to be hungry to eat a piece of cake. Or don't you
like it . . . ?"

"I do. I'm just full. I mean . . ." I was only making things worse.

Silence. Horatio had calmed down. He stretched himself beneath
father's chair and started to nuzzle his penis, licking it vigorously. A
dull yellowish light filled the room. Perhaps they were dead already
and I was visiting them in the underworld. Dutifully, slowly, father
and Ya'el chewed their cake. Gaddi was already having seconds.

"You're not eating yourself," said father gently. "Your cake is
delicious."

Mother didn't answer.

The young nurse rose to collect the dishes, adroitly removing my
plate with what was left on it.

"Would you like some more?" mother asked father.

He nodded, hoisted by his own petard. A new slice of cake appeared on his plate and he set to work chewing that too.

The young nurse placed the dishes on a tray. Someone opened the
door for her. She stepped outside, where waiting hands snatched the
tray, and returned at once. She pulled the cord from the socket in the
wall, wound it around the electric kettle, and took that to the door
too. And again she came right back. Meanwhile the old nurse was
murmuring something to mother while wrapping the remains of the
cake in an old towel. The young nurse opened the door again. Heads

peered in, whispered laughter. They were waiting for the leftovers. The two nurses left and shut the door.

"Who are all those people outside, friends of yours?"

Mother smiled ironically. "Friends . . ."

Horatio crouched next to her, his head turned, his eyes shut, bald patches like burn scars in his mangy red fur. Father gazed at him and reached out to pet him.

"Has 'Ratio been here all along?"

"Since when is he 'Ratio?" we scolded. "His name is *Ho*ratio. You never could get it right."

Father smiled. " 'Ratio . . . Horatio . . ."

"Maybe you should take him back with you to America," said mother abruptly.

Father laughed.

"I hear you've had a particularly hard winter this year. I'm glad I brought a coat with me. At first I didn't plan to, since it would already be spring here, and spring here is as good as summer. But in the end I brought it, and it's a good thing I did . . ."

(Bring himself, he meant.)

Ya'el rose without a sound and handed him the plastic bag that had been lying by his chair.

"Oh yes, I forgot. I brought you a present." He took the bag and went over to her. "It's something that I bought you . . ." But he couldn't remember what it was. He opened the bag to take a peek. "I believe it's a robe and a sweater." He looked at Ya'el for confirmation. "Yes, a sweater."

He pulled out the big wool shawl and spread it on his knees.

"A sweater?" Mother seemed very touched.

Ya'el took the shawl and draped it around her shoulders.

"The colors are perfect for you."

Mother stood up. The two of them helped wrap her in the shawl.

I sat immobile in my chair, thinking what a dangerous thing this tenderness between them was. I glanced at Gaddi, who had not taken his eyes off the dog.

"It's just the thing for you," said father.

"Thank you. You needn't have bothered . . . did I ask for a present? It's really very warm . . ." She wiped away a tear. "Once I had a shawl like this years ago . . . exactly like this one . . . how did you find it again?" She removed it, searching for the missing label.

"You shouldn't have wasted so much money, Yehuda. Really, you shouldn't have. Perhaps you should give it to someone else . . . to Asa . . ."

She made as though to give me the shawl.

But father wouldn't hear of it.

"How can you say such a thing? You don't know how happy it makes me to see you so calm. It's a great change for the better. I would have brought you more, but I left in such a hurry . . ."

"A hurry?"

"As soon as I received your letter . . . and then Kedmi told me . . ."

"Oh."

They were beating around the bush. The afternoon light was fading in the room.

Mother sat down again. "So what's new in America?"

"America?" Father lit a cigarette while he considered. "America is a big place. But nothing is new there. We had a long hard winter too."

"Another one?"

"Another one." He stood dangling his arms, not knowing what to do with them. Was he having an attack of idiocy or of cold feet?

"Are you still in that same place . . . ?"

"Minneapolis."

"But just where is it?"

"Up north."

"Someday I'd like to see where it is on the map. Maybe Asa has a map in his briefcase . . ."

"No. I don't."

"Maybe there's a map in one of those books."

Ya'el was already on her feet, *Homo dutifuliensis.*

"I'll show you where it is sometime, mother. On Passover I'll bring an atlas."

"It's near the Canadian border," explained father anxiously. "Not far from Canada. In the interior. Can you picture it?"

But she could not. Bracing herself, Ya'el threw a despairing glance at the shelves of books. The giant's face peered in once more at the window. Someone, perhaps the old fellow, tried pulling him away. They could be heard quarreling. Father smiled, still groping for Horatio beneath his chair.

"I understand that the doctor says you can leave here soon. Ya'el told me that he's very optimistic . . ."

There was no answer. Arms on her chest, mother watched Ya'el go through the books. She pointed to a corner of the room.

"There must be a map there. Asi's sure to find it."

To suddenly be in her damned clutches again. Hopelessly I rummaged through the books in the corner. Cheap novels. Instant biographies. Lifeless volumes bearing the imprint of the Cultural Division of the National Medical Insurance Plan. Ghost-written memoirs of ex-politicians distributed free of cost by their parties. No one spoke. With a smile of consternation father rose to look too. Nothing could proceed without a map. Finally I found a small one in a children's encyclopedia. I showed it to her, reading out loud the place names near Minneapolis. She bent to get a closer look. Father stood by us, confirming what I read.

"Is it cold there?"

"Very."

"Then you should move down here. Further south." She laid a finger on Brazil.

Father smiled at us uncertainly. But to me it was clear: it was he who brought out the madness in her.

"No, mother. You're already in Brazil."

"Brazil?" she giggled embarrassedly. "I can't see very well. Dear me, Brazil? My glasses broke last week and no one here seems able to fix them."

She took out a folded handkerchief from the pocket of her dress, unrolled it, and showed us her glasses. One lens was shattered. Father took them from her solemnly, carefully, with deep concern.

"We'll get them fixed right away," he told Ya'el. "It's something we must take care of."

The shattered lens fell apart in his hands. He tried fitting it back together.

"It's unimaginable to leave mother without glasses," he repeated scoldingly, rewrapping them in the handkerchief and handing them to Ya'el. Mother watched him with that flickering smile of hers that I had always hated. It vanished when her eyes met mine. The only one in the family who ever stood up to her was me.

"Tell me about the winter there, Yehuda. The last time you were here you described the snow so nicely . . ."

"I did?"

"You don't remember? I was very sick then. I don't remember much, but your description of the snow . . . yes, that I do . . ."

He turned to us for help, glanced at the mass of faces in the window, looked at his watch, gave me a frightened look, reached for Gaddi, held him tight, stroked his hair: trying to fathom what it was that she wanted. On the table, where the kettle had been, lay some folded sheets of paper. No doubt Kedmi's agreement. He started to pick it up, then stopped and sat down next to mother instead, moving his chair closer to her while beginning to tell her about the snow, glancing at us apologetically, failing to comprehend how he had fallen into such a trap. But he had patience. He still felt sure that all would end well. The need to make one's own mistakes. The struggle to resist the historical process as a historical trap.

Take Rhodesia. Sane, pragmatic, unhysterical Anglo-Saxons with a rational outlook and no national mythology to uphold gradually fall victim to the stubbornly lunatic notion that they can twist history's arm. Their immediate motive is obvious, even natural: the wish to retain their productive farmlands and continue to exploit cheap native labor. Slowly, however, they sink into an ever deeper quagmire. There are only two hundred thousand of them and yet, in a world that boasts nearly as many independent nations as people, they are determined to rule over six million blacks in the heart of Africa. At which point the same practical, down-to-earth folk suddenly decide that they have a great, anti-historical mission to perform—the sole purpose of which in reality is to keep them from understanding what should have been understood long ago. And so—sophisticatedly, imaginatively, impetuously, with unbeatable solidarity—they dig in their heels, turning their agricultural acres into a holy land and constructing a global ideology: from now on they are no longer simply white Rhodesians, hardworking farmers who troop off every Sunday to sing sweet hymns in church, they are the vanguard of Freedom, the torchbearers of Truth, stubborn servants of the Lord and of the whole civilized world. Infuriated and embittered, they gaze out through the bars of the cage they have built for themselves, despairing of the world that has condemned them, assuring themselves of the blindness, the pathology, the self-destructiveness, the decline of the West, holding out against embargoes, terrorism, vituperation and ostracization with a military savvy and a messianic passion that are out of all proportion to their true strength, turning themselves into steel, their isolation into a fortress of Western culture. And yet just when the world has begun to get used to their madness and even to learn to live with it, they crack for no apparent reason; they agree to small compromises that lead to larger and larger ones; and, having entrusted their little pinky to the great hand of history, they find themselves dragged along by it with greater and greater force until they voluntarily hand over their power to the most implacable of their enemies.

"And how much do you earn now, Yehuda?"

Father grinned. "A thousand dollars a month."

"How much is that in Israeli pounds?"

"A hundred and twenty thousand."

Mother was staggered. She regarded him with awe.

"That isn't much there. In fact, it's considered a small salary."

"And are you happy?"

"Oh, well . . . happiness . . . what actually is it? It's something I had never dreamt of for myself. The concept itself isn't clear to me. But I do feel at peace there . . . yes, that I have over there, a kind of peace. Not that I don't miss the children terribly . . . all of you . . ."

He eyed us nervously, seeking to gauge the effect his answer had had and whether it had passed the test.

"And that woman . . . did you bring a photograph of her?"

"What woman?"

"That woman of yours . . . the one you live with . . . whose name you never told me . . . maybe . . ."

"Connie," said father hopelessly.

"Connie? Because last time you were here he promised to bring me her picture."

I jumped to my feet but she ignored me. The sudden shift to the third person was always a bad sign. They had to be separated at once. Father looked at us, utterly baffled.

"What do you need a picture of her for, mother? What does it matter?"

"But he promised me last time. I just want to see her picture."

I turned to him furiously. "Do you have her picture with you?"

He crimsoned, rose, pulled out his wallet, and, lo and behold, produced a small color snapshot. Mother took it and studied it at arm's length with Gaddi, who wanted to see what an American woman looked like: plumpish, blond, standing on a patch of lawn by a garage door. The snapshot fell to the floor. Father hurried to retrieve it. He handed it to mother, who declined to take it. Quickly he put it back in his pocket.

"And do you have a picture of the baby too?"

"The baby???"

Ya'el quailed. "What baby, mother?"

"His baby, the new one . . ."

"What are you talking about?"

"Why, about that new baby of his."

"Who said anything about a baby?"

"Tsvi did, yesterday."

"Tsvi???" The three of us were aghast.

"Yes. They were here."

"They?"

"He and a friend. An older man who brought him."

"But what did he come for?"

"To visit me. He hadn't seen me for weeks. He wanted to read those pages that Kedmi brought me . . . he wanted to know what . . . maybe to show his friend . . ."

"And what did he say?"

"Nothing. He told me that you had a baby."

"But he couldn't have!"

"There's no baby, mother," Ya'el pleaded. "Whatever made you think that?"

"But . . ." Mother grabbed her head in deep distress.

Father forced a laugh. "Tsvi misunderstood. He always mixes things up."

"But how . . . ?"

She wrung her hands defensively, blushing, distraught at the unexpected denial.

"And I was so happy that you'd had a baby . . . that you still could . . . Tsvi told me, ask him . . ."

All at once I rose to speak in a clear, dry voice, compelled to put an end to the obscene farce.

"It isn't born yet but it will be . . ." I turned to her, gripping her lightly by the arm. She was afraid to look at me. "It isn't born yet but it will be." I ignored the panic seizing father and Ya'el, the commotion by the door, the faces behind the curtain on the window.

"Father is telling the truth. Tsvi didn't understand. It isn't born yet
but it will be . . . that's why father was in such a hurry to get here.
It isn't born yet but it will be!" I repeated once more, raising my
voice as the deep anger swept over me. "That's why we're here.
Because otherwise what would it have mattered . . . you're separated anyway . . . but because of the child . . . the baby . . .
there's a legal problem there . . . according to the law . . . legally
you need to . . . and you yourself wouldn't want him to . . ."

Only by now I no longer knew what I wanted to say. The word
"law" had gotten into it and stuck there. Mother stared at me, the
old wild glitter in her eyes, the theatrical colors of her makeup a
changed tint.

"We didn't mean to hide it from you . . . you know everything
now . . . father hasn't kept anything back. It isn't born yet but it
will be . . ."

I turned to him in cold fury. "When will it be born?"

"I think"—he could hardly get out the words—"in two
months . . ."

"In two months, did you hear that? Now you know everything.
We're all suffering. You think it's only you but it isn't. It's a disgrace
for us all, but what's done is done. . . . What is it you want to
know now?"

She tried saying something but I cut her short, though her lips
continued to move.

"What more do you want? What good does it do to be stubborn?
Let him go back to America and we'll all stay here with you. All of
us. And you'll be getting out of this hospital soon . . ."

I snatched the agreement lying on the table. Its pages were already
creased and stained.

"What does Tsvi know about it? Kedmi has seen to everything.
I've spoken with him. Just sign!"

She retreated from me with a movement of her brown dress. I
turned the pages of the document until I came to the black line above
her name at the end. I put a light, unsteady hand on her shoulder.
Her smell.

"Are you going to sign?"

She shook her head.

"Why not?"

"I have to think."

"What about?"

"What about?" father exclaimed after me.

She balked stubbornly, staring at us with suspicion.

"What about?" I shouted. "What about?"

Ya'el rose to restrain me.

"You know it's all over with!" I cried, carried away with myself, as though it were my life, not his. "What is there still to think about, mother? But you, you have to know about the snow . . . the snow . . . he should tell you about the snow! And you"—I turned to father with senseless rage while he hung his arms limply with an embarrassed smile like a swindler caught in the act—"you actually start to tell her. I always knew that the two of you enjoyed it. Yes, enjoyed it! This eternal war of yours gives you pleasure. Knifing him, being sick, all your make-believe—there's hidden pleasure in all of it. And you too, father. That's why it's gone on like this for so long. That's why you keep beating around the bush. And Tsvi eggs you on. But Ya'el and I are sick of it, we're so depressed we could die!" Ya'el, her cheeks burning, tried to stop me. "You used to drag me out of bed at night to judge between you. Well, I'm judging now. End it!"

Father grabbed me. "That will do! That's enough."

But I pushed him away, hearing my own steadily rising voice.

"What is there still to think about? Tell us. How much longer can you drag it out? Who has the time? Because there isn't any . . . the time has run out. You wanted to kill him, what more do you still want from him? Why don't you kill me too! Kill me! Go ahead and kill me! . . ."

Overcome by sadness. Her twisted face. Anger snagged on pity. My raised arm. A glance at the dirty curtain at the crazy faces there. I shut my eyes and strike my head here it comes I slap my face hard I drum on my chest with my fists a shudder of joy like desire swept up in the rhythm of it a yellowish light in Gaddi's eyes turned quietly on me at last peace descends the dull pain in my chest now father is acting up too he's caught my hysteria he stutters from anger he buries his face in his hands he shouts out loud he grabs hold of mother who's risen from her chair do you see now do you see all at once he kneels down before her with that terrible hatred of his Ya'el and I both rush to lift him from the bare concrete floor Ya'el shoves me away protecting him from me. Will he hit himself too?

"The child," whispered mother, stony-faced and composed. "Just

take the child outside . . . why should he have to see it? You've
done this on purpose . . . it's all on purpose . . ."

Father and Ya'el pushed me outside while I dragged Gaddi after
me. At once I was surrounded by the patients waiting by the door.
They reached out to touch me, shook my hand, tried grabbing hold
of Gaddi, who shrank against me. Had they seen me lay hands on
myself and now come to give me their blessing? A washed-out, tor-
mented-looking blonde accosted me and tugged at my shoulders. She
stuck a finger in her mouth and shut her eyes. There was a babble of
voices.

"A cigarette . . . Give her a cigarette . . ."

I took out a pack, which was snatched from me by the little old
fellow. A bundle of energy, he nimbly pulled out the cigarettes and
passed them out to the patients. A large gold lighter glittered in their
midst. They bent over it, shielding the flame with their hands, getting
down on all fours to fight the strong wind. At last a lit cigarette
burned in each mouth. I too was given one. I hesitated before sticking its wet tip between my lips. I had no space to move. The old
fellow clung to me, devouring me with his eyes.

"Are you taking her away from here?"

"Not today. Some other time."

"Are you the son from Jerusalem?"

"Yes."

The wind fanned the glowing cigarettes like little engines. The
blonde leaned lightly against me, inhaling greedily.

"They won't let you leave," whispered a morose young man.

"Who won't?"

The old fellow smiled an apology at me and derisively twirled a
finger against his forehead. I noticed dry blood on my hands and felt
my head. There was a scratch there that must have been made by my
watch. A water faucet stood by the path but the long hose connected
to it seemed to end nowhere. I licked the blood clean. Gaddi
squeezed my hand, the locomotive still under his arm, his other hand
working away inside his shirt.

"Does something hurt you, Gaddi?" I asked.

"My heart."

"That's not where your heart is." I smiled. "Let me see."

He slowly moved his hand toward his heart.

"They'll arrest you at the gate," said the morose young man.

"Shhh." The old fellow hushed him with a smile. "No one will be arrested." He tried driving the young man away.

"Your only chance is to escape through the hole," the young man persisted.

"What hole?"

"Over there," said the old fellow, pointing toward an overgrown corner of the fence.

"Over there . . ." echoed everyone, pointing in unison.

"That's enough!" shouted the old fellow angrily. "Clear out of here. . . . Stop bothering him. . . . Don't pay any attention to them."

But they did not clear out. Instead they pressed even closer. The blonde kept rubbing against me, drawing on her cigarette without removing it from her mouth or even opening her eyes, draping herself all over me, soft, light and invertebrate as though her illness had sucked out her insides. Where was I? The breathing in and out around me space. The great bare sea. Red lights twinkling from towers on the Carmel. The world through a glass darkly still it moved. Time can never stop flowing but sometimes there is an air lock in the middle of it. The woman's boneless hand coiled lightly around my stomach. A chill ran down my spine. I tried gently prying her loose but she adhered to me. A uniformed nurse passing by stopped to look at us, wondering if I needed help. But I looked back at her unconcernedly.

"The lawyer isn't coming today?" asked the old fellow.

"He's waiting for us at the gate. This is his son."

"His son?" He was thrilled.

Voices reached us from the library. I fought my way back there, the crowd jostling after me, feeling deeply fatalistic. Father was speaking in Russian to mother, who was answering him with her quaint accent. The sweet Slavic sounds made me shiver. The switch to Russian, her being made by him to speak the language he had taught her, had always signaled a new, more intense stage in their quarrels.

I let the voices draw me on a few steps at a time, the crowd keeping pace with me, enveloping me in thin static. The soft body covered me like a quilt, its gelatinous hand creeping through my clothes, caressing my bare skin. Other bodies swayed heavily against me. A strange, sudden lust stirred in my chest. Someone laughed

madly, half aloud. Now the giant made for us too, eyes riveted on
something in our midst. The crowd tried blocking him but he strode
powerfully through it, slowly yet irresistibly pulled the bright locomotive from under Gaddi's arm, and continued on his way. A cheer
went up from the crowd. He too flashed something like a smile.
Gaddi was shaking all over.

"Don't worry, he'll give it right back," the old fellow reassured us.
"He just wants to look at it . . . I'll get it back for you in a minute . . ."

The library door opened and Horatio emerged, wagging his tail
and shaking scraps of paper from his fur. After him came father, his
face blanched, his tie askew, an extinguished cigarette in his mouth.
A scrap of paper fell from his jacket too. Despair stared from his
eyes. The dog tried ponderously to jump on him and lick him but
father flung him rudely aside.

The crowd of patients ran up to him, shook his hand too, begged
for more cigarettes. The old fellow pushed and pulled, trying to keep
order. Father's eyes met mine above their heads.

"Tsvi ruined everything! He made her think . . . she wants it all
now . . . the house . . . everything. Ya'el is still talking to her inside . . . don't go in . . . damn you, what have you done?"

"Here's the lawyer!" someone shouted.

And indeed up the path in the early twilight came Kedmi, irritably
waving his arms and shouting something. The patients moved back.
The blonde woman released me. A low baying went up like the
sound of hounds scenting prey. Kedmi rapidly approached us.

"What's going on here? What have you been up to? Did you decide to settle down here for good?"

The patients turned to him. The old fellow sought to shake his
hand too, but he rebuffed them, walking right past them.

"Yes? I beg your pardon, gentlemen. Please . . . let's have a little
air . . . give me some room here . . . another time . . ."

They frightened him yet he provoked them, unable to control himself.

"What is this, some kind of happening? What do they all want? At
least let me have my child back. Where's Ya'el?"

He pulled Gaddi toward him, hugging him hard.

"Where's the locomotive?"

"He took it."

"Who did?"

"He'll give it back," cried the old fellow. "He'll give it back right away. I'm responsible."

"Nobody asked you," said Kedmi sharply. Without further ado he flung himself at the giant and tried extricating the toy.

"You should be ashamed of yourself, Gulliver, taking things from little children . . ."

The patients surrounded Kedmi in an uproar. "He'll give it back! He'll give it back!" they shouted while I tried to restrain him. The giant clutched the locomotive with a terrified look, crushing it against his chest with his great paw while Gaddi watched in silent agony.

"That's enough, Kedmi!" shouted father. "I'll buy him another one."

Kedmi was repulsed, flushed with rage.

"Where are all the nurses? Where are all the doctors? Where is the management? This is total bedlam! Come on, Gaddi, let's find mom and get the hell out of here."

Like a whirlwind he spun toward the library, kicking Horatio out of his way and flinging open the door. In the thin, dimming light inside mother was standing and talking to Ya'el, who sat listening quietly, her arms on her chest. The floor was littered with paper. Kedmi bent to pick up a piece of it and laughed bitterly. In a crushed voice he said to father:

"Well, this is the end. Extraordinary . . . she actually finished thinking . . ."

"I tore it," declared father, while fresh anxiety shot through me. "Never mind now. It's none of your business."

"It's none of my business?" marveled Kedmi in his quick, husky voice that was already a thought ahead. "You're right, it's none of my business! I only wish you had told me that a year ago. I couldn't have put it any better myself: it's none of my business and never will be . . . I've had it . . ." He crumpled the scrap of paper, shredding it in his hand. "If I had known you only wanted it to rip it, I would have given you blank pages . . ."

"Knock it off, Kedmi!" I broke in.

He looked at me jeeringly. "Ya'el!" he cried suddenly.

Mother and Ya'el stepped outside. A new light shone in mother's face. She seemed very calm. Ya'el hurried to father and hugged him, whispering excitedly while mother nodded in agreement. All at once the patients surrounded her as though she were their queen, and the old fellow linked arms with her. Kedmi was already hurrying Gaddi away. Mother regarded me timidly, wanting to say something, to explain, but unable to. I backed slowly away as she stepped toward me, my briefcase swinging in my hand. I took a last look at the patients, my eyes lingering on the boneless blonde, who stood leaning against a tree. Next to her on a bench sat the giant, the crushed locomotive at his feet. I turned to go.

Mother whispered something to father. He called to me, his arms limp at his sides. I halted.

"Come over here. Mother asks you to forgive her."

"Never mind. Forget it."

"Forgive me," said mother. "I'm asking for your forgiveness, Asa."

"What for?" I mumbled, turning red. "Forget it."

"Forgive me, Asa."

"All right." I winced. "All right."

"It's my fault . . . all mine . . ." Mother almost managed a smile, glowing with a sadly poignant beauty. "Just don't hit yourself anymore. I thought you had stopped that long ago . . ."

"All right, all right." I bent to kiss her and walked by myself toward the gate. Ya'el and mother followed me arm in arm, while father tagged along at their side, still very pale, absorbed in thought. Further back the crowd of patients trailed slowly after us. We crossed the lawns, Horatio lumbering between us, our sole connecting link. Kedmi's car was waiting at the gate, already faced toward the main road, its radio blasting away. The engine started up and raced nervously.

"Tomorrow . . ." said mother in parting. "Tomorrow . . ."

Ya'el slipped into the front seat. Father was talking Russian again, hurriedly, urgently, intent on finishing his thought. But his words were drowned out by the motor. I got into the back seat with him after me. Horatio tried squeezing in too but the door banged shut on him. He began to howl, clawing at it frantically.

"Ya'el," yelled Kedmi, "if he scratches up that door I'll murder him . . ."

He stepped on the gas.

Horatio chased us. We watched him through the back window as he ran down the middle of the narrow side road, a diminishing point. Smiling to himself, Kedmi glanced in the rearview mirror. He slowed down and the dog began to catch up.

"Drive faster, Kedmi," said Ya'el.

Kedmi sped up a bit and then slowed down again, stopping for a long while when he reached the main road. Horatio loped on down the middle of the side road, behind him the sea and a last gasp of sun setting in a wrinkled orange sky. Eyes narrowed to a slit, red tongue dripping sunlight, he almost touched the car with his wolfish cranium when Kedmi started up again and turned into the main road. Horatio chased us into it, still running down the center line, cars honking and screeching all around him.

"Stop, Kedmi!" cried father. "He'll be run over."

"Don't," said Ya'el. "Drive faster."

But Kedmi neither speeded up nor stopped. All concentration, he led the dog away from the hospital, determined to kill him.

"Kedmi, what are you doing?" pleaded Ya'el. "Drive faster!"

He was deliberately staying behind a slow truck.

"All criticisms of my driving should be typed in triplicate, please . . ."

I said nothing. As soon as we entered Acre we lost sight of the dog among the cars behind us. We were in heavy city traffic now, stopping for lights, passing pedestrians with their packages of matzos and youngsters hanging out on corners between appliance stores and fast-food stands. In Crusader times St.-Jean-d'Acre had been a metropolis the size of London or Paris.

Kedmi stopped to fill the car at a gas station, moving lazily, looking around him. At the last light on the way out of town we caught sight of Horatio in the crosswalk in front of us, his eyes bulging, his tongue grazing the asphalt, a hairy old thing lost in a shuffle of human feet, sniffing the tires of cars. The light turned green, leaving him by himself in the middle of the crosswalk, still searching for our scent. Behind us cars beeped their horns wildly. Kedmi was set to steamroller him when I opened the door and jumped out, grabbing him by the collar and hauling him onto the sidewalk. The traffic flowed past. At first Horatio fought me, but when he saw who I was he licked my hand, more dead than alive, yelping with dumb, hoarse joy. I peered in his eyes. He was exhausted, half crazed from fatigue and the maze of city streets. "Go home, Horatio," I said, pointing north. He looked at me, his skull bones strong but fragile in my palms. "Go home, boy. Go home to mother." He wagged his tail, his eyes a dull wolfish blue. I picked up a small stick, a broken sliver of board, ran it over his dry snout, and threw it as far as I could into a rubbish-strewn abandoned lot. "Go get it, Horatio! Don't you remember how?" He looked at me without budging, drawn to a different scent, wagging his tail some more. "Get it, Horatio!" I shouted. I took another stick and threw it too. "Go fetch, boy, I need it!" He cocked his head wonderingly, then suddenly shook himself as though harking to an ancient call and ran into the lot, vanishing among some two-by-fours. I dashed back to the car, jumped in, and slammed the door.

"Go, Kedmi! For God's sake, step on it. The poor dog."

"Since when have you begun believing in God?"

"Go, Kedmi!" shouted all three of us. "Go!"

"All right, you don't have to shout."

And while the old dog was still hunting for the stick we were already driving south on the highway toward Haifa. Father sat huddled in one corner with his head thrown back, his face swept by headlights, his lips tightly clenched. Suddenly he felt me looking at him and looked back, noticing for the first time the scratch on my forehead, terribly upset, in total despair over me.

"So you're still hitting yourself," he said in a voice barely above a whisper. "But you promised! There'll never be any peace for me now. I shouldn't have brought you today. It's my fault."

I could see Kedmi's beady eyes in the mirror, studying us curiously.

He was struck down by lightning toward evening. His charred body was lifted from the street and laid on a bench at a bus stop, a torn blanket over it. Eventually it was brought to the morgue and left in a corner on the floor. A quiet night passed. In the morning the waiting students filled the lecture hall. A few of them went out to look for him in the corridors. Suddenly, bloodshot, Professor Berger hurried to the dais. He's dead, struck down by lightning, our great genius. What a frightful loss. The most brilliant of all my pupils. Our bright young hope. And just when he was on the verge of the great historical breakthrough. You have no idea what he had in mind, the sheer daring of it. Now only his notes remain. What a painful loss. If only he had had the time. If only he had been given more time. But his parents killed him. A bolt of lightning struck him down. . . . Dina faints at the graveside. Now I know, she says, that I too am to blame. She returns to her parents' home, where she lapses into religious mysticism. In the end she is married off to a dirty old rabbi.

I got out at the Haifa bus station. Father stayed in the car. He'd sleep at Ya'el's tonight and return to the hospital the first thing in the morning. This time by himself. They would call Tsvi immediately; should they phone Dina too and tell her I was on my way? No, I said. You needn't bother. Maybe I'll stay on for a while in Tel Aviv. To punish her. To make her miss me.

Father laid a protective hand on me. My hitting myself had left him one up, he could pity me now. "Well, now you understand me better, don't you? Don't worry, though, I'll let her have her way in the end. Do you want me to give you any money? . . . When will we meet again? . . . You'll have to come on the holiday to say goodbye. . . . We'll be in touch . . ."

Suddenly I was putty in his hands. A burst string. And yet deep down a feeling of tranquillity.

The large concrete station was already dark and silent. In the cafeteria where we had eaten lunch the lights were out and the chairs were stacked on the tables. I boarded the Tel Aviv bus, and it backed slowly out of its stall. A lit-up train traveled parallel to it until it vanished into thin air. The driver turned on the news. The bus was full of sleeping soldiers. A narrow, shrunken patch of sea flickered in the wind. To take some distant period and discuss it in trivial terms —to find a neglected document or manuscript that has yet to be written about and blow up its significance—to burrow through old newspapers in search of unknown facts about some second-rate statesman who lived in a forgotten age—let that be for the rest of them. But I would find the cryptograph, the secret code. The old age has died, the new one has yet to be born, and meanwhile there are morbid pustules everywhere, a bad case of adolescent acne. An age of nostalgia, confusion, anticipation and fear, a twilight zone, an eve of great upheavals, a jumbled time of contradictory processes. Who will find the right cipher, who will see thirty years into the future, not by means of his fallible intuition but clearly and with scientific certainty . . . ?

In Tel Aviv the hard dry wind still blew. A low, orange sky. The bus let us off in a dark, deserted street near the central station. Used

ticket stubs swirled through the darkness. Grains of sand from the
Sahara turned to grit between one's teeth. The passengers scattered
quickly and were gone. I walked down a street lined with shoe stores,
their darkened display windows full of thin, cross-strapped ladies'
models, and emerged in the dimly lit square of the station, by felafel
stands with their mountains of colorful salads and shuwarma joints
with their glowing grills of spitted lamb. On the opposite sidewalk, at
platform number three, a small line of travelers waited to board the
Jerusalem bus, which was almost full. A short, middle-aged man
wearing a striped jacket, elevator heels and a linked chain around his
neck stood by a public phone booth, eyeing me with a warm, pene-
trating glance. May I? I asked. At once he moved aside with a show
of deference, measuring me with his eyes. I dialed Tsvi. An unfamiliar, Levantine voice answered politely. Tsvi had stepped out for a
moment. Did I wish to leave a message? No, I said, there was nothing special. But who was calling? I told him.

"Ah, you're Dr. Asa Kaminka. How do you do? I'm Tsvi's friend,
Refa'el Calderon. Your sister and father telephoned a while ago from
Haifa with the latest news. Can I be of any assistance to you? Would
you care to stop by and rest up here before going on to Jerusalem?"

The same man who brought Tsvi to see mother yesterday. One
more finger in the pie. I hung up.

A dark-complexioned girl in short pants and high-heeled clogs,
apparently a whore, was talking in low tones on the street corner to
the man from the phone booth, who kept looking at me with a
friendly smile. The Jerusalem bus had already left. Waiting for the
next one was a lone traveler, a thick-bearded religious man holding a
suitcase tied with string. I went to get something to eat and bought
myself a felafel and a glass of juice. The short man went on smiling
deferentially, never taking his eyes from me. Two grotesquely
madeup girls wearing Nite-Glo jerseys and swinging luminescent
bags came up to join him. I stood at the felafel stand, garbage cans
all around me, sauerkraut dribbling steadily from the overfilled
pocket bread, eating savagely, my briefcase between my legs, getting
sesame dip all over myself. It was eight o'clock. I hadn't been in Tel
Aviv for weeks; why not seize the opportunity to get in touch with
some friend, someone I could talk to, bounce ideas off? Suddenly I
was in no hurry to get home. I wiped my face with a paper napkin
and bought a new pack of cigarettes, hungry for human contact here

in this no-man's-land, in this no-time and no-place. In my ever-further-away-from-me native town. I thought for a moment of the lunatics I had braved today, of my newly discovered sangfroid in their presence, of the horribly sweet feeling of that soft blonde spilling over me. Perhaps I should give Stern a ring. An old friend who once had studied with me and was now teaching the same period as I was at the University of Tel Aviv: I could never enjoy a relaxed talk with him when calling long-distance from Jerusalem. I searched for another phone token in my pockets but couldn't find one. Still regarding me cordially, the short man with the link chain took out a handful of tokens and offered me one, firmly refusing to let me pay him for it.

"But that would be an insult . . ."

He spoke in a low, quiet, knowing voice. A pusher or a pimp? Well, that wasn't my lookout. I went back to the phone and opened the thick, tattered directory that was attached by a heavy chain to the wall. Its back pages were torn or missing. The letter *S* was gone entirely. I let it drop, the chain creaking loudly, took out a cigarette, and fumbled for a match. At once he stepped up to me, whipped out a small lighter, and lit it for me with a bluish flame.

"Are you looking for something? Perhaps I can be of help."

"No, thanks. The phone book is torn."

"If it's a girl . . ."

"Excuse me?"

"I said if it's a girl . . ."

"No. It isn't a girl."

"Because I have another one for you. She's waiting for you there. She's taken a liking to you."

He pointed to the two whores restlessly swinging their bags.

"No, thank you."

"She asked me to tell you . . . it's just that she's bashful . . ."

"Thanks anyway." I smiled. He talked about the two of them as though they were one person.

"If you think she's too tall for you . . . or too strong . . . if that's it . . . then there are other options . . ."

He spoke quickly, deftly, in a reasonable, businesslike tone.

"It's not a question of that. At the moment I'm . . ."

"Because I have others too. Just tell me what you're looking for . . . explain your wish to me . . . I've got a big selection around

here. I know a sweet, very classy young girl who lives right next door
. . . you might like her . . . she's practically still a child . . . she
may even still be a virgin . . . yes, I believe she is . . . real
class . . ."

He laid a warm, friendly hand on my shoulder. I gave a start.

"There was something I liked about you as soon as I saw you walk
into the station. You only have to say the word to me. Just tell me
what you want. Everything is available. Why don't you have a quiet
cup of coffee and see what I have to show you? . . . Where did you
say you were going? . . . The buses run late, I know because I'm
always here. And if you miss the last one, I'll bring you home in my
own car. Come on . . . you only have to look . . . let me show
you what real service is. There's something about you I like. Don't
be scared . . . it's all aboveboard . . . no obligation, no money
down . . . I just show you the goods, it doesn't cost you a
cent . . ."

He was quiet, reassuring, trustable. And I was out of time, out of
place, plain out of it. Let her wait up for me. She's probably gone to
sleep at her parents' anyway.

"At least you'll join me for some coffee?"

"But I'll pay for it." The words tumbled out by themselves.

He smiled, highly satisfied.

"But of course . . . it's your treat . . . you're the boss. Don't let
me pressure you. I never pressure anyone. It's like window-shopping
. . . just pretend that you're window-shopping . . ."

The coffee was served us at once. I gripped my cup hard, in need
of the hot pick-me-up. A small teen-ager ran up to my new friend
with some message. Everyone in the café knew him. Bazouki music
blared over a radio. He lit a king-sized cigarette and offered me one.
I declined. His face was furrowed with wrinkles. An unplaceable
accent. He managed the conversation with me tactfully, reliably.

"Many people can't explain what they want and end up being
disappointed. It's not something that can be done just like that, automatically. You have to find the right combo. That's my business.
Every dream has its answer. Its fulfillment. Take yourself. You're an
intellectual type, I can see that right away. But you're pressed for
time. You're in a rush, and so are your thoughts. If you'd just say the
word to me . . ."

"What's the price nowadays?" My voice sounded foreign to me, squeaky.

"That depends on how long it's for."

"No, I mean just the usual . . ."

"It depends . . . whatever you feel like paying . . ."

"But what's the going rate?"

"Some people give five . . ."

"Hundred?"

"Thousand. What's a hundred these days?"

"Five *thousand?*"

"But not for you. For you there's no charge. It's on the house. And I have this feeling that she'll go for you . . . that you'll make it with her big . . ."

And supposing just this once. To prove to myself. Not against her but to realize to help us both. For our future. Our child. Another Jerusalem bus pulled out across the street. A new one pulled in after it and was boarded by a crowd of religious Jews. Whenever I want I simply pay for the coffee, cross the street, and get on it.

A couple entered the café and came over to say hello, a chubby girl dressed in white with short-cropped hair and smiling, mischievous eyes and a tall young man whose hand rested on her shoulder. The girl glanced at me inquisitively, her pants stretched tight over her thighs. The little pimp pulled her toward him and she bent down to kiss him, baring for a moment the dark ivory globes of her breasts, before being led by her partner to a table in the corner. Something about her eyes and short hair sent a stab of pain through me. The young man came back to us and whispered a few words to my companion, who listened judiciously.

"She'll be here soon. . . . Would you like to drink something stronger in the meantime?"

"No, thanks. I have to be on my way. I'm in a hurry . . . I'm afraid you've wasted your time on me . . ."

"Why worry about it? It's my time. And I've enjoyed spending it with you . . ."

I noticed him follow my glance to the girl in the corner, who sat smilingly holding her friend's hand and bobbing her head pertly.

"Maybe you like her? Just say the word . . . let me know . . ."

"Who?"

"The one who just said hello to us . . . in the corner . . ."

"Who?" I tried acting innocent. "Oh, her. Yes, I think she's nice
. . . but why do you ask?"

His face lit up all at once.

"Very nice! A real personality . . . she's a student, you know."
He grasped my hand. "Allow me. You won't regret it. Now I see
what your taste is . . . you won't be disappointed . . ."

He rose, crossed the room to the chatting couple, made a sign to
the girl, and whispered something in her ear. She blushed, taken
aback, then glanced my way with her large, gleaming brown eyes
and ducked her head shyly. She was gentle, not at all hardened. And
yet she was pleased. I caught my breath, the blood pounding away in
my heart. My hand shook. I'll punish her. It's my right to. For two
years I've begged and gotten nowhere. The pimp came slowly back
to me, sat down without a word, and offered me a cigarette. I
glanced down and when I looked up again the girl had already
slipped out the back door. Her friend had opened an evening paper
and was reading it. Across the street the bus was still waiting. Two
teen-agers boarded it and then got off again.

Home. She's probably having a fit. Who needs this insanity. And
all the money too.

"Come." He touched me lightly.

I still played innocent. "Where to?"

He threw me a hard look.

"You're just like a child. A stubborn one. Come on, it's only to say
hello to her. Just to say hello. To get to know her."

"Not now . . . some other time," I murmured, rising and putting
a friendly arm around him. We stepped outside, pausing in the doorway for him to regard me with a despairing smile.

"Just come say hello to her. She's waiting for you. You can arrange to meet her some other time . . . it isn't nice to stand her
up . . ."

And patiently, expertly, without losing his calm, he steered me
into a narrow side street. All at once I was back among the shoe
stores, only on the opposite sidewalk. Boots and sneakers filled the
dark display windows. In the back of one of the stores a small bulb
still burned. We stepped into the hallway of an apartment house. The
man pressed the handle of the first door and opened it. "Just say
hello to her. Act your age! What are you afraid of? This is strictly on
the up-and-up."

I was in the lit store. I could see myself reflected in its mirrors, thin and gray, the scratch on my face like a string of tiny pearls, my tie over one shoulder, my jacket badly creased. Next to a divan were some inclined stools for trying on shoes and shelves with samples of ladies' footwear. Empty shoe boxes and white tissue paper lay scattered on the floor. Shoes had been sold here a short while ago, there was still a human smell about the place. She stood at the back of it, near the cash register, examining a shoe with a spiked heel. Close up she was not so pretty; her perfume was cheap and there was a small scar by the side of her mouth; but the special charm of her eyes, that humorous gleam, was still there. No choking up this time. Which thought turned to slow desire. She looked at me calmly, tossing her head with a deep, natural grace so unlike the manner of a whore. She sat on the divan, about my age, perhaps a year or two older, and placed one leg on the stool in front of her, her pant bottom rolled up to reveal a plump, smooth, creamy-white foot. I stepped toward her, still holding my black briefcase. She glanced at it with a bright, intelligent look, waiting smilingly for me to put it down. I laid it on the carpet and sat on the stool like a salesman.

"What's your name?"

"Natalie."

"Natalie? Really? How lovely . . . are you Israeli?"

"For the time being."

I laughed abruptly.

"My name is Tsvi."

"You're not from Tel Aviv?"

"I used to be. Now I live up north, near Acre."

The need to leave a trail of lies in self-defense.

I stroked her foot. Her skin was warm, sweaty, smooth to the touch. I undid the buckle of her old, worn shoe and slipped it off her foot, which she let lie, white and puffy, on the slope of the stool.

"What size do you take, madame?" I asked suddenly, feeling myself go scarlet.

Firmly she set down her other foot, presenting me with it. I unbuckled the shoe, slipped it quickly off, and threw it aside. With an awful lust I fell upon her feet, kissing the dust, the Nubian loess, the faint stink of callused skin, the smooth underarch, the human flesh. Swooning, I licked them, my pants bursting with desire, with my hideous love for her, lifting her feet and sticking them into my mouth, nipping them lightly while she laughed with alarm and strange pleasure, her eyes shutting tight. I dropped from the stool to the carpet, still licking and biting, beside myself, dizzy with desire, grunting like an animal, abandoning myself to the depths. Glassily she stroked my hair and hauled my thin tie in like a rope. Suddenly, though, she took fright and pulled her bare feet away.

"Don't. Stop that! Get up and come over here."

And I did, filled with a passion I had never felt before, struggling to undo her blouse and pants. She pushed my hand away and slipped out of her pants herself. Brown lingerie parted along a hidden zipper, revealing a large, scary brown navel. My love, I whispered. My dearest.

"Help me, please."

She didn't get what I meant.

"Can you help me?"

She made a face. "What do you want?"

"You know. Help me in."

And standing there I began to come even as I went down on her. A failure. Here too? Panic took hold of me. She spread her legs wide, reaching for my wet cock, grimacing with disgust.

"Wait a minute! Hang on there. You're shooting your load. Hang on!"

I buried my face in her, trying to hold it, feeling her warmth, her legs wound around me, shuddering with each jet that squirted as though from a little heart, still coming while I kissed the white fabric of her blouse, searching for her eyes which she denied me.

At last she threw me powerfully off.

"Was I in you?"

"Sure, sure. Don't let it worry you." Her voice was suddenly harsh, impatient. "Don't tell me that this was your first time . . ."

"Of course not. What makes you think that?"

She rose, looking away, and quickly zipped up her pants. She ran a hand through her hair while casting me a querying look of concern. I zipped my pants too, took out my wallet, and gave her the thousand-pound note that I'd gotten from father.

"This is what he and I agreed on."

"Who's he?"

"That man . . ."

"Since when does he do business for me? Hand over another thousand."

"I don't have it."

"You don't have it? What do you mean you don't have it?"

"I don't have it."

"Then give me your watch."

"My watch?" I was flabbergasted. "No way!"

"The hell with it then. Give me five hundred more pounds."

"I tell you I don't have it."

"What's in that briefcase?"

"Just papers."

She sat down by the cash register, slipping her feet back into her unbuckled shoes, her butched head held high. Where had I seen before that look that flared in her eyes?

"Let me see your wallet."

Her voice was dry, tough, but controlled.

I laughed nervously and showed it to her. She went through it quickly, found five hundred pounds, and started to take it.

"Leave me that money. I need it to get to Jerusalem."

"You can hitch."

"No, I can't. No one will stop for me . . ."

I spoke fearfully, fawningly, a stranger to myself.

Someone tried the front door of the store.

She reflected, replaced the money, and handed me back the wallet.

"I'm letting you off this time," she scolded. "But it isn't nice to take advantage like that. You look like a decent type . . . let's have none of your tricks next time . . ."

"I really am sorry . . . next time . . . I didn't realize . . . do you always hang out around here?"

Her eyes smiled.

"You'll find me. But no more funny stuff, please."

A middle-aged man in a custom-made suit opened the door, bowed hurriedly, and shut it again. I took my briefcase and left, walking quickly with my head down, not looking where I was going, losing my way in the vacant streets until I found the station again. I joined the small line of people waiting for the Jerusalem bus. The wind had died down but it was colder now, with fog instead of dust. A few students and tired commuters stood alongside me. Feeling empty inside, I leaned against the metal railing of the platform.

Someone reached out to me across it. It was the short, swarthy man with the link chain.

"How was it?"

"Okay," I murmured. "It was fine. But I don't have any cash left. I gave it all to her."

"How about a watch or a pen . . . ?"

I didn't answer. People turned to look at us. He smiled to himself, fair and patient to the last.

"Never mind, then. It's something else in there with all those shoes, isn't it? A special thrill. I always score well there. Well, never mind . . . next time . . . this is my beat, by the Jerusalem bus . . ."

He shook my hand. I felt shaken. Had he really seen right through me?

The bus lurched into the night, confidently negotiating the narrow streets of south Tel Aviv. To hell with the money. Not against life or beside it but straight into the teeth of it. Home. Home. You'll help her. She'll let you. She's scared and so are you. But to lick her like a dog! From where did it grab me like that? The cheap scent of her perfume still clinging to my face the dust on her feet the sickening horror of it not till my dying day. Alone and by myself. The pairs of shoes in the dark store. An unplumbed reality. And now what? Horatio's head between my palms old and decrepit half dead from chasing after father. I must make order at once. But what made me say my love? Something has happened. Something dreadful has happened and is done. If I'm not careful I'll lose her. Dina my love. My child. My light. My forgiveness. Not against you. With you. But what made me say my love? Yours the decent folk and mine the lunacy. Let him stick to what he's good at. He alone. While he lives and breathes. Let him sit and write.

Take care take care all things are possible never again. Too chancy. Though my heart stirs for it. And you deserved it.

A smell of orange groves in blossom. So spring is breaking out after all. The lights of the houses receding behind us. The last factories. What made me say my love? How did the words slip out? How do I annul them, take them back? What have I done? She must be worried to death. Gone to her parents', called Ya'el, they're at our house now. There'll be hell to pay. What made me say my love?

The three basic rhythms. Contact, release and contraction. The more human beings come to resemble each other under the influence of culture, civilization, commerce and cross-contact, the more they seek freedom, even perversity, but also a greater sense of self via new conflicts. The Peloponnesian Wars. In the midst of such insight, such sophistication, such a blossoming of philosophy, art and religion, the Greek cities declare all-out, bloody wars on each other for no good reason and contract self-destructively.

The roar of the speeding bus into the night, plunging through Judean fog. Surrounded by patients. She leaned on me with such assurance. Did they sense it in me too? A kindred soul. I must be mad to bark like a dog where could it have come from? My students should have seen me. Must get up and bark for them. Her eyes on me. Vera Zasulich. The individual in history. After Passover I'll start straight from the murder of the Tsar. In a subdued tone, with precise, colorful details. The thirteenth of March 1881. Nikolai Riskov pitches a bomb at the horses' feet, not far from the Winter Palace. The cobblestones caked with ice. Sofia Proveskaya, that noble, magnificent soul. And above all, the thrower of the second bomb that killed the tyrant, the blond, curly-headed Pole Ignaty Grynbatski, age twenty-four, an engineering student who refused even to give his name when he lay dying in his own blood. Sitting paralyzed on a bench in the summer garden, Dostoyevsky hears of the planned assassination several months in advance and, despite his reactionary views, neglects to inform the authorities. I'll hook them with the flashy little items and take them quickly on to the big significant ones. They'll learn to love those lost young terrorists yet.

I can't get rid of her smell. The taste of dry felafel and greasy sauerkraut. The smell of diesel fuel. My sticky fingers. First of all a hot bath. What strange stains on my clothes. I'll elude her in the dark. But what made me say my love? And so easily.

The bus is speeding like mad. A cowboy of a driver. A wave of nausea inside me. The other passengers slumped mostly asleep in their seats. I can never learn to sleep on a bus. Horatio. Horatio. Did he ever get back to mother? So terribly sorry for him. Father will go back there tomorrow by himself. And you hit yourself. You'll go mad yet. They'll drive you to it. Genetic insanity awaits you Asa. But give it your all keep a clear head don't take a wrong step. Now I know what my soul stirs for what I need. The sacred tremor within. A woman not a child. Yes my love.

I tripped going down the steps of the bus, the vomit already in my throat, while an old Civil Defense reservist stood looking on. My briefcase had puke on it too. Sick and shivering with chills, I dragged myself to the bus stop, where I waited endlessly for a bus to take me home.

The windows of the apartment were unlit. It was nearly eleven. Her parents must have taken her home with them. I unlocked the front door. The hallway was dark. The guest room was locked. Not a sound. I opened the living-room door, still clutching my briefcase. The blinds were down but bright light struck my eyes. Something was changed in the room. Had the furniture been rearranged? Pillows were scattered all over. Papers lay about the couch. A haze of cigarette smoke. She sat in her jeans with her shoes kicked off, her hair gathered at the back, wide awake, very pretty, looking as if she'd grown smaller during the day. There were more pages in her lap and pens everywhere. A small rag doll sat on the couch among big cushions.

I stopped in the doorway.

"I tried calling the neighbors but no one answered. I had to wait forever for buses. Did you call Ya'el?"

"No."

"Don't get up." She had made no move to. "I threw up in the station in Jerusalem. I feel like I'm dying. What a day! I'm glad you didn't come, you would have gone out of your mind. At least I spared you that. I have to wash up, the briefcase is filthy too. I'm sick. I missed you all day. Were you at your parents'?"

She shook her head with a faraway look, remote, self-absorbed, in a world of her own. She had a new secret. Some new role she'd thought up for herself.

"My mother still won't sign. It's a whole comedy. You can be thankful that your own parents are sane. Better a sane grocer than a . . . what did you do all day long? Wait a minute before you tell me. I want to wash up first."

But I went to the kitchen instead. More pages on the dining table. Dirty breakfast dishes still in the sink and on the counter. Crumpled pages everywhere in her large, clear hand. Something about a young woman with a baby carriage.

"Stop that immediately!" she hissed behind me. "Go wash up. You look as though you'd been rolling in the gutter."

"What did you do all day long? Where were you?"

"Right here."

"Did you go to the bank? Did you take out money?"

"No."

"So what did you do all day?"

"I was here. I wrote a story . . . complete, in one sitting. I was all alone. It felt good to be without you for a change . . ."

I went on collecting the dishes, sorting the silverware and the cups.

"Stop that! Go wash." She raised her voice at me. "You're a filthy, stinking mess!"

I put down the dishes and went to the bedroom. More papers all over the bed. Piles of clothing, hers, mine, on all the chairs: she must have emptied out the whole closet. She followed me silently, careful not to get too close, her light eyes opened wide. I wandered distractedly about the room before going to the bed. On the night table lay an open history book in English that I had been reading in the morning. Portraits of young Russian revolutionaries in cravats and high collars, a photograph of the Tsar in full military regalia, pictures of ladies in long evening dresses, the date of birth and death under each. The earnest face of Vera Zasulich, a gleam of mischief in her dark, deep-set eyes. A flash of fear ran through me as it dawned on me whose eyes they also were.

I went to the closet and began taking out hangers for her clothes.

"Stop it!" she screamed. "Go wash up. You don't know what you look like . . ."

Something happened today. Something will never be the same.

THURSDAY NIGHT

O my love
O my lord
Cherish thou my agony
Lest it be the death of me.
                    Yehuda Halevi

—Tsvi? Tsvi? Is that you, Tsvi? Tsvi?
—Refa'el. Tsvi?
—Refa'el. It's me. Tsvi? Open the door a crack.
—Whom did you think it was?
—Nearly two o'clock. I was afraid at first it was your father.
—Nothing. I just thought I'd drop by. Were you really asleep?
—You don't say! I knocked as lightly as a bird.
—Oh, dear! I'm so sorry. I thought I saw a light.
—There wasn't a light on in the kitchen? But I saw the kitchen light from the street. I'm absolutely sure I did. It's been on for at least half an hour. So I came up and knocked. But really lightly, like a bird.
—Are you sure?
—Perhaps your father left it on.
—But how could I be mistaken? It's weird. Maybe that mouse of yours has been turning the lights on and off. Don't laugh. Once a mouse got into my aunt in Jerusalem's electric box and switched the lights on and off each time he ran around.

—Seriously. That's no joke. They thought the house was haunted until a city repairman caught it. Well, I'll be on my way. I see you really were sleeping. I'm awfully sorry to have woken you. But how was it you heard me? Are you such a light sleeper? I swear I hardly touched the door, just like a . . .

—Are you sure?

—Well, only for a minute. Really, only for a minute. I thank you.

—I don't know what's happened to me. I couldn't catch a wink of sleep tonight. I've been driving around the streets for the past two hours.

—It beats me.

—Why in the kitchen? Go back to bed and I'll sit beside you. Get back into bed. I'll sit by your side and then I'll go.

—Right. I'll talk in a whisper. I'm terribly sorry. I'd forgotten all about him.

—Then we'd better sit in the kitchen with the door shut.

—Eh?

—I don't know.

—What?

—No special reason. I'm just awfully nervous. A total wreck. The bottom's dropped out of my life. Haven't I already told you that you've made a hash out of me? I'll live. But believe me, I'll be a sick man from all this yet.

—No . . .

—Yes.

—Yes.

—Maybe.

—That too.

—You're right. Of course you are. Just try not to mind me. I'll live.

—Tea? No, don't trouble yourself. Go back to bed. You're still half asleep. I'll be on my way . . .

—Are you sure?

—You really do feel like it?

—Only if you do too. I've noticed that you have a thing for tea in the middle of the night. You're always looking for a chance to drink it. Maybe it's come down to you from your ancestors in Russia who sat around the samovar.

—What? Yes. With us tea is like medicine. It's something to drink when you're sick.

—No, no, tea will be fine. By all means, tea. Tea suits me perfectly now.

—No, no. Honestly. Just tea. I'm as good as sick already.

—Any way that you like it. It doesn't matter to me. You're so kind. It pains me to have woken you. I never would have come if I had known you were sleeping. You shouldn't have let me in. That light misled me.

—No . . . never mind . . . I'm angry at myself. Lately I'm angry at myself all the time.

—Thank you. Thank you so much. You know, it's strange to see you without your glasses. I didn't know you could manage without them.

—No, just a bit different. I have to get used to it. Now I understand your eyes better. I mean I see them. I understand them perfectly. Are those new pajamas?

—Very becoming. Soft. Very becoming. Where did you get them?

—Yes. They have lovely things there. Very becoming.

—How much?

—That isn't so bad. They're very becoming. Very handsome on you. So tell me first how your day was. When did he arrive? I phoned three times tonight but got no answer.

—What restaurant?

—Right. How is he? Have there been any new developments? Tell me.

—Just what you suggested to her . . .

—And what did he decide?

—In what way?

—Then . . .

—Congratulations! On Sunday . . . that's the day of the seder . . .

—Are you sure you won't want to be there? I can drive you.

—Never mind, I'll manage . . .

—How can you talk about them like that? You slay me . . . how can you possibly . . . ?

—Their story fascinates me. Not just on your account. I can't get over her face. She made a great impression on me. A noble woman. I was very touched by her.

—Really? I'm glad to hear that. Tell me, do you think I could peek in on him for a second?

—Your father. I'm terribly curious.

—Just for a second.

—In your room? Why?

—Right. Of course. It was his bed. That was thoughtful of you. Just for a second. I won't make a sound.

—Of course, in the dark . . .

—Just a wee bit of light . . .

—He looks like you. Why, he looks just like you. It's astonishing. He's a handsome old man.

—The spitting image of you. As though I were looking at you twenty or thirty years from now, when I'm already in the grave . . .

—No, no, he's a perfect likeness of you. It's amazing. The little one looks like him too.

—Your brother.

—Really amazing!

—Me? Terrible. Can't you see for yourself?

—I don't know. Can't you see? I'm a complete wreck. This is the third time this week that I haven't caught any sleep.

—I don't believe in them. Instead of helping me, they hype me up more. Six hours later they begin to take effect, just when I'm sitting down to the morning conference with Bleicher. Just when we're trying to size up the trends and I need to be at my sharpest. A mistake then can cost the bank millions.

—At nine o'clock.

—Every morning. With today's inflation it should be three times a day.

—That's for sure. And who says a man needs to get seven hours of sleep? Maybe three are enough. Meanwhile I'm getting to know the city by night. There's a lot going on in it. Tel Aviv's become a real metropolis. And now that it's spring and the air is so mild, it's a pleasure to be out. I went to Sami's first. I thought I might find you there, even though I reckoned that you'd be staying in with your father. He wanted me to hang around but what with all the young punks and the music and those whores of his—you wouldn't believe all the whores—I decided that it wasn't for me. So I stepped into *Ma'ariv.*

—*Ma'ariv*, the newspaper. They have a teleprinter there, we get the closing Wall Street averages over it.

—Right. It's a direct line. We get them first thing in the morning. This way I could already start planning for tomorrow. What?

—Of course . . . it's already today . . . I'm in a total fog.

—Does it interest you now? I see you're really into the market.

—Of course. That's the only way.

—What do I think? You want to know now?

—Why should I mind? I think that the dollar is in trouble and is about to take a bad beating. We've been talking about it at the bank for several days now. The way I read the figures coming over the ticker from New York tonight, it could happen anytime.

—A sharp drop.

—More than that. Much more.

—Anything can happen. It's a crazy world. In case you haven't noticed, money is psychology these days.

—What we're planning to do tomorrow is unload a lot of the D series, which is linked sixty percent to the dollar, and buy a large mix of marks, francs and yen. We'll do it even if it knocks the bottom out of IDC, which is the bank's largest money fund. Do you get it?

—Why not? As the dollar drops, so will IDC. Then we'll buy it back at a lower price. Not all at once, of course. We'll spread it over a week or two. That will bring Option 8 back up, which is linked to IDC. It's sort of its weak kid sister.

—The investors? They won't lose. They simply won't make the profit that they're used to.

—Yes. We've been thinking about it for a few days now. But this morning we'll have to decide on the exact amounts. That depends on how we feel about the dollar, and tonight I've come away feeling strongly. Bleicher is looking for a big killing, he's prepared to go all the way. Your water is boiling . . .

—I'd say up to thirty points. The same thing happened in '77, only now it's more dangerous, because it could ruin the stock's credibility and send the market into a nose dive.

—Exactly. Because it's hooked into so many other stocks and bonds, it's a key to the whole market. But he doesn't give a damn.

—Bleicher? Yes. He likes to shake the market up. And the management gives him a free hand. He's one crazy German Jew, always looking for the biggest opening to put his money in. As soon as he finds it he goes in with all he's got, even with closed accounts that he has no business touching. He's perfectly willing to go for broke. Oh, he's a big, dangerous son of a bitch.

—Not always. And if he didn't have us three Sephardim, Atias, me and Ronen (whose name used to be Mizrachi, by the way), to keep an eye on him, he'd land us all in big trouble.

—One spoon.

—Yes. Mizrachi. Did you really think he was born Ronen?

—A pure Iraqi. I'm surprised you didn't sense it. When did you meet him?

—What did he want from you?

—And you didn't pick up on it? It's so obvious. A pure-blooded Iraqi, you'd better watch out for him. I'm surprised at you . . .

—Yes. Terribly nervous, can't you feel it? I don't know what's gotten into me. Maybe it has to do with the theater . . .

—Yes. The theater. We went to see a play tonight. *Uncle Vanya,* you may have heard of it. At the Tel Aviv Chamber Theater.

—Yes. Shekhov.

—How?

—Right. Chekhov. I beg your pardon. It's the first time I'd heard of him. I suppose you must know all about him. I have the playbill at home with his picture and all.

—Yes.

—It was just one of those things. A few days ago the bank offered us tickets at three hundred pounds apiece. What's three hundred pounds nowadays? The sugar and the water in this glass of tea cost more. But our executive organization is terrific at getting discounts.

—Exactly. Maybe because we work for a bank. They want to bribe us, that's the only sense I can make of the bargains we get. The other day, I swear, we had an offer of some big two-door refrigerators for less than the wholesale price.

—It's a shame I didn't know.

—It's a shame I didn't know.

—You should always tell me what you need.

—It really is old and noisy. I'll check if the offer is still on.

—It's a shame I didn't know. It's the same with the theater tickets, you see, and I usually pass them right on to the secretaries. But this time there was no one to take them because of the holiday. My daughters are away too, so I said to her let's go see it, it's been maybe ten years since we saw a play.

—No. I don't know. I'm not saying that they're no good, it's just that I don't care for all those productions about Hasidim and fiddlers on the roof. I don't have any patience for them. And she prefers films anyway, especially French ones. Now and then we go see some comic routine, light things like that. I don't have the nerves for real theater. I always feel embarrassed for the actors, for the crazy kinds of things they're made to say. Don't forget, we're a different generation.

—You know.

—A different generation. It's a fact.

—Don't laugh at me, okay?

—I've already told you but you've forgotten. I wouldn't hide it from you. I told you long ago. I'm going on fifty-six soon after Passover.

—Thank you. But that's the truth. There's nothing to be done about it.

—Because I'm thin and light.

—So I was telling you . . . I said to her come on, let's go and see it, what's there to lose, if we don't like it we'll walk out in the middle, we won't be chained to our seats, why stay home all night eating your heart out over something that God alone is responsible for. Are you listening?

—So she agreed right away and we went.

—Yes. Tonight. A few hours ago. And it was first-rate. I mean the performance. A real surprise. At first I didn't know what it was driving at, all those Russian names kept confusing me too. But we were right near the stage, fourth row center, and we saw everything the actors did close up—each time they laughed or cried or even breathed. You could hear every word. At first I thought that something special was going to happen. It took me a while to realize that it was happening already. I mean that the whole point was that it mattered to those people in the play . . . how should I put it . . . You say it's Chekhov?

—Anton Chekhov. I'll try to remember. But who was he?

—That's all? It sounds so simple.

—No. I never heard of him. It isn't my fault. All we ever learned about in school was that poet who saw God . . . you know, in a pond of water . . .

—Bialik. Right. And a few others like him, that was all. Don't forget, my dear, that my father pulled me out of school in the tenth grade and put me to work. It was during the World War. Remember, we're a different generation. Did you learn about Chekhov in school? I'll buy the book tomorrow—now that I've seen the play, I won't have any trouble reading it. It's something you should see too. I'll take you myself if it doesn't close before the end of the holiday. There wasn't much of an audience tonight, maybe that's why they sold us the tickets so cheaply. After your father has gone. You'll see it for yourself. A really good, natural performance. The main thing was how natural and quiet it was, without any shouting. The actors seemed so real. I have their names at home on the playbill. I must take you to see it. But you're laughing at me . . .

—No. She took it hard too. Already in the intermission I noticed how pale she was. And afterwards in the dark I saw tears on her face. I put my hand out to calm her but she didn't even feel it. And then I started shaking myself. I don't know what it was about it that grabbed me like that. I thought about you too. About us. About the whole desperate situation . . .

—What?

—No. You don't understand. That woman, Helena, Yelena, don't you remember how Uncle Vanya was hopelessly in love with her?

—You've forgotten. I'll take you to see it. Then you'll understand.

—Right. That's just it.

—Believe me, I've been on the verge of tears for days. Even in the bank I feel a lump in my throat as soon as I'm alone in my office. . . . Whenever I think of it, all the desperation of it, all the joy of it, overwhelm me. That's why I say I'm such a wreck. The bottom has dropped out of my life. It has no boundaries anymore. You take it all so easily. It's natural for you but you don't understand what you've done to me. Are you still listening?

—No. I'm beginning to bore you. Your eyes are closing. I can see how tired you are. I'll go now. I'm wide awake.

—No. Never mind. And she has only the desperation, the poor thing. For her this whole business has been . . . and I understand her so well . . . I keep telling myself that if it were the other way around, I'd go out of my mind. But why did that play affect us like that? Maybe we were ready to be shaken up and it just happened to be *Uncle Vanya* that did it. Or maybe it was something else. When the lights came on at curtain time I saw that she was really crying. And it went on and on, she got more and more carried away. I couldn't even bring myself to applaud. We just sat there staring at the floor, waiting for the people around us to get up and leave. And she went right on crying. Are you listening? She cried all the way to the car, and she cried in it too, quietly, as if once she'd started she wasn't going to stop. There wasn't a sign of a letup. And I knew that it was because of me, not the play. All because of me. The same woman who's hardly spoken a word to me since . . . What?

—Since she found out.

—About us . . . that we . . .

—What?

—No.

—Yes.

—No.

—Maybe. But she couldn't stop crying. She was like in a whirlpool of tears. And I decided not to try to make her. I thought it might be good for her to get out what was choking her inside. She's usually a very quiet woman. She has this inner pride.

—It's easy for you to talk. But to stand there and watch her cry . . . and I couldn't even let myself touch her, she's been very sensitive to that since she found out. Not even to comfort her. To have to watch her cry like that . . . But I didn't say a thing. I didn't want to quarrel, even though I knew it was all because of me. I'd sworn to myself never to fight with her—she's suffering enough as it is. So I brought her home and turned on the TV, I thought it might get the misery out of her system. Right away, though, she walked out of the room. I said I'll never bring home any more theater tickets, to add one extra drop of sorrow to your life is the last thing I want to do. She didn't answer. By then she'd stopped crying but she'd stopped talking too. And the girls weren't there to break the ice between us the way they do when they're home. She hasn't said a word about it to them because she doesn't want them to be revolted by me. Those were her words.

—Revolted by me . . . she thinks I'll revolt them . . .

—What more can I do? I've already told her that I'll never leave her. Do you hear me? I want you to know that too.

—I'm glad of that.

—I said, how can I be blamed for what happened to me? It's my fate. Did I ask for it? If it had been a woman, you couldn't be more right. You can even tell me that you'd rather it was one. That you'd have wanted it to be.

—She didn't say anything. Her father was the son of a famous rabbi in Jerusalem. Her fear goes back to that. But I'll take the sin on myself, I told her. I'll pay for it in hell, me and no one else. It's my responsibility.

—I know you don't believe in all that. But I can't take any chances at my age.

—Don't start up with me now, Tsvi. Anything is possible. I'm a wreck. What I wanted to say to her was, a minute with him is worth a thousand years in hell to me, but I didn't. What I said was, it's God who's punishing me. I might have gotten sick. Would you have liked cancer better? It's a deep thing. It came from way down within me, what could I do about it? So then she said to me in this quiet voice—are you listening?—she said, I wish to God it had been cancer. Did you hear that?

—Exactly. That's how desperate she feels.

—I wish to God it had been cancer. That's what she said.

—What?

—Right. I said to her, you're talking like a child now. This is something I may get over, but cancer I never would. I may get over it, I said, it can go away just like it came. So she said, are you crazy? It never will go away. All right, I said, suppose that I'm crazy? You can see that I kept my calm. Suppose I've gone a little crazy, I said, nowadays even crazy people get some consideration. Give me time. Maybe I'll get over it. I feel that I will. That's what I told her, although it isn't what I feel at all—if anything, it keeps getting stronger. Only that I'm telling you, not her. And then she told me that she's following us. What do you say about that?

—Not by herself. She doesn't have the nerve for that. She hired a detective. Just imagine a shy, refined woman like her walking into a private investigator's office and hiring a detective to tail us and take pictures. Have you noticed anything?

—Neither have I. But he followed us all the way to your mother. Just imagine. You didn't notice anything?

—You're laughing. Everything is a joke to you. But I was in shock. Mostly at her. That's what sheer misery will do to a person. Do you know that he photographed you in the street?

—What can I do? She's like a little girl. She tells me she knows everything. And she really does know all sorts of things that even I don't. About your father and your mother, and the names of your sister and her husband in Haifa, and your brother and his wife and her parents in Jerusalem, and all their addresses and telephone numbers. She sat reading it all out to me from a piece of paper to prove God only knows what. But I kept my temper. I said to her, you see, you know everything. If you had asked me I would have told you myself, because there's nothing I'm hiding from you. It's all out in the open. If it were a woman, I said, I might have tried to cheat on you, to do it behind your back. You don't know what some men are capable of. But since it isn't, I can be honest. Because it's not against you, and so it needn't affect you or the tie between us. I don't feel that I'm betraying you or what you are to me. It's not adultery, it's something else. You see the line I took with her. Very special, very logical, but also very true. What do you think of it?

—Exactly.

—Exactly.

—Right. That's just what I thought.

—Yes.

—And without a fuss. That's what I said to her. I'm being honest with you, why must you drag us all through the mud with detectives? It's your good name too. And it's a shame to waste all that money. Not that it concerns me, but you'd do better to buy yourself some new jewelry or a dress with it, and let me tell you whatever you want to know. Are you listening?

—No. Never mind. I have to tell you. So she said she wanted to know what you and I did and how we did it. Did you hear me? That's how desperate she is. I said what do you want to know for, the less you know, the less bad you'll feel. It's thinking about it that's hardest for you . . . you see, she thought I put it into you . . . but the reality is very human, like most things. Because whenever a person gives anything all his pain and emotion, it becomes very human. Do you get the line I took with her? You're tired . . .

—I'll be through in a minute.

—No. In a minute. I have to finish the story. The most famous people, I said to her, all kinds of celebrities, have been through this. I even mentioned a few names I had prepared for her.

—Do you think I remember? Aristotle, for example.

—What?

—Aristotle wasn't?

—Socrates? I never heard of him. I'm weak on names. I looked them up in the encyclopedia. I was sure it said Aristotle. Are you certain?

—Never mind. I just wanted to give her a few examples to cheer her up. You don't understand what this means to her. I might as well be a murderer. Her whole world has caved in. So has mine. But she's simply being destroyed while with me something new is being born.

—Fifty? She'll never see fifty again.

—No. The rest doesn't matter. She started to swear at me terribly. That's something she never dared do before. She's always been a quiet, refined woman, she's always borne herself with dignity even though she has no education—her parents never gave her any. She swore a blue streak and started to cry again.

—I didn't answer back, of course. She said she'd tell her brothers. She has two of them. One is in some high legal position.

—The name doesn't matter.

—What do you need to know it for?

—Some other time. You already know too much.

—No, some other time. Don't make an issue of it now. Please, do me that favor.

—I know, but not now.

—No. Nothing. There's nothing they can do. But I don't want them to know, because from them it will get to the whole family, and worst of all, to the girls. We'll destroy them. Give me time, I said to her, give us both enough time to catch our breaths. Then we'll see. But you must be exhausted. Get back into bed, I'll sit by your side. . . . What?

—It really interests you?

—It must seem like a joke to you. What can I do? Have a good laugh at my expense, my dear.

—No. Go ahead and laugh. Why shouldn't you. We deserve to be laughed at. We're another generation, a world you never knew. How old is your father?

—Going on sixty-five? Well, I'm not far from him then. And where did we ourselves come from? If my own father were alive now, he would want to bury himself. You'll be the death of us all.

—No, don't be angry. I didn't mean you personally. It's just that

. . . even if it's true that . . . that I had it in me all the time . . .
if I hadn't met you it would never have gone beyond a vague longing
for something that I didn't even know I was longing for. But that
there could be such a passion for . . . that there could be this way
of doing it too . . . that it was even possible and not just something
in dirty jokes . . . and then all of a sudden . . . all of a sudden
. . . What?

—No . . . all of a sudden . . . all of a sudden . . . do you hear
me? . . . all of a sudden she wanted me to make love to her, not
because she wanted it but to test me . . . What?

—Exactly. A provocation.

—Exactly. What?

—No. How could I? You must be joking. I said to her, I promise
you tomorrow. I didn't want to insult her, because it's a terrible blow
to the pride. And I haven't . . . done it with her . . . for several
months now . . . and even then it was torture too. I began to be
afraid that I might think that . . . even . . . oh . . . that her
breasts . . . it really frightened me. So I said, I'll be glad to tomorrow, but tonight I'm not up to it, the theater and all your crying
and our quarreling have just knocked me out. Tomorrow I'll do my
best. I tried to be gentle, because I'm sure she didn't want to either, I
just didn't want her to feel rejected. And suddenly she believed me
and didn't say another word. I helped her into bed and hugged her.
It was like she had used up all her strength and had none left, the
way she fell right asleep. And then I looked in her drawer and found
a photograph . . . one taken by the detective . . .

—Just a minute . . . Here it is . . .

—You didn't notice anything? What disgusting professions there
are in this world!

—I think it must be Allenby Street. Here's that store near the
branch of Bank Ha-Poalim . . . Do you see it?

—Yes. Absolutely. But whose arm are you holding there? Who is
that man? Do I know him?

—Who?

—It's the first I've heard of him. Who is he? Look how he's clinging to you!

—No. Not especially. It just seems strange to me, to see him holding on to you like that in the middle of the street.

—No. I mean in the street. It's just that . . . how long have you known him? Does he have a family?

—No. I meant a wife . . . children . . . you never mentioned him to me. I was wondering who he was. Do you see much of him? Where does he work?

—Not especially. But it makes me clutch a bit. I don't know why. Just some damn silliness. Suddenly to see a new face with you in a picture. I must be awfully on edge.

—I don't want anything from you. It's just that suddenly I . . . you know . . . I feel jealous . . . I just do. Please forgive me, Tsvi . . . my dearest . . . my love . . . I know it's ridiculous . . . but I couldn't fall asleep . . . suddenly I felt afraid of you . . .

—No . . . yes . . . afraid . . . don't laugh . . .

—No. But to do nothing but think about you all day long goes against all my beliefs . . . and yet I can't help it . . . you have a kind of power . . . sometimes it's diabolic . . .

—No . . . I beg your pardon . . . no . . . please try to understand . . . I beg your pardon. And then there's the money that I'm giving you. It frightens me too . . .

—I didn't even mention it until now, did I?

—No, but did I? Tell me.

—On the contrary. What frightens me is how much I wanted to let you have it.

—What kind of a loan? Tsvi, my dear, you know you'll never return it.

—No. Deep down I know you won't.

—Fine, so you will. It doesn't matter . . .

—You will, never mind . . . it's not that. I'm just asking you to be careful with me. I've fallen into such a bottomless pit . . . and I don't know if it isn't too much for me. This whole country is too much for me. Just don't destroy me . . . No . . . Don't make me want you too much . . . it's too dangerous. Let me go at my own pace. I can't afford to be enslaved to you. I have a home . . . children . . . responsibility . . . and you're an old hand at all this . . .

—No. Of course it's not your fault. But I feel you're an old hand . . . you may be young, but you're very experienced . . .

—No. Forgive me . . . it's just that, I'm telling you . . . that the boundaries . . . and I'm a child next to your experience . . .

the boundaries are all gone . . . it's like a wall has fallen inside me
. . . there aren't any rules anymore. And I'm afraid to ask too
much, because the more I'll know, the more frightened I'll become.
Who would have thought a few months ago that I could be jealous of
you? I thought it was just some sexual adventure . . . a little bit of
action . . . but it's already gone far beyond that. If it hadn't, everything would be all right now . . . but I fell for you . . . and now I
want you locked up in a room . . .

—I swear I don't know. I'm attracted to your whole family by
now. I was very pleased that you took me to see your mother in the
hospital. It touched me that you weren't ashamed to let me see her or
the two of you together. Your whole story . . . you know, your
father intrigues me too . . . what's happening to me? Have I fallen
in love with you? Can that be? Tell me, you know better than I do. I
know I'm not your first . . . maybe you even have a few other
Refa'el Calderons in a few other banks . . . can that be? You're
killing me. What do you want from me? Is it just the money? Tell
me. You can't just say nothing now. And don't smile . . .

—No. Inside you. I feel that you're laughing at me all the time
there.

—It's crazy for me to be talking like this. And it's almost morning.
—Right.
—But how did you spot me? How did you know? You only saw
me once or twice in the bank, and you already knew that I had it in
me. And then when we went out for lunch you put your hand on my
pants with such assurance. How did you know? I've already asked
you that, but you've never really given me an answer.
—No, no, I won't bring that up again.
—Yes. I beg your pardon. I've gone too far.
—Fine.
—All right. All right.
—I won't say another word.
—No.
—Right.
—Maybe.
—No.
—Yes. You see, what I've told you about the bank verges on a
criminal offense. If they found out about it they'd bust me right away
to some small branch—and they'd be right. Bleicher is always warn-

ing us about leaks . . . what counts most in all these transactions is
the element of surprise . . . because as soon as the word gets out,
you've lost your whole edge. That's why he's lucky to be surrounded
by us Sephardim. He knows we can be trusted to keep our mouths
shut.

—No. No, I'm not prejudiced . . . wait a minute . . . you misunderstood me . . .

—No. He said that himself. That . . . that . . .

—No. But it's an attitude. He's right. If he knew that I had relations with you . . . that I could be blackmailed . . .

—No, try to understand . . .

—No, please try to understand . . .

—No. I didn't mean that. Forgive me.

—No. Forgive me, my dearest . . . my darling . . .

—You keep telling me that and I hear every word and I believe
you. I want to believe you. But you have to understand. Even if I
don't say anything, I'm watching you just like my wife is.

—One minute . . . one minute . . . listen to me, my dear . . .
it's not as though you had a real job . . .

—No . . . one minute . . . oh God . . . what really is that investment company of yours? It's nothing. I've looked into it . . .

—One minute . . . I'm begging you to listen to me. I'm falling off
my feet. Go ahead and reassure me if you can. Go right ahead . . .

—That doesn't matter. But you have no capital. And who is this
Gilat character that you work for? A bank joke. A man who juggles
a few stocks here and there to create an optical illusion. Not that I
mind, but . . .

—Hold on a minute. Listen to me.

—I know all that. I know. But believe me, I'm a specialist in these
things. I know all about them. And I've seen more than one of these
little investment companies come and go like flies. There's no future
in them.

—I didn't say criminal. I said no future, which comes close to
criminality. Not that it's any of my business. It's just that I keep
asking myself . . . it worries me sick that maybe you took up with
me . . . that it's all . . . because otherwise why should you . . .
with an old, worn-out man like me . . . I even have wrinkles . . .

—No . . . just a minute . . . but maybe you're trying to milk
me for . . .

—Inside information. Hold on. Just tell me. I don't care. I never said I wouldn't give it to you. Just tell me if that's what you're after. I don't care. I'll tell you everything, whatever you ask for . . .

—No. I beg your pardon. Just a minute . . .

—Yes, shhh . . . excuse me, I'll lower my voice . . . but what do you need all that for? I can get you a good job in one of our branches. You wouldn't start with a high salary, but you'd be well placed and I'd see to it that you were promoted. I'd take terrific care of you from high up. Stick with me and I'll look after you like my own son . . . because that's how I feel about you . . . as though you were . . . you're the right age, after all . . . but there I go again . . .

—Yes. I'm going right away.

—No. I'm going. I've already ruined your night. My dearest . . . my love . . . my desire . . . oh God, look how I'm ranting at the mouth. I don't know what's happening to me, running around like this in the middle of the night—me, who used to be in bed at nine-thirty, after the evening news, and in my pajamas by eight. I can't go on like this. I beg your pardon, I swore I'd never cry in front of you and here I am doing it again . . . I'm on the verge of tears all the time . . . Hold it, don't move!

—Don't move! He's really there.

—I just saw him!

—The mouse ha ha ha.

—Yes. He ran behind you, by the stove. I swear he stopped to look at us. You were right.

—Hold it, don't move! Don't frighten him. By God, he's a big one. Maybe it's a rat. Or a very old mouse. He was looking at me . . .

—He's in the stove, or behind it, ha ha ha.

—Why do I find it so funny . . . ?

—You thought he was in the closet. But they like stoves.

—I guess the heat doesn't bother them.

—You need a trap and a piece of cheese.

—Leave it to me.

—Me too. But it's the killing that I mind, not the catching. I'll come to spend a night here and catch him for you. It's a real mouse ha ha . . .

—A really big one. I don't know why it makes me laugh. Ha ha ha ha. A mouse . . .

—Yes, shhh . . . I'll be going now. What would you say before
that though to a little . . . it would suit my desperate mood
splendidly . . . I could really go for it now . . . we'll make it
quick and quiet . . .

—Your father? Yes . . . but . . .

—I understand.

—Quietly . . . it would just take a minute or two . . .

—I understand. But suppose we closed the door. He's fast asleep.

—No. I understand. All right.

—I could do it by myself. If you'd just let me do it by myself . . .
you can even fall asleep beside me. All I need is your hand . . .

—It won't take me long. I'll be quiet. I need it so badly now . . .
What?

—You just have to let me lie next to you. I only need to see you
. . . even in your pajamas . . . you needn't undress . . . you
won't even feel me . . . I'll be like a bird. This whole night has
given me the most awful passion . . . I have it so bad . . . I feel all
shook up by it. What a terrible age to be! It's like you're feeling the
beginning of the end. There's an impatience with things . . . I can
understand your father so well. And it's not just physical. It's an
actual psychological need . . . what do you say?

—I don't want to pressure you.

—Never mind. You're killing me. You'll kill me in the end, but
never mind. In the end I'll come down with some terrible illness
. . . I can feel it in my bones . . . or else I'll end up like your
mother . . .

—All right. All right. You've been putting me off for a week now.
And afterwards you'll be tied up with your father.

—I'll live. I just thought . . .

—It's been at her brother's house for the last thirty years. The
whole family gets together. I'm petrified that they'll guess right away
that something is wrong. I can see already that it's going to be a very
hard seder for me. And I'll have to sing too. It gets longer and longer
every year, because her brother keeps getting more religious. Well,
never mind . . .

—Right.

—Yes . . .

—Never mind.

—I've been one my whole life, haven't I?

—My whole life . . . never mind . . .

—No. I mean that I've been a good fellow all my life. I've been a decent husband, a wonderful father, a devoted uncle, a conscientious member of the clan—and now that I want a small time-out for myself, everyone is furious with me. Tsvi? You're asleep . . .

—Yes, you are.

—It's almost three. Get into bed. I'll take a rain check. I'll just stay on a while longer with that ha ha ha mouse of yours. Maybe I'll discover where his hole is. It looks like he's moved in with you. Get into bed, turn out the light . . . I'll sit by myself in the dark . . .

—What?

—At the bank. Why do you ask?

—Phone me at the bank. And if you want those shares, just let me know. I'll take out an option for you.

—Fine. We'll talk about it tomorrow. I mean today. Don't forget that it's Friday. I quit work at one.

—When?

—You want me to wait for you downstairs? I know where it is.

—No problem.

—Let's leave it open. I'm dying to know what you do with him. What you talk about. Is it ever about me?

—I understand. Do you think he could see me sometime too?

—All right. It's something to think about. Try to find out.

—All day?

—When is he going back?

—No. To America.

—Shhh. How can you talk like that?

—Don't expect me to believe you.

—What???

—How can you talk like that? Just the thought of it! If words could kill, there wouldn't be a living soul left in this world. You're groggy. Go to bed. I won't be working on the day of the seder. If you'd like, I can drive you up north.

—That morning.

—Think it over. I'll be glad to do it.

—All right. Now go to sleep. We'll at least be in touch by phone. Thank you for having sat up with me. For being so patient. You're so good to me. I swear, I knocked just like a little bird and you woke up right away . . .

—Go to sleep. You have some hard days ahead of you.

—Never mind, turn out the light. I have the key. I'll lock up when I go. Don't you remember giving it to me a month ago?

—I know I returned it. But I made myself a duplicate.

—In case you might be sick or something and couldn't get out of bed.

—Let me keep it. It makes me feel better about you. I'll never let myself in when you're not here. You can have it back whenever you want.

—Yes.

—No.

—Maybe.

—Fine.

—Don't worry. I won't touch you. Maybe sitting here and thinking will calm me down. I've become like a child again. I'm having a second childhood . . .

—Good night, my dear. Until tomorrow. Just let me give you one hug . . . one kiss . . .

—It's not Tsvi, Mr. Kaminka, but it's all right.

—It's all right, Mr. Kaminka. I'm a friend of his. Tsvi knows that I'm here.

—He's asleep now, but it's all right. We were just having a chat.

—No. Who's Yosef? I'm Refa'el Calderon. He's never mentioned me? We do business together.

—No. I work in a bank.

—I was just passing by and dropped in to chat.

—Refa'el Calderon. I dropped by to help him with something . . . with a mouse . . .

—No, don't be alarmed. There's a mouse here ha ha ha. We just saw him a few minutes ago. Tsvi's known about him for several days, but wasn't sure where he was hiding. So I told him the best thing was to wait for him at night, in the dark. He's a little squeamish, and I don't mind such things. I grew up in the old Jewish quarter of Jerusalem—we were used to mice there . . .

—Yes, a real mouse. It's nothing to be scared of. If you ask me, it's an old one that may have been living here for a long time. It's odd, though, how it should have managed to get up here . . . because you're on the third floor . . .

—A dog?

—Ah, the dog we saw there. I remember him.

—In the hospital.

—I drove Tsvi up there on Tuesday.

—Calderon. Refa'el Calderon.

—No. I didn't take part in their conversation. I was standing off to one side. It was then that I noticed the dog. A big fat one with a tawny coat.

—Yes. Exactly. I thought it was some hospital dog that she had gotten friendly with.

—It lived here? Then you couldn't have had a mouse. A dog would have gotten it.

—Of course. How long has this apartment been yours, if I may be so free as . . .

—Well now, that's quite a while. But please, don't let me bother you. It's very late, and there's nothing to catch a mouse with now anyway.

—Nearly three o'clock. . . . How's that?

—Your wife? In what way?

—No. I was off to the side and didn't hear anything. I know nothing about it . . . What's that?

—Yes. Tsvi had spoken of it vaguely . . . you've come to separate.

—Begging your pardon?

—Yes. To get divorced. Something of the sort. I didn't really discuss it with him. I just drove him up there because the public transportation is so poor.

—In what way?

—I didn't notice anything. She talked sensibly enough. In fact, at first I didn't even know where I was taking Tsvi. I thought it was to some home for the elderly or something . . . I don't know the northern part of the country at all . . .

—Yes. Yes. In the end I realized that it was no home for the elderly.

—From a Jerusalem family. Third generation.

—Exactly. A thoroughbred Sephardi, you might say.

—She is? You don't say. You don't say.

—Half of one? On her mother's side? How didn't I sense it? I always do. I never would have thought . . . she doesn't look it in the least . . . you don't say!

—Come again?

—Abrabanel. Of course. It's a well-known family.

—From Safed? But there was a branch of them in Jerusalem too. How curious. Tsvi never said a word about it. That explains to me something about myself. So Tsvi is also part . . . very interesting! Most agreeable.

—Begging your pardon? No, I just . . .

—The way I talk? In what way?

—I never noticed.

—That's odd. My girls also tell me that I sometimes talk strangely.

—Hebrew too. But not exclusively. I had one grandmother who spoke only Ladino.

—Just Hebrew. There are two girls.

—They're grown up already. I don't know why I keep calling them girls.

—Going on twenty-three. They're twins. Beautiful, fair-skinned girls, you'd never know that they came from a Middle Eastern family. Almost blond . . .

—I'm sorry to say that I was never blessed with a son . . .

—Begging your pardon?

—A Sephardi expression? I didn't know there was such a thing. I thought we all spoke the same Hebrew.

—In what way? I never noticed.

—Yes. We were always careful with our diction.

—A mixture? You may be right.

—I've never paid it much attention. Whatever comes to mind. One takes one's words where one finds them. You're right. Everything today is all mixed up. We live in a mixed-up age . . .

—Now that you mention it. I never thought of it before.

—Mostly newspapers. I have no time for books. Tsvi told me that your field is Hebrew language and style. That explains your ear for it.

—In the investment department of Barclay's Bank. It's an affiliate of the Israel Discount Bank. But I'm truly sorry for keeping you up. Very truly. Tsvi told me how tired out you were by the flight from America. I remember how he called his sister in Haifa several times on Sunday and kept being told that you were still asleep.

—Are you sure?

—For me it's a lost night anyway. I couldn't get any sleep. The later it gets, the more awake I become. But why should you have to stay up because of me . . .

—Yes. It's a hot night. It's suddenly gotten very hot, almost summery. To think that it rained just last night!

—Tea? Surely. I'll put up some water.

—Yes, yes. I know my way around this kitchen. I already said to Tsvi tonight, you Russians like your tea in the middle of the night. We only drink it when we're down with the flu. Black coffee is our brew.

—No, it's no trouble. I'll make it. I know where everything is. There are some chocolate cookies too that I bought yesterday. But perhaps you'd like to drink your tea alone. I'll be on my way then . . . it's a shame for you to lose sleep . . .

—Not at all. It's my pleasure to sit here with you.

—Thank you very much. I believe you've been here for nearly a week, haven't you?

—Yes. I remember. Saturday night. I'm curious to know how you find this country now . . . what you think of it . . .

—In what way?

—That's very interesting. You may be right. When one lives here, one doesn't notice the change.

—Really?

—Yes. All the filth . . . of course . . .

—That too. But don't forget that it's only half a peace. People don't put much credence in it. I myself know nothing about politics. Generally I support the government, whatever it is. I get annoyed when people try obstructing it . . .

—Yes, the one we have now too . . . although I must say . . .

—Yes. A sense of gloom.

—Yes. But it's mostly just talk. Believe me, people are rolling in money. I know them by what they have to invest, not by what they have to say. If it weren't confidential, I could show you now with a pocket calculator what sums are in circulation in this country and who is doing the circulating. Some of them are listed as welfare cases. I get felafel vendors coming to me with wads of five-hundred-pound notes, still smelling of cooking oil. That's why I'm not so critical . . .

—Yes. That's so. There is a group that suffers.

—I hope not.

—We true, old-time Sephardim aren't your troublemakers from North Africa. They really have a wild streak in them . . . and sometimes we're confused with them on TV . . . but we're actually a well-established middle class. You'll find us mainly in the banks, the courts and the police—not at the very top, but in responsible positions. Wherever there's still a semblance of law and order. It goes back to British and even Turkish times, when we were sought out for administrative posts. For desk jobs. That's where we feel best. I once said to Tsvi, this business of a Jewish state, all of Zionism in fact, is really a little too much for us. It's all too fast, too high-powered. We were used to the Turkish pace, to the British sense of decorum . . .

—Yes. I know I'm really talking nonsense. Every country is like that today. Even Turkey is coming apart at the seams—I've read about it in the newspapers. All the lights in Istanbul go out every evening. I suppose that only the English . . .

—The English too? You don't say. Well, well, then there's really no cause to complain . . .

—For about half a year. We met in the bank.

—Yes. It's a sort of investment company.

—His boss's name is Gilat. Have you ever met him?

—Yes, of course, you haven't been in the country. I forgot. I've run into him once or twice. A young, energetic fellow who knows how to play the market. I just hope he doesn't do anything foolish. For Tsvi's sake. All these little firms take lots of risks, but sometimes they grow very nicely. Maybe this one will too, who knows? It's just that the market itself is so volatile these days . . .

—I think Tsvi has a good head for it. He's ready to learn. He's always asking me questions. He has imagination too, and that's important. But one needs a great deal of experience and patience. One has to develop a sixth sense.

—Of course. There's that too.

—No. It's not a science. There's probably nothing that's less scientific. One needs to have a sixth sense. A feeling of what to hold on to and what to let go of, of where to step in and where to lay back. The Israeli market is a small one. Everyone has a finger in it. All kinds of amateurs have gone into it lately too, and that's an extra headache.

Inflation makes the profits seem large but in fact they're on the small side. It's not a big ball game. I don't know how much you know about these things . . .

—In America it's a different story. There you have real gamblers. Not the Jews. They're all over, but strictly in a service capacity. But you'll find some tough, cold-blooded Gentiles who'll risk everything they have on one throw of the dice and calmly step out for a drink while they're rolling. The market's wide open there. A stock can hit bottom . . . practically go below zero . . . or take off all at once like a rocket. Here we're more cautious. And the government interferes a lot too. It can suddenly feel sorry for some company because it has a plant in a depressed area or directors who are friends of a minister. And we're a nervous people in general, we don't know how to hold on to a stock. We're afraid to go for the big gain, because we don't really believe in it. All that will come, though . . . things are just beginning to warm up . . . Is the tea too strong for you?

—The sugar cubes? They're here in the closet. Tsvi likes to suck on them too. Here, is this what you mean?

—No. But I've been here often . . . and I've seen him drink tea like that, with a cube of sugar in his mouth. I suppose he learned from you.

—Yes. Yes. All in all he's just like you. I've already told him that. I too came to look more and more like my father, rest his soul. All of a sudden the resemblance breaks out.

—Right.

—Exactly.

—Begging your pardon?

—Yes. Tsvi told me. It's really a nice apartment. It must be worth quite a few million. The location is excellent, and there are people with money today who are coming back to the city and looking for places to renovate. How far can the ocean be from here? A hundred meters? It does need some work. When there's no woman around, the little things go untended . . .

—How's that?

—Yes. That isn't Tsvi's strong point. What can you expect from a young man these days . . . ?

—Still . . .

—Still. Don't exaggerate. He hasn't seen thirty yet.

—To sell? What for?

—Ah.

—I understand.

—I understand. I see. In principle let me tell you right away that I don't recommend it. I don't recommend it one bit. Not at all, if you're asking me.

—Yes yes. I know. I hear about it every day . . . the most astonishing stories, both kinds of them, about those who made a mint and about those who lost their shirts . . .

—Yes. So I've heard. But here I'm a wee bit conservative. A house isn't just money. It's a home.

—That may be so . . . but I'd still think twice about it . . .

—A car is something else. Don't misunderstand me. A car is something else. When I've seen some opening for a good investment I've advised lots of clients to sell a car, or jewelry, or even the family silver without a moment's thought. But a house . . .

—Yes. But in spite of all that it's a house. You never know.

—But why?

—Ah.

—Ah.

—And Tsvi?

—Ah.

—You think she'll be released someday?

—Aha.

—Begging your pardon?

—In what way?

—I . . . uh . . .

—Begging your pardon?

—No . . . come again?

—Yes . . . something of the sort . . . I mean . . . I didn't know whether you knew or not . . . I didn't dare . . .

—Begging your pardon?

—Yes. I was a bit frightened. I wasn't sure what you knew and what you didn't. And suddenly . . .

—I understand.

—I didn't know.

—I didn't know at all.

—I thought as much.

—I understand.

—Now I understand . . .

—I see. Thank you . . .

—I didn't know. I was suddenly afraid . . . for Tsvi . . .

—Since adolescence? I understand. I suppose that . . .

—Your wife too? How interesting!

—The whole family . . . I understand . . . I'd so like to hear more about it. It fascinates me. Are the others happily married?

—No. I meant are they normal.

—Yes. He told me about him. I haven't had the pleasure of meeting him, but I've been told that he's very gifted. He teaches at the university in Jerusalem . . .

—No.

—Yes.

—No.

—Yes. Naturally I thought that you must know something. I didn't know how you felt about it, though . . . so that when suddenly you came down the hallway in the dark . . . I was frightened . . .

—I'm glad to hear that.

—That's a very sensible way of looking at it. Very refined. No, that isn't the word. What I mean is considerate. So terribly human . . .

—Yes. I'm glad to hear that. Thank you so much.

—I know. That's easy to say. But if I were in your place, Mr. Kaminka . . . I . . . well, never mind. I myself am a novice at this. Until recently I hardly knew that it existed. I never . . . it was Tsvi who introduced me to it. It's all so new to me . . . and at my age . . . that's why I must seem so nervous and distraught to you. This whole last period of my life has been one flood of emotion . . . it's all so new to me . . .

—Just a few months ago . . . after the autumn holidays . . . until then I was perfectly normal. I didn't even know that . . . how can I put it? . . . that it was in me all along. That it was even a possibility. It's only now that it's surfaced that I can look back and see signs of it since I was a boy. Still, it's been a great upheaval . . .

—In the bank. He used to come by my office, because his firm does business with us. He saw through me just from how I talked.

—Just a few days ago . . .

—No. Only my wife.

—It's been very difficult. A real tragedy. You understand that. Very difficult. A terrible tragedy. So distressing.

—No. Absolutely not. It would be the end of both her and me. I can't even imagine it. I could never leave her. Her whole family would murder me.

—Begging your pardon?

—I don't know. Deep down I keep hoping that I'll get over it. That I'm just going through a phase.

—I'm going on fifty-six. I was born in 1923. I'm not much younger than you.

—Yes. You can imagine how this has jolted me. Maybe in America such things are taken more for granted . . . I'm reading an article about it now . . . even among Jews . . .

—Exactly. I've heard about that synagogue in New York. God is truly all-suffering if He can put up with that too.

—You don't say! It's entertaining to read in the evening papers about all the oddballs in this world, but when it suddenly turns up in you . . . when I think of everything I believed in . . . you know, I'm from a religious family myself, I still keep up the traditions. Of course, religion with us isn't as serious a matter as with you . . .

—Yes, I know. But I was thinking of those of you who are. We don't get so ideological about things. You won't ever find us making martyrs of ourselves or of others for some idea. In politics, if you've noticed, we're the first to cross party lines or change sides . . . but when it comes to family affairs, we're terribly uptight. And I'm very much a family man. The family is everything to us. That's the Middle East in us, the family and its honor. We're very uptight about honor. Power doesn't interest us, but honor does, because there was never enough of it in this part of the world. For that we'd go out and kill . . . in theory, I mean . . . I'm not sure you follow me . . .

—I feel that I'm going to cry . . . I beg your pardon, Mr. Kaminka . . . it keeps happening . . . perhaps I'm disturbing you . . .

—I thank you.

—I thank you kindly. Take tonight. I've never had such awful insomnia before. You'll understand me if I tell you that when Tsvi told me about you I said to him, I'm just like your father, only worse. We're a generation that caught fire late . . . maybe the emotions that we feel are a substitute for something else . . . maybe they're in place of some more basic crisis of values. Because we've been a conformist generation. Very conformist, haven't we? Eh?

—In the sense that we never allowed ourselves any crises the way young people, or even older ones, allow themselves today. And we had no generation before us to hand us our crises ready-made the way they're handed nowadays to twenty- and thirty- and forty-year-olds, who are so spoiled that they expect to get a new crisis every week. We're not like that, are we?

—There was no one to do it for us. The old folks kept us on a tight leash.

—Do you mean that seriously? You really find it interesting? It makes me so happy that you understand. I'm not an educated man. Not at all. But I can't help thinking a bit now and then.

—No. They're just little thoughts. Just beginnings. What I must try to understand, though, is why all this has flared up so powerfully, so destructively. All the pain that we're spreading around us . . . when I think what will happen when my two girls find out . . .

—But they're still only twenty-two. What's twenty-two? My father, rest his soul, still whipped me at that age . . .

—I swear, he sometimes did. But it's not just the girls. I'm talking about the whole family. About the old folks too, because we still have them. Yours, you understand, were all killed or left behind in Europe. They don't keep bugging you. You've made your peace with them. You were stronger than they were anyway, and you did what you wanted. Now you have your nostalgic memories, but that's just for the record . . . on Saturday nights you dress up like them on TV in black caftans and beards, and it isn't a bad feeling . . . but if you were suddenly to find them in your living room along with that whole ghetto of theirs, you'd be in a state of shock. Well, with us they're in the house all the time . . .

—A few of them have died, but only recently. Until my father passed away last year I used to go see him practically every day after work. And my wife's mother still lives with my wife's brother in Jerusalem . . . not to mention various aunts here and there who know everything and are told everything and spend the whole day on the telephone, now that they've learned to use it, calling up the whole country. I have one aunt whose monthly phone bill is twenty thousand pounds. That's the equivalent of a small bank branch's . . .

—If you're the type who can travel. But I'm not. Where should I go? Three years ago we went to Europe for a month, and by the end of it I was dying to get back here. Maybe this summer I'll try Egypt for two weeks. We only eat kosher food, and that makes it difficult too . . .

—Yes. I understand you. I certainly do. But where to? In Europe we feel like strangers, even though I speak French. But the air there, that grayness all the time . . . who knows, maybe one day soon the Middle East will open up to us and we'll be able to vacation among the Arabs . . .

—Begging your pardon?

—Yes. When the Messiah comes ha ha. But one mustn't lose faith . . . if only they were a little more civilized. I can't tell you how sympatico you are, Mr. Kaminka. I knew I'd like you. We've been excited since the moment we heard you were coming. It was I who brought Tsvi to the airport Saturday night, but I didn't stay, because I didn't want to intrude. Even tonight I had qualms about dropping in. Your family story attracts me greatly . . . yesterday when Tsvi took me up there to see your wife . . . I was very moved . . . there I was, after feeling that my own family was too much for me, suddenly ready to take on another . . .

—Who?

—What's his name?

—Zhid? A Jew?

—Ah, Gide. A Frenchman.

—A homosexual? I've never heard of him. Was he an important author?

—I've never heard of him.

—Really, he said that? That's very extreme.

—Well, that's not for me. I'm a family man . . . and because of Tsvi . . . because I've gotten so attached to him . . . because I love him . . . and now you too . . .

—What can I do?

—I'm sure he has a future. But he needs looking after. He worries me too. Sometimes I wonder whether he's really suited to the market.

—Yes. He keeps flitting from one thing to another. It is a bit childish . . . but he's still young . . .

—Still . . .

—Still. I would have thought it more advisable for him to take a steady job in the bank. There's a great future in banking. I could have placed him well and seen to his being promoted . . . discreetly, from high up . . . don't underestimate me, I'm a power in the bank . . . my word carries great weight there. I could have taken care of him . . . like a father . . . like his own daddy . . . because after all, you're so far away . . . at the moment, I mean . . .

—Begging your pardon? Come again?

—Yes. I've lent him some money now and then . . . helped him with some difficult transactions . . .

—Yes. It worries me too.

—I don't believe that. No. Don't tell me that, Mr. Kaminka. I have complete confidence in him. Don't tell me . . . and I have his IOUs . . . he'll always be liable . . . no, don't tell me . . . you frighten me . . .

—What makes you say that?

—Yes. I agree. But I can't turn him down. You have to understand, that's my only happiness these days . . .

—I don't want to hear about it. I'll keep a closer eye on him. I'll be more careful. But don't you see, I love him . . . no . . . don't tell me . . .

—You're so sure of yourself. So forthright. It takes a daring man to pick up and leave his family like you did. You must have a great deal of courage . . . although sometimes I ask myself . . .

—I mean . . . I can't help wondering . . . well, never mind . . .

—I mean . . . I beg your pardon . . . I know it's none of my business, but I can't help wondering if it's really necessary for you to get divorced . . . even though . . . that is, I've been thinking of another possibility . . . but of course it's none of my business . . .

—Begging your pardon?

—I don't understand.

—Would you say that again?

—I beg your pardon?

—Are you serious?

—But how? You must mean figuratively . . . in a manner of speaking . . .

—What? I don't understand . . . I beg your pardon . . . one minute . . .

—Here? Where?

—In this kitchen?

—I beg your pardon?

—No. I didn't know about it. Or maybe just a little bit . . . I mean, I no longer know what I really know about you and what I would like to know. Tsvi talks too much, and of course I listen to him . . . it's none of my business, but I do. That's his style, to say whatever is on his mind. It's all so free with you people . . . you have the confidence, the uninhibitedness . . . or maybe it's the innocence . . . you can afford it. Perhaps it's because you stopped believing in God so long ago that there's not a drop of Him left in you. We simply hide things. We're always trying to hide them. The fact is that I did know something about it, but I thought she had merely threatened you, the way people sometimes do . . . that she went crazy for a moment, the way we all can when we're under mental stress. I'm sure she didn't mean it. I saw her, such a refined woman . . . I beg your pardon for intruding, but I'm sure she didn't mean it . . .

—With a knife? No, don't tell me . . .

—I don't believe it. Do you really mean it? I suppose she just waved it about . . .

—Where? Yes, I see a line. But are you sure it's from that?

—I understand. I beg your pardon.

—I understand.

—She must have been under great stress. But what did the rabbis say? Blame not the man who sins in his grief . . .

—Yes.

—It was really right here? And Tsvi witnessed it? It must have been excruciating for him.

—I'm listening.

—Me?

—What would I have done? What can I tell you? In the end I'd have forgiven her. In the end I know I would have. One has to forgive, Mr. Kaminka. One has to think in terms of forgiveness. We're Jews. And there are so few of us that we can't afford not to. If only for the children's sake . . .

—I meant your children.

—It's none of my business, absolutely none of my business, but since you ask . . . and I've become so attached to you . . .

—Yes. I know that there's going to be a baby there. You can see that Tsvi tells me everything. But what can you do? I understand your problem, but there's no point in insisting if she refuses. That's my advice . . . financially you only stand to lose that way. She still has her possessions here . . . I saw her dresses in the closet. It's always difficult to make a clean break . . . and sometimes it's better not to . . . Oops, there it goes again! Just a minute, don't move ha ha ha, it's come out. It must be somewhere over there . . .

—Behind you. It was peeking out at us as though it were listening.

—It must have gone back beneath the burners. They should be taken apart and fumigated inside. If you ask the city to do it, they'll only do the outside. They'll scatter a little poison and that's all.

—There's no need to. I'll take care of it myself.

—No. Not of killing him. That revolts me too. Just of catching him.

—A trap is the best way. Meanwhile try to keep all the food covered. Don't leave anything out. You don't want to eat from his mouth.

—All right. I'll be on my way. Will you still be here tomorrow?

—Yes. I meant today.

—It's already past three. How quiet the city is now. Suddenly I can feel all my tiredness. I'm sorry to have been such a nuisance . . .

—I know. There's a breeze coming up. When do you expect the ceremony to be?

—The di . . .

—Yes.

—Will there be time for it on the day of the seder? The rabbis agreed to it then? Tsvi said you spoke to them this morning.

—Yesterday morning, I beg your pardon. I'm totally disoriented . . . What's that, the telephone?

—It must be my wife. I'm sure of it. Let me have it for a second.

—Yes. She knows the number here. She found it out . . . just a second . . .

—Hello?

—She hung up.

—No. I'm absolutely sure it was her.

—I hope to God that I'm wrong. But I know it was her. She woke up and saw I wasn't there. I'm sure of it . . .

—Let me have it . . . just a second . . . Hello? Hello? . . . She hung up again.

—No. I'm sure of it. It's her. I'm going. If it rings again, don't answer. Say I wasn't here. There it is again . . . I'll take it . . . if it's for you, I'll let you have it . . .

—Hello? Hello?

—Just a minute . . . oh my God . . .

—Have you gone out of your mind? What happened?

—Nothing. I was just passing by.

—Please.

—I beg of you.

—All right.

—All right.

—Fine.

—Whatever you say.

—I'm already on my way home. I couldn't fall asleep.

—What makes you say that?

—No. I'm with his father.

—You'd be surprised.

—I swear.

—As I hope to die.

—No. As I hope to die. By my own dead father.

—It's not what you think.

—That's enough. I beg of you.

—We can be heard.

—Yes. Just a minute . . .

—All right. I'm already half out the door.

—You don't understand.

—You don't even begin to understand.

—All right.

—All right.

—Stop. That's enough.

—I know I'm to blame.

—Only me. I told you.

—All right.

—Later.

—All right. Later.

—How can you say that?

—What an idea!

—You're out of your mind.

—So do I.

—How can you say that?

—I'm listening.

—Not. It's not that.

—I beg you. We can be heard.

—I'll be a sick man from this. I beg you.

—How can you . . . that's insane . . .

—Cut off your breasts . . . ?!

—Whatever you say . . .

—I promise.

—It's too strong for me but I'll get over it . . . I'm in love . . . Give me time . . .

—You can take who . . . ?

—That's fine with me.

—Whatever you say.

—All right.

—Not now.

—Not now.

—So do I.

—Never. Don't you dare.

—All right. Later.

—Then I'll never come home again.

—No. Right away. In ten minutes. I had one foot out the door when you called.

—Don't call again. Promise me.

—I'm hanging up.

—I'm hanging up.

—I'm hanging up.

—I'm hanging up.

—No. He's asleep. There's only his father.

—I swear by the girls.

—You'll pay for this.

—Enough. I've hung up . . .

—It was for me, Tsvi.

—Yes. It was her. I'm sorry, I shouldn't have stayed so long. But everything will be all right. If she calls again, tell her that I'm gone.

Don't talk to her. Goodbye, Mr. Kaminka. I don't know if we'll meet again.

—Yes. Perhaps at the airport. You're flying back Monday night?

—Perhaps. That's a good idea. For sure.

—I'll wait for you there at five.

—I'll live. I'll wait for you at five. Don't worry about me. And in the meantime, good luck. Enough, I'd better get going. I'm so sorry. I didn't even mean to drop in. I just happened to pass by, I knocked like a bird, and you went and heard me . . .

FRIDAY, FOUR
TO FIVE P.M.

We did not sober up, casting off our blindness,
until my father was served up in a dish. He lay
in it, large and distended from cooking, in a
pale grayish aspic, while we sat there as silent
as fish.

Bruno Schulz

"I wonder if I should confess that today I actually felt a twinge of
impatience to see you. I wasn't late this time either, did you notice?"

"Of course."

"Of course . . . of course . . . I needn't have asked. Here I am,
I suppose you must be thinking, caught more and more in your net,
corked in your test tube, pigeonholed in your file cabinet . . . and
yet, if I may comment in a brief parenthesis, your optimism is pre-
mature. How long is it now that I've been coming to you? Two or
three months . . . and each time I've said to myself, well, this is the
last: it's time to end the game, pay the bill and say goodbye. And
apropos the bill, by the way, I haven't asked you yet what you charge
for the right to blabber away here . . . and for the honor, of
course . . ."

"One thousand five hundred."

"Not bad . . . not bad at all . . . but not unreasonable either.

Really not so steep. Some of your colleagues are far more avaricious. I'll pay the bill, then, and we'll part amicably. Oh, I'll pay it, don't worry about that. That is, I think I will . . . yes, I believe I may . . . after all, why shouldn't I? You deserve it . . . if only for having controlled yourself and never made me get to the point. But do you really think I can be trusted to pay you?"

"I think you can be."

"Good for you. Blessed are the faithful. No, don't be alarmed. You needn't think that I take your confidence in me as an undiluted compliment. But I will pay you. And after that, we'll see. . . . The main thing is to have done this too. To have been through it. Because two people can't conduct a civilized conversation nowadays without sooner or later broaching the subject of I and My Shrink, or My Shrink and I. With a mysterious smile and a gleam in one's eye one trades experiences, technical details, fees, descriptions of offices . . . But broaching it only, mind you. It's no disgrace to admit it anymore, but there's still a limit to what can be revealed. And so now I'll be able to join the fun too with my own little adventure. I too was there. And what I found was part shopworn clichés, part sophisticated jargon and part slightly original rephrasing of old, familiar problems. A fifty-minute beauty treatment for one's dried-out ego . . . but harmless. And incapable of causing any harm. With your kind permission, then, I'll withdraw my previous objections."

"Then you did have objections?"

"Up to a point. And please rest assured that I'm perfectly aware of what they meant. My friends couldn't wait to tear into me and explain that any resistance in these matters simply reflects on the resister. I've run into that kind of sophistry before . . . the automatic incorporation of all opposition to a system into the system itself. Oh, it's very clever . . . but as I was saying, I'm officially willing to withdraw my objections as a gesture of social good will. I've paid good money for the privilege of finding out that the system can't do any harm . . . at least not at the hands of the charming young gentleman who has taken me on this brief tour of it . . . and has been kind enough to listen patiently to a stranger like me without betraying the least sign of boredom . . . except, of course, for glancing at his watch once or twice during each session. Yes, and who has been so careful not to be provoked by me . . . is that a smile I detect?"

"Is that another provocation?"

"Perhaps. As you like. But I see that it's simply water off a duck's back. You're an expert at the time-honored technique of returning all questions to the asker for further embellishment. A man who won't commit himself. Who takes care never to involve himself. (Perhaps, I might add in a small parenthesis, because there isn't much to involve, eh?) But still . . . a fair and by no means unintelligent person whom I've done my best to entertain. Normality incarnate has listened to me sympathetically, and since it's offered me a cozy easy chair, a quiet, civilized room and a suitable time . . . well, then . . ."

"Suitable? How so?"

"I mean the time of day that you agreed to see me at, Friday afternoon from four to five. Is there a pleasanter one? Tel Aviv has quieted down, the banks are shut, the buses have nearly stopped running, the crowds are gone, there are less women in the streets too . . . many less. The stores are closed also, though not all of them. Here and there you still can find some old irreligious grocer to sell you a squashed hallah and a liter of milk, or some boutique that goes merrily on selling its flimsy, latest-fashion sport shirts. It's a time for the nut and flower vendors, their stalls surrounded by the heavy weekend papers piled high on the sidewalks . . . a lovely in-between time in which the old week is slowly being packed away. What we haven't managed to do in it will never get done in it now, and the possibilities of the new week don't seem very pressing yet. Even the stock exchange goes into the deep freeze for forty-five long, intractable hours . . . and yet it's still a weekday . . . a sacred one, though. The sad, stupid Sabbath with its hymns and sermons and long looks hasn't arrived yet with that oppressive sense that you're somehow losing out if you don't do something in a hurry. It's a time when, rain or shine, I like to cruise the streets of the north side, not far from the sea . . . to run into the slow singles walking more erectly now because the world suddenly weighs on them less . . . into the lost souls of all sexes whom life has excused from the compulsory family meal . . . a most pleasant time to come to see you, and above all, to leave your office at. It came as a great surprise that you agreed to take me at it . . . in no small measure that's why I chose you . . . I'm just curious to know whether I'm the week's last case or whether you go on working like a beaver right into the Sabbath . . ."

"Would you like to be the last case?"

"Love to. I'm dying to be the last. I've thought several times of hiding behind the stairway to see if anyone came after me, but I didn't want to involve you in a scandal with the neighbors. Yes, I'd be thrilled to know I was the last . . . to be able to think that as soon as I walked out of here the door opened and in came your wife sighing, 'The weekend at last! Is that curly, handsome queer of yours gone? Come, there's cauliflower for supper!' "

"Cauliflower?"

"I smelled it coming up the stairs. Perhaps she hasn't told you yet. You're in for a surprise."

"Do you like cauliflower?"

"I hate it."

"And is that really how you think of yourself—a handsome, curly queer?"

"Curly and handsome, in that order. I'm simply stating a fact."

"Yes. I understand that. I simply wanted to know if that's how you thought of yourself . . . if it was your self-image."

"That's how others think of me too."

"Are you sure?"

"I think so. Do you doubt it?"

"I was only asking."

"But what was I saying . . . you had interrupted me . . ."

"You were saying that because of the suitable hour, the easy chair, the room . . ."

". . . I kept being drawn back here despite my decision to stop."

"And these externals are all that . . . keeps making you come back?"

"The whole atmosphere."

"Yes. The whole atmosphere. Only that?"

"Of course not only that. You too have been clever enough to leave some loose thread at the end of every session . . . some nagging question to bait me with. You'll cut me short in the middle of an idea or even a sentence in order to get me to return . . . you always make sure to leave some buoy afloat for me above the confusion of the week . . . which is why I've kept forgetting to tender you my resignation . . ."

"Forgetting?"

"Yes, yes . . . though I know that there's no such thing as forgetting in this room . . . that everything is significant. My tense young brother, you know, claims that all of human history, the whole hideous compendium of human misery, can be reduced to a few simple laws that he intends to discover. And he will discover them, I have no doubt of it . . . he'll come up with something. All these significance freaks amuse me no end. . . . But what did I want to say?"

"You were saying that this time . . ."

"What about it?"

". . . you felt impatient to see me."

"Righto. Listen, you really do hear and remember everything. You don't lose track of the thread in my wildest associations. I suppose you're glad to be told that I've become less indifferent toward you, maybe even more dependent."

"Do you think that I want you to be dependent on me?"

"Why shouldn't you? It's natural. I like to attach people to me also—provided, of course, that the attachment can always be broken. There are lots of people who would like to tie me to their apron string too."

"Such as?"

"There's a long list of them."

"Your father, for one . . ."

"My father? No, he turned me loose long ago. When the string got too tangled for him. Now he's trying to steal a page from my book and be a free soul like me. You should have seen him getting off the plane . . ."

"He's really here, then?"

"Of course. Why shouldn't he be? A reconditioned father with a brand-new style. Youthful movements, a floppy, offbeat hat, even a snappy-looking valise. What else? Oh, yes, a long mane of hair in the back and color-coordinated clothing that some young lady must have picked out for him. My sister and brother-in-law were waiting for him in the terminal, but I had gone up to the observation deck to get a bird's-eye view . . . to see this sixty-four-year-old psychosexual renovation job step out on Israeli soil and take his first gulp of its humid, gray evening air . . . and above all, to watch him put on his self-pitying mask before passport control . . . our poor murder victim . . ."

"I'm sorry, I didn't catch that."

"It was nothing."

"Didn't you add something under your breath at the end? I didn't hear it."

"No, nothing . . . I was just . . ."

"But you did say something?"

"It's not important."

"Does he make you angry?"

"Not in the least. You're barking up the wrong tree, come down from it. . . . Do I sound angry to you? You're missing the whole point about my relationship with him. He simply doesn't matter to me anymore."

"I had thought that was the reason for your impatience today . . . that you wanted to talk about him . . ."

"But why? You've got your preconceived theories and you have to fit me into them. Father-son relations, oedipal conflicts, primal entanglements . . . I'm sorry to have to spoil it all for you . . ."

"Last session you didn't stop talking about him. You were very tense about his coming."

"Maybe I was. I wouldn't deny it. But it turns out to have been wasted emotion. As far as I'm concerned, his visit hasn't even begun yet . . ."

"In what sense?"

"In the sense that almost a week has gone by without our seeing each other. There was a typical, sentimental Kaminkean moment when he came through customs into the night. We hugged each other hard . . . somewhat harder than I had counted on . . . we even had tears in our eyes, although the real crying was courtesy of my sister. She's been the family's fount of tears ever since childhood. Her lawyerman stood smiling off to one side—I don't believe he even has tear glands. . . . But all this happened very quickly. It had begun to drizzle too. At which point, in the middle of all the suitcases and the packages and the small talk about the flight and the meals and the not having slept, a new leitmotiv emerged: his resemblance to me and mine to him. The three years that had gone by had apparently closed the physical gap between us. I had matured a bit . . . perhaps grown slightly stooped . . . my head had a more profound tilt to it . . . while he'd lost weight, let his curls grow out, and adopted this youthful style. Maybe I had even served as his model from afar. In

short, there were his and my genes showing through at last with a
smile of mutual recognition. The lawyerman couldn't get over it. All
he kept saying was 'Wow! I never knew the two of you looked so
alike!' "

"Did that upset you?"

"Not exactly. But it was a good reason to be glad that we soon
split up. They took him up north with them right away. After all,
there's a reason for this rushed trip of his: the long-promised divorce
. . . the legal termination of their hundred-year war . . ."

"And has it gone through already?"

"Next Sunday, God willing . . . or more precisely, God able. But
I'm not at all sure that He will be able, because so far there's been
nothing but disasters. They've been going about it in the most ass-
backwards, roundabout way, making every possible mistake. To begin with, instead of going straight to her by himself, even on that first
night, throwing himself at her feet and declaring, 'Here I am, you
summoned me . . . forgive me . . . I'm unworthy of you . . . it's
I who have been the true madman . . . ,' he went and fell into a
gargantuan slumber in my sister's house. For a whole day. After
which he sent that comical lawyerman to get her to sign the agreement. I warned them on the phone not to let that joker go alone
because he would screw up everything, but he insisted on it, and
came back that evening totally befuddled. She had made a complete
fool of him. . . . Then on Tuesday, still instead of seeing her by
himself and confessing, 'Here I am . . . I've come . . . you're too
good for me . . . you can have the apartment . . . I'm in a terrible
mess over there . . . have mercy on me . . . ,' he made a pilgrim-
age to the Holy City in order to solicit moral support from my
younger brother and his new wife—a romantic type with literary
delusions whom father had never met, since he never bothered to
come to their wedding. What better time to make amends for having
missed it? So he slept over with them and finally, on Wednesday,
organized a whole delegation to visit my mother—my brother and
my sister and my brother-in-law . . . they even dragged along their
small son. All to soften the blow of having to face her . . ."

"You didn't go too?"

"Absolutely not. The thespian art is not for me—and if I must
indulge in it, then only in solo appearances. Because it was real
theater up there. There was a formal reception, mother had even

baked a cake for it, the patients mobbed them, our old dog recognized father and jumped on him so rapturously that he knocked him head over heels. . . . A gay time was had by all."

"What dog is that?"

"I never told you about him? We had this big, strange, cunning, perverted dog with wild reddish hair and big floppy ears. A mongrel —one-quarter bulldog, one-quarter German shepherd and one-half God only knows what. I used to call him Halves-'n'-Quarters, but mother and Asi called him Horatio and father shortened it to 'Ratio . . . a personality in his own right, whom we sent with mother to the hospital to romp on the lawns and eat the lunatics' leftovers. To make a long story short, he too played a part in the production. My brother had an attack of hysteria and began screaming at my mother and hitting himself . . . my sister tearfully implored her . . . but she still wouldn't sign. So on Thursday my father went back again, this time by himself. He'd finally grasped what he should have understood long ago . . . that is, that if he wants his freedom he has to let her have the whole apartment. It's just his hard luck that she's suddenly in her right mind again and getting righter by the minute. He didn't get back to Haifa until last night . . . this morning he went to see some lawyer friend in Tel Aviv in order to draw up a new agreement. Tomorrow he'll go back to Haifa. On Sunday, if all goes well, they'll get divorced, and Monday night he's jetting back. . . . No, this time I'm under no pressure. It's a casual visit for me. I'm just a spectator. Ya'el and Asi are the official liquidators. I've already done my share. All those last years alone with them in the house . . . I've already told you about them. To have had to be the defendant, the prosecutor, the witness, the judge and the bailiff, all in turn . . . so that this time I've kept out of the way . . . on the sidelines. Did I really talk about him so much in our last session? I don't recall . . ."

"Yes."

"I must have been nervous about his visit. I could still taste the last time he'd been here three years ago, a year and a half after he first left us. He came and moved in with me for a whole month then, a sick, confused, guilt-ridden man torn between two worlds . . . the haunted murder victim returning to the scene of the crime . . . drawn back to all his and her things, to his own bed and home, but scared stiff by the lurid memory. He would get me out of bed in the middle of the night to sob all over me. He couldn't be left alone for a minute—I began to worry that he would never go back to America. . . . And so this time I was afraid of a repeat performance, even though his most recent letters had had a different tone. He had found a woman there, a job, something to do with his life. He was always a terrible square, and yet apparently he had managed to work on himself a bit. . . . Yet who would have thought that he would traipse back and forth in a trance for a whole week between Haifa and Jerusalem without stopping off even once in his beloved Tel Aviv . . . ? Well, I'm sorry to disappoint you. You were hoping that he would deluge me with pressures and shower new conflicts on our reunion. Didn't I warn you in our first meeting that I won't play the neurotic sufferer for you? I told you the whole story of my parents right away so as to clear the table of it . . . to make you realize that I had nothing to hide and that you needn't waste your time digging up ancient history. I didn't come to you with any problems. I came to understand."

"To understand what?"

"The subtle power that I have over people. I want to see myself more clearly in order to be stronger and put my deviancy to work for me. You can't make me feel bad about myself . . . the normality that you're preaching isn't for me . . ."

"You think that I'm preaching normality?"

"All the time. Covertly, of course. You've been smart enough to avoid a frontal attack. Which doesn't mean you won't launch one yet . . . because you still don't know the worst of it . . . sex for sale, the atrocious nexus of pleasure and money . . . only by then you won't be able to mount your self-righteous high horse and denounce me in the name of your social norms, because I'll already be waving goodbye to you from the other side of the door . . ."

"Is it important to you that I should have social norms?"

"You do have them. That's a fact."

"You say that it's a fact because you need it to be one."

"I don't need it to be one. You do. You sit here surrounded by all your books, in one of which there's bound to be some passage that fits my case exactly . . ."

"Which is?"

"Defining it is your job. Why make life easy for you?"

"You keep talking about categories, theories, test tubes that I want to cork you up in. You've drawn yourself a bull's-eye and you keep throwing darts at it. But perhaps it's convenient for you to think that everyone else is square, norm-bound, hyperrational and conformist so that you can enjoy your sense of difference from them, your eternal revolt against them. If I didn't represent normality you wouldn't feel comfortable with me."

"You've never made love to a man . . . and something tells me that you'd never be able to . . ."

"Do you think that I'd have to be able to . . . in order to . . ."

"But I've had women now and then. There are women I can make it with . . . there's a way of doing it . . . maybe I'll let you in on it one day . . . that is, if I'm in the mood. Excuse me, though, for having interrupted you . . ."

"I hear about all kinds of strange experiences in this room, but I don't have to undergo them myself in order to comprehend their significance."

"In order to grasp them intellectually on a very superficial level. I'm talking about in depth."

"No, not just intellectually. Although that too, of course . . . I was wondering a while ago why you pictured me eating cauliflower . . . where you got the idea from . . ."

"There's no cauliflower cooking in your kitchen?"

"No. There never has been."

"I'm sorry if I offended you . . . I smelled something on the stairs . . . I'm sorry . . ."

"That isn't the point. What I'm asking is, why did you pick on cauliflower of all things? What does it symbolize for you? Perhaps it has something to do with the way it looks, its round, white lobed form that resembles a brain. Why cauliflower? I wonder: is it in order to portray me as an utter rationalist, a dyed-in-the-wool intellectual . . . a man who eats brain all the time . . . brain nourished on brain . . . a person who is all cerebral technique? You're constantly sending me some message . . . it's very clear . . . you keep staking out the boundaries of our relationship. You don't trust me emotionally—and you don't believe that I can understand you psychologically. You deny my emotional capacities. To this day you've never given me a real feeling of yours . . . I mean something really intimate . . . despite all your pretending to be candid . . ."

"I simply haven't wanted to embarrass you."

"What makes you think you would embarrass me?"

"Whenever I touch on such things I can feel you wince."

"That's pure projection on your part."

"I've wanted to spare you the gory details of my escapades . . .
you're still so young . . ."

"You needn't spare me. I never asked you to. I'm here to help you
. . . you're even paying me for this. I don't think you understand
my role here. I really am here to help you. Have some faith in me.
Make use of me. If you sought out a young therapist, that too is
significant. One always repeats some family pattern with a father or a
brother or a sister. You chose me to stand for someone whom you
needed to confront. Perhaps your younger brother, who according to
you is a cerebral square just like me. But so far you've merely been
skirmishing with me and avoiding working on yourself. You have
great verbal power, a large vocabulary, a highly manipulative com-
mand of language . . . an ability instantly to translate every experience onto an abstract, conceptual plane . . . while evading the
issue itself, of course . . ."

"I don't follow you . . ."

"You follow me perfectly well. You keep telling me that you're
only here conditionally . . . that maybe you'll pay me and maybe
you won't . . . that each visit here may be your last. You deliberately come late . . . you even picked an odd hour like this because
of its provisional feeling, as though it were a form of weekend enter-
tainment. And you keep insisting that nothing bothers you, that
you're only coming to see how I define what you already know. But
we can't work this way. I've let three months of it go by as an
opening. It's even predictable in a case like yours. But we can't go on
going nowhere . . . your time is too valuable . . . and so is mine
. . ."

"Hey, you're attacking me . . . for the first time . . . I feel almost stunned . . ."

"Don't you think that it's about time?"

"I didn't know you had it in you. You're not as quiet and innocent
as I had thought, then . . . I rather like that. You know, what you
just said about my brother . . . it was an interesting hunch . . .
how old actually are you?"

"Why does it matter to you?"

"Oh no, don't throw the question back at me. Now it's you who are evading. Drop your anonymity for once and tell me how old you are."

"Twenty-seven . . . but why?"

"And you really hope to identify with me?"

"Only in order to understand."

"What an odd profession you've chosen! But all right, I'll tell you a dream. You asked me a few weeks ago if I ever had any . . . well, now I've dreamt one for you, you can't say I'm not trying. In fact, that was the real reason for my impatience to see you today . . . the reason I came on time . . . because I've brought you a fresh dream. I already lost most of it during the day, but something is still left . . . so let's see what you can do with its dehydrated remains. As far as I can see it's completely meaningless, but that's your problem. You see, I must have known that your attack was coming, because I armed myself with a dream. . . . You know, I think we're beginning to form a real tie. Now I'll put you to work, let's see you show your stuff . . ."

"I can only work together with you."

"Together with me, of course. I've already learned the rules of the game. . . . On the whole, you know, last night was rather strange. My father arrived in the late afternoon and insisted on taking me out to eat even though I had cooked a meal for him. He was obsessed with some little restaurant that served a special borscht he had dreamt of all the time in America. . . . Okay, so we went there and the place was closed because of the holiday. But he insisted on finding the owners, and they were so overjoyed to see him that they opened the restaurant especially for him . . . only there wasn't any borscht left. So they sent out for a whole pitcher of it, and for sour cream too, and he sat there putting away the thick red stuff of his dreams, smacking his lips and grunting with pleasure and joking and chattering away. He didn't say much about his meeting with mother, except that he hoped it would all be over with on Sunday and that he was ready to give her the whole apartment . . . after which he began feeling so sick from all the borscht he had eaten that we went home. He washed up, sat down to look at all the letters and journals that had come for him while he'd been away, and then turned on the TV to watch an interview with some new politician he had never heard of before. Halfway through it he began to doze off, so we never did say anything important. I too went to sleep early . . . and then

at two a.m. this old fairy knocked on the door, a big-time banker
from an old Jerusalem family . . . an odd, sentimental character
who's fallen wildly in love with me . . ."

"Calderon?"

"The very same. Which means that I've already mentioned him to
you and that you haven't missed a trick. Exactly. Refa'el Calderon. I
showed him who he really was and since then his life has been one
big mess. It has no structure anymore and his family is falling apart.
He runs after me like a dog, does all kinds of things for me, won't
leave me alone. A case for you. At the stroke of five he'll be waiting
for me below with his chauffered car. A real case for you . . . now
there's suffering . . . mark my word, he'll come to see you yet. In
fact, he's already jealous of you. The man's in a tailspin. . . . But to
get to the point, he knocked on the door and woke me at two a.m.
And I'm such a kind heart that I can't drive types like him away, so
I had to get up and listen to his pre-dawn confession. I too, you see,
have my patients . . . in the long, wee hours of the morning I treat
them free of charge . . . all kinds of oddballs . . . first they wear
me down psychologically, and then they get me into bed and hump
away . . . What?"

"Nothing."

"I thought you said something."

"No."

"I don't know if it's worth starting on that dream now . . . we
haven't much time left . . . all right, I'd better tell it, just so you
don't say I'm evading again. I went back to sleep and Calderon
stayed in the kitchen with my father, who had woken up too. In the
end his wife even called . . . it was either then, or before that, that I
had the dream. I've forgotten a lot of the details, but what I remember . . . what's left for you . . . is more or less this. There was a
small hotel, a building not far from a lake surrounded by distant
mountains . . . it may even not have been in Israel. I don't remember much about it, but I do remember that there were stairs . . . in
fact, two sets of them. The ones I climbed were straight and light-
colored, but nearby, as though they had been built by mistake, were
the original stairs of the building, which weren't in use anymore.
They were made of rough old stone carpeted with an old, reddish rug
that was worn at the edges . . . very windy stairs that led to some
rented rooms, most of them already moved out of. In them I could

see unmade beds and personal possessions that had been left behind —shawls, pins, dirty absorbent cotton, colorful robes . . . On the first floor, which I was trying to climb past, I saw sitting by the window—God knows how he had gotten there—my English teacher from the night school I attended twelve years ago. We called him Mr. Foxy, but that wasn't his real name—he had some German-sounding last name like Neustadt or Freustadt . . . a gloomy old bachelor, a gray, impeccable German Jew who had failed in business and taken up teaching English at night. He always wore a winter suit. He was tall and bald, wore glasses, was round-shouldered, had this yellow skin . . . apart from his fingers, which were green from nicotine . . . and talked only English with us because that gave him the upper hand. . . . Now he was sitting in this hotel in an open white shirt, waiting for someone in a room like a dining room that had tables all around. I didn't know if he remembered me, but I went over to him. He spoke to me in English, but it was an English that I understood, so that I had no trouble following him . . . the words passed into me as easily as though they were Hebrew. Without turning to look at me he explained that he was waiting for his *hunting*. I remember him using that word, and I knew at once what it meant, even how to spell it. *Hunting.* I think he must have been referring to some meat dish, but he called it his *hunting* in English, as though he were a country squire, or pretending to be one. . . . Are you listening?"

"Yes."

"It seemed absurd that this colorless man should be sitting there and telling me about his *hunting* that he expected to be brought from the forest, fresh from the kill, because in the room itself there was no sign of anything like a kitchen. But he kept staring out the window. And there, low down, I saw a thicket of bushes with a hose sticking out of it from which some water was running. Something moved there. It took a step in the bright evening light, and then the water dwindled to a trickle and stopped, as though someone had turned off the faucet or bent the hose . . ."

"Yes?"

"That's it."

"That's it? Did you wake up at that point, or did you go on dreaming?"

"No, I woke up. The telephone rang, and I heard Calderon begging for dear life."

"Did you awake with a feeling of anxiety?"

"Don't you ever give up? No . . . there was no anxiety . . . the phone simply woke me. But had I gone on dreaming, I'm sure I would have climbed down to see what the hose was attached to and who had shut it off."

"And that English teacher . . . what did you say his name was?"

"The students called him Mr. Foxy. He was like a long, gray fox."

"Do you have any associations with him? Have you seen him lately?"

"No. He doesn't mean a thing to me. I didn't even know he still existed in my mind. I haven't seen him for years . . . haven't thought of him . . . why should he suddenly have turned up like that?"

"Were you a good student in English?"

"No. A very bad one. Totally resistant to learning. I don't think I ever took the final exam . . ."

"Were there other courses that you didn't finish?"

"No. I think it was the only one. Once I lost interest in getting my diploma I didn't bother with it anymore."

"When did you start night school?"

"After my junior year in high school."

"Before that you studied in the same school where your father taught?"

"Yes."

"Was he ever your teacher?"

"No. He only taught the seniors."

"Was that why you left?"

"I don't get you."

"So that you wouldn't have to be a student of his."

"Oh. Maybe . . . it's possible . . . that's not how I thought of it then . . . but I wouldn't rule it out. There were several reasons, but that may have been one of them . . . only how does that help us with the dream?"

"This English teacher . . . you say that he was a peripheral figure for you . . . are you sure you haven't run into him lately?"

"Absolutely."

"But in dreams such peripheral, meaningless figures are stand-ins for others. They conceal other, more meaningful figures."

"I'm not sure I follow."

"This Mr. Foxy . . . he's more or less your father's age . . . and like him, a teacher . . . did you ever have a run-in with him?"

"Never."

"But you failed his course. If nothing else, he stands for the one exam you never took, because of which you failed to get your diploma."

"That's of no importance to me."

"But it's inconceivable that it didn't bother you at some point . . ."

"No. I don't buy that. But go on."

"The teacher spoke English, but you understood it as though it were Hebrew. Now your father is in America, with a new, English identity. Behind it, though, his old Hebrew self is still there."

"Go on. I'm listening. I don't say you're right and I don't say you're wrong."

"The teacher in the dream had changed. He always used to wear a heavy winter suit—and here he suddenly was in a summery white shirt. He was different, no longer the same . . . like your father, about the change in whom you keep talking . . . about how young and artsy-looking he's become. You said that the teacher was pretending to be a squire—the same gray personage who used to smoke the cheapest cigarettes . . ."

"The cheapest cigarettes? Hold on there. Who told you that?"

"His nicotine-stained fingers . . ."

"Are you an amateur detective?"

"I was just listening to you . . . to the details that you yourself were giving me. I'm trying to base myself on them. In the dream the teacher is waiting for some kind of meat dish, for his *hunting* . . . while last night your father went hunting for some red borscht. The link is so obvious: red . . . blood . . . Something about your father's appetite evidently upset you. You disguised him as another teacher who meant nothing to you, you put glasses on him and made him bald . . . why was all this camouflage necessary? Perhaps because of what you've been thinking about him . . . because the dream expresses some extreme wish. You need to conceal it in order to protect yourself, while at the same time giving it vent. What it is, though, remains to be discovered."

"I'm still listening. I don't say you're right and I don't say you're wrong. One little question, though: this theory of concealment—is it generally accepted or did you make it up especially for me?"

"Of course it's generally accepted. It's the ABC of our work. Every dream is a concealment, an entire system of them."

"But what was I trying to conceal?"

"Something having to do with your father, or with your intentions toward him. That's up to you to find out. Because from the outset the dream makes clear it's about you too, about a problem of identity that concerns you. I'm referring to the building with the double staircase. Stairs in dreams generally stand for sexual feelings. Ascending or descending them refers to the sexual act itself . . ."

"Now you're putting me on."

"I would never do that."

"Then you're putting yourself on."

"It's an almost classic symbol, and in your case it's expressed most clearly. You ascend one type of stairs, the straight, light ones. But there are others near them—dark winding ones that seem useless to you and are covered by an old, red, worn carpet. Red again, please note. And the stairs pass by a series of rooms that once were inhabited by people who have left behind possessions that are distinctly feminine: shawls, pins, dirty absorbent cotton, colorful robes . . . Between the two sets of stairs is a divide you don't cross—a small, not terribly dangerous one which indeed can perhaps be bridged. What was it you said to me just a few minutes ago? There are women I can make it with . . ."

"This is beginning to sound awfully talmudic."

"But dreams do work talmudically, abstractly, by means of condensation and displacement. You have to interpret them, to take them apart in order to re-establish connections and understand what they are trying to say."

"Following your logic, then, what about the water hose and the bushes?"

"You have no associations with them?"

"None."

"It's not a place you can identify?"

"No. I've already said that something about it didn't seem like Israel."

"Maybe it's some place connected with your childhood?"

"My childhood? Not as far as I can tell . . ."

"Or perhaps it resembles the place where your mother is now."

"My mother? Up there? No . . . those bushes . . . there's no thicket like that there. And on the whole . . ."

"But it is by the sea . . . way up north . . ."

"This wasn't by a sea. It was by a small lake. With mountains around it. Someplace lush, like a Swiss landscape . . . I distinctly remember the mountains ringing it . . ."

"But that could be Haifa Bay. It curves in an arc. In the dream, for reasons of your own, you simply completed the circle."

"You mean that the mountains in the background are the Carmel?"

"Perhaps."

"No. That's not where it was. You can't get me to give in to you here."

"I would never want you to give in to me. I want you to find your own association."

"It was a dreamlike scene . . . can't I create a new place in a dream?"

"You can. But it's generally a composite of old places."

"Well, then this was such a composite."

"Do you remember any other details?"

"No."

"There was no one in the thicket?"

"No. There was a movement that had just taken place. That had to do with . . ."

"The water hose?"

"Yes."

"And does the hose itself suggest anything to you?"

"I don't think so."

"What's the first thought you have about it?"

"I don't know . . . it was a hose that lay on the ground, almost merging with it. It was brown, but quite bright where it protruded from the bushes in the evening light. Water flowed from it and suddenly stopped . . . as though someone had turned off the faucet, or bent it to choke off the flow . . ."

"To choke it off?"

"No, don't make too much of my words . . . someone passing by simply had stepped on it and stopped the water . . ."

"And did the teacher say anything? Did he react?"

"No. I wasn't paying attention to him then. I just had this feeling that it was connected with what he expected to be brought from that damn *hunting* of his . . ."

"And what did you feel when you saw the water stop?"

"I thought that someone was about to appear in the bushes . . . and then I woke up. I must have heard father and Refa'el talking . . . and Refa'el's voice pleading on the telephone . . ."

"Let's go back to that place again. The landscape . . . the mountains . . . the lake . . . the bushes . . . what do they suggest to you?"

"On the contrary, you tell me. Maybe they're symbols too. I rather like that. Don't you have a dictionary . . . some sort of thesaurus with equivalencies like the one you gave for the stairs . . . in which you could look up bushes, a water hose, a sunset . . ."

"I'm afraid it isn't that simple. Try again, quickly. What's your first thought?"

"Quickly, my first thought is nothing. Slowly too . . ."

"You're digging in here . . . taking cover behind your defenses . . ."

"From what?"

"I don't know. But I feel that the real meaning of the dream is concealed here."

"But I really can't think of a thing. I'm a total blank. It was just some kind of fantasy . . ."

"That's the easy way out. You have the key. I can only make suggestions. You thought you were bringing me some pointless, 'dehydrated' dream, that you were throwing me a dry bone . . . but you see now how dreams have their own language and methods of organization. If you can get deeper into it, perhaps we can still find its message."

"It's hard for me to think under pressure."

"Then let's leave it for the time being."

"I feel so blank . . . you've drained me . . . that whole dream took place in such darkness . . ."

"I thought you said it was in bright light."

"Only outside, by the bushes. I was standing by the window in the dark."

"All right. Let's leave it for now. We can come back to it some other time. Are you planning to accompany your father on Sunday?"

"Me? Why should I? Is it my filial duty? They'll be better off by themselves there. I'll see him that evening at my sister's seder."

"And your mother?"

"She'll have to stay in the hospital. What can we do? It's only in fiction that the newly divorced couple spends its first night under the same roof . . . reality is better organized . . ."

"Was she there for the seder last year too?"

"No. She's always been at my sister's. Except for the first year, when I was there with her. After that we got permission to take her out."

"Permission from whom?"

"From the hospital."

"Was she in such bad shape? I thought . . ."

"No. It was a legal matter."

"Legal? How so?"

"Those were the terms of the agreement that got her off from standing trial."

"Standing trial? I don't understand."

"But I've told you all about it."

"Apparently you haven't."

"Father was wounded. There was no way we could hide it."

"I still don't understand. He called the police?"

"I did."

"You did?"

"Didn't I tell you? It's strange that of all things you should have forgotten that . . ."

"Perhaps I didn't realize that you had actually called them."

"I had to. He was in a puddle of blood in the kitchen . . . there was no way of hiding that he had been attacked . . . I thought he was going to die . . ."

"I see."

"They could have pinned it on me."

"On you?"

"They could have said anything. And anyone could have believed it. I was the only one with them. Asi had arranged his life then so that he hardly came home, he was taking exams all the time and doing two years of school in one . . . Ya'el and Kedmi had moved to Haifa . . . and here everything had happened so quickly . . . she was like moving in two parallel tracks, both pretending to be crazy and getting crazier all the time . . . deliberately working herself up to a frenzy and then really being in one. Father was genuinely scared. He was afraid to be left alone with her and begged me to stay with them. He even paid me so that I wouldn't have to go to work. He was terrified, but he kept provoking her too, making fun of her, mimicking her speech. She had started talking with this new musical lilt, almost singing the ends of her sentences, and he would imitate her, singing along with her . . . he couldn't control himself. She would stand there explaining some long matter to him while beginning to sing a little, and he would start singing sarcastically too until he would be frightened by his own self and shut himself up in his room. . . . Sex became a bitter mockery for them too. Oh, I could still feel it was there, and maybe amid all their madness they actually slept together now and then. . . . It went on like that until she began her shoplifting. But I really have told you all about that."

"Yes."

"And about having to keep her from getting her hands on money."

"Yes."

"And about those screwball meals of hers . . . about the big food mill that she bought to grind up everything we ate . . . I've told you all that . . ."

"Yes, you have."

"Looking back on it now, I think she must have been trying to transmit some important message to us by means of that nutty food. She was trying to tell us something through all those weird combinations of hers: cookies stuffed with cucumbers and green peppers, sweet giant meatballs, frozen fish heads, green cocktail spreads, bread ground to smithereens . . . sometimes it would turn out delicious . . . but mostly it was too abominable for words. Once we even found some stew made of dog food on our plates. Father threw up. He became afraid to touch any food. He used to sneak into the kitchen at night to look for bread and cheese. . . . The refrigerator and the closets were overflowing with her food. It smelled bad, the whole house began to stink. And it attracted animals too. All kinds of strange birds kept landing on the windowsills. Ravens turned up in the middle of the night. There were mice. The dog kept barking his head off to drive them away. . . . And then father began seeing doctors to inquire about hospitalization. Ya'el came with Gaddi, and, since mother was especially fond of him, I suggested that Ya'el leave him with her for a while. At first she was afraid to, but in the end she agreed. In the beginning mother was thrilled. She slept with the baby instead of with father and there were a few days of calm. Father took to spending most of his time away from home and locked himself in his study when he returned at night. And then one night all the keys to all the doors disappeared. Gaddi was still with us. Early the next morning we heard father let out this horrible scream and the dog started howling . . . but I really have told you all that . . . I'm simply wasting my money by repeating myself . . ."

"One never simply repeats oneself."

"I'm not so sure about that . . ."

"And then you called the police?"

"He passed out and I was sure he was dead. I phoned them and said excuse me, whom do I inform about a murder? I may have been a bit hasty, but I couldn't think straight with all that blood. And they came right away, as though they had been waiting to hear from me, led by some gung-ho sergeant. Father was conscious by then. He kept clutching his chest and groaning, but I think he was enjoying the sight of his own blood too. They took him to the hospital, and the sergeant went into another room with mother. He talked to her for a long time and then took her away. Ya'el came from Haifa and went straight to see the two of them, and Kedmi arrived later to pick up Gaddi. He prowled around the apartment trying to piece together what had happened, but I didn't give him any help; I just went on mopping up the blood stains. Asi came that afternoon, went to the hospital, and took the dog back with him to Jerusalem. . . . So that by the time evening came I was alone in the apartment with this strange, enormous silence. A few curious neighbors knocked on the door, but I didn't open it. The next morning the bell rang. It was father, all bandaged and sulking. They had sent him home, the knife had barely scratched him. It shocked me afterwards to see how he told all his friends about it. Especially since the police dealt with it so discreetly. The sergeant in charge of the case recommended preven-

tive hospitalization. . . . I really don't see why I should be blamed
for it . . ."

"Who's blaming you?"

"I can feel how you're judging me."

"I'm not your judge and I never will be. I want to understand with
you how your mind worked, what motivated you."

"What is there to understand? They needed to be separated."

"I see."

"I feel that you don't agree with me."

"Whether or not I agree is irrelevant. We're talking about you."

"But you said you wanted to identify with me."

"Just in order to understand you better. Not to decide for you or
take your place."

"They needed to be separated . . . to be removed from their
common hell . . ."

"And she's been there ever since?"

"She preferred it that way. Maybe she needed to punish herself. Or
maybe she was afraid that she would try it again. And once word got
out, there was the public disgrace of it too. She was really quite sick
by then. . . . And when he went abroad, no one knew how long he
would stay. The doctors were skeptical about my taking care of her
at home by myself. She couldn't stay with Ya'el, because Kedmi
didn't want to have anything to do with her then . . . she herself
preferred it that way . . . it's a very decent place, by the sea. Perhaps you're familiar with it. And she's made a lot of friends there—
she helps take care of a few of the patients herself. We even gave her
the dog. At first it was meant to be temporary, but it was a convenient solution for us all and it stuck. . . . Do you think we were
wrong? Perhaps we didn't push hard enough for her release. Perhaps
we wanted to punish her ourselves. Just the other day I asked her
again if she didn't feel it was time to leave."

"You were there the other day?"

"Yes. On Tuesday."

"You didn't tell me."

"You didn't ask."

"Was it for some special reason?"

"No. Why should it have been? Now and then I go see her by
myself . . . every few months. I come for a long visit. It depends on
how she is, on the weather too. I call her in advance, take the day off,

and arrive there in the afternoon. She waits for me by the gate and
we go into town—sometimes to the fisherman's wharf in Acre, and
sometimes in the other direction, to a café in Nahariyya. I take her to
a movie, we eat a meal in a restaurant, and at night I bring her
back."

"But why does she wait for you at the gate? Why don't you go in
to get her?"

"I prefer not to. I don't like hospitals. Mental ones especially give
me the creeps. Once a few years ago I did go inside and the patients
mobbed me. It's hard for me even to be near there . . . oh, I know
it's ridiculous . . . but I sometimes have this fear that they won't let
me out again . . ."

"Who won't?"

"The doctors. It's silly, I know . . . but how can I be sure that
they won't get some crazy idea? There's a book like that by Thomas
Mann, *The Magic Mountain,* in which a young man goes to visit his
cousin in a sanatorium and remains there because they discover that
he's sick too. . . . Why run the risk? There can always be some nut
there who'll decide that I also . . ."

"Did you take her to the movies this Tuesday too?"

"No. We just sat and talked. There wasn't time. I had brought
Calderon with me to read the agreement that Kedmi and father drew
up. I wanted his opinion—he has a good, practical financial head.
And I told her a little about father, to prepare her for meeting him
. . . about this new style of his . . . this great rejuvenation that's
taken place in his life. I said she shouldn't be too quick to sign away
her property now that she's getting divorced and that she shouldn't
let anyone make up her mind for her. We spoke for a while about
their apartment . . . about whether it was wise to let a half-owner-
ship in it go live in America . . . whether it wasn't a better idea to
invest what could be gotten for it in something that would yield a
good return. She isn't all that old, after all . . . who knows what
life still has in store for her. And she's terribly naïve, she has no idea
that uninvested money simply melts away nowadays . . . she lives
in an old-fashioned world . . ."

"And what did she say to all that?"

"She listened. My friend Calderon outlined a few possibilities to
her. The main thing I wanted was to prepare her . . . to make her
realize that she was in a position of strength . . . to keep her from

suddenly feeling sorry for him . . . to give her some existential confidence before her eternal parting . . ."

"From whom?"

"Excuse me?"

"Her eternal parting from whom?"

"From whom?"

"Before her eternal parting from whom?"

"I don't get you."

"You said you wanted to give her confidence before her eternal parting . . . did you mean from your father?"

"What?"

"Your mind is somewhere else."

"What? What did you say?"

"I said your mind is somewhere else."

"It's the strangest thing . . . I suddenly remembered . . . you see, that English teacher . . . that Mr. Foxy who walked into my dream . . . listen, it's incredible . . . a really fantastic thing . . . how could I have forgotten . . . he just died . . . his name . . . how could I have forgotten . . . it's all come back to me now . . . it's amazing . . ."

"When did he die?"

"Just a few weeks ago. Now it comes back to me . . . I noticed a death announcement that the school had placed in the newspaper. He died a short while ago, and I didn't remember! So that's why he was in the dream . . . I raised him from the dead without knowing it . . . I'm literally shaking . . ."

"I suggest that we stop here."

"Excuse me?"

"We'll stop here and continue next time."

"Oh, our hour is over. I see . . . all right then, next week . . ."

"We won't be meeting next week. We'll meet again in two weeks' time. Next week I'll be on vacation."

"You can't see me next week?"

"No. But we'll meet two weeks from now at the usual time."

"But who told you to take a vacation . . . I mean . . ."

"Next week is the Passover holiday."

"You don't work on Passover? Don't tell me you're religious . . ."

"No. I'm just taking a vacation."

"But you'll be in Tel Aviv?"

"I don't know yet."

"Can't you fit me in somewhere? Even at a different hour . . . on a different day . . . it doesn't matter . . ."

"I'm afraid it won't be possible."

"I mean any time that you want . . . any day . . . I'll manage to make it . . ."

"We'll meet again in two weeks."

"I see. Just a minute, I wanted to pay you . . ."

"There's no hurry about it. Next time."

"But I have the money with me now. I owe you . . ."

"Next time. It can wait."

"Excuse me . . . just one more thing . . ."

"Yes?"

"If I want to talk to you next week, just to say a few words, can I phone?"

"I don't think the telephone would be very convenient. Let's wait till we meet again. It won't be long."

"I just . . . I don't know, but . . . I feel that something is going to happen next week. Maybe I'll want to tell you about it . . . doesn't it surprise you that I totally forgot that that teacher had died? . . ."

"We'll talk about that too, of course."

"In a way I feel I've become closer to you today . . . I like you more. I didn't want to tell you, but at first you were very off-putting. I mean physically . . . your being so short and heavy . . . and those muttonchop sideburns of yours . . . why do you let them grow? The style is much shorter these days . . ."

"We can talk about that next time too. Right now I suggest that . . ."

"Yes. I understand. Suddenly I see you in a new light. You really do want to lead me somewhere . . . there's a method to it all . . . a direction . . . you aren't so passive . . ."

"Yes. Today you started to work in earnest. But seriously . . ."

"You felt it too?"

"Yes. But now isn't the time for this. We'll talk about it next time."

"I'm sorry we can't continue now. I just wanted to ask you . . ."

"Perhaps . . ."

". . . just one more thing that's been bothering me. Is insanity genetic? Will I go crazy like her? What do you know about that?"

"We'll talk about it all next time. Here, don't forget your scarf."

"I get it . . . I wanted to leave you something in order to have a reason to come back . . . all right then, I'll be on my way. Just one last question: do you really believe that every single detail has significance . . . that there is no such thing as random, meaningless events . . . just the chaotic surge of life . . . ?"

"No, Tsvi. Really. Not now."

"Just one sentence from you. Please."

"In a sense, there's always a matrix to which the accidents attach themselves. . . . But I promise you that we'll talk about it next time. We still have a long way to go."

"I can't wait. Today was fascinating. What should we start with next time? What would you like me to think about? You must be planning it already . . . no doubt that dead teacher. Although maybe we should go back to the beginning of the dream . . . to that thicket of bushes . . . and the watering hose. You know, you're right. One must never give up . . ."

"We can start with whatever you'd like. Let's leave it open. Whatever is on your mind. Even that dog . . ."

"The dog?"

"Why not? He's part of the story too. But really now, goodbye. If you don't mind leaving this way . . ."

"Someone is behind the door there . . . so I'm not the last, after all . . ."

"Goodbye, Tsvi. Have a good holiday . . ."

"Refa'el, is that you? What are you doing here? I told you to wait for me downstairs."

"Doctor?"

"Excuse me, please."

"Refa'el, not now."

"I wanted to know if you could take me on too. Did you ask him, Tsvi?"

"Not now, Refa'el . . . not now . . . you have to get out of here . . ."

"Please, this really is not the time for it. But you can get in touch with me next month. Tsvi will give you my phone number."

"Thank you so much . . . it's been my pleasure . . . happy

Passover . . . I'll wait for you below . . . begging your pardon . . ."

"You see, I told you. But here I am clinging to you the same way
. . . it really isn't like me. I'm so sorry . . . I'll go now. How did
he put it last night? The boundaries are gone . . . but I'd really
better go. Thank you. Thank you so much. And I'll be seeing you
soon . . ."

SATURDAY?

This is the first time, only lately
Time has not behaved sedately.
                    Uri Bernstein

Saturday? Saturday? Suddenly, halfway through the story, I'm stuck and can't go on. What happened on Saturday three years ago? I hadn't even remembered that there was such a day. It vanished without a trace, without even leaving behind its own phantom pain. Saturday? Somehow I lost it—I, who tended each one of those days like a priestess at the altar; who stubbornly salvaged them, forever frozen in clarity, from the passage of time; who zealously assembled and preserved their story person by person and day by day down to its last detail, color, smell, fragment of conversation, article of clothing, shift of mood and of weather—those last, horrible days of his beamed on a screen in their impossible, in their inevitable unfolding to the distant soundtrack of a faint yet persistent score; who, though none of you ever noticed, have gone on to this day collecting snatches of memories like the last feathers from a torn quilt: from you, Kedmi, from mother, from Tsvi, from Asi, from Dina . . . even poking up the last embers in Gaddi and asking whoever was in the hospital that last dreadful night over and over about it (yes, if only I could find him I would ask the dog too, I would beg him to talk, to join me in my exact, relentless search for those days in their impossible, in their inevitable unfolding from that first moment in ever I had been myself and wherever my imagination had gone for me . . . and yet as soon as I reached Saturday I drew a blank, I blacked out completely, the music stopped, and I stood there saying idiotically, "Saturday? Saturday? I don't remember there being a Saturday at all." My mind wouldn't work. "Are you sure that there was one?" I kept asking. "Maybe that was the first day of Passover, it sometimes happens that way. We'll have to look it up in an old calendar." But she just looked at me with a momentary smile of bewilderment before blushing offendedly, as though I were trying to hide something from her. Where were we on that Saturday? What happened on it? Could I really have forgotten—I, who tended each one of those days like a priestess at the altar, who salvaged them, forever frozen in stubborn clarity, from the passage of time? I almost called you at the office, Kedmi, or else Tsvi. But you, what do you still remember? Why, even what you think you remember is a shadow of the memory itself.

I rose and walked about the room. "Saturday?" I murmured to her with a reassuring smile. "Of course. It will come back to me in a minute. On Sunday he was divorced. He went to the hospital that morning by himself. We never understood how he had convinced the rabbis to perform the ceremony on the day of the seder until weeks later there arrived a receipt from some unknown little yeshiva for a contribution he had given it. What didn't he do to see the thing through! But that still leaves Saturday. Saturday . . . of course. There had to be one." I smiled at her. "We'll find it in a minute. But first let's have some more coffee."

I went to the kitchen, passing through an apartment suspended in time since her coming. Everything was a mess. Dirty dishes were piled in the sink, open pots of food stood on the cold stove, the chairs were up on the tables, a rag lay by a bucket on the filthy floor, the beds were unmade, a record went on spinning silently on the turntable. It wasn't nine o'clock yet when she arrived, and since then everything had come to a stop.

I came back with the coffee and, while she went to the bathroom, her comical notebook left open on the table with its short, heavily underlined sentences in a vexed hand, on each page a date as though she were hunting for something, I slipped off to the children's room to have another look at him in Rakefet's crib. I re-covered his little

the airport when he stepped out to greet us on the rainy, floodli
pavement to the last one on that final night when we arrived too late
at the hospital gate to find him already taken away and the whimper-
ing dog pawing madly at the ground . . . yes, for me that was the
end); who have not forgotten—who will never forget—who will remember for all of you; who was the only one to love him uncondi-
tionally; who was neither for him nor against him but simply quietly
there with whatever warmth and assistance I could give. You can do
what you want, Kedmi; all of you can; I'll always be with you. And
instead of thinking . . . yes, instead of thinking, Kedmi, I'll remember. I'll leave the thinking to you, to Asi, to all of you, but you leave
the remembering to me, because there is no one else to do it. Only
what happened to that Saturday? My God, can I have lost a whole
day without having been aware of it, can my stubborn, insatiable
memory have run right over it on its way to the accident? But how?
Like a fool I sat here this morning and told her about each day, all in
its slow, orderly sequence, in its impossible, its inevitable unfolding,
as though listening to that faint score bring back each minute of it, as
if all the stubborn remembering of the past years had been solely for
this moment and I had known all along that one day some stranger
would walk in out of the blue and demand it all back from me:
someone with a hunger for the tiniest facts and the need to know
everything, so that, if at first I wasn't sure what to tell her and what
not to, not only could I keep back nothing once I began to talk, I was
in an absolute frenzy to cough it all up. Things came back to me that
I had never dreamed I still remembered. At last there was someone
to milk me dry, to turn me over like a bottle and empty me of every
word, sound and movement, to plumb our thoughts and motives, to
keep track of even the most minor characters in my account, refusing
to part from them, clinging to them for dear life. For a while I was
actually alarmed by her passion to know. A small woman in a bonnet
with a big feather, holding a long pencil and a notebook on her knee,
chain-smoking, hanging on every word, jotting down each new expression, nodding incessantly at a fever pitch, in a primitive Hebrew,
while I gave it back to her day by day: Sunday, Monday, Tuesday,
Wednesday . . . following him from place to place and from person
to person . . . from Haifa to Jerusalem and back again, from there
to Tel Aviv . . . morning, afternoon and night . . . everything I
knew, whatever I had garnered from him, from you all . . . wher-

body with the blanket and touched his face. A mystery, I whispered to myself, feeling ready to cry again, because I had started to when they came and never finished, nor do I think I ever will. Brace yourself, Kedmi: it needn't surprise you that I want to cry each time I see the child. And she was so happy when I did. It made her feel better at once, her face glowed. At first she was in such a panic, poor thing, standing there in the doorway with all her suitcases, blushing and stammering, driven to despair by my determined refusal to realize who she was. Until all of a sudden it dawned on me and I hurried them into the house and bent to take the child, bursting into tears when I lifted him. What else could one have done? Could I have done, I mean, not you, of course, Kedmi. What makes me cry makes you laugh, which is all to the good, because that way we're sure to get along. But I mean laughter, Kedmi, not that insufferably aggressive bile of yours. Irony, yes, laughter, as much as you want—as long as it's like this afternoon when, coming home from work, you ran into all her suitcases by the door and turned your surprise so quickly into an amused smile: you knew at once whose they were—you had figured it out in a flash—no, no one will ever pull a fast one on you. And you were so friendly shaking hands with her—yes, really friendly and warm, you needn't deny it. I swear you were—and you can be cold and nasty enough when you come home and find strangers in the house. You went straight to the kitchen, where the child was sitting with the bib I had tied around his neck, all smeared with cereal, banging on the table with a soup spoon and singing in English, and how sweetly you said with a mischievous twinkle to Gaddi and Rakefet, who were watching him dumbfounded, "Well, kids, how do you like your new uncle from America?" You don't know how relieved I was that you didn't go into one of your sulks, that you were ready to share this incredible experience that's come our way, that you'll have the patience to put up with them. Because I know you will. Please, I beg of you: don't already start planning ways to get rid of them during the few days they'll be here. Give me time to hold the child before he's taken away again. My sweetheart, how I love you, how I thank you, how I love you and thank you for the way that you, who have so little use for strange children, went right over to him and fondled him with such a gentle, marvelous smile. You even kissed him, didn't you? Of course you did. And stroked his hair. Admit it, Kedmi, you needn't be ashamed. There's nothing wrong with it. Even you were touched by the mystery.

But I cried and that made her happy. It made her feel so much better, her face glowed. So tense and miserable she was, her first time in Israel and straight from the airport after the long flight from America, having taken a taxi to our house without phoning for fear we would tell her not to come. I ran to answer the doorbell, the whole house in a shambles, still in a fog from the record I'd put on, hypnotized by the soft rain that was falling like gold in the rays of an orange-peel sun, staring at her for what seemed forever, refusing to let it register, sure that there was some mistake and that this bizarre middle-aged woman with a baby in her arms and three rain-spattered valises at her feet—that this flushed, agitated woman who was beseeching me in a rapid-fire English that I didn't even try to understand—that this woman who kept hopelessly repeating a last name that meant nothing to me was someone I didn't know, no, not even when she introduced herself as Connie. And yet gradually I felt myself looking at the child and a shiver ran down my spine. He was a three-year-old Tsvi, perhaps even a three-year-old father . . . not that it had sunk in yet, only now something made me want to fling myself on them and drag them into the house. And still she kept up an incomprehensible stream of English, uncertain whether to come in. Perhaps she'd caught a glimpse of the state of the apartment . . . but the child was already inside, so curious and earnest. And you should have seen how he looked, all in red from tip to toe, as though out of the pages of a fairy tale. He darted from one thing to another and ran off to listen to the music, talking softly to himself, while I tried to catch him with a hot lump in my throat. Why, he was as light as a baby chick, a mere slip of warm air. Already there were tears on my cheeks. And she was so happy to see them. It made her feel better, her face glowed. "That's him?" I whispered. She nodded. "That's him," she repeated in Hebrew, shutting her eyes with a sudden, ceremonious toss of her head.

A strange, peculiar woman, isn't she? You should have seen how she had dressed the child, all in red. . . . Come, let me show you his things: red coat, red jacket and pants—a matching suit, in fact— red socks, even red underpants and red undershirt, all in the exact same shade. And he wore a red velvet skullcap on his head, which she made him put on especially for the trip to Israel, because she thought that everyone here . . . that you had to . . . really weird! The sheer redness of him was too much. And she herself standing next to him in that white bonnet with its long stiff red feather waving back and forth. . . . Come, I'll show you that too, she's left it here. What kind of animal or bird does it come from? Or is it synthetic? Yes, I suppose it must be. . . . She sat across from me for two whole hours with that feather sticking up in the air, an odd, tense, terribly nervous woman. How could we have forgotten about her existence? We must simply have blocked it out. There was a time when I still said to you all that we had to find out what happened to her, that we should write her, but you, Kedmi, were against it, and Tsvi and Asi didn't think much of the idea either. Don't you have enough problems already, you said to me, without asking for more from America? You were afraid of his case being opened again, of raising the issue of the child's paternity and having to re-probate the will. And Tsvi promised us that that little man who followed him around in those days . . . that banker . . . Calderon . . . yes, Refa'el Calderon . . . that he would telephone her in America and tell her the whole story. And he did: she told me today of her talks with him back then and said he behaved like a gentleman and kept in touch with her for a long time, even after Tsvi had broken off with him completely. Would you believe that he even sent her a present in our name when the child was born? She was sure that we knew about it—she, who had been so afraid of us and so certain that we blamed her for what happened, for having driven him to divorce mother so that the child could have his name. And afterwards she felt certain that she would hear from us. She couldn't believe that we wouldn't want to see the child, and she was waiting for him to be old enough to be taken here on a visit. How could we not have an interest in him? Half a year ago she even signed up for an intensive Hebrew course—you can see for yourself that she can really talk. She must be quite gifted, I suppose. I tell you, she sat facing me all the time with that pencil and that notebook, writing down every new word. That's how father had begun to teach her, she said: very thoroughly. An awfully odd woman . . . and not so young anymore, either. She's at least forty-five and has a married son. In fact, she confided in me that she's about to become a grandmother. She ran a real risk to have a

child at her age, she could have given birth to a monster. And yet
she's not a bad-looking woman, is she? A bit tired and lined in the
face, and her hair is dyed a bad color . . . she told me that being
alone with a baby these past three years has been very hard on her
. . . but her body is still full of life. It's a lovely body, I saw it when
I went in to help her with the shower: a young one, with very nice
breasts—I can imagine how happy she must have made father. . . .
It's hard to see all that just from looking at her, though. You're not
used to all that makeup and those loud colors. And she does dress a
bit ridiculously, with those big horn-rimmed glasses and that feather
waving like a red arrow when she walked in. And yet she has a
toughness about her too . . . a dreamy sort of toughness, inside. To
have come straight like that to a strange house, with that little boy
all dressed in red . . . I'm sure those clothes were supposed to
mean something, though I haven't figured out what yet . . . why,
even his shoes were red . . . I don't believe she didn't have something in mind. And the way she sat grilling me about each detail
. . . and then, without even a by-your-leave, went to change and
wash the child, and to take a shower herself, after which she left him
with us and disappeared . . . suddenly it frightens me, Kedmi.
Where has she gone off to? What does she want? The one thing that
reassures me is how totally unexpectedly, how almost peculiarly
calm you are. Do you hear me, Kedmi? I trust you to have thought it
all out, to be in charge here. I'm telling you again that she's a very
odd woman: it's no accident that father was attracted to her. And
she's come here for some hidden reason, not just to find out what
happened. You should have seen how patiently she questioned me,
taking her time, getting details out of me that I never even thought
were still there. And I told her everything, even though it scared me
to: about you, about mother, about father . . . there was nothing
she didn't want to hear. And she'll go see everyone, she'll go to Tel
Aviv and Jerusalem too, she'll follow his tracks everywhere, even to
the hospital. How could we have forgotten her, she sobbed; had we
forgotten him too? I told her everything, she heard things from me I
never thought I still knew, I let her milk me dry. Until suddenly I
got stuck on that Saturday. What happened on it? I remember that
Sunday was the day of the seder, and that father took a bus by
himself to the hospital to get the divorce. He returned that afternoon,
and toward evening Tsvi arrived. But there was a Saturday before it

that I can't for the life of me recall. What happened then, Kedmi? Were we home? I'm trying to think logically about it. What could I have done that day? I suppose I cooked for the seder . . . I must have cooked for it sometime. If only I remembered what I made, I could reconstruct the whole day. What did we eat at the seder, Kedmi? No, don't be annoyed—just tell me if you remember anything. Saturday . . . there must have been something! I'm sure it was nothing . . . I mean, nothing important, just a kind of interlude . . . but still . . . I can't stand not remembering a single thing. That's why I said to her in the end, "Excuse me, are you sure that there was one?" Which got her goat. "I suppose there must have been one," I said, "it will come back to me in a minute." But she wouldn't drop the subject, she kept pursuing it, giving me the third degree. "Of course there was a Saturday," she said. "I even called you on it." "You called us? How did you call us?" "I phoned you," she said. "Early that Saturday morning. I was trying to get hold of him, don't you remember?" "That's impossible," I said. "This time you're wrong. You never phoned. If you did, I'd have remembered. I'm sure of it."

"But it's you who are wrong. She really did phone."

"She phoned when father was here?"

"Yes. In the middle of the night. Now I remember. She told you it was in the morning? Funny lady. She was looking for him in the middle of the night."

"That Saturday?"

"Do you think I can remember now if it was that Saturday or not? Believe me, I have better things to do with myself. I tried to forget that nightmare as quickly as I could, not to arrange it in chronological order."

"But you never said a word to me about any phone call."

"Why should I have? She was looking for him, not for you. I told her that he was in Tel Aviv and gave her the number there. What was I supposed to have told you? You, all of you, were completely freaked out at the time. I had to be careful to keep my distance from you. And you were happy to leave me on the sidelines anyway. You were afraid that my sanity would ruin your lunatic pleasures . . ."

Your sanity? Insufferable insufferable insufferable is how you were then. You tortured us. From the moment that father tore up your agreement and went to see another lawyer in Tel Aviv. You were so insulted . . . so hurt to the quick . . . you raged around the house like a tornado. Insufferable. Insufferable. You tormented everyone, Gaddi too. Yes, you even took it out on Gaddi. You behaved like a barbarian, slamming doors around the house, suddenly disappearing for no good reason. The nightmare was you! It began that Wednesday in the hospital the moment you walked into the library and found your agreement in pieces on the floor. The way you collected them one by one with that caustic smile of yours . . . oh, I could see right away how hurt you were. No, don't deny it. You had a right to be, and it was all so long ago anyway. I should have grabbed it from father when he started tearing it, but everything was happening so fast . . . Asi was screaming and hitting himself in order to goad father on . . . and then suddenly, there you were in the doorway . . . and that document you had worked on for so many days . . . all those times you had run to mother with it, all the telephone calls, all the drafts . . . there it was, in shreds at our feet, with father announcing that he would see some other lawyer whom he knew. I knew we should never have involved you in the whole business. But you insisted on it. You wanted to be involved. You wanted to prove to him, to us all, that you were capable of handling it, and I'm to blame for not having stopped you. It's just that you went into one of your manias that leave us all paralyzed, and me most of all. Not that I'm blaming you. Your intentions were good. You wanted to help, to save father money. And perhaps you thought that he would pay you something for it in the end. No, don't be annoyed at me. Listen. It wasn't your fault that you needed work then. You had just opened that little office of yours, with that moronic secretary who kept messing up. And father didn't help any, either. He certainly shouldn't have fired you in the middle like that and gone to someone else. But the violence of your reaction, the blow to your pride . . . the minute we got back to the car, with that radio blasting away, I could feel your spiteful silence. The way you revved up the engine . . . and do you remember what you did to that dog? No, don't innocently ask me what dog. Our dog. Horatio! The way you cleverly lured him behind you on the main road to make him lose his way and get run over. You played him along, slowing down and speeding up again . . . What do you mean, you don't remember? Mother's friends in the hospital spent five days looking for him in the fields. That little

old man searched for him everywhere. At least let's be honest. I'm
not blaming you now. We all made mistakes then, and together they
kept adding up. It was a mistake to bring Gaddi along too. Yes, I
know, father wanted him to come. But I brought him for mother's
sake, and in the end he had to bear the brunt of it. Only you didn't
spare him any, either. You were merciless with him. You were brutal.
You wanted to punish the whole world for your torn agreement and
for father's loss of faith in you. And you yourself lost control, like a
child having a tantrum. But completely, which is something that
seldom happens to you, because control is the one thing that you
always manage to keep. In every situation, in all your gags, in the
cynical jokes you play on people, in all your loose talk and your
brainstorms that you can't keep to yourself, I always know I can be
sure that you won't go too far. Calm down, I tell myself, it's just a
game, he'll know when to stop and apologize with a smile. Bear with
him, I think, you may as well enjoy his shenanigans. And you do
know that I secretly enjoy them, don't you, because I know that I
can always wait for you to collapse into bed in the evening and curl
up exhausted there . . . that I needn't mind your tongue-lashings
or be hurt by them, because I know another you too: heavy, quiet,
sleepy and warm. . . . But then you were savage with desperation,
you'd been cut to the very quick. No, don't put a brave face on it
now: you simply weren't talking to us then, that's why you never
told me about that phone call. And you had stopped talking because
that was the worst punishment you could give us and the worst
punishment you could give yourself. What could be more terrible for
you than silence? It exasperates you and makes you mean. Not that I
myself would have minded, my thoughts were elsewhere at the time.
But you stopped talking to Gaddi then too. Now you may not remember. Then you didn't say a word to him for days, though, as
though he were to blame for it too . . . Gaddi, who's so used to
your being involved in all he does, and who so admires you . . . no,
I don't mean admires . . . but depends on you and is attached to
you. I'm not saying that explains what happened. But it was hard on
him. Although of course it wasn't only that: it was his being left to
cope by himself in all that confusion, all that anger and grief that
helped bring on the attack. I told her all about it this morning,
because I wanted her to understand what we went through that
week, how we would have lost the boy too if not for you. Yes, if not

for you: I told her in so many words. Only Kedmi, I said. He was the one, I won't forget it as long as I live. If he hadn't kept those marvelously quick wits of his about him and insisted on rushing the boy to the hospital in time . . . if he hadn't read the symptoms correctly as soon as he hit the floor . . . I told her so this morning . . . if it hadn't been for Kedmi . . . because I too hadn't been paying Gaddi enough attention, I was too terrified by what happened to father even to think. And who would have dreamed that a seven-and-a-half-year-old could go and have a heart attack like that? In the middle of all the horror it was Kedmi who saved the boy for us. Who gave him to me again, a second time . . . so that since then I'm willing to be his slave . . . since then I've forgiven you everything. I didn't tell her that, but I'm telling you now. Are you listening?

"Listening to what?"

"To what I've been saying."

"You haven't been saying anything. You've been quiet."

"I've been quiet?"

"You may have been talking to yourself, but as far as I'm concerned you've been quiet."

"I was talking to myself?"

"How should I know? Ask yourself."

"You must have fallen asleep."

"You always seem to think that if I'm not talking I must be asleep, because there is no other possibility. But amazingly enough, Ya'eli, there are times when I do think silently. I wasted so many good thoughts at the office today that I have to stock up again for tomorrow."

"What time is it?"

"Past ten."

"How can you expect to fall asleep so early?"

"I can fall asleep anytime. Haven't I told you the title of my latest book? *Falling Asleep in Ten Easy Lessons.* How does that grab you?"

"I'll be the first to read it, Kedmi."

"Thank you. That's very kind of you. The first lesson will be called, 'Silencing Your Spouse.' "

"She hasn't come back yet, Kedmi. What can she be up to? She hasn't phoned, either. I can't imagine where she is. She's been gone since four o'clock. I'm beginning to worry."

"Worry all you like if you enjoy it, but I don't know what your hurry is. Let it wait until tomorrow. By then you can worry for real."

"Until tomorrow? What are you talking about?"

"A little bird tells me that she's left town. And you know that my little birds are always right."

"Why on earth should she have left town? When? She said that she wanted to look up some acquaintances . . . that she had something to bring them . . ."

"She asked me to drop her off at the central bus station. I rather doubt that she's already made acquaintances there."

"You mean to say you left her off at the central station? You didn't tell me that."

"There are lots of things I didn't tell you. Such as that she bought herself a map of Israel and asked me to show her on it where the hospital was and how to get there . . ."

"She didn't go to the hospital . . . she couldn't have. But where is she? I don't get it. And the child is here . . . what can she be thinking of? I . . ."

"I don't know what she's thinking of, but I do know what you're thinking of, and I'm afraid that it's something silly once again. You're worried that she may have left you the child as a present and absconded . . . but that's really a bit much, Ya'el. A handsome, healthy, light-skinned boy like that, with a religious education to boot, is worth a few thousand dollars in today's market even without his fine clothes. I can't believe she'd pass all that money up . . ."

"How can you talk like that!"

"She'll be back, Ya'el. And if she isn't, we'll give the child to Asi and Dina. I've already told you that we'll never get back from the Christians the Holy Ghost that they stole from us two thousand years ago."

"Will you tell me what's gotten into you? What kind of way is that to talk?"

"A logical way, Ya'el. A cold, quiet, logical way. I leave the fine emotions to you."

"You don't understand . . . you don't see it . . . you've hardly talked to her, but she and I spent a whole morning together. She's an odd, peculiar woman. She came here with some ulterior motive. It's beyond me how you can lie there so calmly. You're beginning to seem peculiar to me too . . ."

"Thank you."

"No, really. How can you be so nonchalant? It isn't like you. What's wrong with you? Don't you see, to turn up suddenly like that without warning . . . with the suitcases and the child . . . and you should have seen how she dressed him . . ."

"Give me three guesses. All in red?"

"Stop that! Just leave me alone. I won't say another word."

"If you expect me to jump out of bed and start running frantically around the room with you . . . I mean if it will help calm you down, I'll be only too happy to do it. Because there is nothing that I wouldn't do for you, my dearest wife. But I do think that it was presumptuous of me to plan on writing *Falling Asleep in Ten Easy Lessons.*"

"That's enough, Kedmi! Cut it out. If you could possibly avoid that tone of yours tonight . . . because I've had enough . . ."

"But what are you getting so worked up about? Do tell me. If somebody brought me a sweet little English-speaking thing like that one fine day I'd be too thrilled for words. The trouble with you is that you take things too much for granted. If you were an only child like me, you'd appreciate what you were given today . . ."

"Leave me alone."

"Maybe you'd like to have a cry now? I think your problem may be that you haven't cried enough today. Let yourself go . . . if you don't, you'll fall apart again the way you did three years ago. Only this time I won't let you. It took me a long time to put you back together, and to this day I'm not sure that a few parts aren't missing."

"Kedmi, please. Not now. I'm nervous as hell."

"She'll come back. She really will, Ya'el. You needn't be so tense."

"Are you sure?"

"The only thing I'm sure of is our great and terrible love. If you weren't so preoccupied, in fact, I'd make you a proposal that more than one lady would be happy to get from me at this hour of the night. But I won't put you to any more trouble. I really did like, though, what you said about my keeping control and about your secretly enjoying my jokes. I wish you'd put it in writing, as we say, so that your admirers would stop accusing me of tormenting you all the time . . ."

"But you are tormenting me. What's happened to put you in such a wonderful mood? I'm all pins and needles, and you're flat on your back without a care. What happened, Kedmi, did you close some big deal at the office today?"

"I may be about to, but that isn't it. I like the deal we've already closed even better. Why, we've enlarged our family today with practically no effort. I've gained a new brother-in-law in diapers and a dynamic, young American mother-in-law. There's a sense in the air of going places. I feel that we've become younger today. You know I think the world of your family . . ."

"All right, I'm leaving. You're out of control for real now."

"You know I'm not. You said yourself that . . ."

"I think the child is crying."

"He isn't. But if you'd like him to, I can arrange it."

"Where did you really take her? Now you're going to tell me the truth!"

"I told you. To the bus station. I didn't ask her, but she must have gone up north to see the hospital. All I did was change some dollars for her. I had no time, I was in a hurry to get to work. I agree with you that she's a rather odd woman. Like a sleepwalker—all there in a dreamlike sort of way. It's hard to believe that your father went all the way to America just to find the same type that he was running away from here . . ."

"Leave my father out of this. Do you hear me? Don't start on him now. That's enough. Just tell me what happened on Saturday."

"On Saturday?"

"Then . . . when my father was here three years ago . . ."

"Oh, no. Now you're really going off the deep end. Don't tell me you're still looking for that day . . ."

"Yes. It matters to me that I've forgotten it."

"God save us all, she's beginning again. What exactly is it that matters?"

"It just does, a great deal. And I feel that you remember what happened and won't tell me."

"*I* remember? That's a good one! Do you think I have nothing else to do than remember what happened three years ago? I hate to imagine where all this will end. I had thought there was a division of labor in this house whereby you were responsible for the past and I took care of the present, so that when the present became the past there would be something for you to remember. You've gone far enough, my dearest: it's time to get over this obsession of yours. . . . And she won't vanish into thin air. Nobody does in this country. Before you can finish jumping off a cliff five helicopters are on their way to save you. . . . Come on, calm down. I still feel like making you a proposal that more than one lady would be happy to get from me at this hour of the night. . . . Hey, where are you going?"

But what did happen on that Saturday? If only I had a clue: a patch of light, a shape of cloud, the way someone looked, a sentence, a few words, a tone of voice, the motion of a child, an item on the radio, one of Kedmi's jokes, the mood I was in, my own face, a single thought. Where are you, day? Where did you get lost? Who made off with you? Somehow I muffed it. And yet there must be a starting point somewhere. Why, that Sunday morning is so hauntingly, so unforgettably, so forever clear in my mind: breakfast in the kitchen . . . a fierce blue sky outside . . . father drinking coffee in a dark suit, his reading glasses perched on his nose, leafing quickly through some papers in front of him, throwing me a worried glance. But when did he return to Haifa? On Friday afternoon he called from Tel Aviv. Kedmi picked up the receiver, said something rude into it, and threw it down again, signaling me to come. It was raining outside. Father's warm, deep voice sounded far away. "Father," I asked, "is it raining in Tel Aviv too?" And he answered, "The sky is blue here. Tel Aviv has never been lovelier." He told me that he was letting her have the apartment, that he had signed it away at the lawyer's a few hours ago. And then he started in on Tsvi. "Watch out for him. He'll take everything. From you too. For those old pederasts of his"—he repeated the phrase several times—"for those old pederasts who hang around him all the time . . ." But between those two memories a whole day is gone, wrapped in white shrouds deep inside me, a missing montage of quick frames, a blank leaven of time between two fixed points. That Saturday. Something has to strike a spark, if only his coming to Haifa. When did he arrive? When could he have arrived? What happened when he did? To think that I've forgotten. If only I could make myself hear the ring of her phone call that morning. Because she really did call, and I must have heard it, even if I didn't know that I did. If only I could hear the phone ring, or remember myself having heard it, I'd have something to latch on to. . . . But no answer. Nothing. A gray void, hollow flecks of foam, unreal hours, a page torn from a calendar. Nothing. And yet that can't be. There must be a way to remember. Right now, deep in this armchair. Turn out the light then, Ya'el. I must find that Saturday. If I let it get away from me now, I'll never retrieve it again.

—What is it, Gaddi? What's wrong? Can't you fall asleep?

—No. I'm not sleeping here. I'm just sitting up a while.

—No special reason. I turned off the light to help me think. No, please don't sprawl on the sofa now . . . go back to bed, it's late . . .

—What hurts? Your foot? That's nothing. It's because you're growing. It's nothing. Your father's gone again and . . .

—I don't know. What do you need him for? I don't think he's asleep yet. He's just thinking in bed.

—You're hungry? But how could you be! All right, tell me what you want to eat. But make it quick.

—Bread? In the middle of the night you have to have bread? All right, I'll slice you a piece. What do you want on it?

—Plain bread?

—No. Your dad won't be angry. He's exaggerating. You needn't worry about it.

—But you're not getting fat again at all.

—Never mind him. He forgets that you have to grow too.

—Ever since the two of you went on that diet together, he thinks that you have to watch every bite. You mustn't pay him any attention.

—That's perfectly all right.

—I know very well what you're allowed to eat and what you aren't. Come, let me spread some butter on it for you. Just a bit, so it won't be so dry in your mouth.

—His mother? She'll be back soon.

—No. He won't stay with us. Just for a few days.

—She wanted us to see him. He's a sweet little boy, isn't he?

—No. She made him wear a skullcap because she didn't know any better. She thought that everyone in Israel wears them.

—All right, I'll tell her. But he is a lovely child, isn't he?

—That doesn't matter. You and Rakefet can teach him some Hebrew words.

—No, don't call him Moshe. He won't know who you're talking to. Call him Moses. That's what he's used to being called.

—Yes, my love. Moses is his real name.

—What makes you think he stutters? You're just imagining it.

—I didn't notice. That's how Americans talk.

—Well, not all of them. But the children.

—Maybe not all the children either. But don't forget that he's really very small. And he's in a strange house now, after a long trip.

—Like who?

—Like Tsvi, yes. He does look an awful lot like him. Sometime I'll show you a picture of Tsvi when he was a baby and you'll see how alike they look.

—Exactly.

—Right. Because he's grandpa's child, even though grandpa never knew him.

—Yes. He died before he was born.

—Here in Israel.

—No. He wasn't that old. He had an accident . . . something ran into him . . . it knocked him down . . . we don't know exactly what . . .

—Something.

—It was a kind of an accident.

—Yes. Like an automobile accident.

—No. He's not a real uncle of yours like Asi or Tsvi. Your dad was just trying to be funny. But he is a half uncle, even though he's very small.

—Exactly.

—That's right. He's grandpa's son.

—Yes. Like me. Like Asi.

—Yes. A kind of uncle. You could say that he was one.

—That's right. Only grandma wasn't his mother.

—Do you still remember grandpa?

—You do? Really? Do you remember him well?

—I'm so glad that you had a chance to meet him. Don't ever forget him.

—You'll remember if you want to. But only if you want to.

—Yes. Rakefet won't remember even if she does want to. But what do you remember?

—Yes, that's right. He slept all day long . . .

—That was the Sunday he arrived.

—That's right. You were left alone with him.

—Right, right. I remember your bathing Rakefet. He was so impressed by how you helped him.

—He cut his hand? No, I don't remember that. But maybe he did.

—It was before you got sick.

—No. Not so fat. You were very sweet. Sometimes I miss how sweet you were then.

—And afterwards? Do you remember the seder with grandpa?

—You don't? But how can that be? Try to remember it . . .

—Then you don't. But you do remember going to visit grandma in the hospital with Asi, don't you?

—Not that either?!

—You were seven and a half. How could you not remember?

—Not even how we all went there together and grandma gave you cake to eat? How did you ever forget . . . ?

—And that locomotive that you got . . . you don't remember that either?

—A big locomotive that grandpa brought you . . . how can that be . . . not even that huge man who tried taking it away from you?

—He was a little crazy. You don't remember him?

—Only that day that grandpa slept here? That's all?

—It was right before Passover. And the Saturday before the seder . . . do you remember anything about that Saturday?

—Never mind.

—Well, if you've finished eating, you'd better go to sleep. It's late already. Come, I'll cover you . . .

The child is standing up without a sound, bathed in moonlight, leaning on the bars of the crib, rubbing his eyes. In a minute he'll cry and ask for his mother. The look of him staggers me: a perfect replica, down to the cut of the jaw, a signed copy. How long has he been standing there so quietly? The room is awfully stuffy, I'd better open a window. Rakefet, all ruddy-faced, has slipped off her mattress onto the floor. If Connie is planning to stay with us, I'll have to look for a folding bed in the morning. There's a strong smell of pee in the air. How sweetly the children filled the crib for him with toys . . .

—Go to sleep, Gaddi. I'll take care of him. Don't worry about it.

Only I can't lift him. The stubborn little thing clings to the bed, regarding me curiously, primed to cry, wondering where in the world he is. My brother. The absurdity of it. Yesterday he spent long hours in the sky. And where has she disappeared to? How can she have done such a thing? Everything is soaking wet: the sheets, the blanket, the whole bed. A copy of father. Incredible. Damned scary too. The identical profile . . . And then, as though over some distant mountain peak, a sudden flash of memory: where on earth has it come from, so stormy-sweet? A moonlit winter night in our old apartment in Tel Aviv. A warm rain falling, a huge moon in the sky. Tsvi, a small child in father and mother's big gilded four-postered bed, wearing those heavy pink pajamas that later were handed down to Asi . . . Tsvi, standing behind the pile of quilts . . . I remember so clearly now . . . his face, the look of him . . . it must have been the middle of the night. They had called me in the middle of the night, or else it was a morning they slept late. Mother was naked beneath a white nightgown, and pregnant. Yes, I'm sure she was. And then father emerged from beneath the quilts too, laughing. They had called me to take Tsvi back to bed. How old could I have been then, ten? The same age as Gaddi. "He'll only go with you," they said. Mother had shut her eyes against the light of the bed lamp. Her hair was loose and she was too absorbed in her own burgeoning self to notice me. I felt that there was some secret pact between them, some deep equilibrium that allowed them to think the same thoughts. They gave Tsvi to me. His long, thin face. And then father kissed mother's feet, and a deep burst of fear took me by storm. When was it? A distant memory. The trees of the avenue in the rain, their large wet leaves glistening in the moonlight. Tsvi's face.

Gaddi curls up beneath his blanket, watching me with his intelligent look. So somber, so serious, a little Kedmi but without the sense of humor, with only that stubbornly logical mind of his. Always having to defend himself from being crushed by Kedmi's attentions. And here is this sweet addition to our family today standing so seriously too, gripping the bars of the crib, his large eyes looking quietly at the clouds adrift in the winter sky, drenched in his pee. How can she have gone and left him like this? It's too much for me even to think about. "Come, let me pick you up," I say. He points to something, speaking in an English that I can't begin to understand.

"Say *boy nice* to him," says Gaddi from under his blanket.

"All right, you go to sleep already. . . . Come," I say to the child. "Come, *good boy.*"

My ridiculously meager English. I take a blanket and wrap him in it to keep him from getting chilled. Absurdly, though, I can't lift him. Suddenly he's dug his little feet into the mattress.

"Come." I pluck him up by force and carry him to the living room, where I stand him in the darkness on the rug. *"One moment,"* I say, going to look for a pair of Rakefet's pajamas. He starts to whimper. Dear God, what should I say to him? *"I change you."* Lord, was that right? Kedmi, come. "There there. *Nice boy. Good boy.* Kedmi! Are you up?"

All at once the telephone rings. It has to be her.

"Kedmi!" I shout. "Answer it! I'll be there in a minute."

"Are you already done talking? Who was it? Was it her?"

"Hello, Moses. How do you do?"

"I'm asking you something! Answer me. Was that Connie?"

"Hello, Moses. Bring him over to the bed here. He really does look like your father. It's amazing . . ."

"Kedmi! Who was that on the telephone? Was it her?"

"Yes."

"Then why the hell did you hang up so fast?"

"Let me have him. . . . You know, your family has this strong, really violent gene in its bloodline. I'm sure glad that Gaddi didn't get it."

"Kedmi, none of that now. What did she say? Why did you hang up on her?"

"I didn't. She finished talking. Will you hand me that child now?"

"What did she say?"

"Nothing special."

"Did she ask about the child?"

"Yes. I told her you were changing him and talking to him in English."

"When is she coming back?"

"She didn't say."

"What do you mean, she didn't say? Didn't you ask?"

"It doesn't look like she'll be back before tomorrow."

"Not before tomorrow? But why . . . ?"

"Why not? Would you prefer her to stay away a whole week?"

"Why didn't you let me talk to her?"

"She didn't ask to talk to you."

"Goddamn you! What are you two up to? Where was she talking from? Did she leave a number?"

"Hello, Moses. Would you hand him to me already? I can't get over how much he looks like your father. Come on, let me have him. Since when does he belong only to you? You know, he stutters a little . . ."

"Kedmi, answer me. Where was she talking from?"

"I don't know."

"How can you not know? Suddenly you're the picture of innocence. What's gotten into you tonight? How can you go on lying passively in bed at a time like this? What did she say to you? Where has she disappeared to?"

"What time is it?"

"Nearly eleven."

"You don't say. It really is late. And you want to get me up and into a chair at this hour? What did we buy a bed for? *Hello, Moses!* Be a sport, let me have him. I want to play with him too."

"Kedmi!"

"Come on now, calm down. She'll be back tomorrow, I promise you. Instead of running around the house like a nervous wreck you should take a look at yourself in the mirror. You're still wearing the apron that you put on this morning . . . you really are a sight. Let me have the child. Why don't you change his bed, and change yourself too while you're at it . . ."

He's hiding something. That smile of his. What's come over him? There's something between them. There has to be. He'd never be so calm otherwise. What is he up to? Can it be . . . is she really capable of running off and leaving us the . . . *but what face superimposes itself?* I can hear the ring of a telephone in the distance . . . how strongly the memory of it flickers on . . . of course! How did I ever forget it? Was it that morning? A call from the prison. That man—that prisoner—that murderer of his—had escaped. I have it! They called that morning. It was raining. It was Saturday. That man—that prisoner—that murderer of his—had escaped. They called from the prison. Of course they did. And it was raining. Now I remember. Saturday. I have it!

All of a sudden the curtain goes up, is lifted, torn asunder. And Saturday shines through. Yes, that Saturday, breaking through just as it was, down to its last color and smell. That morning it rained . . . seize the day, Ya'el! And in the afternoon the sun came out . . . Saturday, the day before the seder, the veil has been rent . . . it can stand on its own feet now, every hour of it . . . and what pandemonium there was. I was cooking in the kitchen for the seder. Rakefet had woken up and was crying. A sour fear churned inside me. Father would soon be leaving, making his getaway: if anything happened to her from now on, I could never turn to him for help. Kedmi had surrounded himself with a pile of weekend papers and still was not talking to me. Tomorrow, at the seder, he was sure to find a way of taking his revenge on father. And just then they called from the prison. I happened to answer. "Something's happened to your murderer," I said, because that's how we called him, that's how he referred to him with us. "I've been to see my murderer." "My murderer said . . ." "My murderer thinks . . ." Kedmi grabbed the phone from me savagely and stood listening to the news. I could tell at once from the look on his face what an awful blow it was.

The children's room is dark. The pungent smell is everywhere. I have to let in some air. To open a window and let the pleasant winter breeze in. Everything is soaked in his pee. You'd think some geyser had erupted inside him. The sheets. The mattress. Rakefet sighs in her sleep, a little flower. Gaddi sucks his thumb, his eyes aflutter. I go over and gently remove the finger from his mouth. He opens his eyes.

"Where is he?"

"With your dad."

"Will he sleep with you?"

"No. I'm just changing his bed."

"Did he only pee, or did he . . . ?"

"He only peed . . . don't worry about it . . . go back to sleep now . . ."

The day of remembrance. The dam has burst. Saturday? Yes, that was it! How strongly, how full of light, it gushes forth now. The tears sting my eyes. How did I ever forget it? And yet I did. In its hurry to get to the accident my memory simply erased it, hectic interlude that it was: the phone calls from the prison, the mess in the kitchen, Kedmi's search for his poor murderer, Kedmi's mother, Rakefet's constant crying, father's arrival that afternoon—an onion shedding its skins one by one, the day shows through on different planes, in different places, unrolling like a sheet of bright tinsel . . . With what should I begin? With Kedmi. In a state of shock, swearing a blue streak, as though his prisoner had escaped for the sole purpose of ruining his career. "Why am I wasting my time being a lawyer? If I were a jailer I could free all the defendants I want." He dressed quickly and rushed to the prison, leaving me—do I hear that faint musical score now?—in the kitchen with a mountain of vegetables and a bloody hunk of raw meat in a bowl, while Gaddi began to complain again of chest pains and Rakefet went on crying. The telephone didn't stop ringing: Kedmi's mother, Tsvi, Asi, the police. The hospital called to ask about the dog and then mother got on the phone to ask too. And soon father was due in the midst of all this madness, and already I could see how the seder night I had had such high hopes for was falling apart before my eyes. . . . Kedmi returned in a vile mood, still cursing like a trooper. "Please tell me what the big tragedy is," I begged him. "You know they'll find him in the end. You yourself said that he just ran away to be with his parents for the seder. When it's through he'll turn himself in." But Kedmi's great fear was that the police would catch him and worm out of him the confession that he had refused to give them so far . . . that Kedmi had desperately been trying to keep from them . . . because the murderer really was one . . . Kedmi didn't believe in him himself . . .

Saturday. Of course. That was it. I have it now with all its colors and smells, down to that light, last morning rain, after which the clouds broke up and a warm wind began to blow. I stood on the terrace hanging up wash, clean sheets and tablecloths, while Kedmi heartrendingly stalked the house like a caged lion, phoning the police every few minutes to advise them, to berate them, to warn them of something new. In the end he decided to drive down to where the prisoner's parents lived and to catch him himself, so that he could return him to jail and go on defending him. What a weird, wild, wacky day it was! I'm still reeling from the force with which the memory of it has hit me . . . to think of me sitting there and idiotically repeating to her, "Saturday, Saturday, are you sure there was a Saturday?" until she was certain that I was trying to hide something crucial from her! Time passed. I waited for father. And then suddenly that afternoon Kedmi called from the office, whispering in a conspiratorial voice. "Come quick, I need your help. My mother's on her way over to baby-sit. I found him but he got away. Come quick, I need you! We'll pick up your father at the taxi stand downtown. I've already spoken to Tsvi."

Saturday afternoon in an empty, drowsy downtown already under the influence of the approaching holiday. . . . Kedmi's mother had come to stay with the children, in a fit over the vanished murderer, terribly piqued by him. How could he have done such a thing after all Kedmi had sacrificed for him? The sheer ingratitude of it! . . . I raced to that dreary office of his that he kept in those days when he was trying to make a go of private practice. The corridors were deserted. A musty smell hung over the stairs. He was waiting for me in the doorway in a white heat, his mind working furiously. He had spotted his murderer in his old neighborhood—where, it turned out, the police hadn't even bothered to search. They had, Kedmi said, spent all day looking in the forests of the Carmel, apparently convinced that the escaped man had gone to pick flowers. But Kedmi had seen him in the street, from an ambush he had set for him not far from his home. Only the murderer took off as soon as he saw Kedmi —the nincompoop must have thought that it was a trap set by the police and all Kedmi's shouting that he was there by himself couldn't keep him from running away. Kedmi was sure he would come back, though. The man simply missed his parents. My job, since he didn't know me, was to wait for him by his house and tell him when he appeared, "Mr. Kedmi wants to talk to you. He has an idea that might help you."

A crazy Saturday, how did I ever forget it? Spring had broken out, the sky lifted quickly. A Saturday of different places, of different people coming and going, of doors opening and shutting, of telephones ringing, of everything happening at once—presiding over all of which was Kedmi, unshaven, disheveled, red in the face, looking like an escaped criminal himself, explaining to me how after the seder he would turn his murderer over to the police at an official press conference. Let them see what a real lawyer was. How his clients obeyed him unquestioningly. How they had perfect faith in him.

Saturday afternoon. Such soft, sweet, sabbathy light, and I utterly exhausted, my head in a whirl. Nothing was ready yet for the seder, and father was getting divorced the next morning and flying back to America two days later, leaving mother to me. I could see myself running through the fields around the hospital in search of her dog, trapped in Kedmi's childish games, having to take Gaddi to the doctor—and meanwhile the hours were going by and nothing had been done. And soon it would be time for the long, deep goodbye to father. . . . By a felafel stand near the station where some teenagers were hanging out we watched him get out of the taxi. Once again I was greeting him—all week long I'd kept dispatching him and welcoming him back. It's all so clear: how did I forget it? The first thing that struck me was the haircut he had gotten in Tel Aviv, which made him look older and grayer. His clothes were rumpled and he walked with a stoop, pulled down by his valise. How it all shoots through me now: his coming that Saturday, his standing there on the sidewalk while I kissed him and hugged him hard, his marveling at the puddles left at the base of the trees by the morning's rain. "With us in Tel Aviv," he said, "it's spring, even summer. The weather has been so hot and dry that people are flocking to the beaches." *With us,* he said, as though he had never left, as though it were I who soon would depart again for who knew how long, as though he had not signed away his home the day before and was about to fly far away. How nice it was of Kedmi, he said, surprised, to relieve him of his bag right away. "There's some dirty laundry in it, Ya'eli. It would be good of you to help me wash it. I haven't any underwear left." Kedmi put a hand on his shoulder, steering him to the car, while we told him all about our murderer. He listened carefully, with a bemused smile, and proposed at once that he come with me, it being unthinkable to send me by myself after an escaped killer, even if Kedmi swore he was a gentle one.

Kedmi drove us to a working-class quarter outside of town, on the road to Tivon, near the big quarry cut by the cement works into the mountainside. He pointed out the house to us, handed me a photograph of the escapee that he had found in his office, and vanished into some side street. And so we found ourselves, father and I, walking at the drop of dusk down a narrow working-class street to meet Kedmi's murderer and talk him into going back to jail. Near the house was a bus stop with a bench on which we sat while keeping a lookout on the entranceway. How could I have forgotten? We might as well have been on another planet, just the two of us sitting there alone. Father spoke and I listened. He was troubled and needed to talk, full of impressions from his days in Tel Aviv and aghast how little time was left him, jumping from one thing to another while the twilight thickened and an occasional passerby stopped to stare at us. . . . "I've signed away my home," he kept saying. "I never want to hear about it again. You'll collect my things there and keep them for me. But don't let Tsvi have the apartment all for himself. He's a degenerate. And he's getting worse. He'll sell it in order to play the market. And you'd better warn mother about him, because she'll never listen to me . . ." His eyes filled with tears. He was on the subject of mother now. "So she's finally driven me away. At last she's managed to uproot me. I'm being punished by her for not being crazy too, for not having gone over the brink with her. She thinks that because we once thought the same way I owe her eternal fealty . . ." All at once he made me get up and stroll in the street with him, holding my hand while he told me again of that morning she had tried killing him and of how Tsvi could not have cared less. I walked by his side, listening in anguish, returning an occasional stare, glancing now and then at the photograph I held so as not to miss our man when he appeared. He was getting emotional, talking with great intensity. We turned and headed back the other way. Children raced by us toward a bonfire of leavened bread that had been lit at the end of the street. Suddenly he gripped me hard. "And you—what do you think? You're the only one who's never expressed an opinion. You just agree with everyone . . . with me, with mother, with us all. How can you be so passive?" And I answered,

"You're right. I really have no opinion. I never have had one." "But I don't understand how that's possible," he protested. "Opinions are too much for me," I said. "I can only feel you. I've never been able to think you. It's as though you both were my babies." Those were my words. It was an odd thing to say and he stood there perplexed while the sun set in the distant bay. But did he really say what comes next or did I imagine it? Yes, he must have said it: "It's you who will kill me in the end." "Me?" I whispered, thunderstruck. "Yes, you. You more than anyone with your silence." Did he say it or did I imagine it? Yes, and then he said, "You've taken my home from me and now you won't let me go." How could I have forgotten? Why? I kept silent then too. Silent as usual. I didn't answer, and then he smiled and hugged me. In its insatiable rush to the accident my memory ran over it all . . . and in the end night came with still no sign of the murderer. We went to look for Kedmi and found him back on the main road, asleep at the wheel.

We came home. Kedmi's mother was gray from the strain and the tension. Father took out his laundry and began to do a wash. Kedmi paced the room again like a beaten dog until he phoned the police and was told to his great joy that the search had been called off. Then he began tidying up around the house and helped me put the children to bed, after which he talked gently to father and even made him some coffee. He couldn't do enough for us now, he was all sweetness and light. . . . And then he suddenly disappeared, only to return an hour later in a state of high excitement. He had, it turned out, paid a call on his murderer's parents—who, though insisting they had no knowledge of their son's escape, seemed definitely to Kedmi to be waiting for him. And poor Kedmi, unable to bear the thought of all his efforts going down the drain, cornered me and begged me to accompany him there again and to wait while he tried one more time.

That Saturday dragged on and on, it seemed to have no end. Who was it who threw a gray blanket over it afterwards? It was almost midnight when Kedmi finally persuaded father and me to go with him again to that working-class quarter, whose streets were deserted now. He sat us on the same unearthly bench, beneath a yellowish streetlight, and drove off to wait around the corner. Father was amused by it all. He was wide awake and kept joking while he toyed with the murderer's photograph in his hand, relating old memories, telling me of his plans for the future, to which I listened drowsily, silently, passively, half dead from exhaustion, smelling his sweat as I leaned on him, forgetting immediately what he said like a bottle that hasn't room for one more drop, letting my glance wander slowly over the tall chimneys of the cement works that glowed with an unnatural, ochroid smoke, over the small, empty street, over the entrance to one of its houses, where I saw Kedmi's murderer detach himself from a wall as though it were the wall itself that had moved: a short, wiry young man, gliding along the housefronts with slow, catlike strides, keeping away from the light. I rose at once. Head down, hands in his pockets, he didn't even look up at me. I stood peering into his unshaven face, into his beady eyes, while father jumped up to join me. "Just a minute," I said. "I'm Mr. Kedmi's wife. He's around the corner, and he wants to talk to you. That's all he wants. It's for your own good. There are no policemen with him."

He froze where he was and studied me and father. He didn't seem frightened. "I have nothing to say to him," he said drily, in a cold voice. "All he ever wants to do is talk. But he doesn't believe what I say. Let him find a real criminal to play with. I've had it with him."

He turned to go with hesitant steps, no longer knowing where to. And then, like a teacher lightly grasping a pupil, father laid a hand on his shoulder and began to talk to him, gesturing broadly with his other hand while the listening man kept walking with his eyes on the ground. They disappeared into the next street and I ran to get Kedmi, who had dozed off again at the wheel. "Kedmi," I said, waking him, "father is talking to him right now." He jumped groggily out of the car and started to run, shouting in the empty street, but the murderer took off again as soon as he saw him, scaling the fence of the cement works and vanishing among its tall chimneys. Father reached for a cigarette and lit it coolly, wide awake and collected. "He promised to come to you after the seder," he told Kedmi, who was in total despair. "He swore he'd turn himself in then. He gave me his word and I believe him. So can you." And Kedmi, perhaps for the first time in all the years I'd known him, stood speechless as a statue, unable to get out a single word.

Now he's fallen asleep, a newspaper over his face, the child looking down on him among the pillows and blankets. He has a funny way of standing, the child, almost hunched, toes dug in, his eyes searching for the moon behind the curtain flapping in the breeze. A tall, skinny little boy who still hasn't spoken to me, who regards me with a suspicious look. I try out my broken English on him again while he cocks his head in wonder.

"That's enough of your Shakespearian diction," grunts Kedmi in his sleep. "Would you kindly put Moses to bed now? He's taking a walk on my head."

I pick him up, carry him to the freshly made but still wet crib, lay him down in it, and cover him up, his sweetness rubbing off on my fingers. And again I try talking to him. Rakefet rolls over on her back, entering a new, more relaxed stage of sleep. Gaddi stirs in bed too, still not sleeping deeply. The room is dark except for the small night light. I'm already on my way out the door when the child stands up again, gripping the crib bars tightly, eyeing me. What does he want? Such a strange, quiet, inward creature. I try laying him down again but he clings defiantly to the bars, grimacing with determination. Where can she be? Has she really gone and left him with us? Can it be, are such aberrations possible too? A portrait of father as a small child.

All at once something makes me recoil, as if father himself had just entered the room from the hallway and left it again via the window. I'm shaking all over, my heart skips a beat and then pounds even faster. How could we have let him go back there? What possessed him to do it? Why did I forget that Saturday, what was I trying to repress? Perhaps meeting that escaped prisoner had some meaning for me . . . only how did we fail to sense it, to know it, to prevent it? What made us leave him like that, looking like he did that Saturday when he stepped out of the taxi, so old, his hair sheared beneath his hat, his valise full of dirty underwear. We had it in for him. Asi despised him. Tsvi wanted vengeance. And I had no opinion. "And you—what do you think?" And I—I didn't answer. "The one person who was genuinely happy to see me was Dina. The rest of you have been hostile, even Gaddi." And still I passively said nothing—I, who identify vicariously with everyone, I, who always will. Indiscriminately I go from one of them to another: Kedmi, Gaddi, mother, even the dog, even that murderer, even Connie the minute she walked in the door. Yes, I identify with whoever comes close to me, I adopt them without thinking, without judging. And so drive them away from me too. And yet did I really drive him away then with my silence . . . with my refusal to say the one thing he wanted to hear . . . back into the horror of that final night?

Saturday. That was it. Slowly it's slipped back into place among those nine days stubbornly salvaged from the passage of time, frozen in hard clarity, beamed by themselves upon a bright screen. At last I've retrieved the lost day. Kedmi didn't want to help me. It was painful for him to remember, I realize that now. Because that murderer of his was not really a murderer after all. Because after we had finally persuaded him to go back to jail the real murderer was found elsewhere, and he was released without the trial that Kedmi had so enthusiastically prepared for. It was that that made him admit failure, close down his practice, and take a job with the district attorney. At no point had he really believed father that the man would turn himself in. And yet all the way back up the mountain, while we sat tiredly in the car, father had to listen to him telling about his murderer and about all his plans for the trial. After which we walked into a house that was a shambles and I had to take father's underwear and hang it on the terrace in the night that had turned to real spring.

When I think of father now I still feel the same pain. The awful sorrow of it stabs me all over again. What did we do wrong? We couldn't get them back together and we couldn't pry them apart. Perhaps all we managed to do was to turn them against one another. . . . Yes, I must take the child to see mother. I'll dress him in his red clothes and bring him to her, maybe he can put some life into her . . .

I take one last peek into the children's room. He's still standing there without a sound, looking for someone. For his mother. Wondering where she's been shanghaied. Suddenly I feel more anxious than ever. Where is she? Kedmi must tell me. I go to our bedroom and undress.

"Kedmi? Yisra'el? Yisra'el, are you sleeping?"

"How can I sleep," he mumbles without opening his eyes, "when I'm already writing my new book, *Staying Awake in Ten Easy Lessons?* Tell me something, must you purposely drive me batty all night long? Why do you keep running circles around me like some big mouse?"

"Are you in a state to hear me, or must you sleep?"

"You've already filled your quota of words for the day. If you're thinking of kisses, though . . ."

"I remembered. Do you hear me? I found that lost Saturday."

"I'm overjoyed. Maybe you can also find someone to buy it from you now."

"Do you know what happened on it? It was the day that poor murderer of yours escaped and we went in the evening to look for him."

He opens his eyes.

"What murderer?"

"The one who escaped. Who turned out in the end not to . . ."

"Stop, stop, don't remind me of him! All the energy I wasted on him . . . it was he who made me close my private practice. Stop . . . when I think of your father chasing him down the street . . ."

"Do you remember how he helped you?"

"Of course I do. Well, you can relax now, you've got all your days back again. And if your mind is at rest, you might let mine get some too . . ."

"Come," I say to him, lying down naked beside him. Startled he throws off the blanket excitedly and begins to embrace me, to kiss me, to fondle my breasts. I hug him back. He wants to come into me. The child starts to cry. I push him away.

"Forget about him!"

"Where has she gone? Tell me the truth now!"

He catches his breath. "Afterwards. I promise."

The child's cries gather strength, piercing the night. Kedmi grows more and more passionate, entering me like a young buck. But I am not with him. My mind is still on that Saturday. Everyone was asleep. I stood on the terrace in the winy, fierce spring night, the starry sky above me, hanging father's laundry on the line and thinking of the days ahead with no idea yet of what lay in store for me. And so the day came to an end. Yes, it did exist after all. Of course it did. At last it has joined all the others, stubbornly salvaged from the passage of time, forever frozen in clarity, beamed with them on that one bright screen down to the last detail.

THE DAY OF THE SEDER

> The light dresses you with its flame of death,
> O enchantress, O pale sick woman, your face turned
> Toward the primeval engines of the evening
> That circles about you.
>
> Pablo Neruda

Violet light seeps from a mortal wound into the broad sky curved
over the bay etched in copper evangelic burning filaments cut into
the pinkish flesh of the infinite day driven westward to the heavily
the slowly the in-triple-time breathing sea sinking into sleep for the
night. The sun-softened water luminescent now warm spray of oily
flame turning slowly to gray in the soft lava of darkness spewn up
from the earth from the great vats hidden in the watered grass over-
run with fierce weeds thorny burnet yellow-blossoming broom creeping up among the treetops fanning out on a breath of wind turning
blue day into a black canopy for this sodden world of wet earth
greedily sipping clinging with lips that suck that kiss stoutly swinging the tongueless bell of evening snuffing out the small spaces between the lines between the words making the pages of my book a
shapeless blob while empty and bloated a giant moon suddenly flips
over in the last window quietly slips into the evening on a weak low
slant. If the dog were here he would cock his head and howl so did
she that first clear winter night we arrived she awoke and sat on the
windowsill gripping the bars letting down her hair her clothes bark-

ing with joyous abandon with secret delight at each little well-aimed yelp until they came with a straitjacket.

"Come on. Let's go! They're beginning . . . the singing has started . . . they've begun to sing . . ."

Yehezkel's voice begs from the door at the far end of the room but I will not answer him I will not move beneath my light blanket.

"You can't stay here all alone for the seder," he says again turning out the light stepping into the room gliding among the beds in his large suit in his hat and new tie a cigarette lit in his mouth. He's hoarse he's been chasing me everywhere for a whole week in a dither over my divorce. And now here he is among the beds in the women's ward where he's never dared intrude at night before desperately glancing fearfully about him his own turmoil driving him on. And only now do I notice that we are alone in the ward. Many patients went home this morning with their families and the others are waiting in the dining room now for the seder. Even the night nurse is gone. Even the doctors' room is locked. And here the silence is broken only by his footsteps small and determined he comes toward me his hands shake the spittle flies when he talks. "Come on! You can't do this to me. The singing has started . . ." He halts by my bed with a violence I never knew was in him he grabs the book from my hands and slams it shut he lays it on the night table and pokes about among my things there pulling out the white parchment divorce and holding it up to the moonlight suddenly angry with me. "Is this how you leave your things, just lying about? You're no better than a baby! What will become of you?" And without asking permission he gathers it all up and crams it in my drawer rattling my lost dog's chain yanking off my blanket in a fit of annoyance with unaccustomed roughness making me get up glaring at me angrily he must think that I'm now public property. "You're ruining our holiday! We're all waiting for you. You're the reason I stayed behind." His light warm hand grips my shoulder. "You can't do this to me!" Cast on the bare wall by the door is Musa's huge shadow motionless except for the hungry movements of his mouth that never stop.

They clustered round me from the moment that Yehuda and the rabbis left the hospital. It was as though they popped out from under the wheels of the taxi when it drove off, a whole gang of them that Yehezkel had inflamed in recent days: Musa and Ahre'le and D'vora and those two young ex-soldiers. "Congratulate her!" he commanded, grabbing my hand and extending it to them. "She's a free, eligible woman now. There's no need to kill him anymore. They've both been saved." Even Musa touched my hand, stammering and blushing with emotion. All day today they followed me everywhere, I couldn't shake them off. The nurses tried to reason with him but he kept stubbornly turning up again at my door, trailing after me as far as the fence, sitting opposite me at lunchtime, passing me platters of food, rolling out the water hose for me. There was no way to unstick him from me and no one to ask to do it. The hospital itself was in a chaos: cars driving in and out around the cottages, families looking for members to take home for the seder, strangers crowding into the wards, dressing the patients, collecting their things, signing forms, memorizing medicines, making a racket, joining us for tea. Yehezkel had a caller too, his son, a carbon copy of him: the same pinched, hangdog look, the same disintegrating face, the same wet cigarette in a corner of the mouth. The only difference between them was that the son's thinning hair was still dark. A future basket case himself. He came in a khaki scooter with a sidecar for his father but Yehezkel wouldn't go. He became so hysterical that no one could talk to him. In the end his son went to the office and brought back a doctor and nurse but Yehezkel was adamant. Absolutely not. It was his duty to stay here with me. "I tell you, he's in love with her," I heard the young doctor say. The blood rushed to my head and I ran off to my deck chair in its clump of trees, put on the glasses that father brought back today from the optometrist's, and opened the book that I've been reading for the past several years while listening to the roar of the departing scooter and the sound of Yehezkel searching for me. I mussed my hair, shut my eyes, pulled my straw hat down over my face and made believe I was asleep. Already I could hear their whispers and the branches stirring around me, could feel the earth shake from Musa's heavy tread. But when they saw me sleeping they grew oh so still and sat down where they were to keep watch. The gentle spring sun ran its rays over me. Slowly the noise of the strangers and the cars died away. A deep, peaceful silence came over me and I thought, here I am with the divorce that I wanted, he's given me his share of the house, never again will I hear him speak to me in that overbearing manner of his that punched my life full of holes. And I thought too, perhaps now is the time for a visit from her to tell me what she thinks. But my breathing grew heavier and the book slipped to the ground while I dozed off, dimly aware of someone taking my glasses and propping my head on a pillow. My mussed hair blew in the wind and I sank deep into a dream at the bottom of which a child's voice spoke in English. From somewhere came a strong smell of cooked mushrooms as though she were really nearby, my murdering-so-filled-with-longing other, and then I felt a light hand and woke with a start to see D'vora's white face framed by its faded blond hair and Yehezkel hiding behind her, holding her arm like a stick with which to stroke me. "Tsvi's come!" he exclaimed right away. "He's here. He's waiting at the gate. He sent us to get you." I had thought Tsvi might call but I never imagined he would come by himself on the day of the seder. I rose feeling woozy but clear-headed inside, as though I'd been scrubbed clean in my sleep. The hospital was completely deserted now. Alone on a path in all his glory, decked out for the holiday in an old, freshly ironed doctor's smock in place of a white shirt and a red bandanna tied around his neck, stood our King Og, our giant Musa. He even wore a black skullcap, fastened by a bobby pin. "Tsvi's at the gate," Yehezkel repeated frantically. "Did you know that he was coming? Have you spoken with him?" The man was in despair. After having stayed behind just for me, here I was running out on him. "Has he come to get you?" But I didn't answer him. Drowsy but so clean inside I walked to the gate, feeling the newly risen breeze that was softly seeding the bright sky with small clouds, followed by the three of them; Yehezkel, Musa and D'vora. (Ahre'le had vanished, someone must have come for him too.) Yehezkel was beside himself. He kept running forward, waiting for me like a faithful dog and running ahead again, as though he were clearing the way. When we passed the closed ward we all stopped at the sight of three unfamiliar children in undershirts and gym shorts, playing as unconcernedly as though they hadn't a notion where in the world they were. Children in the hospital . . . a tall blond girl and a skinny boy rolling their chubby baby brother on the lawn and chattering gaily in English . . .

We reached the gate, from which a row of eucalyptus trees flanked a road that ran ruler-straight through fields stretching out on either side: to its right a green fuzz of cotton that would break out in white blossom toward summer's end, to the left great furrows of plowed earth with huge clods thrown up alongside them. Past them the railroad tracks streamed north to touch the foothills of the Galilee, whose scrub forests cut into strips by firebreaks formed a soft horizon rubbing up against a serenely innocent round sky full of sweet radiance, like a bowl of raspberry syrup mixed with the thin exhaust of the speeding cars on the highway. Somewhere out there, where the orchards and villages ran inland, Horatio loped dirty and hungry through the juicy young thorn shoots, fooled by the intoxicating scent of my wandering wild other no borders could hold, who was making her way steadily eastward.

Beyond the gate, near the darkened guardhouse from which rock music bubbled out, my Tsvi was taking the air by a white automobile, a long cigarette in his mouth, the sleeves of the jacket draped over his shoulders whipping in the breeze to reveal a knit beige shirt above his light bell-bottom pants. He always did have a flair for color that was worthy of a fashion magazine. As soon as he saw us he broke off his small talk with the watchman, bowed casually to my escort and breezily opened the gate for me, shutting it gently in Yehezkel's face even as he thanked him. He threw away his cigarette, turned to have a look at me, took my two hands in his own, flashed a triumphant smile, and embraced me warmly. He kept up a stream of chatter as he hurried me to the car, from whose back seat he took out a bouquet of flowers. He laid them in my arms and grinned again. "You're crazy, Tsvi," I said. "Honestly." He burst into a merry laugh. "Well, you're free at last," he said. "Free as can be. I spoke to Ya'el on the phone, and when she told me it went smoothly I couldn't resist coming up. I had to, and Calderon agreed to drive me. . . . So it's over, then. Whereupon, I've been told, you went and fell peacefully asleep. Hats off to you, mother . . ." He didn't stop running on at the mouth, saying the most fatuous things. And a bouquet of flowers, no less! In the car I could see the banker's eyes glitter anxiously. He nodded imperceptibly, stiff with deference, afraid to intrude on us.

"So it's over," repeated Tsvi, slipping an arm through mine and walking with me down the road between the quiet, pre-holiday fields. "How do you feel? To tell you the truth, I was afraid he'd back out at the last minute." He looked at me. "Or else that you would. Ya'el said something about some rabbi who kept making trouble right down to the wire. But here it's over at last: you've parted honorably and without a fuss. I called Asi to tell him and he was glad too. 'It had to happen . . . sooner or later it had to . . . there was no choice'—he kept saying that over and over. That's his great insight, you know: that everything has to happen. Tomorrow he'll come with Dina to say goodbye to father, and perhaps he'll visit you too. To extend his congratulations . . ."

All at once he came to a halt, winked, and hugged me again. "And now, what do you propose that we do? I thought I would come to take you . . . but where to? I'm torn between the two of you. He's flying back tomorrow night, and I've hardly seen him yet—in fact, I feel that I won't be seeing him again for a long time. He really is leaving us—I finally had to believe it when I saw how calmly he let you have the apartment in the end. And Ya'el asked me to spend the seder with them . . . although Kedmi and his monster mother will be there too . . . and I can't stand the thought of leaving you here with all these people. I did so want to be with you—who would have thought that I'd be the excited one and that you'd have dozed off so quietly? . . . But is everything really all signed and sealed . . . the documents, the bill of divorce . . . you have it all? We have to decide what to do in a hurry, because poor Calderon has to be home for the seder . . . all hell has broken loose there . . . and he keeps deliberately provoking it . . . so what do you say? We could go somewhere by ourselves, just the two of us . . . perhaps to a hotel . . . there must be one with a communal seder around here . . . or should we just go back to Tel Aviv and have our own private holiday meal there? You still have your old clothes in the apartment. . . . Well, what do you think?"

But I stood there without answering, still groggy from my deep sleep and shapeless dream, wondering if she'd come back today, if I'd be able to talk to her, if I still remembered how. My throat and lips felt parched. I let him lead me down the road, looking at the wet, fissured earth, at the plowed-up weeds scattered over it. A single sunny day would burn them all yellow. And he so childishly wanting to celebrate, such a blabbermouth, dragging me as far as a large, rusty plow that stood at the end of the field. He examined its caked blades curiously, wide-eyed.

"What do you say then, mother? What shall we do? We have to make up our minds, we can't keep him any longer . . . his whole family is waiting for him there. His world has caved in on him and he'd like everyone else's to also. Why don't we send him on his way

and go eat by the fisherman's wharf in Acre . . . we'll be the only
Jews there . . . what do you say? You can't possibly stay here by
yourself on the night of the seder . . ."

"Why not?"

"You don't remember?"

"Remember what?"

"How terribly depressed you were that first year. I was with you
here."

"You were with me here for the seder?"

"Of course." He smiled. "You've forgotten. You were very ill then.
You hardly noticed a thing . . . but I was with you, and I'll never
forget what a madhouse it was. It gave me the creeps . . ."

All at once my heart felt for him. He was the only one never to be
afraid of me. To come to see me even then. I took his hand.

"Go be with father. You're right. You won't see him again for a
long time. I've already said my goodbyes to him, but I want you to
be with him. And I want you to help Ya'el. I'd just lie here in bed
and read anyhow. Father brought me back my glasses. Why must
you do all this for me? Everything is finished with . . . you say that
I'm free now . . . I suppose you think that I'm eighteen years old
. . ."

He was moved to sadness. Thoughtfully he knelt by a row of little
sprouts and absently began to pluck them until he realized what he
was doing and stuck them quickly back into the earth with an embarrassed smile. And I thought, was I really with him that seder or
only with her, so alert and enjoying herself? And I lifted my eyes to
the mountains and saw in the soft light of the setting sun a distant
dot that made me freeze. It was she, on the trail in an army windbreaker, her hands in her pockets, traveling light. I couldn't tell if
she was moving toward me or away. And then suddenly I felt the old
throbbing, the urge to have her be part of me again like a heavy
backpack, the joy of her wild otherness between knife thrust and
light flash . . .

Tsvi brushed the dirt from his clothes, out of breath, the first
wrinkles of age in his face. He turned back toward the hospital and
the distant gleam of the sea. "It's so peaceful here. So lovely. I even
dreamt about it. A haunting dream—I'll tell you about it sometime.
But I have to go now. Come say goodbye to Calderon . . . he's
falling apart, he's lost all control of himself. In the end he'll even be

fired from the bank . . ." As he walked me slowly back to the waiting car I could feel that he wanted to say something else but was
keeping it back, could hear her light footsteps behind me. The man
was reading, his crewcut gray head bent over the wheel.

"Calderon," said Tsvi gently. "Say goodbye to my mother."

He roused himself, and when he looked up I saw his face bathed in
tears. He wiped them away as he climbed out of the car, flushing
hotly, in inner conflict.

"Forgive me, Mrs. Kaminka." He shook my hand, nearly falling
all over it. "It's just . . . it's this Chekhov book. Do you know it?
We saw the show of *Uncle Vanya,* and so Tsvi brought me the book.
A tremendous production. Fantastic. And when I think of how everyone cried then it makes me want to cry again . . . although I
know it's silly to shed tears over a bunch of Russians who lived a
hundred years ago and were probably anti-Semites at that. Well, how
are you? I heard that it all went well, praise God. As long as it's over
—sometimes what matters is not what you decide but simply having
decided . . ."

He shook his head, red-eyed with tears that still wet his cheeks.
Suddenly he remembered to say:

"I wanted to wish you a happy Passover. And what lovely spring
weather it is . . . winter is finally over . . ."

"Where will you be for the seder?" I asked.

He glanced at Tsvi. "I don't know yet."

"At home," declared Tsvi sharply. "You'll be at home. Haven't
you gotten that into your head yet?"

"Yes," he sighed, looking back and forth between the two of us. "I
suppose I'll be at home." He gripped his book while stealing a glance
at mine. And again he recalled something:

"Mr. Kaminka told me that on your mother's side . . . that you
. . . I mean, that you have a bit of us in you . . ."

"A bit of who?"

"Of Abrabanel." He pronounced the name grandly. "That you're
part Abrabanel . . . I mean that you have their blood . . ."

When did they meet and what made Yehuda tell him about
Grandmother Abrabanel?

"He was very glad to hear that we're part Sephardi," explained
Tsvi.

"Does that seem important to you?" I asked softly.

He squirmed redly. "It's another way of looking at yourselves . . . a different bloodline . . . the Abrabanels are of very fine stock. Of course, it's not literally the blood . . . I don't believe in that . . . it's something intangible . . ."

He glanced at Tsvi with such deep love that it appalled me. Tsvi smiled mockingly back. And just then I saw her pass quickly by above the treetops. I felt a splitting pain in my head and made a face.

"Is anything wrong?" both asked at once.

"No. Nothing."

"Well, we'd better be off," said Tsvi. "If you're not home soon, they really will murder you."

"Let them," said Calderon with a wry smile.

Tsvi kissed me warmly and said once more, "I'm glad that it's over with." And again I felt that he had left something unsaid. They got into the car, waving goodbye as it turned, and drove off to the east. My clear head was muddled now; it ached all over and things in the distance went fuzzy. The white car headed down the road—and then, by the railroad tracks, in the wet jungle of weeds, someone went flying, a dress shot up in the air, and the car stopped and drove back in reverse. Tsvi jumped out while it was still moving and ran up to me. "Mother, perhaps I should keep those papers that father gave you. It's better not to leave them in the hospital. Someone might take them and lose them."

So that's what he had wanted to say all along. Perhaps even why he had come. "Who will take them?" I asked, not showing him my feelings, my eyes on the jungle of weeds. And he said, "But that's our only document of ownership for the house. Perhaps I should put it in my safe-deposit box because legally it's all we have . . . so that if we ever should want to . . ." "Want to what?" I asked. ". . . It doesn't matter. Whatever. Father won't be here, and . . ." He was breathing heavily, afraid he had said the wrong thing. "It wasn't my idea. It was Calderon's. He's an old hand at these things." But although I didn't say so I knew that he was lying and that the idea wasn't Calderon's. And then all at once, smiling sadly, he relented. Far away a dog barked. "Did you know," I said, "that the dog still hasn't come back?" His arms dangled helplessly. "Yes. I heard. That Kedmi is a bastard. But Horatio has run away before and always returned." "Never for so long, though," I said. "Perhaps tomorrow you should look for him." "All right," he promised. "We'll do that."

He hugged me again. "You look wonderful. It's done you a world of good already." And he gave me a last kiss. Even in the worst of times he was never afraid to kiss me, to hold me tight, to calm and comfort me.

The gate swung open and I walked back in. Only Musa and Yehezkel, who felt greatly relieved that Tsvi hadn't taken me, were still waiting. We walked up the path that went past the closed ward and saw the three strange children still playing fearlessly under the stares from behind the bars. We passed the library, whose door was partly open because I hadn't locked it properly. Something made me want to go inside. A sweet, burned smell hung over the dim room. The reddish light glanced off the rows of books covered with brown wrapping paper and off the dirty teacups and the plate of crackers that still lay on the table. The flowers I had put everywhere this morning were still there too, just softer-looking now, their heads bowed. A hard crust of dried mud covered the floor, which was littered with cigarette butts and a black paper skullcap, while a pair of sunglasses had been forgotten on one of the shelves. I took them and put them on, turning the world a dull brownish gray. This morning the sharp light was as harsh as splinters of broken glass. And since then no one had been in here, everyone was busy preparing for the holiday. I put the flowers on a tray, carried them outside, and handed them to Yehezkel. Then I shut the door, locking it with the key I still had in my pocket, and threw the flowers on the ground with its trampled grass and the tire tracks of the taxi. I had waited by the door for Yehuda to come since early morning. At dawn I was up and around in my white smock, picking flowers and arranging them inside, setting out the teacups and watering around the cottage, which I suddenly noticed was not at all straight but oval with crooked walls. I had my papers in the pocket of my smock and was all there: I never remember feeling so together before. And I was alone because the day nurse, Avigayil, who had been supposed to help me, never appeared for some reason. At eight o'clock the black taxi arrived, cutting like a boat between the lawns, its wheels spraying mud, until Yehuda mistakenly stopped it a hundred meters away. He climbed out of it first, dressed in a dark suit, and led the rabbis to the library, picking his way between the puddles, blinded by the strong sun, sinking into the mud, fording swarms of little insects that flew about newly generated from the light. One of the men, an old

Yemenite with a slight limp and a plastic carrying case, rushed spryly ahead, jabbing his cane in the ground and bending now and then to sniff some flower or pluck the leaf of some plant and crush it between his fingers. After him came round, jolly Rabbi Mashash, who had been to see me several times before, carefully guiding a thin old man in black clothes and dark sunglasses, while slowly bringing up the rear was an odd-looking person in a long, tawny army greatcoat and a visored cap. I hurried to greet them, feeling a twinge when I saw how pale Yehuda looked: this was the third time this week that I had seen him, and each time he looked paler than before. The Yemenite bowed as though performing a lively dance step and shook my hand with a smile before darting quickly into the cottage. I followed him inside and Yehuda ushered in the two older rabbis while the younger one—who had a head of golden curls and a complexion that, though red from the warmth of the woolen scarf around his neck, was as smooth as a girl's—lingered to kiss the mezuzah in the doorway and then entered hesitantly too. I watched the clean floor turn to muck in no time. The men were amazed at how much mud fell from their shoes and made an effort to clean it up. "Never mind," I said to them while they took off their hats, put on skullcaps, wiped their perspiring faces, and exclaimed at the abundance of flowers in the small room. "Never mind." Then Rabbi Mashash introduced his companions. The oldest was Rabbi Avraham Avraham; next came the Yemenite scribe, Rabbi Korach; and last was Rabbi Subotnik, a new immigrant from Russia, a scholarly prodigy straight from a forced-labor camp.

"Are you here by yourself?" asked Rabbi Mashash. "Well, no matter. Dr. Ne'eman said he'd try to make it, but we won't bother waiting for him." Straightaway they began to rearrange the room, moving about chairs, putting the table in a corner, and seating Rabbi Avraham there by a window. The Yemenite scribe made room on it for his implements, paused to sniff some flowers before placing them on the floor, took out several bundles wrapped in large handkerchiefs from his plastic case, undid the knots, and produced an inkpot and some quills. Yehuda helped while the Russian remained by the door, his large blue eyes scanning the room suspiciously, his hands on the scarf still wound around his neck, as though uncertain whether to remove it. And then all at once he spoke, in a soft, melodic voice, with a terribly thick Russian accent.

"But where is she?"

"Where is who?" asked father.

"Your wife. The woman getting divorced."

"My wife? She's right here."

"Her?" asked the Russian in amazement, pointing at me. He had been sure that I was a nurse and that the real wife would be dragged in any minute screaming and tied to a chair, drooling and letting her head loll. "This is her?" he asked again slowly, with disbelief.

"Of course," put in Rabbi Mashash quickly, wiping away his perspiration, his cheeks ruddily blotched. "Of course it is. This is Mrs. Kaminka. Who did you think it was?"

He continued to wrestle with the flowers while, still on the threshold, Rabbi Subotnik threw me a sharp, annoyed glance as though he were the victim of a swindle. Yehuda helped the rabbis out of their coats. "Whew . . . it's hot in here . . . a real spring day . . ." came their low voices while he bowed and scraped before them. When I went to pour the tea, though, he was suddenly in my way, pulling out my glass case from his pocket and murmuring, "Here, Ya'el had them fixed for you. Now you can read again." He handed me a brown envelope from which he took a typed letter. "And this is the house waiver that you asked for. Everything is signed, exactly as you wished." He ran a long finger down the printed lines, talking in a heated whisper. "Here." He took out some more documents. "This is a power of attorney that I've given Asa. If there are any problems, he can act in my place."

"Asa?" I marveled. "Why Asa? Why not Ya'el?"

"Because I didn't want Kedmi butting in again," he answered quickly. "Asa is the stablest of them all. The sanest."

The papers made a rustling sound. I could actually smell his fear. How lucky that she isn't here now, I thought, if she were she'd have a fit. "Why are you so pale?" I asked. He smiled bitterly. And then suddenly we felt how silent it was and saw the four of them watching us in wonder.

A Passover, a pastoral divorce, just a few hours before the seder, in the library of a rustic madhouse purposely garnished by me with flowers and greenery. The Yemenite finished arranging his quills and parchment and rolled himself a cigarette of greenish tobacco while gazing curiously out the window with his shrewd eyes, excited to be in an insane asylum. Rabbi Mashash handed out copies of our file, his jolly roundness filling the room, keen to get through with the ceremony in a hurry. "Professor Kaminka," he called warmly to Yehuda, who winced at the words, making me wonder whether he had really been promoted in America or was simply trying to impress them. I passed among them pouring the tea while he followed me with spoons and sugar, offering them the crackers as though they were guests in our house. At first they balked, glancing at their watches to see if there was still time to eat leavened food, but in the end they each took a cracker, careful to keep the crumbs off their clothes. The Russian sat in a corner with his coat on, smelling unwashed; he had just taken hold of his teacup between two fingers in the ancient way, blown on it, and broken into a blessing in his slow, melodic voice when the door opened and a young woman I didn't know, no doubt from the closed ward, came in with a book. I supposed she must have seen that the library door was open and hurried over to exchange it. At a loss, the men looked at me but I said nothing, not even when father rose to stop her. She slipped quickly past him into the room, and I knew at once that she had a double, that there wasn't one of her but two, and that, though she knew she mustn't come in, it was her double who had made her, who was now forcing her to simper and circle among us as tiny as a bird, studying the rows of books and touching them lightly while glancing at us over her shoulder. Suddenly she said in a violent whisper, "Get your hands off of me, you infantile jerk!" Everyone froze, except for the Yemenite, whose eyes sparkled with mirth. Yehuda made a move to restrain her but I put a hand on him because I knew that her double wouldn't stand for it. Finally she took a book down from a shelf, glanced at it, threw it on the floor as though we weren't there, and fled from the room with an obscene bump and grind.

The Yemenite was enraptured. Like a child he laughed merrily and even went to the window to watch her walk away. Rabbi Mashash, though, was annoyed. "This will never do. Perhaps we had better close the door, because we haven't much time and we'll never finish like this. I told Dr. Ne'eman that we needed a quiet place . . . well, never mind. Let's begin. First, gentlemen, we will identify the divorcing couple."

They opened their files for an identity check. First they asked for our fathers' and mothers' names, then for the names of their parents, and then for their dates and places of birth.

"Since everything is in order, Rabbi Korach," declared Rabbi Mashash, "you can begin to write the divorce."

But just then the young Russian—who had said nothing so far and had not even opened his file but had simply sat staring at me—rose from his place and said:

"One small moment. Not to rush, please. We must not go against law."

And turning to Yehuda, he requested him to leave the room.

"But what is the matter?" Rabbi Mashash angrily protested. "What's wrong?"

"I want to ask something the wife by herself," said the Russian in his thickly accented, odd, melodious Hebrew. He took father by the arm and opened the door for him. "Please, one moment outside." Something hard and domineering seemed to emanate from the gently bright-curled figure.

"But what's wrong?" asked the other rabbis. "What is it you want? Why don't you ask us first?"

He insisted, though, humming some biblical verse and repeating the name of some rabbinical authority. Yehuda grew alarmed. "All right," he said. "All right. I'll leave." The door shut behind him while Rabbi Mashash and Rabbi Avraham jumped angrily up and glared at the troublemaker, moving back and forth in the room like the black hands of a clock, one big and one small, while he, a thin, light second hand, stood still and stared at me.

"I did not think that she . . . that you, madame . . . was in condition . . . that madame was so normal. I was said no choice in matter. But me, I see choice. In no circumstance . . . if mind is free . . . madame understands . . . she has right too, even in asylum . . . if madame says I do not sign . . . here is not Russia . . . here is no . . . *nu* . . . coercion . . ."

By now Rabbi Mashash was furious.

"Coercion? There's been no coercion here, Rabbi Subotnik. What are you talking about? Mrs. Kaminka signed of her own free will. It was her decision. I beg of you. What are you trying to do? She herself asked him to come from America . . . you're putting us in an impossible position . . . an impossible light . . . everything has already been seen to . . . we've given our word of honor . . . Rabbi Vital himself gave us his blessing . . ."

He turned excitedly to old Rabbi Avraham, who, hidden behind his dark sunglasses, had begun to bite his nails worriedly.

But the Russian didn't turn to look at them. With great dignity he bore down on me in his heavy Red Army coat whose big copper buttons bore the head of an eagle, his ritual fringes hanging down to his knees underneath it. He couldn't have been much older than Asi. A smooth, unlined face. A fanatic.

"Is you here . . . is you asked . . . but why? What difference it makes if she . . . *nu,* you, madame . . . is in this place anyway . . . and not young no more too . . . *nu* . . ."

He turned red, flustered, his broken, melodious Hebrew tripping him up. Yehuda had talked just like that when he first came to this country.

"But he's going to have a baby soon," I said.

"Baby? Where is baby?"

"In America."

That lit a fire under him. He turned angrily, sarcastically, to the others.

"Nu. So now we have little bastard on our hands." He thumped the file that he held. "Here says nothing of it . . ."

"Rabbi Subotnik!" Rabbi Mashash was shouting now, pulling at the heavy greatcoat. "Explain yourself!"

But the Russian shook himself free and went on leaning tautly over me, so close I could feel his breath.

"Mrs. Kaminka! Never mind bastard . . . are many, will be one more . . . everywhere is same big mess . . . but marriage is holy . . ."

He was crimson now.

"Holy for whom?" I asked calmly.

"For whom?" For a moment he was taken aback. *"Nu,* for God, of course . . ." He said the word very gently.

At last. It was time. My anger hummed inside me. I had to force myself not to choke on the torrent of words that poured out of me.

"God what are you talking about who is that?"

"Excuse me?"

"I don't want to hear another word about it. Not another meaningless word. Please understand that God means less than nothing to me. I don't want to hear another word about it."

Old Rabbi Avraham sat up stiffly and buried his face in his hands.

As red as a beet now himself, Rabbi Mashash assailed the Russian, who retreated a step with a smile.

"Rabbi Subotnik! That will be enough. How do you think you're making us look? There's a procedure to be followed here. There's a presiding judge. I ask you to keep your philosophy out of it."

He stepped hastily over to me and steered me to the door. "Mrs. Kaminka, there's been a small misunderstanding. We'll continue soon. Please wait outside for a minute."

He led me out into the strong sunlight, closing the door after me. Father was sitting on a rock to one side, smoking. "What's going on?" he asked. If only he would have taken me in his arms now. It was too much to ask. And yet he did that first day, and with such unexpected warmth. "What's going on?" His anxiety was growing. "What do they want?"

The sound of shouts and of someone thumping on the table reached us from behind the door. Father hurried to it just as it opened again.

"Professor Kaminka, come in for a minute. By yourself, please." It was Rabbi Mashash, who gave me a dirty look as he pulled father inside.

My headache felt like an omen, like the first sign of an approaching illness. The words I had managed to get out at last clung like foam to my lips. Inside the cottage the voices grew dim. The young rabbi was examining father now, fighting to save our marriage.

"Professor? Of what? . . . America? Where?"

Yehuda's deep voice answered softly, in that enchanting way of his, while Rabbi Mashash kept intervening and trying to calm the young Russian down. Smoke rose from the hospital kitchen, drifting up into the brightening glare of the sky, and someone stirred in the clump of trees where Yehezkel and his band were watching us. Someone else was there too, a stranger I couldn't place, someone made of branches and leaves. Was it her again? I couldn't believe it. A sudden silence came over the library. Even the whispers had stopped. If only Avigayil were with me. I walked around the cottage, through the high weeds, until I came to the open window and saw father without his jacket, his tie loose, baring his chest while Rabbi Mashash pointed something out to the young Russian and Rabbi Korach rose curiously to look too. I shut my eyes and bit my lips, sinking down on a stoop by the path. After a while the door opened and father was sent back outside. He threw me a tense, angry look, keeping away from me, glancing despairingly at his watch, oblivious of the crisp morning, of the sun and the flowering earth.

"Who asked you about a baby? But you, you had to go tell them . . ."

A faint smile of contempt flecked his face.

"I'm sorry. I didn't realize that . . ."

"Never mind," he interrupted.

". . . they didn't know."

He turned toward me angrily. "Didn't know what? I don't know what baby you're talking about. Because there isn't any. . . ." His voice grew shrill, as though he were crying inside. "Can't you see whom you're dealing with? Why complicate things even more when I've given you everything as it is? Damn it all . . . it's all so humiliating . . ."

His despair was making him cruel. He was afraid that it would all fall through.

"Maybe I should try explaining to them . . ." I tried to rise but could not. I felt as though a stone weighed me down.

"Don't. You'll only make it worse. That Russian rabbi is a nut. He turns every word against you."

I said nothing. I sat with my white smock covering the stoop, cradling my knees, listening to the birds and to the sounds of the awakening hospital, to the tenor voice of the Russian striving fiercely in its pathetic Hebrew to rise above the wheedling tones of Rabbi Mashash: a strange, antisocial man, fighting to save our marriage for reasons known only to himself. Father fell silent, a handsome but weak, degenerate intellectual, straining to hear while his hands went through the pockets of his jacket and his pants, taking out and putting back his passport, his plane tickets, his documents, his wads of money, distractedly rummaging through the mountains of paper he had with him. For a moment our eyes met. Inside the library the voice of the vainly battling Russian was losing ground, while that of the Yemenite, who had entered the fray now too, rose in a keen yodel. Yehuda took out a cigarette and lit it nervously, blind to the world, to the trees, to the hospital, to the sky, fumbling aimlessly, buttoning his shirt which he had noticed was still open, drifting ever further away from me. And I thought, this will be my last picture of him.

"You know, I'm probably the only one who's never seen that scar you show to everyone."

He heard me unwillingly. "What?" he asked, turning hotly toward me.

"You're leaving soon and I'll never see you again. And that scar you have from then . . . from me . . . I've never seen it . . ."

He was annoyed. "It doesn't matter. Why should you want to see it? Let me be, Naomi."

"I'm the only one who hasn't seen it. Tsvi said you show everyone. So why shouldn't I see it too?"

"Please, not now." His voice was entreating. "Some other time. Just let me be."

"But when? We'll never meet again."

"Of course we will. Why shouldn't we? I'll be back . . . there are the children . . . after all, they belong to us both . . ."

But I was tired, impatient. "Show it to me!"

He sensed the threat in my voice, my terrible lust to see it, and debated only briefly before almost gladly yielding. Quickly he unbuttoned his shirt again and showed me in the glaring light the chest I knew so well and had forgotten, with its curly gray hairs and its large, pale mole. Across it ran a hooked line like a reddish beak. A near miss, a swooning memory. Not where I'd meant it to be, he had dodged at the last second. . . . He stood there looking at me quietly, already rebuttoning his shirt. All at once he focused on me sharply, his face lit by that ironic, knowing smile of his.

"But you really did want to kill me!"

He wasn't asking. He was simply musing out loud, struck by the thought.

"Yes," I said quickly, a sweet, dry taste in my mouth.

"But why?"

"Because you disappointed me."

He ran a hand through his hair, content with my answer as though it had confirmed some deep inner truth of his own. With a start I saw her soar through the smoke above the kitchen roof, a small satchel strapped to her back. But just then the door opened and Rabbi Mashash stepped out in his starched white shirt sleeves and invited us back in with open arms. The room was full of smoke. Steam still rose from the electric kettle and a chair lay on its side. Everyone was on edge. As soon as we entered, the ceremony began. Rabbi Mashash read the bill of divorce out loud while the Yemenite scribe at the table copied the words with his quill at breakneck speed. Then Rabbi Mashash led me to a corner and led father to another one near the Russian, who stood crestfallenly by the window. The text was read back to us, after which it was passed around to be signed and handed to father. And then the Yemenite hastened to cup my two hands, the parchment flew through the air and swooped down into them like a small dove, some prayer was growled loudly, and I was divorced.

The Russian opened the door, letting a burst of bright light flood the room, and fled outside, the tails of his army coat flapping behind him, while the Yemenite scribe retied his implements in bundles, Rabbi Mashash went about collecting papers, old Rabbi Avraham groped his way to the exit, and Yehuda approached me with an anguished look. All at once I felt that he could not bear to part from me.

"Mr. Kaminka," they called to him. "There's still a seder to get to today."

He wavered uncertainly. "Perhaps I'll stay on for a while."

"You can't," said the Yemenite, plucking him by the sleeve. "It's forbidden for you two to be together now."

What a softy he suddenly seemed, a desperate old man trying to shake my hand.

"Did I tell you that I've given Asi power of attorney in case any problem comes up?"

He pulled loose from the Yemenite's grasp, wanting to say more.

"Well, so you had your way in the end . . ."

I didn't answer him. But to myself I thought, why, I'll never see him again, he'll really vanish for good now. I was sure that was so. And already they were dragging him swiftly outside, where they sank again into the weeds and wet earth that I had watered in the morning, running into Dr. Ne'eman and Avigayil, who were rushing to get to my divorce. Dr. Ne'eman shook the rabbis' hands and roared at one of his own jokes, while Avigayil hurried breathlessly into the library to join me.

"I was afraid we wouldn't make it," she said.

"It's already over with," I answered, tossing her the parchment.

"What's over with?" she asked. And then all of a sudden she understood and threw her arms around me. "It really is over with? What a crazy day this has been . . ."

"Come, it's begun already."

He tries getting me up lured by my new freedom in the moonlight-silvering dark. Musa too stomps into the ward bumping into all the beds. Yehezkel pulls one of his fainting fits. He falls to the floor he won't open his eyes he says he won't move. And Musa begins to groan again that they're eating already.

I rise from my bed still wearing the white smock over my cotton dress. "All right," I say, "I'll walk you as far as the dining room." They walk on either side as though carrying me while I glide down the path with my book. There is a fresh chill in the air. We pass by the library. A light is on as though someone were waiting inside. I can feel my heart catch but I must go in. The door I had locked is open again the cups are all gone but the floor is still caked with the hard crust of mud the weak light shining on the rude brown curds. How awfully sad. The last vestige of a marriage that here came to an end. He had wanted to ask me something and they took him away. An overflowing ashtray lies on the table a large ink-stained piece of paper sticking out of it. It's from the first agreement that Kedmi brought me that father tore to shreds why right here is where Asi stood hitting himself. Behind me Yehezkel and Musa are waiting like statues once more they start to whine that it's beginning that the singing has started already. Yehezkel turns out the light silhouetting the windows burnished in a glitter of glass-frosted smoke beyond them I see the lights of nearby villages a dog barks far away. Can it be? Already she stands by the hospital gate wrinkled and tanned with her olive green rucksack high hiking boots on her feet neither hunger nor thirst searching for me on her way to me. I want to go hide beneath a blanket but they drag me back to the path that leads to the lit-up dining room joining us on it is a large group of doctors and nurses Dr. Ne'eman too with his great bellylaugh and demoniacally the visored cap of the young Russian rabbi that Subotnik he's back again there's no mistaking his voice he's still in his heavy Red Army coat. They hurry past us and disappear through the large door of the dining room that's as far as I want to go. "Leave me here," I murmur but Yehezkel won't hear of it if I don't come to the seder he'll faint again he'll drop dead right here on the floor. Musa is drawn to the smell of the food but he's bound to Yehezkel too he doesn't dare enter without him. And so I'm swept inside with them into the singing the noise the confusion the tables arranged in a large square and covered with stiffly laundered sheets turned blue from too much starch the stacks of matzos flaking plumily at their browned edges and crackling quietly to themselves the large labelless bottles filled not with wine but with some yellowish glowing freshly-squeezed-looking liquid the patients the nurses the office personnel sitting in groups and making a noise like the sea. At one table dressed in their holiday best are the three children who played today on the lawn their hair slicked and combed. Beside them sits their mother a young rather pretty woman looking bewilderedly around her while her American doctor husband a newcomer to the staff converses gaily this may be their first seder in Israel. And now everyone stands up as though in my honor in my cotton everyday dress beneath my white smock holding my book in one hand the divorcee the divorcer. But it's only the rabbi signaling them to rise he's risen too his glance resting tensely on me his bright blue eyes know who I am. He balances his cup between two fingers as he did this morning all at once his strong mellow tenor voice rings out in the blessing over the wine.

"Blessed art thou O Lord our God, King of the Universe . . ."

But now a nurse hurries up to big portly Dr. Ne'eman who stops the rabbi and whispers into his ear. A side panel opens and into the dining room come the patients from the closed ward nearly a dozen of them I've never seen before escorted by a young doctor and two nurses. Tense and bowed they move in a diagonal line led by a short very squinty-eyed redhead of maybe forty a fireball on his feet dragging the others heavily after him how awfully depressed they seem looking over their shoulders halting in a daze and lurching forward again their skullcaps in their hands the dining hall electric with their invisible split selves all packed into one room as though not twelve but a hundred of them had marched in rattling their chains. The staff helps seat them at a table and fills their glasses. Again the signal is given and the Russian raptly shuts his eyes he too is moved by the occasion perhaps it's his first seder here too. Once more his strong tenor voice rings out.

"Blessed art thou O Lord our God, King of the Universe, who hath chosen us among the nations, and exalted us above all tongues, and sanctified us with His commandments . . ."

Someone screams. The redhead has slipped away from his re-
strainers and jumped on a table squinting at us all with a beaming
festive cross-eyed ecstasy. In no time he's pulled down and dragged
outside a sparking shrieking fireball his harsh muffled sobs like the
grunts of some wild beast can still be heard. Rabbi Subotnik has
turned pale. He starts the blessing all over the kiddush cup poised
between his fingers while everyone rises again. Except me. I stay
seated and open my book how I hate the words of the blessing I
won't wait for it to be done before I drink the sweetish juice in my
cup has some wine mixed in with it after all. Now everyone sits and
the little boy gets up. He faces his family and recites the Four Questions in a heavy American accent as though the words were stones in
his mouth but with blind confidence not knowing what they mean
pulled through in one almost show-offy breath by the anxious love of
his brother and sister without a single mistake while the dining room
gasps in amazement and breaks into applause when he's done. He
makes a loathsome rehearsed bow and the Russian tenor rings out
again hushing the babble of voices. "For slaves were we to Pharaoh
in Egypt, and God redeemed us from there with a strong hand and
outstretched arm . . ." But at once the murmurs and laughter re-
sume I see her face now by the window how thirsty she suddenly is.
Overcome with longing I rise Yehezkel rising with me. I try making
him sit again but the thirst is too much for me I take the bottle and
put it to my lips I guzzle from it greedily while the rabbi goes on
ranting we were slaves . . .

He stood on the watered earth, amidst the rotting leaves, by a strip
of growing grass, bathed in the sharp, splintery light of the violent
spring's flaming sun, the cuffs of his pants stained with mud, too
occupied with himself to notice the world all around him, shifting
papers from pocket to pocket, his tie loose, the soft curly gray hairs
showing through the slit of his shirt by the large pale mole that once
I kissed and the small reddish seam that resembled a hooked beak.
Did you really want to kill me? With such naïve curiosity, yet that
wise smile of his lighting his face. As though it had been simply a
mistake or a dream. He couldn't believe that that morning . . .
only it wasn't morning yet, it was a muggy, lingering summer dawn
with the sea showing through far away like steamy gunmetal. The
kitchen light was still on when I found him at the table in his under-

shirt and pajama bottoms, a tall, skinny, unshaven bird wearing a small apron. He had eaten an early breakfast on the sly and his plate now lay on a yellowed newspaper beside the lock that he had removed from his door, the key to which hung from a string around his neck. He pouted wearily, a cold, withheld man, shut up in the circle of his own self-involved thoughts, his little pots simmering on the stove, full of things he had cooked for himself, while the dog lay under the table, wagging his tail and sniffing at my food that he had thrown him.

He was startled to see me. "How come you got up? Gaddi finally fell asleep again. He sure can scream, he's a loudmouth just like his father. . . . But why don't you go back to bed? We'll have to bring him back to Ya'el. Perhaps you'll take him, and I'll stay here and try to get organized. I haven't read a single line this whole month." Quickly he rose to clear away his plate and hide his pots from me. He brought me my medicine, measured it into a glass with a tablespoon, and handed it to me mechanically, without a word. He was on the verge of collapse. And I thought, what he'll organize is his own despair so that he can get rid of me. I went to the stove to see what he was cooking. He smiled awkwardly but removed the lid to show me a piece of boiled, blackened meat. I lowered the flame, stirred the water with a spoon and stuck a fork in the meat. It was hard as a rock.

"Come, let me help you," I said. "That's not how to do it. Let me have a knife." He looked in the drawer and handed me a large one, which he tried snatching back as soon as he saw how eagerly her hand grabbed the moist handle. He's noticed that there's someone else, I thought, filled with new hope. He recognizes her. He knows who she is. He understands that I'm not just pretending.

The knife was wrenched free from him now. He beat a retreat toward the door.

"I think we'd better wake up Tsvi . . ."

The singing rocks the dining room. *Ve'hi she'amda ve'hi she'amda* everyone happily picks up the tune the personnel the nurses even some of the patients shouting it flinging down the words again with unfathomable delight. Next to me Yehezkel is letting himself go too nudging my arm to make me join in. The rabbi regards the singers with a faint smile on his lips seeking to follow the unfamiliar Israeli melody. I bury myself in my book my head pounding loathing the words the melody thinking of her behind the door in a bathrobe shaking out the drops of water from her loose hair listening happily to the music wanting to join in but too hungry her mouth waters. She notices the stack of matzos and reaches out to them. Go ahead I whisper take one. As though inadvertently she does breaking off a piece and sticking it in her mouth. People are staring at me. I bend over my book and pretend not to see them while I eat reaching for more matzo quickly breaking and chewing it I've hardly eaten all day. The dry flat bread makes a loud crunchy sound in my mouth. And slowly nervously the singing dies down. The rabbi catches my eye and signals me not to but I go right on eating breaking off piece after piece now Musa reaches out and does the same so do the patients from the closed ward across from us all taking their cue from me. "Just a minute there!" somebody shouts trying to retrieve the filched matzos the doctors' table buzzes excitedly. The rabbi turns to it in a whisper he bangs his fist on the table. "One minute, friends! Please wait for the blessing." But calmly spitefully I go on eating cramming matzo into my mouth and chewing it swiftly piece by piece the crumbs raining down on my dress. Dr. Ne'eman smiles and comes over to me big and portly he bends down and hugs me warmly pinning my hands. "Mrs. Kaminka! My dear Naomi. Let's just wait until the blessing. That's all he asks, because it's annoying."

"To whom?" I ask. "God?"

He laughs soundlessly winking at me full of good humor extracting a piece of matzo from my grasp with the same soft warm paws that once used to tie me and give me electric shock. "Never mind. There's just a bit more to go. It's only a ceremony, you know. Just a bit more. I don't believe in it either, but why demoralize people? . . ."

He stood there on the wet earth, lighting a cigarette, rotting leaves and fallen blossoms all around him, pacing the growing grass, bathed in the sharp, splintery light of the violent spring, seeing nothing, oblivious to the blooming earth, self-involved, shifting papers, his tie loose, the soft curly gray hairs showing through the frill of his shirt. Why, for a moment I even saw the pale mole that once I kissed with such passion and the reddish seam they had stitched in him like a hooked beak! He showed them to me, both abashed and amused, a twinkle in his eyes, almost smiling, asking me did I really as though he didn't know. Did I really? Well, now he could afford to, the divorce was almost over on the other side of the door. It pleased him to think that it might all have been a mistake, a passing aberration: that whole brutally muggy summer dawn on which he threw my food to the dog, diddling with his pots, with his constipated, self-involved mind that never would change, that locked itself up with keys swinging from strings, go back to bed, how come you got up, what a night, he sure can scream, we can't go on like this, we should never have had him here . . . and all the time looking for my medicine and so mechanically measuring it and giving it to me, here I was barely risen and already he wanted to drug me, to knock me out, even to drive me away. How quickly he had despaired of me, how disappointingly he had given up on me from the moment he noticed the umbrella I brought home from the store. "What did you buy that for?" he wanted to know. And I said, "I didn't. It got into my shopping bag by mistake. I never paid for it." The next day I returned with two more umbrellas and a brown mug. "How easy it is to steal," I mused. "Not that I was stealing—at least I didn't feel that I was—but perhaps somebody else was doing it for me. I suppose you had better take it all back." He hit the ceiling. "What kind of monkey business are you up to? I want you to stop it at once." I let a few days go by and went to take it all back, but this time they were waiting for me, they had already spotted me the time before. They grabbed me without letting me explain, some young salesman stood me in a corner and insisted on calling the police. In the end they got hold of Yehuda too, who came running from the university to identify me, frightened and as pale as a sheet. I was hungry and tired by then but he didn't even speak to me. He just fawned on the policeman, a fat sergeant who had to calm him down, who understood right away because he knew all the signs and never thought for a moment of pressing charges: a primitive-looking but gloriously humane soul, from the start he behaved gently toward me, he let me go off to the side and only cautioned Yehuda. On our way home we didn't speak to each other. Yehuda was furious, he would only look at me from the corner of his eye as though I were a stranger. We kept quiet in the house too. I ate, washed, and got into bed with the last of my strength, still not exchanging a word with him. But as I was dozing off in the twilight I felt him standing in the doorway with a suspicious stare. "You see," I began to explain to him, "there's someone else here now. It's hard to draw the line but there's an other in me, perhaps a whole extra person. You have two wives now. But don't be afraid. You can cope with her. Just go along with her, don't panic and try to fight her. She may even be the original me. Perhaps she's a virgin. I'm only first getting to know her. I can feel that soon she'll start talking, and then you'll hear her too." He covered his face, not wanting to accept it, refusing to hear anymore. "She's still quite primitive. She isn't used to stores, she can't even tell the difference yet between what's hers and what isn't. She comes from the desert. But you'll see that she can be talked to. That she can even be loved. Just you tell her that too. You have such a good way with words. Make an effort with her. Let her feel your presence. Now that you're retired and have time on your hands, she can give new meaning to your life." "That's enough!" he burst out. "You're doing this on purpose. It's just an act." "But it's not, Yehuda. Listen. She's going to talk to you now, just to demonstrate." And she really did begin to, quickly and in my mother's voice, saying the most complicated, confusing things. He slammed the door and fled, and as soon as she stopped I fell asleep. When I awoke it was the middle of the night. The bedroom door was open and a dim light shone in the house. Someone was singing on the television. Tsvi was up. He came to look in on me and I knew right away that father had told him everything, that he had asked him to come back home to live with us.

Tsvi helped me up and made me something to eat, surrounding me with warmth and concern. He was clearly in the best of spirits. Father was already sleeping on the couch in his study. And only then did I grasp the full extent of his despair, of his fear, of his disappointment, of his surrender. He was handing me over to Tsvi, who was only too glad to get me and to treat me royally. He turned off the TV, made his bed in the guest room, and went off to look for a book to read in it.

Suddenly you can hear a pin drop. I look up from my book to see the rabbi beckon to the pretty young American mother. She rises blushing in her gorgeous dress encouraged by her husband she tiptoes anxiously over to the rabbi he hands her a large porcelain bowl. She holds it in her thin hands while he raises his big wine cup

and begins to list the Ten Plagues in some old chant from the steppes
letting one large red drop of wine fall into the bowl for each plague.
Blood. Frogs. Lice. Locusts. Vermin . . .

The pretty young American smiles she has stage fright and doesn't
understand the bowl shakes slightly in her hands while the rabbi
continues drop by drop flicking each plague off his finger into the
pinkish bowl and chanting as it falls. Boils. Hail. Wild beasts . . .
Hypnotically she smiles at each drop. Darkness. The Killing of the
Firstborn . . . At last he's done. He shuts his eyes and motions her
back to her seat but still she stands there reverently holding the bowl
uncertain what to do with it. And then suddenly she raises it to her
lips and begins to drink. Everyone shouts at once. The bowl of
plagues is snatched from her. Shrieks of laughter accompany her
shamefaced return to her seat where her children crowd around her
and her husband gives her a kiss. And still the tenor voice quavers
on.

"Rabbi Yossi the Galilean hath said . . ."

You paced slowly back and forth on the wet earth, careful not to
sink into it, the divorced divorcing divorcer in the splintery glare of
the raging spring, your pant cuffs stained with mud, your new American suit shiny in the sunlight, someone else was dressing you now,
you never had such a stylish collar before. You lit a cigarette, your
face dissolving into vapor in a puddle of water, you exhaled bluish
smoke, you sank deeper into yourself, shifting papers from pocket to
pocket. Inside the closed cottage, behind drawn curtains, the rabbis
fought over our divorce, but already I was parted from you, sitting
stock-still on the stoop and staring at the soft gray curls over your
heart, at the thin scar hooked like a beak. All at once you stopped
worrying and looked at me. What were you thinking of just then?
Still of yourself as *you* and *he* the way you once used to? You turned
to me so unexpectedly, so openly, so shining with wisdom, yes, even
with humor—why, the worst part of it then was that you completely
lost your sense of humor! "Did you really? You really did? You
wanted to kill me?" Perhaps now that we're parted at last it flattered
you to think that. "Yes," I said. But that wasn't so. I had only
wanted to cut you loose. Can't you understand there's a difference?
To cut you loose from the desperate fear that made you want to run
away, but to leave some part of you too. Because I'm sure there

would have been something left. To cut you loose from your constipated fear, from your self-involved, self-diddling intellect with its
anxieties and its imaginary, self-destructing missions to the world,
Not at that exact spot. Although perhaps there never was a better
one. But I was sure that there must be one, the fulcrum from which
you would come apart. If only you hadn't been so scared. If only you
had waited another moment without moving, you might not have
even felt the pain. But you didn't know who you gave the knife to. It
wasn't to her, as you thought. It was to me, who loved you and
would never have harmed you. Who wanted only to open you up. To
cut you loose but not to kill you. To free you. Oh how gladly I would
have taken apart that mono-self of yours! It broke my heart to see
you with your apron on among those pots, a beginner in the kitchen
trying so hard to cook, the dawn-star Venus upon you, a soft sun of
flame beneath your steamy, boiling meat soup. You gave her the
knife and you panicked because you couldn't see how in a flicker of
thought I took it from her right away. Cut him loose, don't kill him,
I whispered to her. Start with the key on his chest. If only you had
kept still then as you did today, smiling patiently . . . we did, you
know, spend so many years together, even if they were a bitter disappointment . . . what made you grab my hand and wrestle with me,
what made you run away? But you've always run away. Always
surrendered. Always gone to get Tsvi, to wake up the children, not
that they ever did you any good. Because it wasn't a question of
doing justice or of being fair. It was a question of being together. You
shouted when you should have talked. For the longest time you
choked your words to death, you constipated all your sentences.
Who were you shouting at? Why? And in such a high, female voice
that one might almost have thought that my other was in you and
was dragging you off to her wilderness. Groggy as I was I knew I had
to act quickly and so did the loudly barking dog. I knew that it was
either now or never to cut up that stubborn mono-self into its original parts. If only you hadn't moved. If only you had calmed your
mind instead of screaming "Oh, my God!" and springing for the
door. A fresh, clear stream of words would have sprung from you
instead and done the job without a drop of blood. You would have
been cut loose painlessly, joyously. We could have done without the
knife.

Suddenly someone bangs on a table and the murmurs and the laughter die away. Off to the side somebody starts to sing the next passage from the Haggadah and is silenced. From the other end of the room somebody else takes it up and is hushed too. "Shh . . . shh . . . wait a minute . . . the rabbi . . ." I glanced up from my book to see the young Russian standing stiffly at the head table eyes shut one hand on his heart and the other raised in the air. "Shh . . . shh . . ." voices call out. "Quiet, there! The rabbi wants to say a few words . . ."

The silence deepens. At last he looks at us his gaze raking us like a blue torch. All eyes are on him. Here and there the trace of a smile. He takes a step back and quietly begins to make the rounds of the tables one hand still on his chest and the other still in the air. We crane in our chairs to watch him quietly slowly circle behind us two or three times until he deftly slips into the square between the tables and begins to circle that too passing in front of us now staring at the ceiling playing some game that maybe he learned in a Soviet labor camp. All at once he halts in front of me and without even a look at me deftly shuts my book then continues on his way one hand still held high not at all the same man who fought for my marriage this morning. Slowly now he lets his upraised arm drop. No one smiles anymore. We hold our breaths hypnotically. He walks even slower he stops to look at the children he circles some more stopping to study the doctors he walks on and stops again in front of the patients from the closed ward he circles on all at once he too begins to sing from the Haggadah offhandedly in a fine tenor voice like someone singing to himself in a melody nobody knows. Done he circles again lithe and assured on his feet cherubic cheeks pink in the bright light golden curls on his nape fluffing lightly beneath his backward-tipped cap. And again he stops by the children now he sings once more his voice poignant full of longing he circles again halting this time by the patients from the closed ward scrutinizing them slowly while they blink and gape with drooling mouths staring back at him in alarm as though he were about to attack them. Yet instead he begins to speak in his soft quiet voice in his thick odd Russian accent his body arched gracefully backward.

"*Nu* . . . but also you are chosen, do you know? Also you have spark of holiness. Also you belong to God's covenant . . . all of you . . ." He sweeps his hand over the dining room. "A-a-a-ll of you,

even who do not want, who do not believe. All . . . everyone . . ."
He pauses to look straight at me. "A-a-a-ll . . ." he drawls again.
And once more he resumes circling as though lost in thought head
high voice abruptly turning harsh. "*Nu*. For you whole earth is
something to be"—he whips out a pad from his pocket, his voice
dropping to a powerful whisper, and consults it—"trodden underfoot." He smiles to himself. "Underfoot. Underfoot." He forcefully
repeats the word face red with anger everyone sits too dazed to make
a sound. And again he circles round one hand on his heart stalking
softly like a cat the scarf flutters on his neck he runs his other hand
over the white tablecloth such delicate soft skin his curly locks tum-
ble down his neck now I see him from behind and give a start why
it's a woman disguised as a man I hardly can breathe. He stops
across from my table eyeing us. "*Nu, nu.*" He rouses himself. "In
every generation we seek freedom, but only kind of freedom . . .
only kind of freedom . . . is freedom to be slaves . . . freedom to
be slaves of God. Is freedom inside. Only there. Is freedom outside
worth nothing . . ." He reaches again for the book I've reopened
and snatches it from me he looks at it darkly and bangs it shut he
tucks it under his arm and circles some more. But now I jump to my
feet. How didn't I notice before that it was her? It's her disguised as
a rabbi! Desperately I turn to all the people watching him. Hasn't
anyone seen? From a far table he starts to sing again he returns to his
seat and signals us all to join in the melody. It's true, then. She's
back. She's right here. And I bolt outside in a panic.

The vats of night spill over me black and cold already I'm being
chased I fling myself into some bushes falling through the hard
branches I hear feet running down the path Yehezkel is calling in the
darkness I peek out and see a thin little woman puffing on a cigarette
bending down to pick up the skullcap that's fallen from her head as
she hurries toward my cottage. I cut through the bushes scratching
myself breaking loose veering toward the front gate where the road is
swimming in white night light I'm near the guardhouse now there's
Arabic music inside. I turn back toward the office the open door is
swinging in the wind. Inside the rooms are dark. File folders and
telephones gleam in the moonlight. Almost before it has rung Kedmi
answers in his brisk voice.

"Kedmi here."

"It's me."

—Shut up.

—The earth will turn upside down.

—Don't start in on the earth now.

—Then maybe the sky. Maybe the she-sky.

—That's enough. Stop it!

—Because you know what I've been thinking. Godina. Queen of he Universe.

—No. Anything but that . . .

—Godina. It's so simple. So perfect.

—It's insane.

—Godina. What a brilliant idea.

—What nonsense.

—We must remember to tell Tsvi tomorrow.

—You will not say one word to him. Keep away from him.

—But he'll love it. What a beautiful idea. Now that the house is all ours, you'll see that they'll have to put up with me.

—The house was coming to me. What's wrong with that? What do you want from me?

—How easily he let you have it, though.

—Because it was coming to me. He realized that.

—Then Godina!

—If you scream like that I'll kill you. I'll do it with my own two hands. You know I mean it.

—What happiness there will be with Godina.

—Never. Just more miserable depression.

—That isn't so. There was such sweet happiness then too. And now with Godina.

—I'm telling you that's enough!

—Godina! We can't take it back anymore. It's been said. What a shame that Yehuda . . .

—You're crazy. There is no Godina.

—Then just the word. We'll just keep the word. The soft she-ness of it.

—You're not dragging me back there with you. I'll fight. I'll kill you.

—But it's all inside you.

—Nowhere else. Deep down. That's where the war will be. Deep down . . .

"Who? Talk louder."

But suddenly I feel so weak.

"Mother."

"What are you mumbling there? Who are you?"

"Mother," I whisper.

"Whose mother? Oh, it's you . . . What's wrong?"

"Let me talk to Ya'el."

"Is something wrong?"

"Let me talk to Ya'el or to Tsvi!"

"All right, all right. Don't get nervous. I'll let you talk to t
Just tell me first what's wrong."

But from a stack of files in the corner she rises in an old
and galoshes granny glasses falling off her nose tall wrinkled
backed white wool stockings running up her legs cheap chain
neck reaching out an old bony hand to grab the phone w
smile that I hate in another second she'll begin to talk alread
Ya'el's voice. "Mother? What's the matter? Mother?" That
piece of putty is calling me but I hang up and turn to the
how quickly the moon sails through it I stop my ears I don't
hear but I can't stop the murmur that rises escaping from dee
earth.

—They'll have a terrible accident.

—You're starting again. Don't.

—This time they'll be caught.

—You've said that a thousand times and nothing's ever ha

—This time underfoot.

—No. None of your words again.

—Underfoot.

—Underfoot. So underfoot. So what?

—She sings so beautifully.

—He does. Don't say she. I'm warning you.

—No, no, she. You saw yourself all the she there was today
now on if you'd like there'll be only she, lots of she, she
where . . .

—You're out of your mind.

—She. Lots of she. Even Musa will be a she if you'd like.

—I haven't the strength for this. I don't believe it's hap
Anything but having to begin this all over again.

—She everywhere.

—Godina! You better get it straight. Godina. And now I'm going to sing.

—That's enough. I'm not listening. I'm through with you. Go back to the desert. Die!

The telephone rings and I know that it's Ya'el she's worried maybe Tsvi too maybe even father but I'm afraid to answer because I might say something that will only upset them more. I walk outside to the path hearing the phone steadily ringing waiting to come to my senses to be myself again. Around me out among the trees women are stirring dancing up out of the earth. I bury my face in my arms I listen to the wind fan over me like a tender gust in some huge sail billowing bright light into this darkened world. Far off I hear Yehezkel's voice at last the phone stops ringing. I look around me inhaling the cool air slowly pulling myself together watching the world go back to normal the guardhouse the road the lit-up dining room the ticking of the water pump the sound of the surf here and there a lone star I rise my head clearing in the good still night slowly I walk back to the office to phone them perhaps I'll hear Gaddi or the baby I'll ask them how they like the seder.

THE FIRST DAY
OF PASSOVER

> I still am haunted by the knowledge that,
> whether separate or apart, we are one thing.
> Eugenio Montale Xenia

Already it's tomorrow. This is it. A new shadow gleams on the wall like a bar of thin mercury. Good morning last day. Who would have thought they would all pass so quickly? A matter of hours now. At midnight tonight your divorced your divorcing father blasts off. A whirlwind visit but the knot has been cut. Not without mistakes but I'm free. To forget it too. All the dreadful little moments. Perhaps only one of them will remain perhaps not even that the parchment flying through the air into her outstretched palms a spasm of rabbis around us. Old toothless religion you still have the power to shock at the least expected times. A dash of mystery. So farewell my murderess. No fantasy of mine. A few hours from now you will bank steeply over clouds and land in a gray alien dawn straight into a big American kitchen filled with quiet suburban light. Into a cold and peaceful exile. The Return of the Old Israeli laying his now available name beside the swollen white belly. Cold cereal and coffee before stripping to a flabby erection. But with infinite patience. There you do not disappoint. There is only grateful wonder that you exist at all. That you are what you are. But what time is it and what's happened to my watch?

The door opened gently, admitting a quick shaft of reddish light, and Ya'el groped her patient, cumbersome way into the room. Without a sound she made straight for my bed and rolled back the blanket, searching among the sheets. Carefully she moved aside my hand and pulled out a small, limp bundle from beneath my feet.

"Ya'eli?"

"Shhh. Go back to sleep, father. I'm just taking the baby."

"Rakefet? She's still here? I forgot all about her . . . but what happened?"

"She must have put you to sleep."

Night's sweet, stubborn plaything came aloft from the sheets, her clenched fist a last vestige of her nocturnal storm of tears, her head drooping limply, delicately backwards. For a second she blinked, a blue light flashing in the stubbornly idling little engine.

"You should have woken me. How did I miss hearing her?" said Ya'el.

"Don't be silly, what for? I wouldn't give up an extra minute with her, and I couldn't just let her cry. What time is it?"

"It's still early, father. Go to sleep. You have a long, hard day ahead of you."

"But what time is it, Ya'eli?"

"Not even six yet. Go back to sleep."

"I can't find my watch."

I got out of bed and searched for it barefoot among the linen. Ya'el bent and poked a hand into the large, finned diaper just as the little fist opened and a shiny object fell onto the pillow.

"She swiped it from you," laughed Ya'el. "But at least she was fair enough to return it in her sleep."

"Let me have her for a minute. I can't stand to think of leaving her."

I reached out to take her on my lap, planting little kisses on her warm mouth and on the familiar set of her jaw. All at once she sighed deeply.

The door shuts the shaft of light is gone the silent tremor of a shadow resumes its place on the wall. My bare feet still touch the

cold floor the watch is warm and fragrant in my hand its face hidden
from me. Let it be a clockless day. Leave time alone for this once.
Forget it let it lie in your bag by your ticket and passport ticking
away in the dark while you step out of the cold vise of its hands into
the nebulous light now creeping toward the issue of your loins who
will get you through this day let them pilot you in and out of it right
up to the flight gate at midnight Ya'el and Tsvi and Asi and Dina
who promised to come today too let them all have their way with
you. You are theirs today you belong only to them even to Gaddi
who has gotten close to you in his fashion even to the baby even to
Kedmi yes you will put up with him too. Be patient with him today
the man puts his foot in his big nasty mouth each time he opens it yet
since you helped him get his murderer back he's mellowed toward
you. You can put up with him too I'm at your service Kedmi have all
the fun you want with me I'll even put up with your Haifa this
formless town that once used to be a real city but is only the sum of
its neighborhoods now. Yes you can even put up with Haifa today in
this new holiday light this aroma of spring. All winter long you
dreamed of Tel Aviv the people the places in the end it all went down
the drain of coming and going to see her in the hospital but never
mind. The knot has been cut the parchment crossed the room. Next
time. Whenever that will be. It's goodbye for a long while now. My
small maddening land you'll have to wait for me I need to rest. What
was it that little fellow that Calderon said that night in the kitchen
his dark eyes deep in their sockets just give me time. To protect the
chafed exposed surface of your embroiled identity. A nervous land.
And how quickly without even thinking he agreed to give her his
share. Just give me time. But the knot has been cut. A new freedom.
The shadow moves on the wall the windowpane shakes a bus starts
its motor in the street startling the morning's deep quietude. I lift the
blinds and open the window letting a breeze slip inside. A dawn mist
swaddles the bay. The newspapers vivisect this country on each page
merrily they wonder if it has a future Kedmi makes hash of it ten
times a day but here it is stretching so peaceful and safe its smoke-
stacks exhaling lazy gray smoke into a low sky. Reality is stronger
than all thought it even surprises itself.

Not even Kedmi believed it until they rang the doorbell halfway
through the seder. We were sitting with our Haggadahs, and for a

moment I was terrified that it was her on the heels of her phone call. But Kedmi ran to the door and there he was in the dim light of the hallway, come to turn himself in. I didn't recognize him at first in a white shirt, freshly shaven and combed, his beady chimp's eyes gleaming fiercely, until Kedmi broke out in a crafty smile and grabbed him with both hands as though to make sure he stayed put. He was already talking a blue streak. "Well, well, well, what an honored guest! Just look at what we have here, everyone! Now that we've made two happy people of father and mother, it's time to cheer up the police. . . . But do come in. We'll have to think quick if we're to keep this night off of yours from costing you another two years."

The young man stood silently, sullenly in the doorway, recoiling from Kedmi's grasp, a great fatigue in his eyes. He turned back toward the dark stairway from which two more figures emerged, one of a short, sturdy old workingman wearing a threadbare suit and gray cap and clutching a plastic bag, and the other of a swarthy, unkempt, gypsyish-looking woman of undefinable origin. Kedmi divined at once who they were and hurried toward them.

"This way, please, Mr. and Mrs. Miller. Come right in, it's no imposition at all. I'm sure God won't mind if we take a break and finish the seder later. Come in, have a seat."

I felt a twinge of pity for the father standing so awkwardly with his dark wife, who looked too young to be the boy's mother. I rose to make room for them and offer them my seat, as did Ya'el, while Kedmi's mother sat up and smiled indulgently and Tsvi slumped deeper in his chair, looking the murderer over. More chairs were brought but the couple seemed uncertain whether to join us or not. Both kept looking at their son, unprepared to have to part with him again.

"Sit down, have something to drink," said Kedmi, suddenly in one of his manic moods. "Perhaps you'd like some wine . . . you can have the cup we saved for Elijah . . ."

"You haven't informed the police yet?" asked the father in a thick German accent.

"No. I decided to wait and see whether your son would really show up. I thought he might want to spend the whole holiday with you, ha ha . . . but never mind . . . never mind . . . we'll give it a religious twist, eh? We can say that he ran away to pray I

hope you at least attended services . . . what, you didn't? But we'll
still make a born-again Jew of him! We'll have him wear a skullcap
. . . we'll give him a new image in the very best contemporary style.
Do you know, I phoned the prison this afternoon and they were still
hunting for you in the woods . . . they're absolutely determined to
find you there . . . they even brought some dog to track you, just
like in the movies, and flew over in a helicopter. Oh, they're playing
a real fine game of cops and robbers. I tell you, this family seder of
yours will cost the government a quarter of a million pounds . . .
but never mind, they'll run it off the press as soon as the holiday is
over. . . . Come, sit down, ladies and gentlemen, don't be afraid.
There's no extra charge for any of this. I'm still waiting for your
uncle from Belgium . . . perhaps the police will find him in the
woods too, ha ha ha . . ."

Kedmi Kedmi where did they ever find you? With your supercil-
ious sarcasm your total tactlessness your diarrhea of the mouth your
weird pointless but still surprising even sometimes anarchistic jokes.
And yet Ya'el does love you I never realized that until this visit. And
controls you too with that passive silence of hers that manipulates
you by some hidden force. Who really are you Kedmi? And such a
home-brewed Israeli concoction always shoving to the front of the
line . . .

The morning mist is breaking up dissolving northward a clean
light washes the bay. How quickly day is born here. And out there in
the west darkness awaits you or rather it creeps up behind you in a
few more gratuitous hours it will have caught up with you again. A
free gift that you needn't pay back. What time is it? What time can it
be? You open the door of the darkened guest room Tsvi is curled up
on the living-room couch fast asleep his pale arm dangling down his
wristwatch catching the light you can't resist picking up the thin
hand he lets you have it in his sleep you twist it to look it's five after
six. He opens his eyes for a moment with a smile then curls up like a
fetus again. You walk to the dining room nothing is left on its ex-
panded table but the soiled cloth you drop into the seat at the head of
it where you sat last night your head in your hands from somewhere
comes the flicker of a thought.

Here next to you, a few hours ago, sat the uncommunicative parents. At first they wouldn't hear of joining us but I insisted until they did. Kedmi took the young man aside for "a quick briefing," as he put it, telling him what to admit and what not, the main thing being to dispel all suspicion that he had escaped to stash away the loot from the robbery. Once again it struck me that he thought the fellow was guilty and was defending a client whom he didn't believe in. In the end he made him sign some document stating that he was turning himself in of his own free will, after which he hastened to phone the police, refusing to talk to anyone but a certain officer he knew. Meanwhile the murderer's parents sat with us at the seder table, frantic with worry, not touching the wine cup placed in front of them, the woman staring at the table, the man watching us with hard, alert eyes. Gaddi looked back at them hostilely, while I sought to smile sympathetically.

"He simply wanted to spend the seder with us," the woman explained to Ya'el. "He's an only son, he didn't want us to be alone . . ."

"Are you his mother?" Ya'el wondered softly. The woman nodded in an admission of guilt. When you began to question the father you discovered a stubborn but naïve German Jew who had somehow fallen by the wayside due to his own self-limiting rigidity and had remained a simple blue-collar type all his life. Now he was in total, unremitting conflict with the world, and economically slowly going under.

"Don't you worry," said Kedmi's mother, beatifically inspired to feel that via Kedmi they had come under her patronage. "You'll see. My son will save him."

The woman regarded her trustingly, murmuring her gratitude, but the father burst out irately:

"There's nothing to save him from because he never did anything in the first place!"

Kedmi's mother gave him a knowing smile, mystified by his stubbornness but ceding nothing. "You'll see. Even if he did murder her, Yisra'el will save him."

"Murder who, grandpa?" asked Gaddi, who was sitting next to you, in an excited whisper.

"No one," we all exclaimed together. "No one at all."

Tsvi smiled, still slumped in his chair, toying with the little Haggadah that he held.

"Then why are the police coming to get him?" Gaddi persisted.

"Because they think that he murdered someone. But your father
will prove that they're wrong."

The murderer's father looked angrily at Gaddi and we all fell
silent, listening to Kedmi rant over the telephone with his customary
know-it-all aggressiveness and uncalled-for provocations. Tsvi alone
sat there untroubled, taking it all in with an ironic smile, his fingers
constructing a small pile of matzo crumbs on the white tablecloth.
At last Kedmi returned to the dining room, beamingly dragging the
escaped man after him as if afraid to let go of him for a second. It
had taken a while for the morons at police headquarters to get it, but
soon they would arrive. "Come on now, let's finish the seder in a
hurry before the fun begins . . ."

The parents jumped up in alarm. "Well then, we'd better go," they
said sorrowfully. "We've bothered you enough as it is."

"But how can you say that?" asked Tsvi. "You've been no trouble
at all!" He got gallantly to his feet. "Stay with us until the police
come. You'll want to say goodbye to him then."

"Yes, do," agreed Ya'el. "Perhaps you'd like to wait in the living
room. You can be there quietly by yourselves."

"But why should they?" protested Tsvi, who had come suddenly,
mysteriously to life. "Come sit with us if you can stand it." He
smiled at me. "You'll have the experience of hearing my father sing
Passover songs." And he made room for Kedmi's murderer, brought
him a chair and helped him into it, and redistributed all the Haggadahs.

I felt a burst of fear when I saw how he looked at the fellow.
Kedmi was taken aback for a moment but quickly gave his assent;
perhaps he was afraid that the escaped prisoner would disappear
again if left alone in the next room. Hesitantly the guests resumed
their seats and listened to the weak, uncertain singing led by me with
Kedmi's mother and Gaddi joining in while the others just hummed
along. Thus the seder came to an end, leaving us at the table still
waiting for the police.

Kedmi went to open the front door. "For Elijah." He winked.
Suddenly there wasn't a sound. We sat there unaccountably silent,
except for Tsvi, who whispered something to the murderer with

glowing cheeks, to which the escaped man replied with an annoyed, uncomprehending look. And so we waited until at last we heard heavy steps on the stairs. Kedmi hurried back to the door. "Listen to them drag their feet," he mocked. "The only place you'll ever see a cop run is on TV."

Finally a fat, mustachioed sergeant appeared in the doorway gasping for breath. He had a piece of paper in his hand and a big pistol strapped to his waist. "Does Yisra'el Kedmi live here?" he asked.

"Yes," answered Kedmi rapidly, "and it's about time you've come. It's only on TV that you people ever move fast. In reality you're as slow as molas . . ."

The words were still in midsentence when the sergeant pulled out a pair of handcuffs from his pocket and slipped them with startling speed onto the astonished Kedmi's wrists.

"That's enough of your wisecracks," he said, dragging Kedmi to the door. "Move!"

Kedmi went wild. "Just a minute, you nut, I'm the lawyer! Why don't you read that note through to the end . . ."

Tsvi let out a loud, strange guffaw while the rest of us crowded around the sergeant. Next to me Gaddi was biting his lips. The murderer grabbed the policeman and said calmly:

"Hey, it's me. I'm the one."

But imperturbably, stubbornly, the sergeant refused to admit his mistake. He stood there slow and stolid, his humorous eyes the only sign that he was enjoying the scene he had caused.

"What do you mean, it's you?"

"I'm the one who escaped."

"Are you Yisra'el Kedmi?"

"No, I'm Yoram Miller."

"Who the hell is that?"

"That's me."

"No one said anything to me about any Miller. But if you care to join us, come along."

Kedmi went totally beserk, rattling his handcuffs and screaming, "You let me out of these at once, you moron, I'm his lawyer!"

The sergeant gave him a sharp yank, twisting his cuffed wrists savagely. "Stop calling me names, you! I've got Yisra'el Kedmi written here. Is that you? . . . It is? That's all I want to know."

At which point I approached him, gripped him lightly by the arm, and set him straight simply and clearly. He listened to me, beginning to comprehend, while Kedmi watched pale with anger, his eyes darting hatefully back and forth. The sergeant took a walkie-talkie from his belt and tried to get headquarters. There was a crackle of static. He asked Ya'el for a glass of water, laid the set on the table, took the glass with his free hand and gulped it down. A young woman's voice spoke. "What did you say the name of the apprehended party was?"

The sergeant told her. A brief silence ensued while Kedmi stared hard at the set. "Is there a Yoram Miller there?" asked the voice.

"Yes," said the sergeant.

"Then apprehend him. He's the escapee. And be advised that he's dangerous."

With a smile the sergeant let Kedmi go and handcuffed the murderer. "Sorry about that," he said.

Kedmi sprang away from him, massaging his freed hand. "If anyone should be sorry, it's the parents who gave birth to you. Now please sign this statement that I'm turning him over to you of his own free will."

The sergeant didn't even look at the paper extended to him. "I'm not signing anything. The last statement I signed cost me two more years of waiting for my sergeant's stripes. If you want, you can come with me to the precinct." He smiled genially again. "I really am sorry, but all I had written here was Yisra'el Kedmi."

"Why be sorry?" reiterated Kedmi in a quiet, hate-filled, profoundly injured voice. "It's not your fault. Your parents should be sorry. The police force should be sorry. You're not to blame that you were born a cretin."

"I'd watch it if I were you, Mr. Kedmi," said the sergeant, still smiling unflappably.

But Kedmi wasn't through with his tantrum. "*I* should watch it? *I?* It's you who better watch it. . . . If you think you've seen the last of me, I've got news for you! But enough of this clowning around . . . I'm coming with you. You too, mother. And the rest of you . . ."

He was in a white heat. How quick the man was to take offense. But I was less mindful of him than I was of the boy, who had taken the sight of his handcuffed father hard and was clinging to me in confusion, his hand in mine, in search of support. You're going to miss him, I thought. When you first saw him the night you arrived and they woke him to show you, you were almost frightened by how fat he was. A miniature Kedmi, but without Kedmi's manic spirits, so somber and strange. And then when he woke you that overcast afternoon with rain streaming down the window you were scared again by the sight of him standing there in a black trenchcoat with an old leather hat jammed down on his head, holding a pair of sugar tongs. You were sure that the boy was retarded or at least emotionally disturbed. But in the end you came to understand him, to appreciate his clarity of mind. Oh he was somber all right, seldom smiling, a little pessimist squelched by a father to whom he was very attached and yet whom he judged all the time. It amazed you to hear him talk about his parents, whom he saw so complexly, so accurately. And all along, in that brooding silence of his, he must have been judging you too. How foolish it was to take him with us to the hospital. We must have seemed ridiculous to him—and yet even when he saw Asa hit himself, even when you went down on your knees, he didn't bat an eyelash—no, not even when that giant snatched his toy away. Will he at least remember you and this hectic crazy week until you come again? Only when will that be?

The shadow beside me sticks steadfastly to the wall a dark ragged strip of gauze that will dissolve in the morning light. Behind you before you the darkness deepens over the sea. Already a dull feeling of fatigue but better a tired day than a flight without sleep. Distractedly my fingers knead the scar Connie calls it my psychosomatic itch and takes my hand away tonguing it with a kiss. With such American goodness such bold givingness. All at once Dina wanted to see it. Good and scared I was. No fantasy then. The need to show everyone. The compulsion. Even you found it odd the way you opened your shirt for her in that crowded café. Asa was furious he couldn't understand the petty mind. Why did you have to go tell her? What a luminous smile. She was happy you did though not frightened at all even secretly made a note in her little pad maybe you and your scar will turn up in some story of hers. No more than a child. A beauty unaware of her own power but she liked you. The joy of seeing her again. Coming especially to say goodbye. The slow trickle of time what surprises has it in store for you today? What time is it?

The sleepers tossed in their rooms. Soft morning stirrings. A warm, cozy hour. Everyone had gone to sleep late. Tsvi made up his mind to go to the police station. Kedmi took his mother and the murderer's parents home. Ya'el went to put Gaddi to bed. And so I was left by myself at the head of the deserted table while, as though materialized by magic, across from me sat a young reporter from a local newspaper who had tiptoed in the open door. Never one to miss a trick, Kedmi had gotten him to cover the story in order to get some free publicity. "They're all gone," I said, "but I'll tell you exactly what happened." And I sat him across from me like a student and gave him his scoop.

A heavy shuffle of feet. Gaddi emerged drowsily from his room and walked blindly to the bathroom, his shadow trailing after him on the floor until swallowed up by the rug.

"Gaddi," I whispered.

He paused for a second as though hearing voices and continued to the bathroom. The water was flushed and he came back the other way.

"Gaddi," I whispered again without getting up.

He paused again, scanning the darkness with shut eyes as though called by a ghost. Slipping his hand through his pajama tops like a little Napoleon, he laid it on his chest and went back to bed without a word.

My heart went out to him. I followed him into his room. Curled up beneath his blanket, he opened one eye and regarded me. Would he remember me? How delve deep enough into him to keep him from forgetting? I sat on his bed, feeling his warm body, smelling a faint odor of pee. "Do you know that I'm leaving today?"

He nodded.

"Will you remember your grandpa?"

He considered and nodded again.

"Didn't you hear me calling you before?"

He didn't answer. Calmly he observed me with his big eyes, realizing now that the ghost was only grandpa. Beneath the blanket his hand groped back toward his chest.

"Where does it hurt you? Your mother said she'd take you to the doctor tomorrow and that you'd write me what he said. You're just not active enough. You don't exercise. You don't walk."

"Where to?" he asked.

"I mean in general."

"No, that won't help," he answered hopelessly, with a maturity that seemed beyond his years. "It's because of my glands. They have to be taken out."

"That's nonsense. Nothing has to be taken out. You're a fine, healthy boy. You just have to do more with yourself. Come on, get up. Maybe you'd like to take a walk with me now."

"Where to?"

"Just out in the morning air. We'll be the only ones out at this hour."

"All right," he said, still making no move to rise.

I went to get dressed, watching the thinning, gauzy shadow that had breezed in through the blinds turn to a flap of sky blue. Parting. Only eighteen more hours. The knot was cut. The border sealed and receding the wounds that would quickly heal. No more of her and her other. No more lunacy. I washed and shaved with slow movements. And out there the darkness was moving behind before the slowly revolving light. I peaked in on Gaddi, who was still in bed with his eyes shut. Asleep. I went to the small kitchen and shut the door behind me. The washed dishes were stacked in the drying rack, the leftovers were all neatly covered. I put up water to boil. Opening a closet, I found a hidden cache of bread that Kedmi had put away for the holiday. Alongside it lay the long bread knife. What had I promised that disappointed her so?

I was drinking my coffee when the door opened and in walked Gaddi in his school uniform, rubbing his eyes.

"So you're up! That's great. Would you like something to eat? . . . No? Are you sure?"

He debated with himself.

"No. Then how about a glass of milk at least?"

He consented. I poured it for him. He drained it quickly, reaching out without thinking for some matzo, breaking off a piece and sticking it silently into his mouth.

"Eat," I said. "You don't want to be hungry."

He ate the rest of the matzo. I put the dirty dishes in the sink and we left, passing by Ya'el's bedroom, through whose slightly open door I saw Kedmi's great bulk sprawled on its back, one hand on Ya'el's face.

"We'd better leave a note," I said. I found a piece of paper and

wrote: *We've gone for a morning walk. We'll be back soon. Grandpa.*
"You sign too," I said to Gaddi. He wrote his name gladly.

It was already full morning outside, but still very chilly. Spring
was having a hard time deciding. What time could it be?

Gaddi seemed pleased to find the street so still. "Everyone is sleeping off the seder," he said. "What time is it?"

"I left my watch in my valise. I'll spend the day without it."

"How come?"

"Because I don't want to see time running to the finish line of my
visit."

He smiled.

"You don't have a watch of your own? I'll leave you some money
and tomorrow you can buy one with it."

He wanted to show me his school. We walked down the hill and
entered a large, rectangular yard that was caked with a layer of well-
trodden mud. On the wall of the school building hung a large clock
that said eight.

"It always says that," said Gaddi, who was full of life now. He was
searching for something around him, bending to dig in the hard
mud. Suddenly he kneeled and scooped up a big colored marble that
he put into his pocket.

"I found it!" he murmured under his breath.

He went on looking, enjoying the unfamiliar quiet in this familiar
place, feeling at home. At one end of the yard was a small stone
platform on which he jumped and walked about importantly.

"Where's your classroom?" I asked.

He pointed up at it and after unsuccessfully trying several locks
found a door at the back of the building that swung open. We
stepped inside, walking down long corridors whose walls were
decked with portraits of national heroes, dried flowers, slogans and
verses from the Bible, maps of a post-1967 Israel. A homeland still
struggling to be a homeland. A squashed-banana, public-school
smell. I hadn't set foot in such a place since the children grew up. I
began to tell Gaddi that I too was a teacher, but a teacher who
taught teachers to teach. He nodded, satisfied with the information,
and led me up some stairs to his second-floor classroom, whose door
was disappointingly locked. Through its glass pane we saw desks and
chairs stacked against the wall. He led me back down to the yard,
trying all the doors on the way. The sun was shining brightly. The

blinds on the houses across the street were still drawn. He jumped happily on the stone platform, ruddy and fat, excitedly talking to himself, playing at being the principal or some teacher. From afar I watched the sunrays glance off his face that resembled an overfed boxer's.

"Who's your principal?" I asked when he rejoined me.

"It's a woman," he murmured shyly.

"Your heart doesn't hurt anymore?"

"No."

Less than a thought. We left the schoolyard and he proposed showing me his old kindergarten. We walked back up the street until we came to a small stone building tucked into the side of a ravine. Stone stairs descended to it. He hurried down them, cutting across the play area with its seesaw and sandbox and trying the door. It was open. I followed him.

"Someone's in there," he whispered.

We entered, hearing voices, and found that the kindergarten had been converted into a makeshift synagogue.

"Excuse us," I said to the small group of men who were standing inside and stretching a rope across the room to mark off the women's section.

"Please come in," said one of them. "There'll be enough of us to start the service soon."

"Oh, no," I stammered. "We had no idea . . . my grandson just wanted to show me his old kindergarten . . . we didn't come prepared for prayer . . ."

But they wouldn't relinquish us, they had everything we needed, from a cardboard box they produced, all brand-new, prayer shawls and prayer books and skullcaps. "Come on in, sit down, if you don't mind waiting. This is the first time that we're holding services here. The municipality let us have the building for the holiday . . . there's a need for it in the neighborhood . . . we'll be starting soon . . ."

I glanced at Gaddi, who was watching with interest as his old nursery school turned into a house of worship.

"Would you like to stay a bit and see a service? Have you ever been to a synagogue before?"

"No."

"Your father never took you?"

"No."

"Then let's stay a while. It will give us a chance to rest. What time is it?"

We sat on the tiny chairs. The four or five young men around us went on setting up the room, arranging the chairs in rows, making an ark for the Torah out of the doll closet, placing a Torah scroll in it that they removed from a carton, improvising a podium for the cantor, joking amusedly about the kindergarten they had invaded while a young, dynamic rabbi with an English accent directed them. Someone banged cymbals. For years I hadn't bothered to attend a synagogue service in Israel. And here was one being held by these young people—and very unreligious-looking young people they were, with their skullcaps that kept slipping off their heads—who seemed so normal and with it.

"Do you live around here?"

"No, but I'm visiting my daughter, who does."

Still glistening from the last rains the green ravine could be seen through the window in the brightening light. Silvery-green olive trees dotted its slopes, which here and there were darkened by the mouth of a limestone cave. Large, gaily colored toy blocks lay around us, and here too slogans, accompanied by photographs of dogs, papered the walls. Already Gaddi was excitedly checking the names of the children by the coat hangers and helping the rabbi to find things, while I, on my little kindergarten-turned-synagogue chair, bore inadvertent witness to the contemporary religious revival . . .

Only a few hours left now. One last Israeli day under way. And there behind you before you the thickening darkness waits. Not a fantasy after all. Sitting there in her wide cotton dress beneath her white smock so strong so big so serene that crazy fanatic fighting for our marriage beyond the thin wooden door playing for time. For a burned-out wick. Smiling not at all sorry clinging to her madness as though to the leash of some great crouching beast. I don't believe in her getting better children watch out for her you have no idea how deep it goes. You disappointed me. So calmly so lucidly. I did did I? Disappointed you that I didn't go crazy too. Forgive me but that far I wouldn't go. And did I ever really promise?

Two of the young men, scientists from the Haifa Technion, it
seemed, were talking about some laboratory experiment of theirs.
Gaddi came and sat beside me, his heavy profile with its double chin
suddenly reminding me of Ya'el when she was a girl. His eyes darted
curiously about him while his hand unconsciously crept up to his
chest again, exploring, squeezing lightly.

"Why do you keep putting your hand there? Does it hurt?"

"No."

"Then why?"

"If it starts to I'll squeeze it."

"Squeeze what?"

"The pain."

"Tomorrow your mother is taking you to the doctor. I don't like
this one bit. And he'll explain to you how to lose weight and how to
keep away from fattening foods. The next time I'm here . . ."

"Are you coming back?"

"Of course I am."

Three young women entered the room with a whoop. The men
rose to greet them. "Good to see you here!" They joked about their
kindergarten, showed them the little washrooms, and sat them behind the rope they had strung. "Here. You are absolutely forbidden
to cross it." More laughter. It was an adventure for them, this trying
on of religion for size. More worshippers arrived, descending the
stairs and exclaiming at their surroundings. The young rabbi had the
men put on prayer shawls and taught them the blessing to recite.
"There are ten men here now," someone said. "We can start to
pray."

There's a bit of ocean too in the splendid view in the window. My
first year abroad I missed this landscape terribly afterwards I grew
attached to others so breathtaking especially in autumn and in
spring. We who saw this country being born thought we could always bend it to our will always correct it if it went off course yet here
it was out of control full of strange mutations different people odd
permutations new sources of unexpected energy. The clear lines have
been hopelessly smudged. If only it could at least be a homeland
when will it settle down to be one. Asa go easy with your historical
chaos don't force too much of it on us.

The scented women regard you from behind their rope. It was in

America that you first discovered your powers of attraction. They didn't miss a lecture not even in midwinter not even during a blizzard. The old Israeli Valentino. The Apostle to the Exile who re-exiled himself and now spends his days in heated underground shopping centers fingering the fabric of dresses checking out the millinery aisles waiting for Connie. Connie I've given away my half of the house. Like a corpse tied to the bedposts and you so patient such a gentleman.

And still there were only ten men.

"I'm sorry," I whispered to the rabbi. "I didn't come to pray. I just happened by."

"At least stay for the beginning," he pleaded. "There'll be more of us. Just for the beginning."

He went to the improvised ark, explained briefly to those gathered the nature of the morning's prayer, and began to sing the old hymn in a mild, clear voice:

> *Great King of All Whose reign began*
> *E'er was there any living thing,*
> *And Who, when All's done by His will,*
> *Forever still will be called King;*
>
> *When All is gone and is no more,*
> *Still will He rule eternally;*
> *Imperially glorious,*
> *He was, He is, and He will be;*
>
> *And He is One, beside Him none . . .*

A young couple arrived and stood looking on in the entrance. I felt rooted to my chair. Exhausted. Time was trickling away. But what time was it? The room began filling up. The box of prayer shawls was empty. The sun glared through the window. Hymned clarity. Stubborn flicker of thought. Fear-constricted. Gaddi turned uncomfortably to the rear. A small boy had entered the room, recognized him and pointed him out in a whisper to his father, who was wearing an officer's uniform. He tugged at my sleeve, ill at ease.

"When are we going?"

"Soon."

I shut my eyes, in thrall to the liturgy, around me the decorous

silence of these non-observant Jews unaccustomed to the constant
drone that accompanies prayer in an Orthodox synagogue.

"Mom and dad will worry," Gaddi persisted, rising from his chair.

"All right, let's go. Excuse me," I said to a young man sitting next
to me, "do you happen to know the time?" He showed me his watch,
afraid to utter a word.

I took off my prayer shawl and skullcap and handed them without
glancing up to a new congregant who had just arrived. The small boy
rose too and made his way toward us, but Gaddi hurried up the
stairs away from him and we stepped out into the spring day. The
street was filled now with both adults and children. Cars streamed
down the hill. I walked still staring down at the ground. What guilt
they managed to infuse in you. Not that you ever believed but for a
long while you didn't disbelieve either. Leave God out of this Naomi
said right away.

We continued back up the street. Gaddi strayed into a field and
returned with a bent metal pipe. He stopped by a tree to pick leaves
for his last silkworm that hadn't yet spun a cocoon. Suddenly I felt
that we were being followed by a car driving slowly behind us. I
stopped. So did it. The light reflected from its windshield was too
blinding for me to make out the driver. We turned into Ya'el's narrow street and climbed the stairs to the apartment. The living room
was still dark. Ya'el and Kedmi were in the kitchen, sitting at a table
piled high with breakfast, with matzos and pitas side by side, both
eating ravenously. Kedmi still wore his pajamas and was in high
spirits.

"Last night you made off with our daughter and this morning it's
our son, eh, grandpa?"

"Gaddi keeps having these pains in his chest. You have to take
him to the doctor tomorrow."

"It's nothing," said Ya'el. "He's just imagining it."

"Still . . ."

"All right, we'll take him," said Kedmi.

"Is that a promise?"

He looked at me, amused.

"It's a promise. Where have you been?"

We told him about the new synagogue in the kindergarten.

"Didn't I tell you they were taking over this country?" he shot back. "Before long we won't even be allowed to drive a car on Saturday. We'll have to get around on roller skates."

I asked him what happened last night at the police station. He had actually filed a complaint against the sergeant, who would, he claimed, retain that rank for the rest of his life. I asked him again about his murderer. Did he really think that he was guilty?

"Do I think that he's guilty? What difference would it make if I did? My job is to keep the judge from thinking it."

Ya'el brought me my breakfast.

"What time is it?"

"Did Rakefet break your watch after all?"

"No. I just left it in my room."

"It's half past eight. Have you begun counting the hours?"

"No. Why?"

The phone rang. Ya'el answered it and returned. It was Asi calling from the bus station in Tel Aviv. They were on their way. I returned to my room on a wave of emotion, knelt by my little valise, took out my passport and ticket, and checked the time of departure again. I reread the power of attorney that I had prepared for Asa and glanced again at the signed certificate of divorce. A shadow flashed across the ceiling. Mine or some object's in the room? I folded my pajamas and packed them away. The sky outside was bright blue. Below on the corner I caught sight again of the white car that had followed us. Its driver loitered beside it, a slender man in a white suit.

I hurried to Tsvi, who was still sleeping in the dim living room, his white arm trailing on the floor. He open his eyes with a luxuriating sigh.

"Father? What time is it?"

"Already past nine."

He sighed again deeply.

"Tsvi, get up. I think that man is waiting for you downstairs."

"Who?"

"That man . . . of yours. You know who I mean . . . Calderon. . . ."

"Oh my God. He's here already? He's really too much."

"Are you getting up?"

"In a minute. What's the rush? It's only nine, and today's a holiday."

"Perhaps I should invite him up then."

"Don't. Let him wait. He's used to it."

He snuggled back under the blanket and shut his eyes again.

"I still think you should get up."

"All right. In a minute. There's plenty of time. Do you have the travel jitters?"

"Not especially."

"Are you glad to be going back?"

"It's not easy to leave you all."

"Oh . . ." He turned over on his other side.

Kedmi sat down to read a newpaper. Ya'el cleaned the house. I looked out the window at the slender man, who was still in the same place, smoking a cigarette. I debated for a moment and made up my mind to go to him. He was standing and gazing up at the windows of the apartment when I approached him. Suddenly he noticed me. He made a movement as though to flee, recalled it immediately, smiled and held out his hand.

"Hello, Mr. Kaminka. I didn't realize you had recognized me. How was your seder?"

"Pleasant enough. And yours?"

"The main thing is that it's over. It dragged on and on. That's because of my wife's eldest brother . . . every year he makes it longer. But we got through it in the end . . ."

"Are you waiting for Tsvi? He's still asleep."

"Of course, of course, I knew he'd be. Let him sleep. I have something to tell him. Something new that may interest him. But never mind. Let him sleep."

"Something new?"

"Oh, it's just a business matter. Nothing very dramatic . . . it can wait . . . it's not really that important. But how are you, Mr. Kaminka? I heard that the divorce went smoothly. I drove Tsvi up there yesterday and had the impression that she took it well."

"Would you like to come upstairs with me?"

"Oh, I couldn't do that! Not at an hour like this. I'll wait here in the car. I have a radio and whatever I need. I simply misread my watch, and so I came early . . . but never mind . . . and after all, this is your last day here . . ."

"No, Mr. Calderon, I insist. We'll wake Tsvi up."

"Absolutely not! It's just that . . . just that I . . ."

He began to shake all over.

"It's just that I . . . I actually had meant to go to synagogue . . . I never travel on holidays . . . I have my prayer shawl and prayer book with me in the car . . . that is, I was on my way to synagogue when suddenly the thought crossed my mind . . . that it's hopeless . . . that he wants to leave me . . . tell me it's not so! You were a source of so much strength to me that night, that's what's kept me going until now . . ."

I touched his light, warm arm and he sheltered against me, his lined face blotchy as though rouged, his eyes two bits of sunken coals.

"Come up anyway."

His face lit up.

"He didn't say anything of the sort about me . . . Tsvi . . . he didn't say . . . ?"

"No. Not as far as I know. But come up and have something to drink. We'll wake him. He's slept enough."

"It's no good for him, this sleeping late of his. It keeps him from getting ahead. I've told him that he can't wake up an hour before the market opens and think that there's still time to size it up. But today's a holiday, why shouldn't he sleep? Never mind . . . he'll only be annoyed if we wake him . . . and perhaps I can still find some place around here to pray in . . ."

He wiped his eyes.

"Come, then, let me show you a little synagogue that just opened today. Gaddi and I were out walking this morning and we found it in his old kindergarten . . . some people in the neighborhood have gotten interested in religion . . ."

He wavered. "I'm sure they're not Sephardim . . . it's only the Ashkenazim who are returning to religion now . . . and I'm not up to a whole lot of new melodies. Never mind, though, I'll go . . . where is it?"

He took his prayer shawl from the car and donned it, placed a black skullcap on his head, rolled up the windows, and locked the doors.

"When I got into the car this morning and started out on the highway I felt like I was driving on fire. I've never traveled on a holiday or a Sabbath before. It's a good thing that my father is dead and doesn't know. But I'll make it up . . . I'll give God back what I've taken from Him . . . I'm keeping accounts. It's just that I feel so hopeless. The bottom has fallen out of my life. I'll be good and sick from this yet, I know I will."

He grabbed my hand.

"He really said nothing to you? He hasn't told you what he intends to do?"

"No."

"But I know it . . . no, don't try telling me . . . I know that he wants to ditch me . . . I can feel it. If he were a woman . . . but where am I going to find another man to fall in love with? This whole thing has been such a disaster for me, right from the start . . ."

He stood in the sunlight by the stone stairs of the synagogue, raving with a nasal whine. Down below it seemed like a regular service now: children ran about, voices were lifted in prayer, men lounged by the entrance in their prayer shawls. I wanted to comfort him, to make room for him in me too.

"Let me talk to Tsvi about it . . ."

"But you mustn't! He'll be furious with me . . . and you've had enough worries as it is, quite apart from your leaving tonight. By the way, I told Tsvi that I would be happy to drive you to the airport. I'll miss you, Mr. Kaminka . . . we all will. Well, I'll see you later. Maybe praying will calm me down a bit. Tell Tsvi that I'll be over soon."

His long crooked shadow snaps on the descending stairs he vanishes into the kindergarten and is gone. And you where are you? Your shadow frozen on the concrete wall plastered there larger than life laced with foliage like a frilly dress. I'll miss you. How quickly farce turns to tragedy. I'll miss you. Whose shadow is now blotted out. The chill light. A sky arrayed in the deepest of blues. The softly stirring air. We all will. Your guts are hanging out your flattery gets you nowhere you are a run-down washed-up old man. And nevertheless. Straight simple streets avenues of eucalyptus trees. March on. March on. Homeland can you be a homeland. A small dog with its tail in the air leads a large dog nose-down after it. Children people the traffic in the street. What time is it? The jungly green ravine between two houses. A sense of depth now. It mustn't be said must not even be said but the state of Israel is an episode. Or will history have mercy? Asa do you hear historical mercy there's a concept for

you to work on. March on. March on. Easy. A matter of hours. Or
else to stop time in its tracks. You who thought to slink away in the
night will be missed. Not even angry with you. Overwhelmed by
your generous concession. Asa and Dina are coming all this way
they feel close to you after all. Down down into the ravine oh to
disappear there following a path through the fragrant tangle of
bushes to where the bay opens up at a new angle. Far away dogs
bark. The squat buildings of the Technion across from me. To remember. To cleanse my tired eyes in this light. At first the longing
for another landscape you saw then that landscapes were replaceable.
Sitting on this rock unbuttoning your shirt airing out your scar contemplating it pleasurably scratching it here by yourself in this lush
moist brush. Dawn knife flash. No fantasy no nor regret. Promiscu-
ously doubling herself demanding the impossible from me to keep a
promise meant only as a metaphor as a landmark of longing. But is it
thinkable? And suppose that I did disappoint that I was afraid but I
wasn't ask the dog. One day the children will understand what really
happened.

"Hey, someone's down there!" shouted a youthful voice above me.
"Some old man." All at once a column of youngsters filed overhead,
slithering out of the bushes like a colorful snake and tramping down
the path a few inches from me with giggled whispers.
"What time is it, kids?"
"Almost eleven."
The column continued down the ravine and vanished in the under-
growth. I climbed back up, passing the synagogue, which was now a
kindergarten again. A heavy lock glinted on the door. The white car
was gone. Dressed in old clothes Kedmi stood in front of his house
with a hose, rags and bucket, washing his car and barking orders at
Gaddi, who was assisting him.
"Are Asa and Dina here yet?"
"No."
"Is Tsvi up?"
"Why should he be? Is the stock market open today?"
"What time is it?"
"Time enough for you to take a few more walks."
I quickly climbed the stairs. The door of the apartment was open,
admitting the sounds of the neighbors and of someone's radio. Ya'el

stood washing dishes in the kitchen while the baby sat gaily in her armchair at the table, waving a big-nippled bottle.

"Tsvi's still sleeping?"

Ya'el smiled serenely. "He doesn't want to wake up. You know what he's like in the morning."

"But we can't let him lie around all day. I'll wake him."

And I stormed into the darkened living room, pulling open curtains, raising blinds, shaking him back and forth. "That's enough, you lazy bum! On your feet!" An obscure anger swept over me. "Up, you brute!" I pulled off the blankets with one jerk. The smell of his bedclothes. He sat up in a daze, groggy and annoyed.

"What's going on?"

"Get up! What's going on is that I'm leaving for America soon, Asi and Dina are about to arrive, and you're wallowing in sleep right in the middle of everything!"

He tried pulling the blanket back over him but I jerked it wildly away. His degenerate, smooth, unsullied face. A portrait of me as a young man.

"What's gotten into you, father? Are you out of your mind? What time is it?"

"That's enough, can't you understand! The rest of us have been up for ages . . . that's enough . . ."

He sat up, squatting on his haunches among the crumpled sheets, holding his head, regarding me with a troubled look.

"I think I dreamed about you again . . ."

"You dreamed about me?" I broke into a hysterical laugh. "God help us all! Now get up."

"Don't you want to hear about it?"

"Later. First get up."

I turned on the radio full blast, rocking the house with loud choral music, and hurried back to Ya'el, who was in the bathroom getting ready to wash the baby.

"Here," I offered eagerly, "let me help you."

"Why bother, father? Go lie down. You've been on your feet all morning, and you still have a long day ahead of you."

"I don't want to lie down. I want to be with you all I can. Here, hand her over. I'll hold her."

I carefully undressed the baby, laying her on a fresh diaper, while Ya'el filled the little tub with water. Steam rose from it and fogged the mirrors. I removed her tiny shirt and undid her diaper, smelling her thin, odorous BM. I prepared the soap and baby powder and checked the temperature of the water. Outside we heard Gaddi and Kedmi, who had come back upstairs. The kibbutz choir on the radio sang even louder, celebrating the Festival of Spring. An announcer read verses from the Bible. Who would have imagined that all these old rituals were still kept up? Amazing. More voices of neighbors, someone stepped in to borrow a cup of milk. An Israeli morning. I took off my shirt to keep from wetting it and swung the baby's rosy little body over the water, lowering her slowly into it, crooning to her and trying to make her laugh. Ya'el sought to help me but I waved her away. She watched my deft, vigorous movements with astonishment.

"We'll miss you."

"You'll what?"

"We'll miss you, father. I mean it. I never realized . . ."

"Don't be silly. You'll finally have a little peace and quiet when I'm gone."

"No, it will be sad without you tomorrow."

"Not for Kedmi."

"For Kedmi too. He's gotten to feel close to you these past few days. I can sense it. He doesn't let it show but still . . ."

"Oh, I know that. He's really not a bad sort. I've gotten more used to him too."

"He really isn't. It just seems that way because of how he talks . . ."

She blushed, afraid of having said the wrong thing.

I smiled and said nothing. Rakefet gaily slapped the water with her hands, sending it spraying. Her chaste, dainty pudenda. With a start I recalled Gaddi had said she looked like Naomi. I gripped her little form hard to keep it from slipping. Tsvi came in to wash and shave, fully dressed, making his way between us to the sink, where he stood watching me in amazement. The baby shut her eyes while I took her for a swim in the water.

To have room enough for them all. Crazy thought. Out there peaking now the behind you before you darkness. Brave widow turned corpselike in the huge bed. Illimitable desires. Taking off from them a few hours from now perhaps really making them sad. Left to wish you were here. To miss you. But will they?

"That's enough, father."

"Just a little more. Can't you see how she's enjoying it?"

The choir was still going strong, soprano voices raised in an Israeli oratorio. Kedmi entered the bathroom too and watched me float the baby with superior amusement.

"We'll miss you, grandpa. How will we manage without you tomorrow?"

"I just said the same thing to him."

He walked out again, switching off the light and leaving us in moist, vaporous darkness. Ya'el spread a large red towel.

"That's enough, father."

I fished the baby from the water and handed her to Ya'el, who wrapped her quickly in the towel. The doorbell rang. Someone entered the apartment. Gaddi knocked on the bathroom door.

"They're here from Jerusalem!"

I felt honestly moved to be seeing them both again and hurried down the hallway half naked, my hands dripping water. Timidly, like strangers, they were standing in the doorway's square patch of light. She had had her hair cut boyishly short and looked different in her old-fashioned, puritanically long-sleeved black dress with its white, nunlike collar; tall in high-heeled black shoes, a black patent-leather bag in one hand and a bouquet of flowers in the other, she might have been paying a condolence call. A pale black candle. Older-looking than when I last saw her, she stood chatting with Kedmi and threw me an anxious glance when she caught sight of me. Something in the beauty of her extraordinarily chiseled face with its high cheekbones and large bright eyes had changed, grown deeper and more inward. She stared at the floor, nervous to be meeting me again, while Asa, oblivious of my presence, made straight for the living room, where he halted by Tsvi's unmade bed to examine the books on the shelves. I hastened after them, my heart pounding for no good reason, thrilled by her beauty as first I was in that Jerusalem street by the taxi.

"It's so good to see you children. We were in the middle of bathing Rakefet. I'm soaking wet."

Kedmi stood hulkingly in the middle of the room and winked at them. "He's doing his internship with us."

They smiled uncomfortably.

"Have a seat, have a seat. The mess you see is pure Kaminka."

He himself sat down first in the big armchair.

The two of them looked at me silently, a great gulf between them. I should have gone to my room but instead I stepped up to them in my state of undress and hugged and kissed Asi, feeling him draw back from me.

"Don't be afraid, it's only water. And thank you for coming," I murmured emotionally. He didn't answer. I turned to her, reaching out to grasp her too, but she too recoiled from my nakedness. I smiled and bent to sniff the flowers that she held. She clutched them tighter, extending a rather cool hand.

"How are you, Yehuda?" she asked.

"You can see for yourself . . . it's my last day . . . how was your seder?"

"Very sederlike," snapped Asi with a sharp sideways look at us. She didn't turn to look at him.

"And how are your dear parents?"

"Fine, thank you."

"I mustn't forget to say goodbye to them. Perhaps I should call them now."

"That would make them very happy. But not now . . . tonight . . . they don't answer the phone on religious holidays . . ."

"Of course not. Tonight, then. I must make a note of it."

I put an arm around her thin shoulder.

Ya'el emerged from the bathroom with the baby, all scrubbed, combed and snugly wrapped in snow-white diapers. With a quick cry of admiration Dina turned to hand her the flowers, taking Rakefet in return with a graceful movement. Just then Tsvi stepped into the room, freshly shaven and nattily dressed. He nodded to Dina.

"Was it still dark out when you left Jerusalem?"

He went over to embrace his distinguished younger brother, who shrunk back from him too while casting a glance at Ya'el. Shyly he went over and kissed her warmly, clinging to her like a mother. I felt a sharp pang. For a moment we were all too disconcerted to speak. Kedmi alone remained seated in his armchair.

"Go on, kiss away, you Commie Russians," I heard him mumble under his breath. "Later you can knife each other and drink tea."

I was so stunned I couldn't move. What a vile character after all. How could he talk that way? But the others didn't seem to have heard him. I felt befuddled. The cold breeze coming through the window made me shiver. I hurried to my room and took out a folded white shirt from my valise. My fingers touched my watch. It still said eight o'clock, it must have stopped. I held it uncertainly for a moment, then put it back. I checked my passport and ticket again and found the power of attorney for Asa, which I folded and stuck in my pants pocket. Suddenly I felt dizzy. How to find room for them all?

The line that runs between them all at once there are tears in my eyes my shadow leaps out from under the bed I shove the valise back beneath it making some order around me. A few more hours. Chin up. They came especially to make you happy. Your power over them. And yet you feared the disgrace. The loss of you beginning to sink in. Why shouldn't you? Not in their wildest dreams. A thought to tear you all apart. Naked lies the hairless Jewish widow. The frigid whirlwind. And you namelessly kissing each cell. The terrible tender lust. But who would have thought that there would be a baby?

Gaddi came into the room.

"Mom wants to know if you'd like some tea."

"Of course I would, old buddy. Come over here."

I squeezed his fat, heavy frame.

"Go show Asi your worms and cocoons. When he was your age he also liked experiments."

I wiped away my tears, put on the shirt and a tie, combed my hair and rejoined them. Ya'el and Dina were in the children's room with the baby. Tsvi was making his bed under Kedmi's supervision. Asa stood alone on the terrace, smoking and staring at the view, gloomily preoccupied. So calmly hitting himself in the little library. The parchment flying through the air. What's wrong with him? Torn apart, devastated by her beauty. Gaddi approached him with his shoe box of white cocoons. Asi nodded absentmindedly and glanced at me. I went to him.

"Well, we didn't get to spend much time together, did we? Such a short visit."

"How did it go?"

"Where?"

"Up there."

"Pretty well. I already told you on the phone. The actual ceremony was very brief."

"As long as it's over with."

"Yes."

"And mother?"

"What about her?"

"She was all right too?"

"In what sense? Yes . . ."

"She kept calm?"

"Yes. Why shouldn't she have?"

"Ya'el told me that some rabbi tried making trouble."

"It wasn't anything much. He was a young fanatic . . . but Rabbi Mashash handled him well . . ."

"And does she really want to be let out? Will they agree . . . ?" An anxious note crept into his dry voice.

"I don't know. Maybe. The doctor said that there wasn't any reason not to . . ."

"But where will she go?" he interrupted.

"I really don't know, Asa. Wherever she wants. She's yours now, not mine."

"Did she drop any hints about her plans?"

"No. I didn't ask her about them, either."

"She didn't say anything about Jerusalem?"

"Jerusalem?"

"Never mind."

He truly hated her.

"You know, I have to give you my power of attorney so that you can officially transfer my share of the house to her."

"Why give it to me? Why not to Tsvi or to Kedmi?"

"Because I want you to have it. Tsvi might do something rash—you know what he's like when it comes to money. And it's none of Kedmi's business. I want you to take care of it. It won't demand much of your time."

He regarded me quietly.

"But how are things with you on the whole, Asa? How is your Vera Zasulich?"

He flushed hotly, taken aback.

"What does Vera Zasulich have to do with it?"

"I just happened to think of her. Your students . . . I still remember the few minutes of your lecture that I heard . . . I'm all admiration for how you teach . . . for the ideas you have . . . really I am. I was very moved by it all. Please don't forget to send me all your publications. This time I promise to respond . . . I'm so sorry I didn't then . . . I can't forgive myself . . ."

"Forget it."

Tsvi re-entered the room, animatedly talking to Dina. Kedmi still sat provocatively in the armchair with his newspaper, his mocking little eyes darting back and forth, ready to strike without notice.

Ya'el served tea. The light had grown dim and the air felt less warm; a soft curtain screened the sun; almost at its prime, the day had suddenly faltered. A weak-willed spring. From beyond the windows, with their view of white houses and wooded slopes, came the muffled sound of traffic. Ya'el set out the teacups, her heavy face aglow, while Dina helped her with unobtrusive grace. I smiled at her, seeking to strike up a conversation, but she continued to avoid me behind a wall of reserve. Gaddi brought a tray of hot pita bread. Asi questioned Kedmi about the view and received an explanation. Tsvi began to crack jokes. I let my eyes linger on my progeny, all gathered together with me here, then glanced out the window at the north end of the bay and at the white cliffs of the Lebanese border clearly visible in the distance beyond it.

Homeland will you ever be a homeland. Out there my concupiscent horizon. My ears register only a faint buzz such tiredness they drink the tea they chew the round warm bread. Weak trickle of light. Half hearing Tsvi tell of his therapy. His graphic much too clever tongue. Did I disappoint them too? No longer my judges. A fact. Their odd dispossessed father. Kedmi steers the talk toward politics. Asi's face lights up. Before Kedmi's cynicism his thoughts retreat then quickly counterattack. A flanking movement. Speculations historical examples from different times different places taking the long view. Such a precise wealth of language that much at least I did give them. Language. A tongue. Tsvi in a puddle of light basking in sunshine gripping his teacup like me between thumb and forefinger joining handsomely in with that shiny inner shallowness of his laughing someone's at the door.

Gaddi answered the doorbell and came back for Tsvi.

"Somebody wants you."

Tsvi sighed without getting to his feet and shut his eyes in despair.

"What can I do? Tell him to come in."

Calderon entered hesitantly, not daring to look at us. I quickly rose to take him under my wing, afraid that Kedmi might make some rude remark. Yet when I introduced him to the family, he already seemed to know everyone, hastening to shake hands with them all and to identify each by name.

"Yes, yes, I know . . ." he murmured. "Pleased to meet you, Mrs. Kaminka. So you got here from Jerusalem . . . and you too, Dr. Kaminka . . . Mr. and Mrs. Kedmi, how do you do . . ." He patted Gaddi's head and handed him a bar of chocolate from his pocket. "I'm honored to meet you all." His eyes avoided Tsvi's. "I see we're all here except Rakefet. Where is she?"

"In bed," smiled Ya'el.

"Well, did you manage to get in some praying?" I asked in a low voice.

"Yes. Thank you. A bit of the *musaf*."

He took out a pack of cigarettes and offered it around, stealing a glance at Tsvi.

"Would you like tea or coffee?"

"No, nothing, thank you. I only came for a few minutes. The weather is changing again. When is your plane taking off?"

Ya'el went over to whisper something to Kedmi, who remained ensconced in his chair, enjoying the scene.

"Who needs to buy anything?" he answered her impatiently. "We have all we need here."

Ya'el pulled his hand, trying to make him get up.

"Can I be of any help, Ya'eli?" I asked. "Why don't you let me cook. You can ask Asi and Dina to recommend me."

Dina too wanted to help. Ya'el, though, kept tugging at Kedmi, who refused to leave his chair.

"Get up!"

"Forget it, Ya'el," said Asi. "We'll eat what there is. We're not hungry anyway."

Calderon jumped up. "Perhaps I could take you all out to a res-taurant that I know of near here. Let it be my treat. A lovely place to eat, in a garden in the woods."

Ya'el declined:

"Thank you all the same, but we'll eat here."

Kedmi, however, came out in favor. "Maybe we really should eat out. Why not?"

"Let it be on me," insisted Calderon eagerly. "It's my pleasure to invite you all. A farewell dinner for Mr. Kaminka . . . provided, of course, that I'm allowed to foot the bill . . ."

"But it's not a question of that," smiled Ya'el. "I've already pre-pared a meal here . . . you're invited to it too . . ."

And again she tried pulling Kedmi out of his armchair. Carried away by his own idea, though, Calderon now tried persuading Tsvi, who sat grinning in his corner at Ya'el.

"It's fine with me," he said. "Whatever you prefer. His restaurant will be a good one, that much I can promise you. Money is no object with him . . ."

"It's a very distinguished place, with good, digestible food . . . and served in a garden . . . real European cuisine . . . our bank takes its customers there . . ."

Yet Ya'el wouldn't hear of it.

"No, we'll eat here. Everything is ready."

Which only stiffened Calderon's resolve. He was getting hysterical now.

"It's in a garden, we'll have a quiet corner to ourselves . . . no-body will bother us . . . why put yourself to all that trouble, Mrs. Kedmi . . . it's father's last day, let it be my treat . . . I'd be only too happy to have you as my guests . . ."

His agitation was incomprehensible and his reference to "father" made us all feel uneasy. Only Kedmi was entertained by it. Yet he too looked mystified, his mouth agape as though waiting for the next burst of laughter.

I rose and put an arm around Ya'el, my shadow surging up the bars of the balcony on the terrace.

"Why don't we go out then? It's really not a bad idea."

Dina sat in her corner dressed in black, cold, upright and with-drawn, her incredible face a bright pennant aloft.

All your children. The knife turned at dawn. Would they have cared? The Case of the Early-Morning Scream. And how slow Tsvi was.

Kedmi rose at last. "A jolly good idea! Why don't we? What's the point of fussing with pots in the kitchen all day long? The food here won't go to waste, Gaddi and I will polish it off tomorrow. And you have only a few hours left with your father."

Ya'el was confused. She wasn't used to putting up a fight. She turned again to Calderon:

"Really, it's very kind of you, but we have whatever we need here. You'll join us."

He literally began to shake.

"I would love to join you, but don't you see I can't because of . . . the bread. Not that it's any of my business . . . it's your right . . . this is a free country . . . but I can't sit at such a table. Perhaps Mrs. Kaminka too . . . not that I'm naïve enough to think that anything will happen . . . here, I'm touching it"—he lifted a pita from the tray with his fingertips and gingerly put it down again —"you all see that I wasn't struck down by lightning . . . but still . . ."

"Ya'el," I said, "why don't we go out. It will be nice."

"And the children?"

"We'll take them with us . . . of course we will!" exclaimed Calderon. "The place is perfect for them . . . special arrangements can be made . . . I'll hold them on my lap . . ."

Kedmi let out a great roar.

"I suppose I'm just being a nuisance."

He stood there mortified, looking at Tsvi, who said nothing.

Kedmi grabbed hold of him good-naturedly and backed him into a corner. "*Now* that occurs to you? No, no, it's quite all right . . . I didn't mean any harm . . . what bank do you work for . . . tell me, how old did you say that you were?"

Oh they'll make a happy man out of you yet today.

It really was a pleasant place, high on the Carmel, in a small pine woods reached by a narrow path whose small bits of gray gravel crunched beneath our soles, a well-tended, countryish boardinghouse inhabited by elderly people with a bit of sea like a small kerchief in the distance between two houses. Buxom old women in flowery dresses sat about the garden, through which, looking peaceful and bursting with health, two little old men in dark suits strolled while regarding us fondly. The wood-paneled restaurant was a bit worse for the wear but very clean. Its Arab waiters, dressed in black with white bow ties, hurried to greet us.

"Where should we sit, inside or out? . . . Will it be too cold here for Rakefet? . . . It's not that bad, let's sit outside . . ."

Calderon ran inside to get the manager, who immediately ordered a large table set out. "We'll start you in the garden," he said. "If it gets too chilly, you can always come inside."

And indeed the skies had begun to cloud over, turning from blue to gray, while the air was growing colder. From inside the restaurant emerged two large, thin, white-goateed, very hairy dogs, evidently twins: they circled us slowly, their tails like weak pendulums, their noses down to get a whiff of us, dropping exhaustedly on the gravel path as soon as we reached out to pet them. Chairs were brought quickly and someone spread a white tablecloth. Calderon ran back and forth. Asa bent over one of the dogs, lightly scratching its head.

"Did 'Ratio ever turn up again?" I asked Tsvi.

"Why must you insist on calling him 'Ratio? His name is *Ho*ratio, father. No. I was there yesterday. He's been gone for four days now. But he'll turn up in the end. He always does."

"You really are a bastard," said Asa straight to Kedmi's face. "Why did you have to lure him on like that? What did you get out of it?"

Kedmi was hurt. "That dog could drive a person nuts. Don't you people have enough problems without him?"

"But what did you have against him?"

"Me?" inquired Kedmi innocently. "What did I do? Is it my fault that he ran after my car? It's hard enough to keep track of who runs in front of it."

"It's lovely, here, isn't it?" Calderon kept asking. "You must admit that it's lovely here, Mrs. Kedmi."

"Yes, it is," conceded Ya'el with a sad smile.

"Father at the head of the table!" called Calderon, seating me first. "Father goes at the head! You decide where to seat the rest of them . . ."

"Come, girls, sit next to me," I said to Dina and Ya'el. "And you, Gaddi, you sit near me too."

Tsvi took a turn about the garden, walking in the shady light of the trees and nodding haughtily to the old people, who had fallen silent and were watching us with interest. Calderon hurried over to confide something to him; he sought to take his arm, choked by his own love, but Tsvi brushed him off without looking. Two waiters set the table with silverware and plates, smiling at the baby, who had been placed on a second table next to us beside a large wicker basket of matzo, while staring at Dina out of the corners of their eyes, overwhelmed by her beauty, honored to be able to serve her. Asa went off to have a look at something, then returned and sat down at the far end of the table. Kedmi took a seat too. Tsvi was the last to join us. He picked up his knife and tested it carefully on his fingertips, looking at me hard as he stood by his chair.

"When I think, father, that in a few hours from now you'll be gone . . . we really will miss you this time . . ."

I smiled, my cheeks red, a queasy feeling in my stomach, and turned to Dina, who was sitting next to me thin and virginal, her perfumed skin contrasting whitely with her mysterious black dress. She was involved with the baby, still oddly remote.

"What's wrong?" I asked her, glancing at Asa sitting by himself at the table's other end. Suddenly it struck me that they weren't talking to each other. They hadn't exchanged a word since they had come.

"Is anything the matter?" I asked again.

"No, nothing." She smiled.

"This really is a lovely spot. Thank you, Calderon. It was a good choice."

"I told you. Didn't I tell you? You could be in Europe here."

Flushed and bright-eyed Dina leaned toward me in a low voice:

"Will you have some time for me later?"

"Of course. What a question! But what for?"

"I have something to read to you."

"What? Ah . . . something of yours?"

She nodded.

"Of course. I'd be glad to. Whenever you'd like . . ."

"It's long, though."

"Don't worry about it. We'll find the time."

I squeezed her arm.

"I'm so glad you came today. This whole visit has been like a quick dream. The evening I spent with you in Jerusalem already seems so far away . . . is everything all right with you two?"

"Yes."

She wouldn't unbend. And meanwhile the table was filling up with baskets of matzo, bottles of wine, condiments, platters of raw vegetables. The waiters poured the wine and silently handed us our menus.

Kedmi scanned his quickly. "The prices aren't half bad," he murmured.

"What did I tell you?" crowed Calderon.

The headwaiter appeared, a heavyset, immaculate, middle-aged Arab, and positioned himself next to me.

"Good afternoon, please. Would you care to order? I'll bet it's grandfather's birthday . . ."

"You lose," Kedmi shot back. "It's actually a divorce party."

The headwaiter laughed incredulously.

"Grandpa is leaving Israel. Aren't you glad? There'll be one less of us here."

The man was stark raving mad. You never knew what he would come up with next. Calderon was alarmed. Ya'el laid a hand on Kedmi's arm. This time he had really gone too far. But the headwaiter smiled imperturbably.

"The gentleman can't be serious. Why leave Israel? What's so bad about it?"

"Maybe it's not so bad for you," Kedmi answered with unaccountable, poker-faced vitriol. "After all, you people think you own it."

This time the headwaiter frowned. The smile froze on his lips.

"Cut it out, Kedmi! That's enough!" disgustedly hissed Asi and Tsvi.

The man was too much.

"Well, then, what will you have?"

We conferred. Calderon insisted that we all order appetizers. Even Gaddi. Even the baby.

"I'm asking you for my sake . . ." he pleaded. "Please do it for me . . ."

"Calm down there, Refa'el," snapped Tsvi angrily.

Calderon shut up.

The meal was tasty, though: consommé, chopped liver, tender chicken breasts, crisp-roasted meat, vegetables done to perfection, big white potatoes. Asi and Tsvi chatted at their end of the table and

Calderon sat in the middle talking with Kedmi, who was eating voraciously while pumping him about the bank. The wine was dry and subtle, lit now and again by tumbling drifts of light. Rakefet rocked back and forth in her high chair, a big piece of matzo in one hand, singing to herself as she ate it. The dogs minced down the gravel paths, along which some elderly boarders in their holiday best slowly led a small lady leaning on a walker while conversing in spirited tones. More tables were set for the oldsters and the waiters ran back and forth among them with little glasses of schnapps. They murmured brief instructions to each other in Arabic and served us pleasantly and politely. Ya'el sat tranquilly next to me, eating hungrily. Gaddi kept looking about him, hardly aware of what went into his mouth. A chill wind blew, stirring the branches. Ya'el talked about Rakefet to Dina, who kept wanting to know more and suddenly pulled out a small notebook and quickly scribbled something in it.

I laid a hand on her and winked. "So the little pad is still with you."

She returned a friendly smile. "Always."

The wine was going to my head. Kedmi had made peace with the headwaiter and was joking with him now, trying out his Arabic on him. I would have loved to know what Tsvi and Asi were talking about at the other end of the table. Kedmi praised the food, piling more and more of it on his plate until he was red in the face. Calderon's worried eyes ran back and forth; from time to time he made some motion to a waiter while Kedmi jotted down on a napkin the names of stocks he was giving him and Asi and Tsvi lit up cigarettes.

"No smoking in the middle of the meal, boys," I called out to them.

"Who do you think we learned from?" laughed Tsvi.

"But what are you two talking about? Speak louder, I want to hear too."

"About history," laughed Tsvi again in his winning way.

"History?" asked Kedmi. "What's that?"

"Everything," answered. Tsvi. "At least according to Asi."

"What do you mean, everything?"

"Even this meal that we're eating."

"Even this meal? I like that." Kedmi lifted a fork with a slice of meat on it and slid it into his mouth. "Yummm . . . what a delicious piece of history . . ."

The vulgar, twisted mind of the man.

"But if it's everything," asked Calderon wonderingly, "what can you learn from it?"

"Nothing," Kedmi shot back. "You just keep eating it till you die . . ."

"No, really," Calderon persisted, turning to Asa. "Is it possible, Dr. Kaminka, to understand what's going to happen . . . perhaps even to draw conclusions about the future and prevent mistakes . . . ?"

Asa nodded seriously.

"Really?"

"Not to prevent them, but to inoculate against them."

"To inoculate???"

"To isolate the meaning, the secret code of the past, and distill from it a serum that can be injected into human beings to prepare them for the coming catastrophe: that's the study of history in a nutshell."

"What catastrophe is that, Asi?" I asked, startled.

"The coming one . . . the one that can't be helped . . ."

Dina broke off her conversation with Ya'el and turned to look at Asa as though seeing him for the first time. An uncomfortable silence set in. It was clear that they weren't on speaking terms.

Rakefet began to whimper. Calderon rose to pick her up but I reached her first and lifted her in my arms.

"Would someone pass me the meat, please," said Kedmi, beet-colored by now. "And you, Asa, none of your horror tales, please . . ."

All at once exhaustion. You feel like you're going under. The wine percolates through your limbs. What time is it? I grip Dina's thin hand and twist it lightly to look at her gold watch with its Hebrew letters in place of numerals. A Jewish wristwatch. *Alef zayin.* One thirty-five. Before you behind you the darkness cleft by a strip of purple light. Snow in the streets stubborn icy snow packed hard against the quick plows. A divorce party. How could he. Taking liberties. Mother why. Her very words. Disappointed her how? I was afraid I always feared her even those first years when we made love.

And suddenly two of her. The spirit is weak. Perhaps. I promised too much is that it? All at once the full weight of the thought O wondrous oppressiveness. So many things at one time. The cleft dawn. Soft sounds of German among the trees. She sits on the stoop she walks she reads she may get out any day. The dog in some city street or already run over and dead. A limp erection. The parchment in the air. Connie in the air suspended nude. A Jewish dish. You give me something realer than mere values. Behind me the headwaiter filling my glass with more wine. I smile back at him. He gives me a friendly look. For a moment the urge to open my shirt and show my scar to him too. Tsvi whispers something to Asa Kedmi bends crimsonly forward to listen. Gaddi is still putting it away how can they let him someone has to stop him. Ya'el and Dina confide in low voices. Only Calderon turns his washed-out face toward me wanting to say something wanting to hear.

I recalled our midnight meeting.

"Say, whatever happened to that mouse?"

"I finally caught it. In a trap I brought. We heard it snap shut in the morning."

"What did you do with it?"

"I gave it to the city."

"To the city?"

"I left it by the entrance to city hall. I thought I'd let them decide what to do next."

"Ha ha. Too much!"

"I'm afraid, though, that it isn't the last mouse running around there. I heard another."

"What isn't the last mouse?" asked Gaddi.

"Mr. Calderon discovered a mouse in the kitchen and caught it."

"In whose kitchen?"

"In my and grandma's old apartment in Tel Aviv."

"But it isn't yours anymore. You signed away your share."

"Yes, I heard about that," chimed in Calderon. "A surprising, I might even say dramatic, decision . . ."

"Dramatic." I smiled at him. "That's the word."

"To sign away five million pounds just like that . . ."

"Five million? You're exaggerating, Calderon."

"No, it really is worth that."

"That old place? It's barely worth four."

"I'm sorry but you're wrong," said Calderon heatedly. "It may be old but it's in an excellent location. Right in downtown Tel Aviv, in the most promising block of real estate in the whole city . . ."

"It still can't be worth that much."

"But it is. I happen to know for a fact that Tsvi has a buyer who's offered him that, and that isn't his last word either."

"What?" I was aghast. "Tsvi wants to sell?"

An easy killing. I glanced at him, leaning comfortably back in his chair and talking to Asa with that remote shadow of a smile. Soft-throated. Winsome. Calderon threw a longing look at him. He would try to pull a fast one on us yet. But I was leaving everything behind. Out there the land of frozen lakes was lit by a fiery dawn now, the red-bulbed trucks were thundering down the turnpikes like flying Christmas trees. Suddenly the sky darkened. A small black cloud had covered the sun. We all looked up at it. The old boarders let out a cry of joy in German, reminded no doubt of European climes. And I was to be left with nothing, my lifeblood running low. Except for my now available, my divorced name. To have to begin again from scratch. Rakefet gave a start on my lap and screamed in her sleep. I tried to gentle her while Ya'el hurried to take her from me, but her screaming only grew louder as she pushed away the bottle that Ya'el gave her. Now Dina rose to take her from Ya'el and walk with her in the garden, rocking her in her arms while the old boarders looked on excitedly and cooed advice. But Rakefet continued her deep, heart-rending cries. Ya'el took her back again and undid her diaper but the crying didn't stop.

"Ya'el," grumbled Kedmi, "do something."

Rakefet shrieked still louder, as though possessed. Gaddi jumped up and down with excitement.

"It's just like it was then, just like it was then, only then I was alone with her! You see that you can't make her stop! Only then I was alone with her!"

Rakefet was passed from hand to hand, keys were jangled in front of her, even the headwaiter tried his luck with some old toy dog made of wool that he brought from the kitchen. Rakefet wouldn't even look at it. She shrieked till she was blue in the face. Ya'el was alarmed.

"We have to go home," she said to Kedmi.

"Just a minute. What about dessert . . . ?"

Calderon leaped up to order the desserts but Rakefet's screams were deafening. In a panic Ya'el began to shout at Kedmi. We all got to our feet.

We tried to calm her. "It's nothing . . . she'll get over it . . ."

But Ya'el was adamant. "I want us to go home this minute."

I went over to join Asa and Tsvi, who were still chatting off to the side.

"You two should get together more often. What have you been talking about all this time?"

"The assassination of the Tsar," laughed Tsvi. "Asi was telling me how he was killed. Which one did you say it was?"

"Alexander II."

I laughed too.

"All right," said Kedmi, giving in. "Let's go."

"What a pity," said Calderon. "Perhaps I should take her for a drive in my car. That's how I put my own girls to sleep when they were babies."

"Don't trouble yourself. We'll all go home."

Dina and Ya'el busied themselves with Rakefet and gathered up her things.

"We'll drive to the hospital, father," said Tsvi. "You go rest. You're pale, and you still have a long day ahead of you. Maybe we'll look for the dog while we're up there. Soon mother will get out, and if Horatio goes back there he won't find her. He doesn't deserve to have to stay there by himself. Are you coming with us, Asi?"

Asi wavered.

"Go to her, Asi," I encouraged him. "She'll be very happy to see you."

"All right."

"And Dina?"

"She'll stay here. There's no point in taking her with us."

"When will you be back?"

"By six. We have plenty of time. Your flight doesn't leave until midnight."

Calderon made his way into the circle. "So, what have you decided?"

"We're going to the hospital. Can you drive us?"

"Certainly."

"Your wife in Tel Aviv must be going out of her mind."

He shut his eyes in anguish, the flicker of a smile on his thin lips. "So supposing I've changed families for the holiday?"

The waiter came over with the bill and said something to him in a whisper.

"How about splitting it," I suggested.

"Absolutely not. It's my pleasure."

Tsvi smiled. "It's his pleasure."

I looked him in the eyes. "Are you really trying to sell the apartment?"

He blanched and turned to Calderon.

"You have to blab about everything, don't you, you old tattletale!"

"I beg your pardon . . . forgive me . . . I was sure your father already knew . . ."

"You want to own our minds too, it's not enough that . . ."

"Don't . . . I . . . just a minute . . . Tsvi . . ."

"That's enough out of you, you traitor!"

Gaddi tugged at my clothes. "We're waiting for you." Kedmi honked his horn.

Dina and Ya'el were already in the car with the baby, who was still screaming. Dina hadn't said goodbye to Asi. The motor started up. I got in.

"What is it, Rakefet? What?"

The car backed out through the gate. For a second I caught sight of the three of them standing there, Asi holding on to Calderon, who was struggling to go down on his knees before Tsvi.

"He fell down," said Gaddi.

What time was it?

Suddenly, just like that, Rakefet grew still. All at once.

"That's just how it was then!" exclaimed Gaddi, unable to get over it.

Kedmi stopped the car. *"Now* she quiets down. She just didn't want me to have my dessert. It was damned nice there. Maybe we should go back."

"For God's sake, Kedmi," shouted Ya'el, "drive home!"

"You call him Kedmi too?" asked Dina in surprise.

"No one likes to call me by my first name . . . one Israel is enough. That old fellow is damned nice too . . . why does he torture him like that?"

"Let's not talk about it now, Kedmi."

But that failed to put a damper on his mood. He whistled merrily, the car's shadow darting from curb to curb as he drove. The streets were deserted. A quiet holiday afternoon. The weather was changing again and looked like rain. Rakefet sat without a peep, staring straight ahead with dry, wide-open eyes.

"What's wrong with her?" asked Ya'el anxiously.

"Not a thing."

"What time is it?" I asked.

"Almost time for you to fly off into the wild blue yonder, Yehuda. You're a lucky man. The rest of us will be left behind here with Begin . . ."

"But didn't you vote for him?" asked Ya'el, puzzled.

"What does that have to do with it?" He burst out laughing, his hands dancing on the steering wheel.

The apartment was growing dim. Rakefet slept with her head thrown back. Ya'el seemed less worried now. "What did she want?" she asked. "What was the matter with her?" She put her to bed. Gaddi entered the children's room too and lay down on his back, one hand on his chest. All at once the place seemed so untidy. The dirty teacups. Tsvi's open suitcase. Kedmi went to the refrigerator and took out some chocolate to eat. "Have some," he said. "Sweets to the sweet."

"Dina and I will be in my bedroom for a while," I said to Ya'el. "She wants to show me something."

Ya'el and Kedmi went off to their room. Dina sat on my bed, kicked off her shoes, and tucked her legs, golden in their silk stockings, beneath her. She sat upright, her slender shadow a blur on the wall. My head was still spinning from the wine. She took a thick packet of closely written pages from her bag and looked at me glowingly.

"You're the first," she said softly.

"How come? Hasn't Asi read it?"

"No."

"But why not?"

She shrugged. A strange girl. Like a black candle burning with a bluish flame.

"Has something happened between the two of you?"

"What makes you ask?"

"I can feel it. It's like there's a tug-of-war between you. You
haven't said a word to each other all day."

"That's true. We haven't been talking much."

"Why not?"

"It's just one of those things."

"Is there anything I can do?"

"Not in this case."

"But how long have you . . . not been talking?"

"Since Wednesday."

"Of last week?"

"Yes."

"But that's the day he went with me to the hospital!"

"Yes."

"He must have come back in a bad mood. He had a hard time
there. It wasn't his fault."

"Yes. I know. He told me that he hit himself in front of you."

"He told you that?"

"Yes. I know all about it. But it isn't that."

"Then what is it?"

"I can't tell you now." She was suddenly impatient. "Are you
ready to listen?"

"To listen?"

"Yes. To what I want to read."

"Ah, you want to read it out loud. . . . All right, that's not a bad
idea. If that's what you'd prefer, fine. I'll sit here. What's the story
called?"

"It has no name yet. But that's not important . . . you just have
to promise to tell me what you really think . . ."

She took a pair of glasses from her bag and put them on, accenting
her beauty even more. Solemnly she began to read in a slow, barely
audible, slightly husky voice, her eyes glued to the text, a soft crease
appearing in her pale forehead. Her prose was complex, its sentence
long and involved. An eclectic style. Sometimes nouns without verbs.
A Jerusalem evening seen through the eyes of a woman, a not so
young secretary on her way home from the office, walking down
street, going into a bank, thinking of having a baby. Long descriptiv
passages that occasionally repeated themselves but had a definit
sensuous tone of their own and a steady cadence, three or four beat
to the phrase. Outside the window the sky was turning grayer. A

cozy silence reigned in the apartment. Dina kept her thin, almost matchlike legs tucked beneath her and didn't take her eyes off her manuscript, from which she read slowly and quietly, enunciating each word clearly, never once looking up, as though afraid to catch my glance.

"Excuse me, Dina. Perhaps we should turn on the light."

She shook her head and went on reading.

I struggled to concentrate. The thought of the Tel Aviv apartment bothered me. If Asi let him sell it she would be left without a home, and then I'd be sent for again. There wasn't a sound in the house. Suddenly I heard a hoarse gasp through the wall next to me . . . was it Kedmi's? I froze. They were making love, I could hear his voice whispering, "What are you doing to me?" No doubt of it . . . and the passionate one, so it seemed, was Ya'el . . . well, at least they had that much between them. I rose uncomfortably from my chair and went to stand by the window. Dina glanced up at me, annoyed at the interruption, her voice quivering in a light rebuke.

"Are you still listening? Should I go on?"

"Of course."

And she did. The secretary, a nameless woman of about thirty who had once been briefly married, was planning to kidnap a baby and took a bus to some new section of Jerusalem to look for one. A description of it that sounded very much like the neighborhood in which Dina and Asi lived. She attached herself to a woman with a baby carriage and followed her into a supermarket. The descriptions grew more and more detailed.

On the other side of the wall the noises grew louder. Kedmi was snorting now. How like him to come like an animal. Had we not always felt, though, that Ya'el, for all her docility, had in her a tough, dark kernel of passion? She never even got through high school. The snorting sounds reached a comical crescendo. A lunatic scene. Afraid that Dina would hear, I crossed quietly back across the room and leaned my body against the wall to cushion the sound.

But she was too absorbed in her own bizarre story to hear anything. The flow of words didn't stop. Descriptions of counters, of foods, of shopping lists. There was something undeveloped, held in, still juvenile about the emotions she was expressing but she definitely did have talent. The power to titillate with language, to let a plot slowly unfold. Only what was this fantasy of hers really about? What was she getting at?

Beyond the wall I heard Ya'el's soft sobs and Kedmi's devilish laugh. Dina took off her glasses and glanced up with a troubled look. I felt myself go red. She studied me severely, puzzled to find me standing with my back to the wall.

"Is something wrong?"

"No."

"You're still with me?"

"Of course I am."

But my thoughts strayed. Don't pin your hopes on me I said to her I'm not a stand-in for the man you don't believe in and never will. And I can't love the second woman any more than I do the first. A waste of time. And out of guilt you let her have it. Out of fear that you'd make a dreadful mess. Disgrace yourself. The tears formed a lump in my throat.

The woman quickly paid for two liters of milk and went to the checkroom, by the counter of which stood the baby carriage. With one motion she lifted the infant and hurried outside to the bus stop, where she boarded the first bus. A description of the sky. She changed buses, got off again, and climbed the stairs to her apartment. A thorough description of a stairwell, on which stood a bucket and a mop. She laid the kidnapped baby in her bed. More straightforward narrative, the pace quickened. But what a weird plot!

I sat down again in the chair. A small tuft of absorbent cotton lay on the floor and I picked it up absentmindedly and rolled it between my fingers. Strange as it was, Dina's story moved me. She continued to read, her blue eyes deepening a shade, her soft breast rising and falling with her breath, her cheeks rosy with color, her voice growing stronger and more intense. A description of the night passed by the woman in her apartment with the crying, kidnapped child. Suddenly a knock on the door. An unexpected visit from her father, an old pest in a fedora, a slightly bohemian type. With a start I realized that he was partly modeled on me. The woman hid the baby in the bathtub. She turned the radio on full blast and finally managed to get rid of the old man.

My fingers were coated with slime. I stared at them. The absorbent cotton oozed a living, sticky jelly that might have been a squashed butterfly or a worm. I shuddered. One of Gaddi's cocoons must have fallen on the floor and was now crushed between my fingers. I hurried to throw it in the wastebasket and to wipe my hand on a piece of paper.

But Dina hadn't even noticed. She went on with her obstinate narration, continuing the story. Days went by and the woman remained imprisoned in her little apartment, afraid to leave it for anything. Only at night did she venture out to get food. Time passed, no one came to look for the child, and little by little the suspicion dawned on her that it might be slightly retarded. An odd, messy denouement. Possibly symbolic. An ending that didn't really end.

It was getting darker out. The day had turned. The pages rustled in Dina's hands as she collected them, still avoiding my glance. She took off her glasses and stretched herself, a feverish glow in her cheeks.

"You were bored."

"I most certainly was not!"

"Then talk!"

Confusedly I began to relate my impressions, analyzing the story like a student before a professor, telling her what I thought of it. She listened tensely, hanging silently on every word, her fingers playing with the edge of the blanket. I tried to be honest while also being careful what I said. "I'm overwhelmed. . . . Awfully moved. . . . You have great power. . . . I need to read it again. . . . The end isn't clear. . . . Still unresolved. . . . It needs more thought. . . . A slightly childish fantasy, but complex. . . . It's true that there are repetitive passages, but there are also unforgettable descriptions, such as the one of the bucket and mop at the bottom of the stairs. . . . And at the same time there's something frightening about it. . . . That moment when the father arrives and she puts the child in the bathtub. . . . I was scared of her then, of what she might do . . ."

She looked up, intrigued. "You were scared of her? How odd!"

"Yes. For a moment I thought that she was going to kill the child."

"Kill it?" She seemed amused. "And you never once felt sorry for her during the entire story?"

"Sorry? No . . . something else . . . I'll have to think about it . . ."

All at once she stood up radiantly, very satisfied, even blissful. She hugged and kissed me, pressing herself against me.

"And I was so afraid of what you would say . . ."

"You were afraid of me? But why, silly girl?"

"We'll miss you a lot . . . Tsvi was right . . ."

I stood there distractedly stroking her cropped hair. Yes, parting was going to be harder than I'd thought. You've made a happy man of me today.

"The only one who doesn't care is Asi . . ."

"Oh, no, he does too. He's just too proud to admit it."

All of a sudden she let go of me, ran to her bag, pulled out her pad, leafed through it, and wrote something down. So infantile. I looked down at my stained fingers, on which was smeared something shaped like a wing. I went to the bathroom to wash my hands. A few more hours. And I had let Naomi have my share. Soon she would be free, might even remarry. Where does the thought keep coming from? On again off again. I washed my hands thoroughly, looking at myself in the dark mirror: the tired face, the dry, gray hair, the bloodshot eyes. I took my toothbrush and cleaned my teeth. Phantasmagoric. A few more hours. Perhaps I should shave, the flight would be a long one. And there dawn had broken by now. Connie was counting the hours. Not a young woman anymore and soon to have a child. And me with my bridges burned. Disinherited. Homeland why weren't you a homeland. I left the bathroom and passed down the hall, peeking in on Gaddi, who lay open-eyed in bed with a suffering look on his face. I kissed him without a word and returned to my room. Dina was still on the bed in stockinged feet, her glasses back on, rereading her story, pleased as punch with it. An ambitious little thing. One of your do-nothing won't-work don't-want-children scribblers. He'd have his hands full with her. Fantasies. I went to the living room. The house like the still echo of a no longer thrumming bowstring. Outside it really was gray now. Maybe it would rain. I went to the bathroom to pee. My face shook and was gone in the dim toilet. What really do you want? Five million just like that as though it weren't mine. Back in the hallway I bumped into Kedmi in his undershirt, drowsy, sour-smelling, sleep-disheveled, smiling to himself as he stepped into the bathroom.

I returned to my room. Dina was still too absorbed in herself to notice me. I bent over my valise and took out my passport and ticket, putting them in my pocket. I took out my last dollars too and stuck them in my wallet. I put on my jacket and hat.

"I'll be right back. Tell Asa and Tsvi that I won't be long."

Some boys and girls in the blue shirts of a youth movement were
drifting slowly down the street below. By the newsstand on the corner was a taxi stand. I jumped into the first cab, whose driver was a
sullen-looking, middle-aged man. What time was it?

"Take me to Acre. I'll direct you from there."

He started the motor.

"Wait a minute." I tapped him on the shoulder. "Will you take
dollars?"

"Don't you have any pounds?"

"I'm afraid not. But we'll check the exchange rate in the paper.
You won't lose a cent."

The taxi's shadow bolted ahead of it. It headed downhill toward
the bay and then took the main road running east. The traffic picked
up. The city itself had been quiet but the roads were full of vacation-
ers. At the old British checkpost outside of town we turned north to
follow the curve of the bay, passing through its industrial zone and
suburbs, the traffic lights slowing us up. The driver kept silent, and I
was thankful that he didn't turn on the radio. To my left, in the west,
I caught sight of the sea, the last sunlight glinting off the foam of its
strong, steady surf. Clearly visible behind us was Mount Carmel,
massive and lush, a large cloud sinking over it. Pinkish light. The
same now here as in Minneapolis. The cab picked up speed. Northward toward the minarets of Acre. We approached them and crossed
some railroad tracks. The traffic kept getting thicker.

"Don't drive through the town. Bypass it to the right."

"But where do you want to go?"

"I'll guide you. Keep heading north past the town."

"But where to?"

I told him the name of the hospital.

"So how come you didn't want to tell me? What's to hide?"

"I didn't realize that you were familiar with the place."

"Of course I am. You're not the first fare I've taken there, and you
won't be the last."

The taxi swung around Acre to the right. Soft pastel colors, a row
of eucalyptus trees, stands selling wicker furniture. We passed the old
railroad station with its freight cars gleaming in the waxing golden
light of sunset. Dusty streets, Arabs selling pitas, cars backed up in a
row. A crossroads. To the right the road ran eastward to the Galilee
but we drove straight ahead. We crossed the railroad tracks where

they swerved toward the sea, the western horizon all awash, the sun slipping free of the clouds, dropping as they rose. The taxi slowed. The traffic ground to a halt, cars honked. Something must have happened ahead. I leaned impatiently forward and glimpsed a pack of dogs blocking traffic while cars beeped their horns and tried to shoulder them off the road. At last we came to the yellow sign of the hospital and stopped to turn left, waiting for the line of southbound cars to pass. More dogs ran by wagging their tails, careening off the car and into the fields. Finally we turned into the narrow approach road that led to the hospital gate. Back again. For the fourth time this trip. Yesterday you were certain that you would never return. The sea. The sun at eye level near the horizon. The mountains at your back. In a few hours I would be taking off. The cottages. The trees like paper cutouts, a slender form standing by them in the brackish, yellow, crinkly evening light.

"Stop!" I cried.

The taxi slowed down.

"Stop right here, driver!" I said again, grabbing him by the shoulder. He turned to me angrily.

"What's wrong?"

By the distant gate I had made out Calderon's white car and several figures standing by it. Tsvi, I recalled, made a point of never entering the hospital.

"Stop right here."

"What's the matter?"

"Wait for me here. I'll be back in fifteen minutes."

"I can bring you right to the cottages. They always let me drive into this crazy house."

"You needn't bother. Stop here and wait. I'll be back in fifteen minutes, half an hour at the most. Can you wait?"

"Nope."

"Why not?"

"Because I once waited here for half the day for someone who was supposed to be coming right out. For all I know he's still in there."

"No, listen here, I'm not a patient . . . I just have to deliver some document. Here, let me pay you for the return trip."

"Keep it, mister. Pay me for coming here and for the wait. Let's call it an hour."

"That will be fine. Would you happen to know what time it is?"

The sunrays glance off the green dollar bills he holds them up to the light pretending to know what to look for. I get out and stride into the fields leaving the road behind me cutting through rows of young sprouts in the moist earth bearing traces of sand from the sea heading for the hole in the fence that the patients told me about. The yellowish light gives the sprouts a blue tint I'm walking through a sprouting sea on my right to the north the houses of a village. A tractor pulls a cart piled high with long irrigation pipes and drops them off at intervals in a field. Behind me my huge shadow plows the ground. Homeland why can't you be a homeland. No fantasy then she wanted to kill me. Had she just gone mad I would have stayed to nurse her but she used her madness to settle old scores. I disappointed her? Wait till she sees what I do now. And there it's morning Connie grinding coffee in her gadget-filled kitchen. A pregnant woman by herself she wonders how. I'll take back what's mine. I reach the old concrete wall festooned with dead vines looping up from its base an imposing barricade of barbed wire but where is the hole in it? All at once the wall stops but the gap is sealed with barbed wire too. Have I been misled? I press on. The wall resumes again it's lower now the concrete yielding to ancient stones perhaps the ruins of a Roman aqueduct of the kind often found in these parts. I clamber up its broad stairlike headers there's the hospital below me the lawns the paths even the little library. The parchment flying through the air. I turn to look at the black taxicab parked now in front of the railroad tracks next to Calderon's car.

Hurry.

Not really dusk yet it's the clash of clouds and sun that's ground the light to smithereens. Already you're on the hospital grounds you know your way from here. Your fourth time in ten days. Once more into the breach. Collect yourself. The right to change your mind. The clump of trees. The rubber hose snakes upon the ground someone is standing there and slowly hoeing a small dead bush it's that mute giant hard at work. I pass close by him but he doesn't see me. Be quick. Ask her for the waiver and destroy it have the lawyer cancel it in Tel Aviv. I jam my hat down on my head. The library door is open the puddles of mud have dried to hard earth. No one here. Silence. Soft light of fear. Born-again balminess of the spring evening. Here's her cottage. Three years ago when I first came to visit it was pouring cats and dogs she sat layered in clothes by the kerosene stove listen-

ing to me tell her about the snow in America. It was then that I
promised to write her.

Stealthily I enter the cottage ready for anything. The beds in rows
some made some not a small overly tailored lady of about forty
sitting on a chair by a window next to a very big suitcase reading a
woman's magazine. She glances up at me her face twitches quickly. I
take off my hat and nod.

"Excuse me. Perhaps you could tell me which bed is Naomi
Kaminka's."

"I'm sorry but I just got here myself. I don't know anyone."

But I've already found it by the broad straw hat upon it. I hurry to
her locker here are her dresses her red robe the shawl that Ya'el
brought her for me. I open the drawer and go through it rattling the
dog's chain. Bottles of perfume salves bags full of medicines here are
some papers a packet of letters from me the parchment divorce a
peaceful white dove the waiver on the house a copy of the power of
attorney for Asa. I fold the last two and stick them in my pocket I
turn to leave passing by the small lady again she hasn't stopped
looking at me.

"Excuse me . . ."

"Yes?"

"How were you allowed in here?"

I smile. "What do you mean, how was I allowed? That's my wife's
bed over there . . ."

"But didn't you need special permission?"

"Not at all."

"Men are allowed in here?"

"Of course."

"Because my husband said he wasn't. Perhaps they misinformed
him, or else he misunderstood . . ."

"He must have misunderstood."

"Because suddenly he left me . . ."

She rises and comes over to me perfumed rather scared suddenly
she whispers:

"Do you happen to know by any chance if this is a religious institution?"

"A religious institution? What gave you that idea?"

"We came here so quicky. I had a sort of breakdown at the seder,
and the doctor from the health plan sent us here. But I think . . .

I'm afraid . . . that they sent us to a religious institution. My husband is an army officer and knows nothing about these things . . ."

"But what makes you think that it's religious?"

"It looks like it is. The walls . . . these beds . . ."

"Well, it isn't. Some of the patients may be observant, but . . ."

"And the management? How about the management?"

"No. There's no reason to think . . . it's a government hospital, after all, it's run by the department of health . . . it's not a private institution at all . . ."

She smiles sadly reassured.

"Excuse me," I say. "Do you happen to know what time it is?"

"Half past five."

I nod goodbye to her I tip and wave my hat she sits down again in her chair reaching out to touch her suitcase hesitantly sticking her thumb in her mouth. Dusk now. I head back toward the front gate the giant still standing there without moving limply holding a pitchfork waiting for something. He's recognized me. I retrace my steps cutting back through the ward with its rows of beds smiling pleasantly to the tailored lady who watches me bare legs pertly crossed hesitantly taking her thumb from her mouth. I enter the small kitchen at the far end of the ward and slip out through the back door. A new perspective. The sound of surf. Dogs bark. The green cottage of the library seen from behind. The bench in the garden beneath the tall eucalyptus trees where we stood. Nearby another cottage with bars a dim light shining inside. The gathering darkness. I make a leisurely detour around the lawn to my left no need to run I bend down and pluck a leaf chewing it inhaling its fresh green smell. I reach the southern end of the fence and cut back eastward plunging into the bushes planted alongside it the barking growing louder one dog is howling now as though it were hurt I never was afraid of dogs but this is an eerie sound. The concrete wall ends. Here must be the hole I head toward it through the bushes but I'm wrong it's the barbed wire again the sealed gap some hairy mangy thing is thrashing about in its loops and kicking up dust. Beyond the bushes more dogs bark. And human voices too. It's 'Ratio he's caught in there he's howling pawing up earth. All of a sudden I feel my heart break for our old dog.

" 'Ratio!" I shout. " 'Ratio! Horatio!"

He stops what he's doing and looks up at me. Our eyes meet. He wags his tail madly. From beyond the bushes I hear Tsvi calling him too.

"Horatio! Horatio! . . . He's stuck in there, mother."

And Naomi's voice from afar:

"Where?"

Dogs bark in a frenzy.

"Git!" shouts Asi furiously.

I crouch and hide behind a bush hearing them struggle in the red sunset.

"He's over there! He must have smelled him."

"Father??"

"He's stuck in there, pull him back this way!"

Above the branches I glimpse Naomi's white hair.

"Grab his chain!"

"He's gone crazy! How did he ever get in there?"

I don't move at all seeing the road far away the black taxi waiting by the railroad tracks facing east toward the main road a line of cars turning in there toward the hospital. They're shouting outside the fence and I'm hiding inside what a reversal of roles.

Now! I take the documents from my pocket I read them quickly and tear them into little pieces I dig a small hole in the ground and stick them in it covering them with stones and earth. A sense of inner peace. I'll have to call the lawyer from the airport. Divorce yes. The house no. My inalienable rights. I disappointed you? What did I ever promise? I rise and head back the way I've come doubled over. Hide-and-seek. I'll leave by the sea side. Soul colors in the fiery pageant of sunset far away. What time is it? Time enough. Time enough. I finger my ticket and my passport in my pocket. Cars enter the hospital bringing back patients from their seder day at home. A noisy bustle of people lights go on in the wards. I cross the lawns again the giant's still there poking his pitchfork at the dead bush. Dumbfounded to see me. I smile at him. Amazingly he has a big watch on. "What time is it?" I ask. He looks at me in a trance not answering. I tip my hat and walk on.

Your head is spinning but inside you you're at peace. A bit much though all that tipping of your hat. You enter the ward again the tailored lady hurries toward you.

"Oh, it's you," she says. "I'm glad you're back. I can't seem to turn on the light."

I flick the switch but nothing happens.

"There must be a short," I explain. "Someone will come to fix it soon."

No fantasy then. What you love is what you kill the spirit listeth where it will. And supposing I did disappoint? Divorce yes. The house no. We'll bargain again. Two women. No less. Maybe you'd like to kill me again please. I fling myself on Naomi's bed. Saber-sharp thought. I push aside her straw hat and stretch out on her bedclothes. The last rays of the sun glint on the white sheets. I'll wait for them here. The wretched lady hovers by the bed.

"Excuse me, Mr. . . ."

"Kaminka."

"I don't remember what you said about supper."

"Supper?"

"When is it served? And where?"

"Usually here on the ward, but because of the holiday it's in the big dining room tonight."

She nods wringing her hands.

"I feel so lost here. I can't even get myself to unpack my suitcase. This whole place makes me sick . . . they didn't allow my husband in, and so he left me . . . he's an officer, he's always in a hurry . . . he has to get back to his regiment . . ."

"You'll get used to it." I nod back with my head on the pillow my mind somewhere else. "You'll see that you will."

"But how?" she asks hopelessly. "How?"

"You'll see. They'll take good care of you."

"I certainly hope so." She smiles childishly. "Do you think they'll let me swim in the ocean? . . . I like that so much . . ."

"Why shouldn't they?"

She regards me sharply stricken with new anxiety.

"But where is your wife? Where is she?"

"She'll be here any minute."

"What kind of woman is she? Do you think that we'll be friends?"

"Of course you will. She's a very nice woman. You'll get to know each other."

Suddenly the sound of people running. I jump up instinctively and dash to the kitchen seeing Yehezkel hearing him call from the door:

"I tell you, that wasn't him! You're wrong."

He runs to Naomi's bed he opens the drawer he takes out the broken half of the dog's chain he runs back out again.

I return to the bed. All things mesh together. The sun enmeshed in the middle of the square windowpane. The tailored lady sits there helplessly tears running down her cheeks.

All at once gripped by the thought.

"Why are you crying? What are you here for?"

"They thought I wanted to kill myself. But I didn't. I only wanted to try it . . . to frighten them . . . and they thought I meant it . . ."

"There, there. Look, they'll take good care of you here. And soon you'll be able to leave."

I can't tear myself away from Naomi's bed I don't lie down on it though I just stand there looking at the straw hat on the pillows at the open drawer. Fragile inner workings of. Thinking of your regained half a house. Half a guest room half a bedroom half a kitchen half a bathroom the whole place halved by an imaginary line. Taking off my soft felt hat and putting on her straw one in its place. The lady in the corner looks at me but there's no turning back now. I lift Naomi's cotton dress I finger it crinkling the fabric I sniff it she's lost her old smell these last five years and gotten a new one. I can't put down the dress. Shaken annoyed at myself I wriggle out of my jacket I hold up the dress and slip into it struggling with the fabric caught for a dark moment but then it falls freely over me stiff and clean. I see the little face in the corner fill with terror the lips are trying to speak.

"Oh, no . . . why are you . . . you're frightening me . . . oh, don't! Don't frighten me, please . . . why didn't you tell me you were sick too?"

I frown at her watching the dress swirl lightly around my legs bending to roll up my pants until my white ankles show. The sun sinks slowly beneath the square window I take the soft gray shawl and cast it over my shoulders looking for a mirror. The woman trembles bites her fingers sobs.

"Don't . . . don't . . . please . . ."

I walk to the door the giant is standing there limply holding his pitchfork listening. Cars keep coming down the road now Asi rushes up too. I run back to hide in the corner the woman watching every move white-faced falling apart eyes sputtering in the dark. Asi steps inside and gropes for the light switch. History as closure? No children there is always a way out. I freeze in my corner the hem of the dress flutters slightly while he steps warily into the dark room and finds my jacket on the bed.

"Father?" He halts calling softly. "Father . . ."

He senses me for sure but doesn't dare come closer he stops I'm ready now. Murder me. I am that I am. Let her rip. I've done all I could. Suddenly I dart from my place I spin around and race to the kitchen and out the back door. In the open again. I have plenty of time my ticket my passport my money. Plenty of it. And half the house mine again. The taxi is waiting. I hurry down the path by cars unloading patients more depressed than ever after a day with their families. In female garb I slip past them an unaccustomed draft around my ankles suddenly a flood of lunar light. The dogs are still barking faintly but the howling has stopped. 'Ratio must have been freed he's galloping toward me I mustn't miss the hole in the fence.

I head straight for it the outline of my plump woman's shadow trailing clearly after me. A cool wind. Scudding clouds. All symbols. I know and smile to myself. And supposing that the pleasure that it gives me does destroy my very self?

All at once I see him before me the giant mute colossus of a man just standing there moving in slow motion as though remote-controlled he faces me on the little path blocking my way staring at me hard. They call him by some Arab name Musa I think that must be it but I'm sure that he's a Jew. Well what's on your mind? Have I disappointed you too? "Naomi . . ." he mutters. "Naomi . . ." Meaning you or trying to warn her? Can he really have confused us? He mutters some more or rather groans it's all too much for him I'd better calm him down he's humorless that's your original your unilateral your unadulterated form of madness. I take off the shawl and toss it on the ground I unbutton the dress but it just puts him into a Neanderthal rage. He's actually growling now. The main thing's not to panic not to touch them they're like dogs fear only makes it worse. Perhaps he needs to be scolded. A fateful man. Better to humor him. But now he's waving his arms he doesn't even know he's got a pitchfork in them. What a predicament. Suddenly you're in a dreadful mess.

DAT